JIMMY HOPE

A NOVEL

# SMITTY

## A TRUE AMERICAN HERO

A STORY OF WAR AND LOVE

*Smitty, A True American Hero*

Cover design by Jimmy Hope
Author photo by Judy Hope



This is a work of fiction. Names, characters, businesses, places and events are either the products of the author's imagination or are used in a fictitious manner. Any resemblance to actual persons living or dead, or actual events, is purely coincidental.



ISBN-13: 978-1-64204-301-3

Printed in the United States of America

2021 - First Edition

# DEDICATION & THANKS

To my wonderful wife, Judy: I still cannot help falling in love with you.

I want to thank the members of my family. Your support in my life is beyond measure. I love you all. I have a forever family of people I love that I have shared my faith and my life with for many years. You are my life treasures. Thank you to all of my pre-readers and editing helpers, and to Pat McWhorter who helped put everything together.

Most of all I want to praise and thank my Lord and Savior Jesus Christ for the abundant and blessed life He has allowed me to live. He is my life.

Johnny
You are one of the finest men
I have ever met. A true
gentleman. Your influence on our
city and its citizens could never
be known. You added to my life.
Thank you for who you are.
Your written words through
past decades have produced
a wonderful story.
Blessings,
[illegible signature]

# CHAPTER ONE

The slamming of a fresh ammo clip into an M-1 carbine shattered the silence of the night. The eight bullets in the clip should bring death to at least four German soldiers. In the third watch on a snow-covered battlefield in France, William "Smitty" Smith was overwhelmed with sadness as he looked back at past days. He had considered suicide to escape his suffering and possible death. Still, in his final hours, he decided he wanted to live more than die. He took a deep breath of bitter, cold air, hoping to slow his run-away heartbeat. Despite the frigid temperature, perspiration covered his face with his body's tightness, feeling the world was pressing him. He could no longer feel his hands or feet and knew frostbite was devouring his tissue and would soon take its toll.

With thousands of German soldiers surrounding his convoy, he faced imminent death, with little hope of surviving. He sighed, knowing his end was near. With over four hundred wounded and dead American soldiers scattered around him, he was seeking answers and grasping for hope. He was horrified, witnessing so many of his fellow warriors pay the ultimate price for freedom; he expected to join them before sunrise. He had often wondered what it would be like on the day he died, realizing he could soon find out.

With a handful of men facing half a division of fully armed enemy soldiers, he and Bravo Company members had little chance to survive. Their first wall of defense had crumbled with the enemy's surprise assault slaughtering a third of his men. His enemies and Mother Nature would soon strike the final blows, and nothing he could do could prevent death and defeat. He struggled to hold his faith and hope. Still, without headquarters knowing their exact location, aid and assistance could not be dispatched. He kept praying deliverance would come from God and the Command.

He paused to reflect on his journey into the war, and in his final hours, he wanted to die in peace. He teared up, with his heart aching at the possibility of never seeing his family or the Smith farm again. He might never again hold or kiss the love of his life, even though he had promised her he would return home alive. He had searched and found his forever love, and the possibility of losing her was worse than death.

The temperature sat at zero as the killer cold pushed him toward lifelessness. Questions roared through his mind. Would he die as he had visualized in repetitive nightmares, or would God deliver him from this valley of the shadow of death? Would he live to see another day, or would he soon stand before his Maker? Would he keep his promise to return to the woman he loved? What would his future hold?" Question after question raced through his mind without a single answer.

Desperately wanting to make it through the night, he prayed, with his last thoughts on how brief his life had been. At nineteen, he felt his entire life should be waiting before him. With an overpowering enemy encompassing him, he closed his eyes in the quietness and stillness of the night as his thoughts returned to a scorching July day in Ringgold, Georgia.

***

The sun was blazing on a small Georgia farm located

seventeen miles from Chattanooga, Tennessee. The red clay field absorbed and radiated the unbearable heat, driving the temperature to over one hundred degrees. The summer sun created heat waves in the open fields without a cloud in the brilliant indigo sky.

The long rows being plowed for winter corn seemed endless as William Bryan Smith, III, gazed at the majestic oak tree at the field's edge. "Smitty" was the latest member of the Smith family to farm the fertile bottomland.

A drink of spring water would cool the burning in his throat, but he would not surrender his determination to complete his work before stopping to drink. His family's need for the crop came first, and with rains looming in the weeks ahead, the seeds had to be in the ground before the first of August or his labor would be in vain.

Like his father and grandfather before him, Smitty stood over six feet tall. But, unlike their fragile builds, which resulted in part from their fondness for rotgut whiskey, he weighed well over two hundred pounds. The sixth and next-to-last child of William Bryan (who everyone called Junior) Smith and Hannah Everett Smith, Smitty was strong enough to keep his family fed. However, he was often required to do two men's work.

He muttered to himself, "I desperately need help, but my good-for-nothing Daddy won't lift a finger. He is content to let me work alone since he knows I will keep the farm going at all costs. I can't depend on him for anything, never knowing if he will be too drunk or too lazy to get up from the couch."

Old Mindy, the family mule pulling the plow in front of him, was old and worn out. She had moved progressively slower as the day dragged on, and the heat grew more intense. He sensed Mindy was nearing the end of her farming days and realized they desperately needed a younger mule. Purchasing a new mule was out of the question with the war raging and money scarce.

"Get up, Mindy," he mumbled through habit every few minutes. He snapped the leather reins against the old mule's rump to keep her moving as the plow struggled to break through the baked, rock-hard clay. The long row seemed to lengthen in the shimmering heat as Mindy slowed and then stopped. He snapped the reins again.

"Get up, Mindy!" he yelled, irritated that she was more cantankerous than usual.

When he jerked the reins once more, slapping them against her back, Mindy reared and bolted, the plow handles flying from his hands. The old mule, infused with sudden strength, bulled her way toward the large oak tree with the plow bouncing wildly behind her. As she reached the shade, she shuddered and fell to the ground.

Smitty stood motionless in shock and uttered, "Mindy's down. How can I save her?"

He raced to the spring, grabbed his drinking bucket, and dipped it into the spring head's shallow pool. He hurried to Mindy and found her massive body quivering, her visible eye fixed, and her mouth open. She drew in a deep breath and stopped breathing. He searched for any sign of life, but she did not move a muscle.

"Don't die, Mindy, he screamed as he held the bucket near her head and splashed water toward her mouth. Come on, girl. Drink. Come on, Mindy!"

Water combining with sweat glistened over her head, ran over her unblinking eye, and trickled into her mouth.

"Mindy!" he uttered while lifting the bucket and pouring most of the remaining water over her lips. The old mule did not move.

"Don't you die, Mindy! We need you! We need you bad!"

Despite his attempts to persuade the mule to live, Mindy would not breathe again.

He stared in disbelief for several minutes before unhitching the plow and removing the bit, bridle, and harness. He slammed them to the ground in anger and kicked a clump of dirt, looking toward the battered farmhouse he called home. His grief, pain, and loss overwhelmed him as his mind flooded with concerns of how Mindy's death would affect him and his family.

Smitty looked up to Heaven and shook his fist at God with his anger and disappointment exploding.

"Why, God? Why would you allow this to happen? Ain't our lives hopeless enough without you adding this to our struggles? I don't understand why you want to make our lives so difficult. I love you, but you keep acting like you are not even there. What can I do to persuade you to give us some blessings instead of trials?"

He dropped to his knees, settled back on a pile of rocks at the base of the tree, and took a drink from what little water remained in the bucket. Sadness and concern flooded him as he covered his eyes and wept. He knew it would be impossible to work the farm without a mule. He worried about how his family could survive without Mindy and money from the crops. He struggled to find an answer to how they could overcome such a devastating event and was at a loss for words, with his emotions swirling like a gale.

He had been feeling the uselessness of plowing and planting day after day for just enough money to survive. He stayed discouraged and often cried in the field, with his tears mixing with sweat and dirt flowing down his cheeks. Hopelessness and discouragement had become his constant companions as his daily efforts were never enough. He never seemed to get ahead.

He had often thought, "I will be dirt poor the rest of my

life if I continue working this farm. Some way, somehow, my life has to change, and I have to believe the good Lord will bless me soon."

He clenched his fist and bit his lip, fighting back his anger and disappointment. "I'm doing my best to keep a positive outlook, to stop looking at what my family doesn't have, and focus on what we do have. We have been blessed!"

And now, after the old mule's death, all hope was gone as he threw the bit, bridle, and harness over his shoulder. Standing in the partially plowed field, he felt the immense difficulties and impossible situations facing him. Tears continued to run down his face as he questioned if he was crying over Mindy's death or the emptiness, hardness, and hopelessness of his life.

He glanced up the hill at the farmhouse, weathered to a dull gray. It had been painted white until time, weather, lack of money, and lack of care by a drunken father had taken their toll. Keeping the house maintained lost its importance with so much work in the fields. Despite his best efforts, the house, the barn, and the yards gave testimony that the occupants had given up on life and were waiting for death to deliver them from their misery.

His slow walk from the bottoms to the house seemed to take forever as he pondered how to tell his parents the devastating news. His mind continued to race with his thoughts running wild. He prayed in preparation for his daddy's anger and his mother's tears. The information would be difficult, but nothing anyone could say or do would bring Mindy back. He knew that even when things were difficult, truth was always the best choice.

He had always attempted to be honest and truthful. His life had been shaped and influenced by his grandpa, Henry Everett, who had lived with the Smiths after his wife died of cancer. Henry and Edith Everett were married for sixty years. He admired how his grandfather had lived his life the right way. After being called to preach at an early age, he never became a full-time pastor and never took on a church. He chose to live his faith more than preach it and was a quiet and humble man whose actions spoke louder than his words.

He always told Smitty, "I want to be Jesus with skin on, and I want my life to preach my message. I don't want to preach the good news; I want to be the good news. I don't want to go to church; I want to be the church."

His Grandpa Everett trained him to work with his hands. He taught him to live by the Good Book and shared his integrity, honesty, and truthfulness. He imparted to Smitty what his father should have given him. For all the bad Junior sowed into Smitty's life, his Grandpa Everett had deposited ten times more good.

Wanting to delay the delivery of the bad news, he decided he would check the mail. He walked to the rusty old mailbox covered in dust from the dirt road. He seldom went to the mailbox anymore since they rarely received any letters. Relatives used to write until time, responsibilities, and lack of caring took the importance of letters away. Most family members had forgotten Hannah and Junior and sent letters when they needed money or help. There hadn't been a letter in the mailbox for weeks.

Smitty had considered replacing the dilapidated mailbox but the lack of funds and other pressing needs had prevented it. He kept hoping the mailman would deliver an important letter bringing good news of hope and opportunity.

He pulled open the bent and rusty door and was shocked to find a letter. He gazed at the official-looking brown envelope addressed to William Bryan Smith, III, Box

211 Maple Road, Ringgold, Georgia. In the top left corner, two words grabbed his attention, "Selective Service." He ripped open the letter and saw "Greetings."

His heart raced as he gasped for breath, with his thoughts and feelings running wild. His hands shook and trembled, making it difficult for him to hold the notice.

He read the letter and discovered startling news; he had been drafted. He realized from the moment he opened the letter his life had radically changed. The envelope not only contained his draft notice, but a mountain of uncertainty. The news slammed and stunned him as he weighed it as either a terrible turn of events or deliverance from his hopeless future.

He tried to forget Mindy's death, farming, and his problems. He had been drafted and would soon be inducted into the United States Army.

He had followed the war on the Crosley radio his family listened to after supper, had heard the reports of the attack on Pearl Harbor, and knew President Roosevelt had declared war. Men from Ringgold, Dalton, Chatsworth, Calhoun, Resaca, and nearby areas had been drafted, and many young men had enlisted.

His draft notice had been delivered and he could not ignore it. The realization he could soon be a soldier shook him to his core. He shuttered and grieved when he considered leaving the Smith farm and the only life he had ever known. An array of emotions surged forth. From the moment he opened his draft notice, he knew his life would change and could only hope and pray it would change for better and not for worse.

Making his way to the house in a daze, he looked at his life, his family, and what was happening. He paused for a moment on the front steps to think about his news and, with his mind spinning, he attempted to stir up enough courage to face his fears and uncertainties.

# CHAPTER TWO

Smitty's father, "Junior," had been born and raised on the Smith farm and had been held firmly in the grip of rotgut whiskey most of his life. Excessive drinking had been a curse on Junior's people. Smitty had never tasted alcohol, hating the destruction, loss, and hard times alcohol had brought to his family.

Junior had made and consumed hard liquor through the years and had reached the point where he had to drink every day to function. He had once kicked the habit for a year but allowed it to return with a vengeance. He not only fell off the wagon, he burned it.

Smitty carried shame over his father's bootlegging endeavors and often disagreed with him brewing illegal whiskey with his whiskey-peddling buddies. He refused to help Junior run his still in the Smith bottoms. Junior had sold whiskey most of his life, even serving several sentences in the county jail. He and his whiskey-making friends were called moonshiners, brewing rotgut whiskey in copper stills by moonlight.

Revenue agents in northwest Georgia had worked to end the running of white lightning from Ringgold to Chattanooga, Atlanta, Macon, Columbus, and Savannah. Junior had been a significant target for years with the revenuers watching for any unusual activity around the Smith farm.

His moonshine skills were exceptional and everyone wanted his services. People around Ringgold always said, "Junior Smith cooks up the best mash and makes the best corn liquor north of Atlanta."

He stayed angry and frustrated because his bootlegging career had been curtailed by the revenuers' increased enforcement. At his age, he did not want to be arrested and spend more time in jail. He stayed concerned and carried guilt over the lost income from his whiskey-making operations, making his family's life difficult. Setting up stills and distilling spirits had always allowed him to make more money than his family needed. Junior was aware this chapter in his life had ended.

Most people around Ringgold liked Junior even though he was a drunkard. He was always willing to share a swig from the bottle he always carried in his overalls. His family would often say of him, "Junior likes to guzzle a little liquor now and then."

"Now and then" had turned into several times a day.

***

Smitty's mother, Hannah, was a good woman who was dedicated to her family and loved attending Shiloh Baptist Church. Besides her family, God and her church were the most important things in her life. She prayed daily for Junior and her children. At one time, Junior's life had improved and he had attended church with her until they received the tragic news their oldest son Billy had been murdered in a fracas at the Red Light Bar near Dalton. Witnesses said Billy was killed in an argument over money from a poker game, while others said his murder resulted from a lover's conflict involving him, Sandra Stone, and Robert Vickers.

Junior knew the truth regarding Billy's death, but never shared it. He felt it was too horrible to speak of, even when he was drinking. Everyone had wondered why Billy's casket was not open at his funeral. Some of the witnesses at

Robert Vickers' murder trial had testified Billy's face had been mutilated beyond recognition.

As the firstborn and Junior's favorite, Billy was his daddy's drinking buddy. He always brought Junior a pint of liquor or a fifth of home-brew whenever he returned home from his drunkenness bouts.

He had a wild nature that caused him to stay in trouble with the city police and county deputies. He had broken the law on numerous occasions and had served considerable time in jail on various charges. He often looked for trouble, until trouble found him one night in a bar outside Dalton.

Smitty had never been close to any of his brothers because he was very different from Bobby, Tommy, and Billy. He carried strong feelings about his older brother, Tommy.

He was disappointed in him and had never approved of him or his values.

Tommy became wealthy after he married Ella Taylor, the daughter of the president of the Calhoun National Bank. Tommy married Ella after her mother and father found them in her bed when they returned early from a banking conference in Atlanta. Tommy relocated to Calhoun to live a successful, but boring life, helping Clinton Taylor guard and count his money. Ella delivered a baby girl six months after a Justice of the Peace presided over their wedding.

He felt Tommy was a weakling, the way he allowed his wife and Clint Taylor to control his life. He considered his actions and compromises a disgrace to his manhood. After seeing Tommy's lapse in sound thinking, he believed they even told Tommy when he could or could not go to the bathroom.

He had often said, "I will never sell my values or self-respect for sex, money, or position. I will never be like Tommy and I consider him a disgrace to the Smith family."

Tommy lived in a large house, drove a new car, and, in all probability, would own the bank someday. Sadly, Tommy and Ella were too rich and socially prominent to associate with the lower class Smith family.

His sister Evelyn was the oldest Smith girl. She had babied Smitty like a second mother and taught him to read and write before he started school. He and Evelyn spent summer days and cool evenings playing together. She loved him as his sister and his friend.

Evelyn won beauty contests all over Northwest Georgia with the beauty she inherited from her mother. Several young men pursued Evelyn, but she and TJ McCord had loved each other from childhood. Even though they were in love, they never married while they were young. Hannah kept insisting her daughter graduate high school before there could be a wedding.

They could not marry after TJ got drunk in Chattanooga, took a bar waitress to the Justice of the Peace and married her. He would have had the marriage annulled, but felt guilty after his wife, Beatrice, became pregnant. He brought his bride back to Ringgold, with their days and nights filled with fighting and separations. They stayed apart more than they lived together, with jealousy and rage causing Beatrice to badger TJ about his past relationship with Evelyn. TJ regretted his mistake, but did not file for divorce even though the baby boy had freckles, red hair, and little resemblance to him.

As for Evelyn, she could never release her anger and resentment over TJ's actions and married a drifter named Tommy Hall. She never loved Tommy and only married him to get even with TJ. Tommy moved Evelyn to New York City where he left her on the streets and he sailed to South America to find his fortune. He never returned. A rumor circulated that Evelyn worked as a prostitute in the city's red-light district and the stories were amplified after a salesman from Ringgold saw her working there. The witness fed the fires of gossip about Evelyn Hall's prostitution for months.

The drama took an even stranger turn when Evelyn returned home. Within a few days after her return, she and TJ ran off to Florida in the middle of the night without telling anyone. Hannah spent many days and nights worrying about them realizing they would never return home.

Beatrice vowed to kill them when she located them and even hired a private investigator from Atlanta to search for them. After a year of searching and having spent all her money, the investigator told Beatrice the errant couple had moved to Miami or Panama City, changed their names, and disappeared from the face of the Earth.

For her part, Beatrice did not mourn long. After securing a cheap divorce in TJ's absence, she hooked up with TJ's best friend, Hubert Whelchel. In Ringgold, people said Hubert's immediate presence and marriage weren't a coincidence, since he had a reputation of bar-hopping in Chattanooga, had freckles, and flaming red hair.

Bobby was the wild one in the family. He was highly intelligent but too unpredictable. He grew up with peculiar ways, a strong will, and rock hard opinions. His independent nature caused him to never listen to anyone. He quit school in the fifth grade after cursing his teacher and threatening to whip the principal. Smitty always said, "Bobby is as stubborn as Mindy. He has to be the most hard-headed person that ever lived, and would stand and argue with a signpost."

Bobby ran away from home at sixteen and hitchhiked over a hundred miles to find work in Atlanta. After reaching Atlanta, no one saw or heard from him again.

People always said, "Bobby is in Atlanta," whenever his name came up. He had been a loner and would remain alone. People in Ringgold questioned what Bobby could be doing in the big city. Rumors had him selling white lightning, like Junior, while some people believed he was serving time behind bars in the Atlanta Penitentiary. Hannah and Junior felt Bobby might have been murdered on the streets of Atlanta and never identified.

No one ever saw or heard from him, and if he were dead or alive, it made little difference. The Smiths seldom thought of him or even mentioned him. To the Smiths and most people in Ringgold, Bobby might as well have been deceased.

The baby of the family, Maria, arrived late in her parents' life. Her arrival surprised and stunned Hannah and Junior. With them in their late forties, they never expected another child.

Hannah had a difficult time with Maria's birth. The doctors in Chattanooga had said, "It's a miracle Maria survived with the obstacles she faced and the length of Hannah's labor."

Maria had always been frail, sickly, and slow. Hannah justified her problems by saying, "Maria is a slow learner; she'll outgrow this."

Smitty had seen Junior, in drunkenness, verbally and physically abuse Hannah during her pregnancy. He believed Hannah and Maria had been permanently damaged by Junior's rough treatment. Because of this, he never had a relationship with Junior, never loved him, or even cared for him. He could only tolerate him because he was his father.

People in Ringgold knew Maria acted peculiar around strangers. She would not communicate with anyone but her family members. Hannah kept Maria by her side and always blamed herself for Maria's problems. Maria's health was fragile, with her daily seizures difficult for Hannah and Smitty to handle.

Even though he knew Maria had severe health and life issues, he would never face the truth. He loved her and did everything within his power to improve her life, spending time teaching her to read, write, and spell, since she was unable to attend school. In his spare time, he read her stories, drew her pictures, and taught her songs and rhymes.

With Billy, Tommy, Evelyn, and Bobby gone, the Smith family consisted of Junior, Hannah, Smitty, and Maria.

As the lone son remaining at home and the most responsible person in the Smith family, Smitty lived as Hannah's pride and joy. He had used his above-average intelligence to graduate with honors from Ringgold School and was selected as valedictorian of his graduating class. The faculty at the school loved Smitty and had encouraged him to attend college. He was given an academic scholarship to help with tuition, but he knew the struggles of the farm and lack of money left him without any opportunity for a college education or better life. His deep love and concern for his family would never allow him to leave the Smith farm to enroll in college or pursue a career. He had reconciled himself to being a struggling farmer the remainder of his life.

He had deep concerns for Hannah and Maria's safety when he departed for the service. If Junior became drunk or abusive, he would not be there to restrain him. He realized he would have to be Maria's caregiver if Hannah died, knowing Junior would never care for Hannah or Maria since he spent all his time and energy only watching after Junior.

Thinking back to better days, he had memories of when

Junior stayed sober, worked at the corn mill, and cultivated the farm. He remembered times when all the family members were happy and he cherished the times the Smith children worked, played, and romped through the four-hundred-acre farm William Bryan Smith had left to his only son.

When hard times came or money was needed, Junior would sell ten acres. With alcohol of such importance to him, the Smith farm had dwindled to a little over fifty acres. So few acres made it difficult to make ends meet and had forced the Smiths to struggle for every penny they could earn.

# CHAPTER THREE

Smitty's mind was racing, and his head spinning as he stepped into the house. His heart was breaking at the possibility of leaving his mama, his daddy, and Maria. He questioned how they could survive without having someone to work the farm, plant the crops, and harvest the fields.

He had thought his being drafted could be a blessing since he could send most of his Army pay home for his family's support. With his pay, his mama might be able to hire someone to work the farm if Junior could not or would not.

He found Junior on the couch; whether passed out drunk or sleeping, he could not tell. He was nervous about telling them the news about the mule's death and his being drafted. He dreaded telling Junior because of his lightning temper and explosive anger. Junior had a short fuse, but it did not take long for him to get over his fury after a drink or two. He decided to give Junior the news after supper since Junior always ran from problems and would never face any issues. He realized Junior had lived his life as a weak person and emotional cripple.

Hannah paused from cooking supper on their wood stove when he walked into the dimly lit kitchen. Seeing the stove reminded him of the difficulty of keeping firewood supplied, another reason to dread leaving home.

One whiff of the kitchen smells told him they would be eating soup beans and cornbread, with onions, sliced potatoes, and sweet tea if his mama had sugar. Government rationing had made sugar a luxury.

He walked to his mama and leaned over her shoulder. "Mama, he whispered. Old Mindy just died."

Hannah turned to him in disbelief. As his words sank in, tears flooded her eyes. She knew what the loss of the mule would mean.

"Oh, no! Her face paled. What will we do? We can't afford another mule, and we don't have any more land we can sell."

"I'm sorry, Mama."

"Aw, it ain't your fault, Honey." She wiped her eyes with her apron. "Old Mindy's sure been a good mule. I've been worried a long time she might die. Maybe the Lord's been preparin' me."

"There's something else," he said, his eyes tearing up.

"What?" He could tell she knew by his downcast expression that she wasn't going to like 'something else.' He had prepared himself for her reaction to the bad news.

"I got my draft notice in the mail, and I will be going into the Army. I am in perfect physical condition, and there's no way I will be rejected."

Hannah's tears welled up as she moaned and took him in her arms. "No, no, no, Smitty!"

Maria rushed into the room, upset at her mother's crying. Her hand reached for her mother's shoulder, and in her confusion and lack of understanding, she asked. "What's the matter, Mama?"

Hannah drew her apron to her eyes again and tried to compose herself, but continue to sob, moan, and shake her head.

"Smitty?" Maria persisted. "What's wrong with Mama?"

"Old Mindy has died," he whispered, not wanting to tell the worse news.

"Oh, no," said Maria. "Just now?"

Smitty nodded.

Maria did not understand why the mule's death would cause such weeping. She took her mother's hand and patted her brother's shoulder.

Hannah turned to Maria and ran her hand over her hair. "And your brother might be going into the Army, Baby."

"The Army?" Maria was filled with fear. "Why?"

"I got drafted," said Smitty. "But I'll be all right, Maria. Don't worry."

Maria was confused as she clung to her mama and Smitty.

Later, at supper, he broke the news about Mindy and his draft notice to his father, and he took it as well as could be expected. After he mentioned sending money home every month, Junior remarked, with a comforted tone, "We will have to make the best of a bad situation. Life will go on."

Junior's mind started spinning as he worked to figure out what would be best for Junior.

Junior leaned back in his chair as his mind returned to his Army days. His time in the Army was one of the few things he could take pride in.

"You'll have to go. It's the law," Junior drawled. I know what will happen. The same things that happened to me will happen to you. They'll take you to Atlanta for your physical and your swearin'-in. The Army will examine you like they did me when I went to Europe to fight the Germans. We whipped 'em good, we did."

When no one commented on his part in the war, Junior pressed on. "Your mama, Maria, and I will miss you, but you'll have to go. You don't mess with Uncle Sam, and we don't want no cowards in the Smith family. I fought and gave my best to my country, and I'm expecting you to do the same."

***

The Selective Service Board gave Smitty two weeks to report to Atlanta for his physical exam, on the first day of August, to be accepted for military service or rejected. As healthy as he had been, never sick a day in his life, he was confident he would pass his physical exam and be called to active duty.

Old Mindy's death did not seem as important as it had been earlier in the afternoon. The Smith family wouldn't be farming anymore except for a small vegetable garden Hannah might plant. With him sending his monthly allotment home, Mindy would not be needed. He knew Junior would not hire anyone to work the fields and save the crops. From that perspective, Mindy's death was a blessing, since she wouldn't have to be fed, watered, and cared for.

Amid the day's bad news, the Smith family had overlooked an important event. It was Smitty's nineteenth birthday. Hannah had always baked a cake, and everyone would sing "Happy Birthday." They never had the money for presents, so missing out on that aspect did not bother him. He wasn't disappointed when Hannah came and apologized for forgetting his special day. She had been so upset with all the bad news she had sat in her rocking chair and cried.

Junior had not shown any emotions or said a word. Smitty had not noticed when he slipped out to visit the Cantrell brothers. In tough times his daddy had always turned to the bottle. Smitty was sad the way alcohol had robbed his daddy of all God's blessings.

After the day's emotional struggles and awful news, Smitty did not want to celebrate and felt his birthday could not compare to the day's events' importance. As bedtime neared, he stopped to consider the impact of his draft notice." This is a dream, this isn't happening. It has to be a nightmare or misunderstanding."

Gazing about his bedroom, he experienced sadness at the thought he might never sleep there again. He looked around the room that could soon become a memory. He saw the kerosene lamp he often used at night to do homework he failed to do earlier in the day because of farm chores. He hadn't lit it much since they got electricity and only used it when Junior could not pay the electric bill, and their power was turned off for non-payment.

He studied his eighth-grade pencil drawing of a horse on the wall above his bed and looked at the feather mattress his Grandmother Everett had made for Junior and Hannah as a wedding gift. It had been handed down from child to child until it had reached him. Junior and Hannah had first given it to Bobby after they purchased a store-bought mattress with money from the sale of some farmland.

Even a cracked window pane, damaged when he threw a boot at a wasp, held a memory for him. He thought back to former years when youth still burned in his eyes and his heart. He had experienced some long and challenging periods in his life.

He was heart-broken over leaving his lifelong friend, Johnny Little, and did not want to think about leaving Janice Miller. Janice was the love of his life and the center of his world. Leaving them stirred as many emotions and feelings as leaving his family.

Johnny was more like a brother than his real brothers, and Smitty loved him with a special love. They had been pals since before first grade, when they waded in Little Chickamauga Creek, picked blackberries, and fished together. Whenever you saw one, you saw the other. They were inseparable, as if they had been tied together with invisible cords.

Smitty thought Johnny had the perfect name since he had little sense. Johnny did not have a serious bone in his body or brain in his head and often got the pair in trouble.

He thought of when they got revenge on old man Beasley for shooting Johnny's blue tick hound, Worthless.

He knew Johnny wasn't right when he gave his dog that name. The first month after Johnny got his dog, all the hound would do was eat, sleep, and stay on the porch. Johnny would take him in the woods to hunt, and the dog would beat him back home. All the good for nothing dog did was cause Johnny a ton of problems. He once dug up all the plants Louise Little had worked for a week planting her garden.

Johnny told him, "That dog ain't worth nothing; he is worthless. That's it! That's his name, Worthless."

From that day on, the dog went by the name of Worthless and would not go to the woods and stay until he and Johnny had slept in the outdoors several nights to get him used to hunting. He had grown to be one of the best coon dogs in the county.

Mr. Beasley had lied and told everyone he killed Worthless for chasing cattle and killing chickens. He and Johnny knew the only things Worthless ever chased were deer, coons, squirrels, rabbits, and the two of them. The old man's dislike for Johnny caused him to kill Worthless.

Their opportunity for revenge came on a dark, cold, and rainy Halloween night.

They took the biggest and freshest pile of Old Mindy's manure they could find, shoveled it into a paper sack, then placed the manure-filled bag on Mr. Beasley's porch by his front door. They lit it with a stick match, knocked on his door, then ran across the yard to hide in the bushes. By the time Mr. Beasley opened his front door, the sack had blazed. They were ecstatic when Mr. Beasley jumped up and down on the burning sack to stomp out the flames. They felt the smell of mule manure on his boots would reach downtown Ringgold.

He smiled as he remembered them laughing until they could not laugh anymore. Mr. Beasley heard their laughter and threatened to shoot them like he had shot Worthless. He screamed with anger while he attempted to put out the fire and scrape the manure from his boots. He swore he would get even, yelling to the top of his lungs, "I'm calling the law and have you locked up in the county jail."

He and Johnny were spared from punishment after Mr. Beasley failed to call the sheriff or tell their mothers. The boys saw him the next day at Brown's grocery, purchasing a new pair of boots to replace the ones scorched by the fire from the burning sack. They broke into laughter and told everyone in Ringgold about their revenge and Mr. Beasley's dance on his front porch. Their revenge was sweet. As long as he and Johnny lived, they would never forget the night Mr. Beasley did "the manure stomp."

Johnny caused him to receive a ton of whippings. One of the worst involved Bertie Seymour, wife of Reverend Artis Seymour, the pastor of Shiloh Baptist Church. As Hannah's closest friend and companion, she spent a lot of time at the Smiths' house. One morning she came to visit Hannah just as Johnny and Smitty finished making a mongoose box. Johnny talked him into playing a trick on Bertie and for her to be the first person to see his mongoose.

The wooden box had been built to look like an animal cage. The boys had tied a raccoon tail inside and rigged it so that when the box lid swung open, the tail would fly out toward the person examining the box. Johnny had placed grass, leaves, and what was suppose to be mongoose food in the box.

Mrs. Bertie arrived at the perfect time. As soon as she saw the boys, she asked, "Good morning, young men. What's in the box?"

"A mongoose," said Johnny. "It's the meanest and deadliest creature in the world. It kills anything it fights, and when a mongoose attacks, it never stops until it or its victim dies."

"I've never seen a mongoose, and I've been to several zoos. Let me take a look at your mongoose." She moved nearer the box to get a closer look. She had fallen into Johnny's snare and had asked the perfect question.

When she bent over to see the mongoose, Johnny flipped the lid, and the coon tail flew out of the box, striking Bertie in the middle of her over-sized bosom. She jumped on the sofa and then crawled up on the back like a wild animal, screaming, "Kill the S.O.B.!" over and over.

She fainted on the couch and lay there like a dead woman. He and Johnny panicked, thinking she might have died of a heart attack and were terrified that the mongoose had killed her. Johnny asked, "Reckon the law will arrest us for murdering her?"

Hannah heard the screaming and rushed from the kitchen into the living room, slipping in a puddle of suspicious liquid where Bertie had been standing, and she hit the floor. After Hannah pulled herself up, she looked to see why her dress was wet. Anger flooded her when she discovered it was Mrs. Bertie's urine. Mrs. Bertie was so frightened she had wet her pants. Bertie regained consciousness and stormed out of the house without saying a word, slamming the front door in a rage.

Pastor Seymour resigned his pastorate due to the rumors of Bertie's language and humiliation. Within a week, the Seymours moved to Resaca, where Mr. Seymour became an insurance salesman for the Carolina Life

Insurance Company. Few in the community missed Mrs. Seymour, with most people happy to see her go.

He got the worst whipping of his life despite his numerous declarations of innocence. He wondered why he got the whipping when it was Johnny who lured Bertie into the snare. He was an innocent bystander. He would have taken another whipping to witness Bertie Seymour's mongoose attack again. It was the funniest thing he ever saw.

As for his girlfriend, Janice Miller, he could not wait to see her and share the news of his draft notice. She might love him even more with the prospect of him becoming a soldier. He dreaded the thought of leaving her.

He had another issue swirling in his mind regarding Janice. His most profound concern did not concern leaving her, but involved Roger Brown, a brat from the town's wealthiest family. He hated Roger Brown and had seen evidence he had his sights set on Janice.

Janice had been Smitty's first love and only love. He had loved her since first grade at Ringgold School when she shared her beautiful smile and her mother's fried peach pies. From then on, she had been his girl, and fried peach pies were among his favorite things in the world.

He remembered the Shiloh Baptist Church's summer picnic when he and Janice walked by Little Chickamauga Creek holding hands. Janice wrapped her arms around him and kissed him with a long passionate kiss. He never forgot the feelings her kiss stirred inside him.

Janice's beauty awed him. He considered her movie-star beautiful with golden blonde hair, sky blue eyes, and a perfect figure. He loved her despite her having some significant issues. Her foul mouth and quick temper concerned him, and he hated the possibility she might become like her mother, Eunice.

Eunice Miller stayed involved in everyone's business. To classify her as a gossiper and a busybody would be understatements. Mr. Miller traveled with his company and used his sales trips as opportunities for time to get away from his wife. Eunice could drive a person crazy with her continual gossiping, complaining, and shouting. She never closed her mouth, was never satisfied and was always unhappy.

However, she did make some fantastic fried peach pies!

His goal in life was to marry Janice. He believed she would change for the better after they married, but he still worried about her attitude. He had decided if she didn't change after their wedding, he would become a traveling salesman like Mr. Miller. He stayed concerned after being told the fruit never falls far from the tree.

Another reason Janice held a special place in his heart was she saved his life after Mindy tossed him into Little Chickamauga Creek. She found him floating at the edge of the water and dragged him to the bank. He felt he owed her his life as well as his love.

He decided to visit Johnny first and then walk to Janice's house at the right time to secure an invitation to lunch - and possibly a couple of Eunice's fried pies.

Smitty set out his clean dungarees across a straight-back chair and turned down his bed. His mind raced, and he knew he would have difficulty sleeping with all his excitement.

# *CHAPTER FOUR*

The crowing of Hannah's bantam rooster in the Smiths' front yard cut through the stillness of early morning. The rooster's cry woke him at daybreak, but the emotions of the previous day and a long restless night had left him exhausted. He had turned back over, fallen asleep, and dreamed about getting married to Janice after the war. When he stumbled out of bed, the sun was a ball of fire with the July day's scorching heat promising to soar to a hundred degrees again. He had little sleep, tossing and turning all night with his thoughts and feelings weighing heavily upon him.

He had forgotten Mindy would have to be buried before he could visit Johnny and see Janice. He realized he should have buried her right after she died, but he did not have the willingness or energy to endure it.

As he stepped from his bedroom, he smelled fried streak-o'-lean, sow-belly as Junior called it. Hannah had it frying in a black iron skillet on the woodstove. Stumbling into the hot kitchen, he smelled fresh-perked coffee and biscuits in the oven spreading a mouthwatering aroma throughout the house.

"Good morning," Hannah chirped as brightly as she could. "I've been praying for you all night and most of the morning."

"Thanks, Mama." He did not speak another word for the sake of crying.

"I'm concerned the Army will send you to France to fight the Germans or someplace where so many of our men are being killed. I'm afraid you will never come home," she said tearfully. "I could not live if anything happened to you and would just lay down and die. I can't believe you graduated high school in June and have been drafted in July. I wish we had more time together."

"Mama, I haven't even been to Atlanta for my physical, and you have me dying in France or on some battlefield in a foreign country." He leaned over, hugged her, and kissed her on her cheek.

Hannah seemed frail, small, and old when he took a closer look at her face and hands. Her life hurts, trials, tests, tribulations of wayward children, and living with an abusive, alcoholic husband had exacted a high price.

Hannah's beauty was known throughout Ringgold. Like her daughter, Evelyn, she had won every beauty contest she entered and was voted the most beautiful girl in Ringgold school. At her age, she was still a beautiful woman. Everyone told him he got his good looks and fine qualities from his mother. He loved his mother more than anyone.

Over breakfast, Junior told stories about his Army duty and explained to him, "When you go to Atlanta, the Army doctors will work you over. They'll examine every inch of your body, and you'd better be prepared for what they'll put you through."

Junior leaned back in his chair, stared into space again, and thought back to his war. "I wish I could go to fight the Germans with you, Son. The two of us together could whip any ten soldiers in their stinking Army."

Smitty often considered Junior's involvement in the war had contributed to his drinking problem, with him suffering tormenting dreams most of his life. There were times he would wake everyone in the middle of the night, screaming and fighting. Junior had fought in many horrible battles, killed many Germans, and seemed to live some days like he was still in the Army.

He rose from the table, and Junior said, "Smitty."

"Yes, sir?" Smitty answered

"You'll have to bury Old Mindy since you were plowing the old mule when she died."

He knew Junior would not help dig Mindy's grave or have any part in her burial. Junior would use every excuse he could think of to avoid work. Smitty stayed angry and frustrated with his father's constant complaining about his injured back and migraine headaches. Junior was a hypochondriac who made sure people knew he was sick and injured. Junior always came up with a medical reason for avoiding work, which Smitty had diagnosed as a bad case of laziness.

He often said, "Junior is allergic to all manual labor and the hot sun. You never know what he will be down with next. If he went to the doctor with all his ailments, he would have to move into the doctor's office."

It was a known fact Junior would not lift a finger to help bury Mindy, so he decided not to ask.

On the way to the barn, his head swirled when he considered how large a hole it would take to bury a dead mule. He dreaded the heat of another scorching day. He chastised himself for not getting up before dawn to do the deed in the cool morning air. He wanted to hurry with the burial so he could see Janice and Johnny and share his news.

He could not tolerate the idea of buzzards and other critters feeding on Mindy, so he pulled tools from the rickety old barn and headed for the bottoms, grabbing a couple of pieces of scrap wood on the way. He hurried to the field to complete his duty.

He swung the pick at the hardened earth, and it bounced off the ground leaving him feeling he was breaking up concrete. The pick careened off the rock-hard ground and struck him on his shin. He hopped around for a few minutes screaming at himself for being so careless.

The buzzards were circling the mule when he placed his foot on the rusty shovel and turned the red clay. The ground was baked. He shook his head, realizing the work could take the remainder of the day.

Knowing he could not move Mindy even an inch, he decided to bury the mule on the spot where she had died. He dug under her to roll her into a shallow hole. He struck a massive layer of rock and could not dig deeper. He reconsidered the amount of work needed and concluded it would take five men over a half a day to finish the job with so much rock and the blistering heat. He decided to cover Mindy with rocks thinking the rocks would keep animals from digging down to her. Using the rocks he had removed from the field, he could leave most of Mindy's carcass above ground and would not be forced to dig a deeper grave. He worked more than two hours stacking rocks to give Mindy a proper burial.

After finishing the burial, he took his Barlow pocket knife and carved 'Old Mindy' in the scrap wood he had fashioned into a cross. He said a few words, ended with a short prayer and cried after lifting the pick and shovel and walking away. It was tough leaving Mindy in the ground, but it was time for him to visit Johnny and Janice.

He left his sadness, farming life, and Ringgold life at Mindy's grave, realizing he might never plow, plant, or harvest another crop on the Smith farm. He knew the corn he had worked so hard to plant would soon be overgrown with weeds and briers. He knew there would not be a harvest in the fall after Junior allowed the corn to rot in the fields. He buried more than Mindy that hot July morning; he buried his old life.

He headed to Johnny's house, thinking it best to visit Janice at lunchtime. After a quick walk, he reached the Littles' place, where Johnny's mother, Louise, met him at the door. She shook her head when she told him, "Johnny's gone fishing down at the Coosa River. He promised he would catch a mess of catfish and bluegill for supper. He's supposed to be fishing near the old bridge off Chickamauga Road. You tell him if he wants any supper, he had better fish and not loaf."

He reached the bridge and found Johnny asleep on the river bank naked. Johnny raised up, nodded, and mumbled, "I want a full-body tan like the movie stars in mama's Hollywood magazines. Women will love and worship my golden body."

Johnny had spent the morning swimming, sunning, and sleeping and had not caught a fish. His fishing poles weren't baited, and he did not have a line in the river. Without any fish, the Littles would not have what Louise wanted for supper. They would have tomato sandwiches or warmed-up soup beans and cornbread. If Louise was angry at Johnny, they would have cornbread and buttermilk.

Smitty taunted Johnny, "You can't catch anything if your lines aren't in the river."

Johnny fired back, "It's too hot for the fish to bite. Nothing's biting but flies and mosquitoes."

Johnny showed him a large mosquito whelp on his arm. "That sucker took a pint of blood! He must be holding his own blood drive for the Red Cross. I ain't a full-blooded American anymore; I'm a little low." Johnny roared with laughter at his joke.

"Seeing all the insects reminds me of my life," Johnny said. Smitty could not believe Johnny was getting philosophical.

He asked, "What do insects have to do with your life?"

"Well, it's like this. Sometimes you are the windshield, and sometimes you are the bugs. Today I am not sure which one I am."

Johnny had stood up and moved closer to Smitty. Suddenly he lunged at him and grabbed him in a headlock, attempting to throw him into the river. Smitty recovered and overpowered Johnny. He broke free and threw Johnny into the river, laughing at Johnny's fake screams.

"I'm drowning!" Johnny yelled as he floundered and flailed in the water. "I've got a cramp. Pull me out, or I'm going under for the last time!"

Smitty knew if he tried to help, Johnny would pull him into the river. When Johnny saw he wasn't coming to his rescue, he crawled from the river and slid on his overalls.

In the shade of an old Chestnut tree, Smitty told Johnny about Mindy dying while plowing the field. "She must have had a heat stroke or heart attack. She was way too old to be plowing on a hundred-degree day. She was always one of the best mules anyone could want."

Johnny frowned and replied, "I'm sorry about Mindy. Your family has loved that mule for over twenty years. I remember we used to have fun riding her, pretending we were cowboys, Indians, outlaws, and rustlers. Those memories were so long ago."

"Got something else to tell you, Johnny. The mailman delivered my draft notice yesterday. I may be going into the Army. I am scheduled to go to Atlanta for my physical August first. What do you think?"

"Dang, Smitty, butter my butt and call me a biscuit," Johnny shouted as he started hitting Smitty on his back. "The Army? You are going to be a G.I.!" He paused a moment and grinned. "Well, shoot fire! I'll join, too!"

"You will?"

"Yep, I'll walk down to the draft board and sign up this

afternoon. We can go to war together! Man, will we have fun! We'll turn Atlanta upside down, and I know Atlanta ain't ready for Johnny Little and Smitty Smith!"

Time flew by with Johnny's funny stories and corny jokes. Smitty looked at the sun and knew it was past time to head toward Janice's house.

"Hey, I better go. I've got to give Janice my news."

"Why don't we make like a bakery truck and get our buns out of here?" quipped Johnny. They laughed and hurried to the Little's house since Smitty had to walk that direction to reach the Millers.

As fate would have it, Johnny was in for a shock. He stopped by the mailbox and almost fainted when he pulled out his draft notice delivered the day before. He held it in his hand, looked at it for a moment, and had difficulty believing his eyes.

Johnny jumped up and down, yelling, "I'm going in the Army and be a soldier. I'm going to Atlanta with Smitty. Ain't that something! I won't have to enlist; I've been drafted.".

They would travel to Atlanta for their physicals with August first looming as a big day for the close friends.

***

Smitty covered the two miles to the Millers' home in less than twenty minutes. He had planned to be there before lunchtime, but the events of the morning made him late. With it being almost two o'clock, his lunch would be leftovers, but he decided Eunice's warm-ups would be fine with him.

The Millers' house always looked like a picture, painted yellow with a large porch, white rocking chairs, and a white swing. Janice's mother, Eunice, loved flowers, and their front yard was a rainbow of colors, forming a beautiful tapestry. The yard exploded with so much beauty and brilliance, it looked like a floral shop. The smell of gardenias filled the summer air. He thought they smelled like expensive French perfume even though he had never smelled any such thing.

Before he reached the Millers' house, Roger Brown's car rumbled down the dirt road and covered Smitty in a dust cloud. Roger was his enemy and rival for Janice's love. He appeared to be headed to the Millers' house, but he sped past after seeing Smitty.

Roger knew Smitty would be angry if he found him with Janice. The last time he and Roger fought over Janice, Smitty had put the fear of God in him. They had a come-to-Jesus moment.

Roger had richer-than-thou and better-than-thou attitudes and had been raised with a silver spoon in his big mouth. The Browns had money and flaunted it. Roger's mother, Claudine Brown, enjoyed life as a wealthy socialite and valued social standing more than money, power, or wealth. Her goal in life was for the Browns to be the leading family in Ringgold, and she was doing everything in her power to attain her goal.

# *CHAPTER FIVE*

The Browns had spoiled their only child by giving him everything he wanted, and he always had the best of everything. He was prideful, haughty, and looked down on everyone, acting like the king of Ringgold.

As he walked up to the Millers' house, he saw the most gorgeous creature God ever created. Janice looked like a fashion model sitting on the swing wearing a sky blue dress that matched her eyes. Her gold ponytail was tied with a light blue ribbon, and her beautiful skin was glowing in the sunlight. Compared to all the flowers in the garden, she was the most beautiful. His heart skipped a beat, and the male thing inside him stirred. He flushed with the anticipation of holding and kissing such a gorgeous woman.

Janice jumped from the swing, ran to him, leaping into his arms. She hugged him tightly, and he could feel the warmth of her body, with his heart racing as his mind filled with passion and desire.

He could not wait to tell her his news and blurted out, "Janice, I've been drafted into the Army, and I could be dispatched to the war."

Alarmed and shocked, she pulled back, looking into his eyes. She was speechless as she took a deep breath. Overwhelmed by the tragic news, she started shaking and became agitated.

Janice's temper exploded as she raised her voice and screamed, "NO! You can't go. You might never return from the war, and we might never see each other again." She took his hand and led him to the front porch swing. "I won't allow you to go. You have to stay with me and be my lover. There has to be a way to keep you out of the war."

She sobbed as she laid her head on his shoulder. He knew Janice wanted him to kiss her, so he leaned forward with anticipation, just as Eunice opened the front door. She had come outside to put cotton in the door screen to fill some torn places. The cotton would fill the holes and keep flies from entering the house.

"Hello, Smitty," she said. "How's your day going? We have been washing and cleaning all morning and are about to have a late lunch. Would you like to join us?"

He walked to Eunice, hugged her, with a warm feeling inside. Any day became a wonderful day when you were invited to eat with the Millers.

"I made fried peach pies this morning in case you came to visit today. Janice said you might come to see her. We've missed seeing you with all your plowing and planting."

Smitty had difficulty deciding which he wanted more: kisses from Janice or fried peach pies from Eunice's wood stove. He could kiss Janice later, so he said, "Yes, Ma'am, I would love to eat lunch with y'all. It would be my highest honor and greatest pleasure to slide these feet under Eunice Miller's table. You're one of the finest cooks in Northwest Georgia." He smiled, knowing his plan had worked.

He knew better than to say "the finest" cook because his mama was the best cook in the world with Eunice rating second best. He held on to the possibility his compliment might secure him a couple of fried pies to take home after he stuffed himself at lunch.

He loaded his plate with white, half-runner green beans, fried okra, fried squash, and vine-grown tomatoes picked that morning from the Millers' vast vegetable garden. He went back for seconds on the fat-back meat Eunice used to flavor the green beans, deciding the fat-back tasted better than the beans. Eunice's sweet tea washed down bite after bite. Janice's beauty and Eunice's fried peach pies filled his mind and his stomach with pleasure.

He told Mrs. Miller about his draft notice and Mindy dying. Her sympathy lasted a minute before she turned to her favorite topic and began criticizing her husband as the scum of the Earth. She loved to tear him down and expound on his every fault. Smitty liked Mr. Miller and admired him for his continual battle to avoid becoming a henpecked husband. The thought occurred to Smitty, given Mrs. Miller's tirades against her husband, that Janice could inherit some of her bad traits.

After lunch, Janice wanted to walk with him to Little Chickamauga Creek, saying, "I want to see Old Mindy's grave." Her request raised his curiosity because she had never shown any affection for the mule. He concluded Janice might have other plans.

He and Janice strolled toward the bottoms and waded in Little Chickamauga Creek's chilly water. Janice decided to go swimming. In a flash, she lifted her dress over her head, and to his surprise, she stunned him with her naked body. He hadn't realized she wasn't wearing anything underneath her clothing.

Shocked and speechless, he debated whether to run or move closer. He froze with all kinds of thoughts and concerns flashing through his mind.

He remembered what had happened to his brother Tommy in Emma's bed and a drunken TJ McCord in Chattanooga. He thought of how their actions had ruined their lives and how unhappy they were after yielding to their temptations. A moment of pleasure had cost them a lifetime of pain, loss, and unhappiness.

He thought back to his Sunday School lessons at church, He remembered a seducing woman named Eve seduced Adam, the first man. A Shulamite beauty outwitted and seduced the wisest man in the world, Solomon. Samson, the strongest man in the world, was overpowered and seduced by a cutie named Delilah and Bathsheba outsmarted and attracted the most spiritual man in the world, David, and caused him to fall.

A beautiful, seductive woman was now rushing to seduce him! His future and his faith were at stake, and he did not want to throw them away.

He felt he could not take Janice as his lover, knowing how great his mama's disappointment and hurt would be with a child out of wedlock. He did not want to sin before God and could feel the pressure of Mr. Miller's shotgun as he and Janice would be forced into a wedding before the Justice of the Peace. He did not want to ruin his, Janice's, or their families' reputations.

He had a few seconds to make his decision. All those realizations flashed through his mind instantly, and he decided he did not want to risk becoming a father or be involved in a shotgun wedding.

He leaped from the creek and ran through the bottoms as fast as his legs could carry him, glancing back to see Janice completely startled. He acted on the first excuse that popped into his head. He screamed at the top of his lungs, "The buzzards are over Mindy's grave and want to eat her body."

It wasn't a lie with several low flying buzzards circling Mindy's grave. The sight of him jumping around the pile of rocks and shouting at a flock of circling buzzards would have been hilarious to anyone other than Janice Miller, who had quickly dressed.

Janice stormed up to him at the big oak tree mad as fire with her hands on her hips. "If you don't want me, I'll find someone who does!" she ranted. "I thought you loved me, and I can't believe you refused my offer and did not want me at all. There are plenty of other fish, and I'm going fishing."

He became upset, angry, and flustered as he reached for her hand. She jerked it away and stood glaring at him. Her anger spewed out at him, with her fuming and vindictive at not getting her way.

"I do love you," he insisted. "I do want you, but I want you the right way. I want you when we are married, and you become my wife."

Janice shot back, "You're going to want me someday, and I'm going to run from you the way you ran from me today!"

She turned away, stopped, and stared at him with narrowed, steely eyes. "I'm going to find a man who wants me and won't be afraid to take me. I'm going home so you can be on your way to the stinking Army." She turned and stormed off without looking back.

He realized he had to walk around Janice like walking around quicksand or a land mine ready to explode.

***

Wednesday, August, first seemed to take forever to arrive. He and Johnny counted down every day before their trip to Atlanta for their physicals. They both had slept fitfully the night before and were up before the crack of dawn.

He had tossed and turned most of the night broken-hearted with thoughts he could be spending his last day with Hannah, Junior, and Maria. The possibility of not returning home filled his mind with the dangers and changes facing him, feeling like lead weights on his shoulders. He struggled to control his emotions with dread, sadness, and fear flooding in.

He needed a suitcase or traveling bag, but knew he would travel without one since no one in his family had ever used a suitcase. Junior was the only family member to spend time away from home, and that, when he was in the county jail and served in the war.

Without money to purchase a suitcase or traveling bag, Hannah removed a pillowcase from Smitty's feather bed. She sewed a string around it to pull it tight. He was embarrassed with the homemade bag but knew he would be forced to carry it.

He folded his Sunday shirt and pants and placed them in the bag. As he packed his razor and a few personal things, he realized everything he owned could fit in the sack. He took a wrinkled five-dollar bill he had saved for emergencies and placed it in his sock, knowing his foot odor would prevent anyone from touching it. His shoes smelled like something had crawled into them and died. He felt his money would be safer in his sock than locked in the Calhoun National Bank vault with Tommy Smith and Clinton Taylor guarding it.

Sadness and sorrow kept pulling him down. He did not want to leave the farm, his family, or Janice. It would be hard to leave Janice with so many unanswered questions about her aggressive sexual actions. His wants and desires did not enter the picture since he would belong to Uncle Sam and would have to obey any orders the Army would issue.

He kept his composure until Maria walked into the living room and placed a new red pencil in his hand. He quickly realized she wanted him to use the pencil to write her letters. Tears filled her eyes as she wrapped her arms around him. Her love brought his tears, and he held Maria so close he could feel her heart beating.

With Maria's health declining, he felt she might not live very long and might not be alive if he returned. He swallowed hard and took a deep breath, thinking he could be seeing her for the last time. The thought of her possible death crushed him.

He took Maria's hands and promised, "I'll write to you every week and tell you about my new adventure. I promise I will. Cross my heart and hope-to-die promise."

As he peered into her brown eyes, he noticed the black circles. Her seizures came more frequently, were more debilitating, and her medicine did not seem to be working. He knew Hannah would have a difficult time dealing with Maria's declining health and possible death.

He had been the one to care for Maria when she suffered her seizures. He kept a wooden spoon on the mantle to put between her teeth to prevent her from chewing her tongue. Each episode had become more severe with him thinking each one could be her last. During some of her worst seizures, she would lose her breath. He knew Hannah couldn't handle Maria's attacks alone. He was concerned Maria could be left without anyone to care for her.

He wanted Junior to step up and help, but he knew Junior would always be Junior. Whenever Maria had a problem, Junior would disappear without supporting anyone. He ran from problems and issues straight to his bottle.

He reconciled himself to the closing of one chapter in his life and the opening of another. He was concerned with what the new era could bring. He never liked uncertainty and always wanted things in his life to be perfect and in order.

After visiting with Maria, he walked to his bedroom, reached into a dresser drawer, and removed a toy train his rich aunt, Betty Everett, had given him on his eighth Christmas. He was abandoning his hope to keep his treasured possession and pass it on to his son, but he saw a higher purpose for the toy.

He wound up the spring-mechanized train and handed it to Maria. She sat down on the floor and watched the train go around as she smiled and laughed. He had never allowed anyone, not even Johnny, to touch his train. He knew Maria would treasure the gift and spend hours and days enjoying it. He had a feeling the train might be his last gift to his sister. He dried his tears, swallowed hard, and left Maria playing.

As he walked through the living room, he heard someone talking, but could only see his mama in her chair. He stood listening as she prayed for God to protect her son. She looked up and smiled.

"Son, it may get tough, and things may look hopeless, but God will be with you every step of the way. You will make it through. I want you to know you will make it through."

Hannah reached into her apron pocket and pulled out a small Bible with a metal cover, with William Bryan Smith, II engraved on it. "This Bible belongs to your daddy. The Army issued it to him when he entered World War One. He carried it through the war and brought it home."

Hannah gazed at him and said, "I want you to carry this with you wherever you go and read it when you can. Draw strength from it when you need strengthening. This little Bible may save your life. I want you to bring it back to me when you come home."

He answered, "I promise you, and you know I have never lied to you." When he took the Bible from Hannah's hand, they were both crying. "I will come back to you when the war is over, he whispered, kissing his mama on the cheek. I promise I will."

He glanced around for Junior as he picked up the full pillowcase. Junior never liked anything emotional. Smitty suspected he had slipped out to the barn to take a few shots of white lightning. Smitty realized his father was an emotional cripple who could not handle his son's departure and could not even see him off.

He thought about his dad and decided to tell him goodbye. He determined he would not be wounded by the man who should love him the most. He had decided he would not follow his daddy into an early grave. He walked out the back door and crossed the swept dirt yard to the barn. As he stepped into the ram-shackle structure, he could not believe what was awaiting him. Junior leaned against the loft ladder, holding a whiskey jar in his right hand with tears running down his cheeks.

Seeing Junior cry stunned him and stopped him in his tracks. Smitty walked over to his daddy and hugged him for the first time in his life. He had never realized how frail, and bony Junior's body was. Alcohol had taken his strength, and Smitty realized it could soon take his life.

He reached for his daddy's hand and held it, "Thank you for being my father. I love you, Daddy."

He suddenly knew that, despite all the junk in Junior's life, he loved his father. He understood the silence when Junior opened his mouth but could not speak. The hug and Smitty's words had broken something in his father's heart. He walked back to the house, looked around, wanting to remember his life and the things he would leave behind. He hugged Hannah and Maria for the last time.

He kissed his mother on the cheek and said, "You're the most wonderful mother in the world. I thank God he chose you for me." Pausing a moment, he added, "Thank you for your love and the care you've given me through the years. I love you, Mama, with all my heart."

As they walked to the front door, he kept holding his mama's hand and released it when he pushed open the screen door and walked into the sunlight.

Even as he descended the rickety steps into the yard, he still heard Hannah repeating, "You'll make it. You will make it through. You will make it through."

Looking back, he nodded when she said, "Trust God and keep your faith. You will make it through."

***

As he strolled across the dusty front yard, he noticed the absence of flowers. The yard had once been filled with beautiful flowers and shrubs. He looked at the stumps where giant shade trees once thrived, having long since been cut and split for firewood. Not a blade of grass had survived the summer's heat, with only chickweeds and nut weeds growing in the yard.

The Greyhound bus from Ringgold was scheduled to leave for Atlanta at 10:15. He would have time to see Janice and tell her goodbye before leaving - if she would talk to him after he had rejected and embarrassed her.

As he walked away, he took one last look at 211 Maple Road and teared up. Little Blackie, a mutt he had found injured and abandoned on the roadside, followed at his heels. The cocker spaniel was small and black as midnight, so he had named him Little Blackie. The dog did not yelp or bark but was content to walk with him and seemed to sense he might be taking his last walk with Smitty.

He patted his dog on the head, rubbed his ears, then shooed him back to the house, before continuing down the road. His dog returning home heightened his feelings of being alone. He took one last look at the Smith house as he rounded a curve and choked back his sorrow and grief as his home disappeared from view.

The farther he walked from the house, the more he cried. With no one around, he released his feelings and sadness from his difficult life. He was overcome with grief over leaving his family.

As he walked down Maple Road, he allowed his mind to wander to thoughts of battle. He thought about his family's heritage and how it had been filled with war. Smitty had spent time researching historical events around Ringgold and the Smith farm. His love for history became evident when he won the Outstanding History Student Award at Ringgold High. The faculty had presented him a certificate, a trophy, and a small scholarship he knew he would never utilize.

He loved history books and had used his mind and imagination to experience historical events. He had spent thousands of hours plowing the bottoms, passing the time in vicarious visits to history-rich times and places.

His love of Civil War history had grown after he studied battles fought around Ringgold. The Smiths' front porch overlooked Ringgold Gap. On this site, Confederate General Patrick Cleburne used four thousand troops around the Ringgold Train Depot to hold off twelve thousand Union troops under Union General Jack Hooker. General Cleburne always credited God for his victory. Even though the Confederate troops were outnumbered over three to one, they held firm to gain an impossible triumph.

This battle taught Smitty a significant life lesson. No matter how outnumbered you are, you always can win if you do not surrender. He understood looking to God instead of circumstances could change the direction of any battle. He prayed he would never forget that lesson if he ever faced that scenario in this war.

He thought back to when he and Johnny hiked up East Chickamauga Creek and over Ringgold Gap, pretending to be soldiers. He thought about them using their Barlow pocket knives to dig musket balls from the trees.

They found many artifacts from the battles on the Smith farm. Johnny even found bones he swore were from a fallen soldier, though Smitty believed they were from a deer or some other animal. Nevertheless, Johnny vowed to keep the bones the remainder of his life.

"These bones are part of history," he declared. "They represent a soldier giving his life for his country."

As far as he knew, Johnny still had the bones in a leather bag in a dresser drawer.

As he crossed the railroad tracks at the edge of town, another piece of history came to mind. In 1862, a Union spy named James J. Andrews stole a train called the General from Big Shanty near Atlanta. Another locomotive named The Texas chased the stolen locomotive in reverse until the General ran out of water in the Smith farm's shadow.

The Union soldiers abandoned the General and scattered into the woods. Most of the soldiers, known as Andrews' Raiders, were captured and tried as spies. Smitty's grandfather, William Bryan Smith, claimed his father was one of the spies from the General who hid in a root cellar on the Holcomb farm. Even though he was a Yankee, he later married a Holcomb girl and inherited the farm. While most of the twenty-six members of the raiders were caught and hung, the Confederate Army never apprehended William Smith.

William Smith was Smitty's great-grandfather, who later received the Medal of Honor from the United States Congress. He was James J. Andrews' right-hand man in the raid. A fire destroyed his medal when the original Smith home burned in 1870. Smitty's spirit was stirred to become a hero whenever he heard stories about his great-grandfather.

***

The town clock showed 9:20, and he knew he would have just enough time to visit Janice since it only took a few minutes to walk from the Miller home to the town square.

As he plodded down the dirt road toward Janice's house, Roger Brown almost ran him down again. Red dust swirled from under Roger's Plymouth, covered him, and left him coughing, wheezing, and fighting mad.

He had one last opportunity to see Janice, and he was determined Roger was not going to spoil it. He sprinted up the Millers' driveway as Roger stepped from his car.

He stomped over to Roger, "If you don't leave right now, I'm going to wipe that dirt road with your face. If I find you've been with Janice while I'm gone, I'll put you in the hospital in Chattanooga or in a casket at Jones Brothers Funeral Home. Do you understand what I'm saying?"

Roger flushed with anger and stopped in his tracks, shaking with fear, and claiming his innocence. "You had better leave me alone. I have told you I'm not interested in Janice, and I stopped to see if Eunice needed any groceries. I've got more important things to do than waste my time with you."

He jumped into the Plymouth and roared down the drive breathing a sigh of relief that he could lie his way out of a dangerous confrontation with Smitty. He knew if he fought him, there would be two hits. Smitty would hit him, and he would hit the ground.

Smitty knew Roger was a coward and a mama's boy and felt he wouldn't have to worry about Roger, but he would have to be very concerned with Janice. He was having second thoughts about their relationship. He doubted he could trust her, having realized you can't change a person; you can only change their circumstances. Though he knew he could not alter her behavior, he held out hope marriage might make a difference.

Janice came through the screen door without any signs of anger. She had been so irate with him, he did not know if she would speak to him again. To his surprise, she welcomed him with a smile, a hug, and a kiss.

He apologized for being rude, "I am sorry about yesterday. With me going to the Army, I did not want to risk anything and leave you in trouble. I had hoped you would understand."

He changed the subject to his trip to Atlanta and his departure to the Army.

Janice took his hands and said, "I don't want you to go. I love you, and I want you. I understand your concerns, but I want to give you something to make you return to me. I don't know if you will come home or not, so I want you to be my lover before you leave for the war."

She pressed against him and whispered, "Daddy is on a business trip to Nashville, and mama is at the women's Tuesday morning church fellowship." She raised her eyebrow and said, "We are all alone! There isn't anyone within miles of here."

She motioned him inside, but he suggested they sit on the swing.

He sat down and expected Janice to sit beside him, but to his surprise, she slid into his lap, wrapped her arms around his neck, and kissed him. Each kiss was more prolonged and more passionate. They were breathing heavily, with him resisting her with all his strength and determination.

She blew in his ear and whispered, "Remember

yesterday? I'm ready, I'm willing, and I'm available."

Janice's actions shocked him and set him on his heels with her making another attempt to seduce him. She was acting like a cheap, low-class hussy he did not know or care for. What she did at the creek and on the front porch made her look like a tramp. He decided Janice was too hot and too fast for him to handle. He was seeing her real side, and he did not like it at all.

He had heard whispers and stories about Janice but never believed them. He always stood up and defended her. He had to face the truth with so many rumors from so many people. Janice had provided enough evidence to validate the stories. He had been blind and unwilling to believe anything wrong about her, but her urging him to have sex in broad daylight on the Millers' front porch convince him. He had been hoodwinked and deceived.

He pulled back from her with reality and disappointment flooding him and leaving him feeling someone had slammed him in his face. This was not the Janice he had always loved.

She looked at him and said, "I love you, Smitty. I've loved you since we were children. I have always wanted you, but I am not sure you want me. Are you going to turn me down and run again?" She started unbuttoning her blouse.

He gained his composure and whispered, "I do love you."

He decided Janice was a conniver and manipulator with him thinking she could have an ulterior motive to her actions. He felt she might have a sinister plan involving him, a quick marriage, and Army pay. The way she seemed to be forcing herself on him made him wonder if she might be pregnant and seeking a way to name him the child's father. He couldn't be called the father if he never accepted her offer. He definitely had second thoughts about Janice and decided he would no longer blame his thoughts on his imagination.

He wished he could forget the Army, the Greyhound bus, and the world but knew he had to leave. He had spent too much time with Janice. The Army, the bus, and the trip to Atlanta became urgent matters. The possibility of missing his bus jarred him to reality. To be absent without leave and miss his physical would not sit well with the Army. He didn't have any desire to be punished at the start of his military service.

After realizing it was past time to get to the bus station, he panicked, knowing the bus would leave at 10:15 with or without him. He grabbed Janice, kissed her in his most passionate way, and held her tight. He would never face anything as stressful as leaving Janice but knew he had to flee now, or he might not flee at all.

He broke from her embrace, leaped off the porch, and headed down the dirt road. He yelled, "I think I've missed my bus!"

He stopped in his tracks after he glancing back to see Janice weeping. He ran back to the porch and kissed her again. He wanted to chuck the Army and surrender to his passions. With great inner conflict, he changed his mind and decided he would accept Janice's offer. She had worn his resistance and determination down.

He said to himself, "To heck with the Army and whatever punishment they give me. I don't care anymore. I will yield to Janice and give her what she wants. He walked to the porch, sat down on the swing, and said, "I am ready to be your lover."

He took her in his arms and kissed her just as Rodney O' Dell, the mailman, pulled up with Eunice's package. He greeted them with a smile that indicated he suspected what he had interrupted after seeing Janice's open blouse. Everyone in Ringgold would soon know what they were doing on the Millers' porch.

He was shaken and came to his senses. He leaped from the porch, lifted his pillow bag, and ran as fast and as far as possible, never looking back. The buzzards and the mailman had kept him from making a huge mistake. He was crushed and kept kicking himself for running from the thing he wanted most in life, to make Janice his wife. He sprinted into Ringgold, knowing he only had a few minutes to make arrangements, secure his ticket, and board the south-bound bus.

# CHAPTER SIX

Smitty rushed down Nashville Street, racing past Bishop's Cafe, Whelchel's Barber Shop, Rime's Drugs, and McClelland's Five and Dime. He slowed at Brown's Grocery when he saw Roger glaring through the front window. He didn't have time for Roger, so he raced on.

He headed for Jerry's Sinclair station. The bus ran twice a day, once in the morning to Atlanta and once from Atlanta in the afternoon. Without a bus depot in Ringgold, Jerry's wife, Billi, handled bus service tickets.

When he didn't see a bus waiting, he panicked, afraid the bus had left already. Then he saw someone with a small brown suitcase thrown over his shoulder running toward him. As the pair converged, he slowed down, but Johnny kept racing toward him. He saw Johnny's silly grin half a second before Johnny tackled him and threw him to the ground.

Smitty jumped up, shoving Johnny aside. "What the heck is the matter with you, Johnny?" he shouted.

Johnny stumbled to his feet, laughing. "I send my mother to whip tougher men than you," he roared. "You're not much of a soldier if I can knock you down in the street. You've got to get tougher if you're going to fight in the United States Army." He laughed and punched Smitty. "Those krauts will beat the devil out of you. Come on, Smitty, get tough."

Johnny tousled Smitty's hair, put him in a headlock, and asked, "Are you ready for Atlanta? Do you think Atlanta is ready for us? Hot dog, let's head south for the big city!"

Again, Smitty brushed off Johnny's rough-housing

efforts, grabbed his arm, and led him to one of the benches outside the filling station. Before the two could sit down, Larry Garth, the star quarterback of the Ringgold School football team, walked out of the restroom.

"You get drafted, too, Garth?" Johnny asked.

Larry had been the best baseball pitcher the Ringgold Lions ever had. He had told everyone he would not be drafted since the University of Georgia Bulldogs wanted him to play football and baseball. Most people believed him, but Smitty did not fall for his lies and thought he was blowing smoke.

Larry frowned and said, "I should be getting ready for the season's first game, but the Army has priority."

They were sitting on the bench jawing when the Greyhound bus rolled into the parking lot and blasted the horn. Billi met the boys at the bus and handed them tickets to Atlanta, compliments of Uncle Sam. A sickly-looking bus driver opened the storage compartment and threw in two suitcases and a sewed-up pillowcase. Three young men boarded the bus before it roared to life and headed south for Atlanta.

Johnny went for the back of the bus, pulling Smitty to where the black people sat. Larry found a seat up front since he did not care about sitting in the back.

Ulysses Johnson, a black farm worker, worked the fields on the Little farm for years. After Johnny's father, Henry, was hit by a truck and killed when Johnny was four, Ulysses and his family came alongside the Littles to help. After Johnny grew old enough to take over as man of the house, the Johnsons moved on. They were like family to Johnny and Louise. Ulysses and Johnny were very close, with Ulysses planting in his heart a love for black people. Ulysses was the closest thing Johnny ever had to a father.

Johnny felt the people at the rear of the bus were

friendlier than those at the front and felt more comfortable sharing the bus ride with them.

Neither Smitty nor Johnny agreed with the way blacks were being treated in the South. Most towns had separate schools, restrooms, and water fountains for blacks and whites. Johnny never understood why black people had to sit at the back of the bus, so he would sit with them to show his support.

Johnny and Louise had taken the bus to Chattanooga many times to visit Johnny's aunt Olive. Johnny had ridden in the back of the bus on his first trip and always sat in the back on other trips.

Smitty and Johnny had talked about how a person should never be treated differently because of their skin color. They had experienced a sharp cultural shift for young men whose fathers had worn the white robes and hoods of the Ku Klux Klan and burned crosses.

Smitty told Johnny, "I don't see any difference in white and black people. Jesus did not come to save skin, He came to save souls. We should love each other regardless of the color of our skin. I feel this world would be a better place if people would love each other and get along. God is no respecter of persons, and neither should we be."

Johnny never met a stranger, could talk to a fence post, and moved from seat to seat talking to every passenger. He made sure he spoke to every person, "How y'all doing? We're on our way to Atlanta to go in the Army, and we're going to fight. This is Smitty Smith, who will soon be a hero. I'm Johnny Little, and I'm going to help the United States win the war and beat the devil out of the Germans."

Smitty listened to Johnny ramble on while he enjoyed his window seat with a view. He had waited all his life to visit Atlanta and was amazed to be on a bus flying down the road at thirty miles an hour, heading for the big city.

Larry considered himself too good to sit at the back of the bus, so he took a seat behind the driver. Smitty did not care for Larry, knowing he was full of pride and arrogance with a Roger Brown kind of attitude.

Smitty looked toward the front of the bus to locate Larry. Johnny beat him to the punch and said, "Look at lucky Larry, he's sitting by a looker, and from her looks, the looker may be a hooker."

Johnny laughed at his witty observation. The lady qualified as a looker, and they could not keep their eyes off her. She drove them crazy when she stood up to stretch in her tight-fitting black dress and black hose. They were drawn to her shiny black hair in a tightly wound bun. They could not comprehend why a looker like her would be traveling on a Greyhound bus through rural Northwest Georgia.

Johnny said, "I don't know if she's a looker or a hooker. I think she's both. Don't let her have a close look at me, or she'll have to have me. I wish I could show her my all-over Hollywood tan. I bet she's never seen anything like my golden body!"

When the two visited with her during a bathroom stop, they discovered she was headed to Atlanta to be the star entertainer at the Martinique Club. She introduced herself as Lila Leigh from Raleigh, North Carolina. She told them, "I've been headlining in New York City, and I am headed to Atlanta after spending a week with my mother in Chattanooga."

She told the two future GIs, "Come to the club and be my guests. I'll entertain you and buy the drinks."

Lila Leigh's beauty overwhelmed Smitty and left him thinking no one could compare to her except Janice. He considered Janice a young beauty, but Lila was a full-bodied woman. He decided she was drop-dead, knock-your-eyes-out gorgeous, feeling she had movie star beauty that exceeded any star he had seen on the big screen at the Ritz Theater.

Larry wanted to visit with Johnny to pass the time, so he and Smitty switched seats. Lila found Smitty adorable with his good looks and Georgia charm. They chatted a few minutes, and Smitty was shocked when she took a pencil and paper and jotted down her phone number. He swallowed his gum when she placed her hand on his leg and began stroking it.

Nothing like that had ever happened to him except Janice's antics at Little Chickamauga Creek and on her front porch. With two beautiful women showing interest in him, he started to feel like a lady's man.

He could not believe Janice and Lila had made a move on him and asked himself, "How much better can my life get?"

Larry grew tired of Johnny's talking and returned to his seat. Lila grabbed Smitty's hand and wouldn't turn loose. Larry grew angry, cursed Smitty, and was ready to fight. He grabbed Smitty's shirt attempting to jerk him from his seat. He had always considered himself a tough guy, but he had never faced anyone like Smitty before.

He said, "So, you think you're quite a lady's man! What about Janice Miller? You ain't the first guy she's thrown herself at. She chased after me for months before I gave in. I considered her a smoking-hot number, but to tell the truth, she's nothing but a tramp."

Smitty could not respond after Janice's recent actions had shown him he could no longer ignore what Larry and others said.

He wanted to punch Larry's lights out and thought about whipping him until he decided his best action would be to move out of his way and not get thrown off the bus.

He knew he could take Larry with a single punch and knew he was more of a man than Larry would ever be. He pushed Larry out of his way and backed down from a fight.

Smitty told Lila, "This is Larry's seat, and Johnny and I need to make plans." He was shocked when she reached up from her seat, took his face in her hands, and gave him a long passionate kiss. After their kiss, Larry had little doubt Smitty had become a ladies' man.

Johnny clapped, whistled, and screamed at the sight. "Romeo, O Romeo, where art thou, Romeo? Smitty has become a Romeo!"

# *CHAPTER SEVEN*

The Greyhound bus rambled through the crowded streets of Atlanta. Smitty had visited Chattanooga but had never seen such a place as Atlanta. Craning to see the tall structures, some over ten stories high, he strained his neck. He saw the state capitol, Rich's department store, hotels, and office buildings, and even streetcars running through the heart of the city. He decided Ringgold could fit in one block in Atlanta.

The bus rolled into the Greyhound station with Smitty fighting his nerves and anxiety over what his destination and future might hold. He, Johnny, and Larry were unloading their luggage when three soldiers dashed to greet them. With the largest soldier snapping, "Smith, Little, Garth?"

They shouted in unison, "Yes, sir!"

One of the soldiers looked them over from head to toe and stated, "We've been expecting you, boys. Welcome to Atlanta!"

The boys were so naive they thought they were getting special treatment until they were ordered to wait in an old olive drab bus parked at the rear of the station. The bus, parked in full sun, was like an oven, and the men were ordered to remain on the bus until all draftees arrived.

The temperature was over a hundred and ten degrees in the bus with the August heat, making Smitty feel like he was standing too close to the woodstove at home. About twenty recruits were sitting on black leather seats hot enough to burn their butts through their pants. When Smitty sat down, he thought his pants would catch fire.

The three soldiers in charge were waiting for more inductees before departing for Fort McPherson. The bus from Valdosta was behind schedule by over three hours, and the soldiers' mood worsened as time passed. The soldiers came to the bus, ordered everyone off, and made them stand in the hot sun to use the toilet.

Johnny told Smitty, "I have TB."

" Tuberculosis?" Smitty couldn't believe his ears.

Johnny laughed and said, "TB, tiny bladder! I'm about to die to take a leak. Can you see if I've wet my pants?" His pants were as wet as if he had fallen into Little Chickamauga Creek.

He laughed at Johnny's humor before realizing everyone was soaked with perspiration. The men looked like they had taken showers with their clothes on.

Johnny complained about the line, the time, the heat, the misery, and pain from holding his water. He let everyone know he was agitated at his discomfort and poor treatment.

Sergeant Booker, one of the three soldiers walking by, overheard Johnny and jerked him up by his shirt's front. He snarled, "You're mine now, and you can be sure I'm not the one you want to complain to. You belong to me, and I want you to know I'm not your mama. You don't tell me what you want or don't want to do, son. You obey my orders and pray you don't have questions. You're now on my bad side, and my trouble makers list, and I can assure you that's not the place you want to be. You keep on, and I'll jerk a knot in your chain. If you're looking for hell, you've found it. Do you understand me?"

Johnny's response was, "Yes, sir."

"Don't call me 'sir.' It's Sergeant Booker to you."

"Yes, Sergeant Booker."

The sergeant put Johnny at the rear of the toilet line and

made him wait until every man on the bus had relieved himself in the one commode bathroom. Smitty and Johnny did not care for Sergeant Booker or the other two sergeants.

Johnny was fuming, and said, "I don't care for military life and never dreamed it would be like this. I'm ready to re-board the bus and head for home, but I know its too late, and we have to accept whatever the Army hands us. It doesn't matter how we feel since nothing will change our situation or the Army's power."

Sergeant Booker acted like a tyrant with him and Johnny knowing beyond a shadow of a doubt he wasn't their mama or their friend. They decided he was a mad man ready to explode and did not care who would be hurt, wounded, or killed in the explosion.

After the bus from Valdosta pulled into the station, they learned the driver had to change a flat tire. Afterward, the bus overheated near Macon, requiring the thermostat to be replaced. Twenty-six South Georgia draftees rambled from the bus and hurried to sort their bags.

The lead sergeant barked out orders. "Get your bags and get your rears on the bus. You don't want to make us angry by lollygagging around. You whining babies better be on the bus in three minutes or we're going to leave you here."

The orders were filled with profanity, threats, insults, and coarse sarcasm. They got in the recruits' faces, chewed them out, and wouldn't even let them use the toilet. They were introducing the draftees to military life in the United States Army.

Sergeant Booker's attitude and disposition were worse than the other two combined. His actions were wake-up calls for the recruits, and their responses had to be, "Yes, Sergeant Booker!"

After leaving the station, the bus driver seldom traveled

more than twenty miles an hour. Smitty felt that was as fast as the worn-out bus could travel with a full load of recruits, their luggage, three sergeants, and the driver. They were almost four hours late, had not eaten, the body odor in the bus took their breath, and the bus driver was driving like he was in a hearse leading a funeral procession.

The draftees cheered, clapped, and whistled as they passed the Fort McPherson entrance sign. They had endured enough pain and discomfort and were ready to complete their physicals, be shipped out, or returned home.

Smitty, Johnny, and Larry were directed into a vast assembly building where about a thousand draftees had gathered. They were greeted by Colonel Thomas Oliver, who said, "Welcome to Fort Mac. We're glad you answered your country's call, and you can see from your bus ride, we'll try to make your stay as comfortable as possible."

The men roared with laughter, moans, and groans.

"I have good news and bad news," he continued. Many of our buses have arrived late, and slow check-ins have affected our examination schedules. Some of you will be required to stay an extra day for your tests, examinations, and classification. I assure you, you'll be examined soon. Some of you will be tested Wednesday, and the remainder will be tested Thursday morning. The latter will be free Wednesday afternoon and have an opportunity to visit Atlanta. Atlanta is a rough city, so be careful where you go. Good luck, men."

He and Johnny were placed in the Thursday morning group with Wednesday afternoon and night free. The clerk assigned Larry Garth to the Wednesday group and dispatched him to a different area. After signing in and completing a couple of forms, the draftees were dismissed.

The next morning the soldiers gathered to complete the paperwork for their examinations. They sat in hard chairs for four hours while the Army staff taught the recruits to hurry up and wait. Johnny complained about his sore rear and reconfirmed his dislike of the Army. The Army kept them four hours to sign five forms and released them before noon.

Johnny could not get his mind off Lila Leigh at the Club Martinique. Even though Smitty did not want to go to the club, Johnny kept pressuring him. Johnny was persistent, could aggravate a person to death, and never backed off from anything once he got it in his head.

"You have to go, Smitty. You don't want to miss the fun and excitement of a nightclub, and you might even get a kiss or two from Lila, Romeo."

# CHAPTER EIGHT

He and Johnny toured the base in the afternoon. The boys couldn't comprehend the size of the base. Johnny fell in love with the tanks and military vehicles. He talked about driving a tank and taking on the entire German army by himself. Smitty chuckled when he told Johnny, "Your mind just ain't right and never will be. You never realize when you're talking crazy and pushing your luck."

Johnny kept talking about visiting Atlanta and pressured Smitty until he caved in. They boarded a bus pulling away from the main bus stop, with Atlanta looming on the horizon.

Johnny told the bus driver, "Take us to the big city. Atlanta can't be hot enough for us, and we're going to burn it down like General Sherman did."

The bus driver dropped the men off in the center of downtown. Without a clue where they were, they flagged a taxi. Johnny told the driver, "Take us to the front door of the Club Martinique. We have a hot number who can't wait to get her hands on us."

Johnny had all kinds of plans and expectations, and Smitty had never seen him so excited. He was burning with anticipation of what his big night in Atlanta could bring.

They rode the taxi for thirty minutes and saw parts of Atlanta most people would never see. They rode by some places two and three times. The cab driver, Bernie Fieldstein, had bragged, "I know Atlanta like the back of my hand."

The truth was, it was Bernie's first day driving a taxi, and Smitty and Johnny were his first fares. He had hoped to stall until he stumbled on their destination but never found the club and put them out back on Peachtree Street.

Bernie charged a dollar for a cab ride that should have cost a quarter. The boys glanced around and realized they were a block from where they had boarded Bernie's taxi.

Johnny asked a couple of people for directions to the Club Martinique. An old drunk sitting on a street corner raised his bony finger and pointed north. On a main street, off the next intersection, a neon sign flashed "Club Martinique."

Johnny made a joke about taking a personal, chauffeured tour of Atlanta. Of course, he wouldn't tell anyone it was in a taxi with a lost driver that had overcharged them for the ride.

They could've walked two blocks from the bus stop and reached the club in a couple of minutes. If they had looked northward at the next block, they would have seen the sign. Johnny slapped Smitty on the back, flashed a grin, and said, "Welcome to the big city!"

In minutes, they were outside the club, and the crowd of people lined up validated it was Atlanta's hottest nightspot. A long line was pressing at the doors to get inside with two bouncers attempting to manage the crowd.

Johnny broke for the front door when Smitty noticed a sign: "Two Dollar Cover Charge. Drinks not Included."

They could not believe admission was two dollars without a free drink.

"I'm going in no matter what it costs," Johnny said. "I've waited all my life to drink a cocktail in a night club, and nothing's going to stop me. I'm going to let the women see a real man. They would die seeing my all-over Hollywood tan."

Smitty thought Johnny was obsessed with his tan and actually considered it his most striking quality.

Johnny slicked back his hair, wet his lips, did a little dance, and headed for the front door.

Smitty stopped Johnny and said, "All I have is a five-dollar bill, and it's in my sock. I'll have to sit down on the sidewalk and take off my shoe and sock to get the money. I won't drink any cocktails, even if they are free. I've seen Junior drink enough alcohol to make me despise it. I will never touch a drop of alcohol in my lifetime."

Johnny came up with one of his big ideas. "I'll talk to the doorman and let him know we're friends with Lila Leigh. I'll pay my two dollars and see if I can talk him into letting you in free. I'll see if he'll be generous to two future soldiers on their way to the war."

They were surprised and shocked when the doorman said, "Miss Leigh left Smitty Smith's name on her guest list. You gentlemen follow me to the VIP entrance."

Johnny concluded Smitty had more charm and good looks than he had thought and decided he had a way with women.

The lights were dim in the club. In the darkness, Johnny tripped over a chair and fell on his face. Everyone in the club turned to the commotion. Johnny's fall sounded like a bomb had exploded.

A large man in a dark blue suit, starched white shirt, and red tie made some cutting remarks about Johnny. "When the good Lord said brains, this bum thought he said rain and ran for cover."

Everyone near the man laughed with the drunk's remarks embarrassing Johnny. He became furious at being mocked in front of the women and was ready to fight. He blurted a few choice words in the drunk's direction and raised his fists ready for a fight.

Johnny could fight like a savage; he would spit, bite, claw, throw dirt into an opponent's eyes, and do whatever it took to punish his opponent. He topped six-foot-three and tipped the scales at two hundred and forty pounds. He was as strong as an ox from being raised on a farm and always found a way to win a fight.

After his temper boiled with his anger spewing forth, people in the club prepared for a brawl. He kept mumbling threats and throwing punches into the air. Smitty grabbed him and pulled him away from the drunk just before two large bouncers came and warned Johnny, Smitty, and the troublemaker they had to quieten down or leave.

Smitty tried to calm Johnny. "Dang, Johnny, don't act like a redneck farmer come to the big city and left all his manners at home. Mind your temper and your tongue, or I'm leaving. I did not come here for trouble, and you're going to get us hurt or killed if you don't stop jawing. You are overestimating the advantage of brute force and never realize when you are pressing your luck. You are acting like there's no way for you to get in trouble, and you feel you are invincible."

Johnny looked around and turned Smitty toward the elaborate stage at the club's front, where Lila was dancing in a skimpy exotic outfit. She ended her act by dropping a red scarf from her arms. Smitty and Johnny were shocked when she finished her show wearing nothing. She wasn't an entertainer or singer, she was a professional stripper.

Johnny and Smitty competed for whose eyes popped out the farthest. They got more than an eyeful of Lila, and there was more than an eyeful to see. Johnny grabbed his chest, moaned, and pretended, he was having a heart attack after seeing Lila naked.

Once she completed her act, she came from backstage wearing nothing but a thin white silk robe and a wide smile. She rushed to Smitty, wrapped her arms around him, and delivered a passionate kiss.

"I knew you would come to see me," she said. I wanted to be with you again. In fact, I would like to see a lot more of you if you know what I mean. Can we get together after I get off work?"

"I am sorry, but I can't stay the night. I have orders to return to Fort Mac by midnight, and the club won't close until 2 AM. I wish I could, but I won't be able to make it work."

Johnny could not understand what Smitty had that he did not have. Lila shook hands with him breaking his heart. Johnny was expecting the same kind of welcome kiss Smitty had received, with her handshake not what he expected from his hot night in Atlanta.

Lila asked, "Can I get you a drink? Whiskey, beer, a cocktail? It's on the house, and I'm buying drinks tonight to celebrate seeing Smitty."

Johnny lit up and said, "Let's have a party and get wild. I'll have a cocktail with whiskey. The stronger, the better. Do you have any girlfriends around here? Let's party till we drop."

Johnny's mouth fell open when Lila told him, "I'll introduce you to some of the girls at the break. They need to meet a real man like you."

Johnny's chest pushed out as he filled with anticipation and excitement. A nightclub, a cocktail, and maybe a dance with a beautiful woman would be everything he had expected from Atlanta.

Smitty whispered, "I would like a Coca Cola."

When Lila motioned for the hostess to seat them at her private table, the guys realized they were VIP guests of the club's major attraction and headliner. Lila had arrived in Atlanta as a rising star and had packed out the club after being recognized as one of the top three strippers in America.

Lila's private table was beside the drunk Johnny had a problem with when they entered the club. The drunk had too much to drink, was loud, obnoxious, and insisted on dancing with Lila. He had been obnoxious before but had passed that stage. He raised his voice calling Johnny and Smitty a couple of names and reached for Lila's robe.

Johnny reacted, grabbing the thug by his throat and throwing him over his table against the wall. Neither Johnny nor Smitty heard the snap of a switchblade knife when the angry drunk stood up, staggered forward, and stabbed Johnny in the heart.

Shocked, Smitty jumped to his friend's aid, but Johnny collapsed to the floor before he could catch him. Blood seeped from Johnny's chest and dribbled from the corner of his mouth as he lay gasping with his eyes darting side to side.

Smitty was horrified and screamed out, realizing Johnny could be dying, and there wasn't anything he could do. He felt as helpless as the day Mindy died.

He grabbed Johnny's shoulders, attempting to lift him from the floor. He pulled Johnny close to him, holding him in his arms.

"Johnny, Johnny! Get up, Johnny! Don't you die on me! Don't you stop breathing! You can't die, Johnny! You can't die! Call the police!" Smitty shouted. "Get help now! Get a doctor!"

Looking into his friend's eyes, Smitty prayed, "Lord, help! O, Lord, please let Johnny live!"

With the realization he could be dying, Johnny's eyes focused on Smitty as he found Smitty's hand and gripped it.

He forced a smile and said, "I guess we weren't ready for Atlanta after all. I did listen to you when you shared with me about Jesus. One night in my bed, I prayed and asked Jesus to save me. I have not been baptized, but I know I believe in Him and believe He will allow me into Heaven. I'll see you there. I love you, Smitty."

Johnny closed his eyes, took his last breath, and died in Smitty's arms. Smitty held him close and whispered, "I love you, my special friend. I will always love you."

Smitty sobbed and shook at the shock of Johnny's death. Lila pulled Smitty from Johnny's body and comforted him in her arms as she held him, kissed him, and cried with him. Johnny had died on the liquor-soaked floor of the Club Martinique in Atlanta at the age of nineteen.

Smitty lost control and broke from Lila's arms. In a rage, he searched for the man who stabbed Johnny and saw him hiding under a table, the knife in his hand. Smitty grabbed him with enough fury to kill him with his bare hands. He struck the man with his right fist and then his left, and the knife flew from his hand. He laid into the man with both fists flying furiously. His punches spun the drunk around, each blow taking its toll on some part of his body. Smitty beat the man unmercifully until two bouncers and a club employee pulled him off the killer.

Smitty searched for the switchblade that had been knocked away, but could not find it. Wanting to inflict more punishment, he broke away from those restraining him and dove for the killer with an urge to take his life. The club employees slammed Smitty to the floor and pinned him down until his anger and fury subsided.

Smitty wanted revenge, a life for a life. The killer ended up on the floor face down in a pool of his and Johnny's blood. The man's face was so cut and mangled it left everyone in the club thinking Smitty had beaten the man to death with him motionless on the floor.

The Atlanta police rushed into the club, examined Johnny's body, and declared him deceased. They interviewed witnesses, took statements, and filled out reports. A sergeant covered Johnny's body with a white sheet as other police officers arrested the drunk for murder. The police identified him as Gino Marcellie. People in the club knew him as part of the Marcellie crime syndicate in New York City. One of the club's employees told the police Gino was a powerful man and controlled the mob's gambling operations and prostitution ring.

Smitty knew Marcellie would be taken to jail. He feared he would not be held long but would post bond and be back on the streets within a few hours after the mob's lawyers used their money, influence, and connections to free him. Mr. Marcellie would never do time, see a rope, or be strapped into an electric chair. With his powerful connections, he would never spend a day or a night behind prison bars. At least Smitty had taken the opportunity to give him a beating he would always remember.

The police were putting Marcellie into a police car when he collapsed and fell unconscious to the pavement. They transported him by ambulance to Grady Memorial Hospital for emergency treatment. At one point, they thought Gino Marcellie had died.

A second ambulance arrived. The attendants placed Johnny's body on a gurney and loaded it into the back of the vehicle to transport him to the morgue.

Smitty continued to weep, his heart breaking and filled with denial that Johnny had died.

Lila held Smitty's hand and said, "Why don't you call the base and tell them what happened. You can spend the night with me and report in the morning. I want to make sure you are alright."

Smitty declined and reminded her, "I have orders to report back to Fort Mac by midnight. I don't want to get the Army involved. I don't think that would not be wise. I will take care of the Army issues in the morning."

He dreaded the call to Louise Little to tell her Johnny had been killed. He thought about asking one of the policemen to call but knew he should be the one to give her the horrible news. Smitty was overwhelmed, trying to decide how to break the news to Louise. He chose not to tell her Johnny had lost his life after being stabbed by a drunk in a nightclub. He would delay the call as long as he could.

As Smitty walked out of the Club Martinique, he vowed to never go into another bar, cocktail lounge, night club, or strip club again. He also renewed his vow to never drink alcohol. His anger and hatred were still raging when he vowed he would kill Gino Marcellie after the war.

In bed, Smitty was tormented with nightmares. He relived Johnny's murder over and over. When he closed his eyes, he could see Johnny's dying face and smell the fresh red blood oozing from his heart. He experienced periods of anger, fear, loss, sorrow, and grief. He had lost a lifelong friend and felt Johnny's shortened life wasn't long enough. Smitty had expected he and Johnny would live happy lives and grow old together.

His hands were skinned, scraped, and throbbing from his violent attempt to beat Johnny's killer to death. No matter the pain or price, he would have paid whatever he had to pay to take his revenge.

# *CHAPTER NINE*

He watched the sunrise as sadness and grief overtook him. He glanced at the small brown suitcase on the empty bunk next to him and fell into a well of emotions sobbing and moaning. No one in the barracks said anything about his weeping and understood it was from his deep love for his friend. Smitty had never been so happy for a night to end after experiencing a dark night for his soul and the darkest, saddest, and most horrendous night of his life.

After breakfast, two military policemen questioned Smitty about Johnny's murder. They took his statement and filed a formal report. The MPs informed him that Colonel Oliver, the base commander, wanted to meet with him later in the morning after the police reports were reviewed. He questioned what the big brass at the base could want from him.

Colonel Oliver asked him about the events of the night before. After hearing him out, he looked across his desk with great compassion and said, "I'm sorry about your friend. I know it's a terrible loss, and I know how you must be feeling. I have lost too many friends in this crazy war. I'm going to postpone your physical for five days to return home for your friend's funeral.

"I see from the reports you had nothing to do with the murder. I wish you boys had not visited the Club Martinique. And I hate you had to use so much force disarming his killer. I understand the doctors at Grady are struggling to keep the man alive. He is in critical condition in the intensive care unit with a brain bleed. If he survives, he may never walk again, confined to a wheelchair for the rest of his life. Please see me when you return to Fort Mac and tell me about Johnny's funeral. I would like to be there, but I won't be able to attend. I wish I could bring Johnny back, but I can't. Time and the good Lord does a lot of healing. You're dismissed, Smitty."

Johnny's funeral was sad, heart-breaking, and the most painful funeral Smitty had ever endured. At Jones Brothers Funeral Home, Louise Little moaned and cried so loud people could hear her in the parking lot. She wailed over Johnny's casket as though the louder she screamed, groaned, and cried, the more people would think she loved Johnny.

At the funeral, four pews at Shiloh Baptist Church were occupied. The preacher preached about walking through the valley of the shadow of death and how Christian believers should fear no evil because Jesus Christ is with them. Smitty knew he was walking through the shadow of Johnny's death.

Smitty, Janice, Roger, and a couple of young men Johnny's age who lived near the Little farm were the only young people in attendance. Johnny did not have many friends or loved ones. In fact, he and Johnny were such good friends they did not need any others. It occurred to Smitty that only a few people would attend his funeral if he was killed in the war. Smitty sat between Louise and Janice, feeling very uncomfortable and weeping through the service.

He attempted to hold Janice's hand, but she kept moving it to brush back her hair or pull at the hem of her dress. She acted strangely, with Smitty feeling she was still angry at him for rejecting her sexual advances. He cared for Janice but could feel their relationship changing. He decided he would not raise any issues with his life filled with too many complications and frustrations to open

Janice's bag of problems and issues.

The funeral lasted fifteen minutes, the shortest he could remember. A few people followed the preacher and pallbearers to the cemetery where, after a scripture and short prayer, the pallbearers lowered Johnny into his grave. His brief life on Earth had tragically ended.

Smitty had worried about Johnny's soul and prayed Johnny would make it to Heaven. Every time he had attempted to talk to Johnny about his faith, he would make a joke about having reservations in the other place. Johnny thought he would live forever.

It broke Smitty's heart to think Johnny could have died without being saved. He decided to believe God had enough grace, love, and mercy for Johnny to allow him to enter Heaven. He confessed he had been saved. After all, Johnny's last words were, "Smitty, I believe in Jesus. I believe He will let me in, and I will see you there."

Johnny's last statements provided some comfort to Smitty. He believed God's mercy and grace were deeper than people could comprehend, and he was holding his faith that he and Johnny would be reunited.

After everyone left the cemetery, Smitty stood before Johnny's grave with tears flowing. He whispered, "I love you, Johnny Little. I will never forget you. You've been the best friend any man could have, and I'm going to miss you. Goodbye, my special and forever friend."

Tears rolled onto his shirt as he walked from the grave, knowing he had lost a rare and valuable treasure. He realized any man with a friend like Johnny was a blessed man. A spirit of loneliness swept over him as he continued weeping. He had cried for Johnny, and now he was grieving for himself.

Smitty was shocked to see Mr. Beasley show up after the funeral. He approached Louise Little and said, "I want to tell you how sorry I am about your son. I want to apologize for the way I treated Johnny. I lied to justify shooting his dog. Worthless never chased any of my cows or chickens. I got mad at Johnny and took my anger out on his dog. Please forgive me for what I did. If Johnny were here today, I would ask his forgiveness, too."

Beasley lifted his old felt hat, placed it on his head, and walked away. Smitty followed him, shook his hand, and said, "I'm sorry for what Johnny and I did to you that Halloween night. I don't know the cost of new boots, but I'm willing to buy you a pair to make it up. Can you meet me at Brown's store early tomorrow morning?"

Mr. Beasley looked at Smitty and said, "I've already been repaid by talking to Johnny's mother and receiving her forgiveness. What I did has been difficult to carry. I have already forgiven you and Johnny for the trick you played on me. I deserved that and a lot more. I have been a hateful and grouchy old man, but I am leaving here different than when I came."

He wished Johnny could've heard Mr. Beasley's apology. He would've jumped up and down shouting, "I told you so. I told you Worthless was a good dog who never chased any cattle or killed any chickens."

Watching the old man walk away, he realized the power of forgiveness. He felt guilty he had vowed to kill Gino Marcellie after the war, and his unforgiveness weighed upon him. He knew his thoughts were hateful, unforgiving, and ungodly. Smitty felt if he did not forgive Gino, he could be locked in an emotional prison.

He whispered, "If I don't forgive him, I will not be forgiven. I know forgiving him benefits me more than him. He could care less. Forgiveness will break Gino's hold on me and will free me. I will have to allow God to take care of Gino Marcellie."

He released his hatred, looked to Heaven, and said, "God, I choose to forgive Gino Marcellie for killing Johnny. Forgive me for hating him and wanting to murder him. I cannot live with hatred and murder in my heart."

He felt the release of God's forgiveness and realized his way forward should never be revenge but forgiveness. He knew vengeance and murder were terrible roads to travel. Nevertheless, he still felt angry.

# CHAPTER TEN

Smitty had the Janice issue to work through. He had watched Janice and Roger arrive at Johnny's funeral in the Browns' black Plymouth. Janice told Smitty Roger had driven her to the funeral because her mother was sick and unable to attend.

Regardless of her excuses, Smitty felt Janice had written him off and counted him gone to die in the war. He felt there was more to the Janice and Roger situation and suspected they were lovers. Roger might have consummated with Janice what Smitty had determined not to do. He concluded Roger had not run away from Janice but ran to her. He was convinced Roger no longer feared his threats or a shotgun wedding.

Smitty attempted to push his anger down and deal with his disgust with the world and everyone in it. His anger raged toward Roger and Janice, toward Johnny for dying, at the drunk with the knife, at the Army for drafting him, and at God for allowing all the things to happen.

His life grew more miserable, leaving him unable to handle the emotional turmoil spilling from his soul's deepest recesses. Johnny's funeral had been depressing and somber, and losing Johnny had crushed his heart and filled him with sadness and grief. The funeral left him depressed to a level he had never experienced before.

Smitty felt like he was living out a nightmare on his bus ride back to Atlanta with rain driven by the wind, forcing the wiper blades to struggle to keep the windshield clear. The bus had encountered a dangerous situation with gusty winds blowing it all over the road. The driver was fighting to stay right of the center line and keep the bus out of the ditches. The driver was exhausted in his efforts to maintain his lane. The bus traveled five to ten miles an hour with Smitty feeling they were traveling through a monsoon. The high winds shook the bus with him feeling it could go airborne at any second. Smitty observed dark swirling clouds in the distance and concluded they had traveled through some severe thunderstorms or tornadoes. The area they traveled through was known as tornado alley.

While traveling on the bus, Smitty experienced a range of emotions, being mad, sad, glad, and afraid. His sadness made him feel the heavens were crying over Johnny's death.

One of the sergeants from his first trip picked Smitty up at the bus station, and they passed through Atlanta in a new military Jeep. Even though the Jeep's canvas was snapped in place, the torrential rain blew around the flaps and soaked Smitty. He felt like he had taken a shower with his clothes on when they reached the base.

# CHAPTER ELEVEN

On his arrival at the base, Smitty ran through pouring rain to his barracks and found the only things different were the men. He asked about Larry Garth and was informed he was classified 1A and sent home. Smitty said to himself, "So much for Larry playing football and baseball for the Georgia Bulldogs! I knew he was not telling the truth, just wanting to look like a big man."

Larry had told Smitty and Johnny he would request duty in the Pacific to fight the Japanese. He had said, "I don't like cold weather, and I prefer to do my duty on a Pacific island with sparkling waters and beautiful beaches. I hope they station me in Hawaii."

Smitty glanced at the bunk next to him where Johnny might have slept had he lived. He turned to his own bunk in deep sadness, fell face down on his pillow, and cried until he could not cry anymore. He was sick and tired of what his life had become, felt he was living out an endless nightmare, and wanted to wake up.

Smitty had never been to a doctor and did not know what to expect when people said "physical examination."

He followed the yellow lines on the floor in only his undershorts. He walked down a long corridor with examination rooms realizing he would be examined in every room. He obeyed the doctors' orders, "Open wide, look this way, breathe deep, close your eyes, cough."

The doctors and medical corpsmen examined every part of his anatomy. He handled the examination well until one of the doctors had him lower his shorts, bend over an examination table, and cough. Smitty resisted until he realized the doctor's actions were part of everyone's examination. He had never heard the word prostate and had no idea what it was or where it was located. Smitty wasn't prepared for the battery of medical tests and extensive examinations with the tests seeming to last forever.

He made friends with Jerome Dean from Perry, Georgia, and they discussed the exams. Jerome reminded him of Johnny with his continual griping and complaining.

Jerome frowned and said, "I've been examined every place but under my tongue. I have been punched, jabbed, and poked all over my body. Is this a medical facility or a torture chamber?"

Smitty agreed with Jerome and responded, "My daddy tried to tell me how this would be, but I did not believe him. I'm beginning to think this will never end. If this is how we start our Army life, what will the future bring?"

Smitty turned red with embarrassment when the doctors had everyone strip naked. A country boy from Ringgold was seldom naked in anyone's presence. He had never been naked before anyone except when swimming with Johnny or bathing. He fumbled around, very uncomfortable, and not knowing how to respond. He kept his hands over his private parts and tried not to turn red with embarrassment. He continued counting the minutes until his physical would end.

During his examination, Smitty kept looking at his feet. He was embarrassed at his size twelve feet that were wide, long, and stained from going barefoot on the farm. Over time, black dirt and red Georgia clay had created permanent stains, and his feet would not come clean no matter how much he soaked and scrubbed them.

He thought if Johnny had been there, he would've said, "Smitty, you must be an Indian. I can see by your feet you're a member of the Blackfoot tribe." Smitty smiled at his remembrance of Johnny.

Smitty passed his Army physical with "1A" stamped in bold, black letters at the top of his file. The last doctor looked at Smitty and said, "You're in perfect health. You should live to be a hundred if you survive this war."

"If" he survived the war, that was the big question. He had survived the medical examination, but could not imagine what difficulties were awaiting him on the battlefields. Smitty did not want to consider the "Ifs." He wanted to go on to the next chapter and close the current one.

His orders required him to report for basic training in less than a month and become Private William Bryan Smith, III. The Army would train him for combat and send him to war. He would become one of the ninety-day wonders the Army churned out, going from farm boy civilian to trained combat soldier in less than three months. Life had changed for Smitty, and he did not like the changes.

The war wasn't going well in Europe or the Pacific, with the United States needing every soldier they could train and deploy. The number of casualties and wounded combat soldiers increased daily. All branches of the armed services were under tremendous pressure to produce more fighting men in a shorter time.

Before he left Fort McPherson, he attended a briefing where eligible draftees were gathered to discuss future options. They were informed they had two choices. Their first option involved going home and waiting for orders with them receiving their final orders within four weeks.

With the second option, they would report immediately to basic training. Smitty learned early reporting would benefit him with additional opportunities for advancement and a cash bonus.

He thought about the second offer for a few minutes and decided it would be too difficult and painful to return home. He was not prepared for more disappointments and heartaches.

When the Major asked potential early signees to remain, Smitty and about a hundred men stayed. The other draftees gathered their belongings and headed for the green buses.

Smitty took a set of forms and filled them out. He printed Hannah and Junior Smith on the first line identifying them as people to notify in case of accident or death. He entered Janice Miller's name on the second line. Other than Hannah and Junior, he wanted her to know if anything happened. He was sworn in the following morning and departed by train for basic training at Fort Benning in Columbus, Georgia, in the afternoon.

His signing bonus and monthly pay exceeded what he would have made in two years working the farm. He designated the largest portion of his pay to be mailed to Hannah. Knowing his family had provision lifted his spirit and re-confirmed his decision for early reporting.

He hoped Hannah and Junior would use the bonus money for winter expenses since there wouldn't be any farm income. Junior could find hired help, but he knew that was never going to happen.

Deep-seated resentment for his father's laziness attempted to rise up, but he pushed it down. Junior would always be Junior, and there wasn't anything he could do about him.

"Raise your right hand and repeat after me," ordered the sergeant who swore Smitty in.

"I, William Bryan Smith, do solemnly swear that I will support and defend the Constitution of the United States of America against all enemies, foreign and domestic, that I will bear true faith and allegiance to the same, so help me

God."

After taking his oath and being sworn in, Smitty officially became a soldier in the United States Army. In minutes, he became Private William Bryan Smith, III.

He realized he had taken an oath to fight and even kill to protect his nation. After he attempted to kill Gino Marcellie, he sometimes wondered if he could shed another man's blood or take an enemy soldier's life. He had concerns about killing someone in hand to hand combat or looking down his carbine sights to kill a man. Could he shoot a man and watch him die like he had watched Johnny die? He was not sure but would soon find out. He muttered, "Sometimes, a good soldier has to pull the trigger, but he never wants to."

The next day Smitty wrote Hannah and Janice about his early reporting and scribbled a short note to Maria to fulfill his promise. By the time they received his letters, he would be in basic training at Fort Benning.

# CHAPTER TWELVE

The Army was working fervently to produce ninety-day wonders, with the Ground Infantry soldiers trained for combat in three months. This basic training prepared men to fight, use weapons, protect themselves, and survive on various battlefields. The comprehensive combat training was producing quality fighting men in excellent physical condition.

Basic training in places like Fort Benning would be the only training a GI would receive. They were trained to fight and survive in dangerous areas where thousands of enemy soldiers would fight to the death attempting to take their lives. No vocational or skill training was given.

So many GIs were being killed and wounded in Europe and the Pacific, troop production had become the primary focus of the armed forces with thousands of replacements needed daily. When a soldier was killed or wounded, another armed and ready soldier had to step up.

Smitty felt he would be trained to be a good soldier but decided to secure books and training materials to study on his own. He utilized some of his off-duty hours to learn combat techniques, leadership training, and survival skills.

After he arrived at the base, he discovered Sergeant Benjamin Rylee was the meanest, most uncaring, foul-mouthed human he had ever encountered. He rated him worse than Sergeant Booker at Fort MacPherson. Sergeant Rylee stayed on their backs and in their faces from a recruit's first step off the bus. Throughout basic training, he pushed his recruits to the limit. He had deep concerns about his men dying on the battlefield and trained them to survive.

"Come on down, you bunch of sissies! I'm going to make real men out of you or kill you trying. You're mine now and don't you forget it! You can whine and cry all you want, but I'm not going to warm any bottles or change any diapers on this base. You're going to grow up or get out.

War is hell, and I'm going to let you taste it here. Before this training is over, you're going to hate my guts. But what I do may make the difference in whether you live or die. Give me a hard time, and I'll break your neck. I'm the toughest drill sergeant in the United States Army. You're going to be the toughest soldiers this country can put on the battlefield. Do you understand? Drop and give me twenty push-ups!"

Smitty not only disliked Sergeant Rylee, but he also hated his guts - more than he hated Roger Brown and more than Gino Marcelli. Smitty understood Sergeant Rylee was giving his best to train and equip the recruits for war. As a career soldier and a giant of a figure, he was committed to the Army way. Smitty understood his dedication and performance of his duty, but that didn't make him likable.

Rylee stood well over six feet and was a monster of a man. At times Smitty had difficulty understanding him or his actions with him growling when he talked and often shouting at the top of his voice. His face was scarred and battered from hand-to-hand combat and cleaning out his share of bars and clubs.

He had forgotten more about the Army than Smitty could learn in a lifetime. Rylee had trained some of the best soldiers in the war under his watch. As a true patriot, he loved the Army, his country, and his men.

The area around Fort Benning reminded him of the woods on the Smith farm, but hotter. The air stayed steamy hot, struggle-to-get-your-breath hot. Excessive humidity from the nearby Chattahoochee River added to the trainees' discomfort and made the heat unbearable.

On the day of the first twenty-five-mile hike in full field gear, Sergeant Rylee took pleasure telling the trainees the temperature could reach over one hundred degrees and the humidity, over ninety percent. He raised his voice when he added, "The temperature on the hike today will feel like a hundred and twenty degrees." He enjoyed playing mind games with the recruits and putting tremendous pressure and fear in the men.

Rylee knew some of his trainees from the easy city life could be in trouble. Some of the over-weight soldiers had arrived in poor physical condition. They had experienced dehydration, heat exhaustion, and heat strokes in physical training. Several heat-related deaths occurred during the summer, with Smitty fearing some of his fellow soldiers could die from the harsh physical elements of training. The southwest Georgia heat was murderous in July, August, and September and kept Smitty praying he would not die or witness any deaths in the field.

The hike took its toll on most soldiers, but not Smitty. He had learned the hardships of life on the Smith farm, where he had become tough and lean. He watched as soldier after soldier fell out on the trail, unable to tolerate the hike's heat and physical demands. Smitty stayed step for step with Sergeant Rylee, and at the end of the hike, the sergeant asked to see him in his office.

Sergeant Rylee raised his eyes from his paperwork and growled, "You think you're a tough man, don't you? I watched you stay with me today, and you never slowed down. I don't think you're as tough as you think you are. I want to find out what you are made of, farm boy, and how they raised you in those Georgia hills. I have assigned you

Kitchen Patrol tonight, and you are doing the obstacle course tomorrow morning. Yes, sir, we'll see how tough Private Smith is tomorrow."

When Smitty reported for Kitchen Patrol or KP as the Army called it, he received a rude awakening and shocking reality. Smitty had never seen so many pots, pans, glasses, trays, dishes, and silverware in his life. There were piles of dishes to be washed, dried, and stacked for breakfast the next morning, and he had been chosen as one of the few men for the duty. His legs were tired, his back was hurting, his arms were heavy with fatigue, and he had been assigned an all-nighter. He needed to be in his bunk, sleeping and preparing for the obstacle course. He had genuine concerns about whether he could last the night and knew he would fall out on the obstacle course.

After Smitty walked into the kitchen, he met and shook hands with a soldier named Leonard Kowalski. Leonard was a big man, tall and broad, with a shaved head covered in black stubble from his Army haircut. He had been ordered to Fort Benning from the Polish neighborhoods of Chicago.

Leonard's parents had immigrated to America after World War I. They had worked long and hard in the meatpacking plants around the city. Leonard had four brothers, and three of them were American soldiers. The Kowalskis were proud of their sons' military service. They valued, loved, and cherished the freedom they had found and were flag-waving Americans who cried when the National Anthem was played.

Leonard - or Lenny as everyone called him - lacked education, but had an abundance of sympathy and caring. He offered Smitty a cigarette, but Smitty said, "No, thanks. I've never smoked a cigarette in my life. In fact, I've never lit one, and I can't stand the smoke. Smoking may not send someone to hell, but it will make them smell like they have been there. Smitty grinned, "I think smoking is sending up burnt offerings to the nicotine god."

Lenny laughed at Smitty's jokes, but he did not tell Lenny he had heard most of them from his friend Johnny.

Lenny and Smitty talked about the Army, home, and life after the war, with the first few hours passing quickly as they laughed and joked. They attempted to top each other's stories and jokes as they washed pot after pot, the friendly banter helping pass the time. They sounded like a comedy duo on a USO tour.

Smitty shared, "I just graduated from high school in June and was drafted in July. I can't believe my school life is over, and I have been drafted."

Lenny told Smitty, "I never graduated from high school and went to work when I was fifteen. I graduated with honors from Southside reform school with an A+ in fighting, cursing, and gambling."

Smitty told Lenny, "I completed a twenty-five-mile hike today, and I'm struggling to stand. Sergeant Rylee has me on the obstacle course tomorrow morning to see how tough I am. I don't know if I can even make it to midnight."

Lenny wasn't scheduled for the obstacle course until the following week. He had compassion for his new friend and wanted to help him. "Say, go in the storage closet, get some sleep, and I'll do your share. You need to rest for what you'll be facing in a few hours."

Smitty was shocked and overwhelmed at Lenny's offer. He had wondered what he could do to get some rest and regain his strength. He laughed and told Lenny, "Yes, sir, I'll show Sergeant Rylee how tough I am and how this Georgia farm boy can take anything he can dish out. Lenny, this means the world to me, and I can't tell you how much I appreciate your kindness and help."

Smitty stretched out on some boxes in a storage closet and fell asleep. He was exhausted from the hike and facing one of the most strenuous elements of basic training in a matter of hours. He needed rest.

Smitty woke up with the first rays of sunlight breaking through the night sky. He felt somewhat rested and strengthened. He walked into the kitchen and found Lenny drying the last of the pots and pans. Lenny did not seem to mind the work and wanted to see Smitty succeed. He knew Smitty would benefit from catching some shut-eye and was aware of how rest would help his new friend.

Lenny laughed when he told Smitty, "I'm an experienced dishwasher and was promoted to head dishwasher at the Imperial Hotel and Restaurant in Chicago when I turned sixteen. I consider myself one of the best dishwashers in the world. Yes, sir, I consider myself world-class in washing dishes, and it has to be one of my best talents."

Sergeant Rylee strolled into the kitchen at 0500 hours for his morning coffee. He looked around, expecting the worst and could not believe his eyes when he saw stack after stack of clean dishes and trays. Every pot and pan had been scrubbed, polished, and hung in place. Smitty and Lenny were standing at the sink. They snapped to attention and gave the sergeant a crisp salute. Rylee returned the salute, smiled, and nodded.

He turned to Smitty and said, "I'll see you on the course in full gear at 0630 sharp. You had better be ready, have your boots shined, and your rifle cleaned. By the way, we're using live rounds today. I'm ready to check you out, but I believe you will fold before the course is finished, farm boy. I believe the obstacle course will whip a Georgia cracker like you to hell and back, and I can't wait to see it."

Smitty and Lenny glanced at each other and smiled.

They had a surprise for Sergeant Rylee, and the joke would be on him.

The obstacle course was stressful enough when blank ammunition was used but became even more difficult and dangerous with live rounds. Live fire training increased the danger and made it one of the most demanding elements of basic training. Every trainee in boot camp dreaded live-fire training. Smitty found it hard to believe Sergeant Rylee would use live rounds and realized he would have to move slower and use extreme care. This new element on the course would slow him down.

He shook hands with Lenny and expressed his thanks and appreciation for his opportunity to sleep. He felt prepared for the test, believed he could beat the crap out of the course, and show foul-mouthed Rylee what a tough Georgia farm boy could accomplish. He was tired of Rylee's sarcasm about him being from a farm in Georgia. Rylee had handed him additional motivation to show what he could do. He was determined to earn the sergeant's respect before the day was over.

At 0625, Smitty arrived at the obstacle course shining like new money. He looked like a recruiting poster soldier, and from head to toe, every element was better than regulation. Sergeant Rylee looked his way without uttering a word. Smitty joined his fellow soldiers at the starting line and waited for the timer to set his stopwatch. Trainees were required to meet a designated time or repeat the course until they met the requirement.

Smitty tightened the strap on his helmet, pulled his carbine close, drew in a deep breath, and, as soon as the starting gun fired, sprinted. He climbed over the wall, up the ropes, into the foxhole, and through the trenches.

Live artillery exploded nearby. Machine gun bullets roared over his head, and small arms fire streaked just above the barbed wire, with Smitty slithering on his belly like a snake.

His heart pounded, and his mouth was as dry as an empty paint can. He was craving a drink of cold water like from the springs under the oak tree in the Smith's bottoms. The obstacle course was painful and punishing, and he was ready to get it behind him.

Running the course, Smitty appreciated his days plowing the burning hot Smith fields and days spent following Mindy down row after row in the bottoms. Difficult times on the farm had prepared him for tests and trials in his life with the obstacle course at Fort Benning being one of his most punishing ones.

"Run, run, run, run," Sergeant Rylee's voice boomed and brought him to reality.

Smitty still had to swim the river and traverse the swamp. He knew he had an excellent time when he could not see any soldiers behind him. He slid under more barbed wire, veered around a fake minefield, and hit the river in a full run. A log floated by, so he lay across it and paddled toward the opposite shore. He was relieved he would not have to use all his energy to swim the river, with the log providing a tremendous advantage. With the log, he did not have to stop and take off his combat boots and put them back on. The river crossing wasn't easy. He was drawing deep, painful breaths when his feet hit the far bank.

As he jumped from the river, he landed on a rusty nail in a buried piece of lumber. He moaned with pain as he placed his other foot on the board to pull his foot from the concealed board. The injury stopped him in his tracks, but he was determined to finish the course.

Limping with every step, he struggled on. The swamp loomed ahead and was the killer part of the challenge. Standing at the edge of the swamp, he was sweating profusely, his heart was pounding, and he felt like throwing up. He froze in fear at the dangers of the swamp.

Deadly cottonmouth moccasins inhabited the swamps around Fort Benning. More than twenty soldiers had died from snake bites in the swamps in recent years. Smitty hated snakes more than anything in the world, even more than Roger Brown.

His fear of snakes started his ninth summer when Junior and his brothers took him on a fishing outing to the Coosa River. He remembered the hot summer day and how the clear, cold water flowed freely. Smitty caught a large shoal bass and fought it to the bank. When he leaned down to string his fish, he was eyeball to eyeball with the largest snake he had ever seen.

The snake was huge, as large as a grown man's arm, coiled on a log, mad at being disturbed, and ready to strike. Smitty froze with fear and attempted to roll away from the snake and the river. He crept through a thicket of blackberry bushes, and the thorns made it appear he had been bitten several times. Smitty turned sick, and Junior and his brothers were forced to carry him to Junior's truck. They feared he had been bitten by the snake and would soon die.

The snake did not strike him, but his fear was worse than any snake bite. The episode created great respect for and a deep fear of snakes. No matter what color, size, or kind, to Smitty, the only good snake was a dead snake.

To make matters worse, Sergeant Rylee had taken thirty minutes to make his men fear the snakes in the Georgia swamps. He made the draftees believe the swamps were crawling with giant water moccasins waiting for the next soldier to enter their territory. Smitty had chills as Sergeant Rylee told about soldiers falling into dens of snakes and being eaten alive. The training pictures had giant snakes coiled and ready to strike and actual images of soldiers who had been bitten by the snakes.

Smitty paused for a second at the swamp's edge, though it seemed more like an hour. He jumped in and waded waist-deep through the stagnant green water. The ground trembled under his feet with the swamp dark, miry, and scary.

Johnny once told him to walk on the mossy side of the trees around swamps and bogs. He moved to the mossy side and found sound footing. With sure footing, he picked up his speed and plodded through the swamp. With his injured foot throbbing and his head pounding, he was forced to dig deep into his spirit for strength and added determination.

He had learned to glide through the bottomlands in the Northwest Georgia mountains coon hunting with Johnny and his dog, Worthless, but he always avoided the swamps. Johnny did not have any fear of swamps or snakes.

He would not glance down for fear of seeing a lurking cottonmouth. If a snake was to move nearby, he knew he would panic. His imagination kept playing tricks on him as he jumped out of the water at any sound or movement.

He pushed harder to increase his speed. The more fearful he got, the faster he ran. His heart was beating so rapidly he felt it would explode from his chest.

When he limped across the finish line, Sergeant Rylee was the first person to greet him. He was staring at his stopwatch looking angry, and Smitty wondered if he had made an error or missed something. A smile stretched across Sergeant Rylee's face as he said, "I can't believe a sissy like you can run like you did. Son, you have brought the camp record for the obstacle course to Bravo Company, and I'm proud of you. You didn't just break the record, you shattered it.

"I can't believe you accomplished this after a twenty-five-mile hike yesterday and no sleep last night. You are one of the toughest soldiers to ever come through Benning. I'm thinking about grooming you for squad leader since you are a natural-born soldier. I was wrong about the farm life; your preparations for becoming a soldier began many years ago."

Honor, goodness, and courage had been planted in his life and had brought forth a mighty and well-prepared soldier.

Smitty was struggling to keep his breath with his heart beating like a drum in his chest. "Thank you, Sergeant. I want to be a good soldier like you." He took another deep breath and said, "I want you to teach me everything you know, so when I reach the battlefield I can help save others. You've been tough on me, but I know you're preparing me for what lies ahead."

"I take it that's affirmative."

Smitty nodded. He felt sorry about not telling Sergeant Rylee he had slept, but he had promised Lenny it would be their secret. He decided some things are best left unsaid. Sergeant Rylee would always wonder how fast Smitty could've run the obstacle course without the hike, the kitchen duty, and not having a full night's sleep.

The sergeant noticed Smitty limping and asked, "You have a problem, Smith? Are you injured? Let's have a look at your foot."

When Smitty removed his combat boot, blood had saturated his sock. The wound was still pouring blood with the nail hole larger than Smitty had thought. He knew it would be necessary for a medic to treat his injury.

Sergeant Rylee put Smitty's arm over his shoulder and told him, "Lean on me, and I'll take you to my jeep. This makes your run even more amazing. You did the course in record time with an injured foot. I am speechless!"

When Smitty walked into the mess hall for chow, the nine men in his squad stood and cheered. Rylee gave him and the men a half-day off as a reward for Smitty setting the new camp record on the obstacle course. He became an instant hero in his barracks after he and his men were allowed to go first in the chow line.

All Smitty wanted to do was eat and hit his bunk. He was more interested in sleep than being a hero. He was walking and acting like a drunk with his body numb. His foot was still throbbing, and his head was still hurting. He was so exhausted he could not think and hoped he could find the right bunk.

He dragged himself into his barracks and fell on his bed. Before lying down, he glanced at the red pencil Maria had given him and realized he had not written her in a week. He wanted to keep his promise, so he arose from his bunk, picked up the pencil, and began writing. He knew she would enjoy his story about the obstacle course and did not want to wait another day to post her letter.

He went to sleep thinking of Maria, Hannah, Junior, Janice, and Johnny. He slept with the smell of crispy-fried bacon, home-made buttermilk biscuits, and fresh peach fried pies in his dreams. He was homesick and kept thinking about how good it would be to go home.

With Janice's seductive actions and questionable morals, Smitty reassessed his love for her and his dream of marrying her. His feelings for Janice were changing. He could never trust her in marriage. Even though he thought he loved her, something inside kept telling him it would never work. She had violated his trust and destroyed his dream.

After the Janice fiasco, Smitty was hesitant about trusting anyone. That changed on his first visit to the Post

Exchange when the cashier's smile and friendliness drew Smitty to her. Patricia Owens had a winning personality and a dentist-advertisement smile. Business was slow in the store, so he and Patricia had time to visit. In his loneliness, he opened up to her after realizing how special she was. Sometimes even a stranger can find their way into someone's heart.

She helped him select a new razor, advised him on the best aftershave, and checked out his purchases with her employee discount. Their encounters gave Smitty something to look forward to on his time off. She redeposited a lot of good things that had been removed from his difficult life. He discovered that a friend in need is a friend indeed.

His mistrust for Janice was replaced with the joy of spending time with a nice person. Patricia had values, virtue, and discipline in her life. Her father was a major on the base, and she had been raised properly. She wasn't as beautiful as Janice, but Smitty realized there was more to a woman than beauty.

Even though Smitty knew he would be shipped out shortly, he enjoyed the time they shared. They did not share a romantic relationship even though with time, it might have been. Of all the things he needed, a healthy non-romantic relationship with a female was near the top of his list.

Movies, walks, and time by the river filled a void in Smitty's life. Patricia had allowed him to hold her hand and kiss her goodnight at her door. She told Smitty, "I don't want to rush things in my life. I am not looking for love or romance. My goals are to live right, get my college degree, and then find the man I want to marry. I like you, Smitty, but I only want us to be friends."

Smitty realized rebounding from a broken relationship

could be dangerous for him. Still, he liked and valued the attention and caring Patricia had given him. She became a friend he would not forget and felt he might want to renew their relationship after the war.

# *CHAPTER THIRTEEN*

In any war, even peculiar people are drafted and ordered to basic training. People of every shape, size, vocation, personality, social standing, nationality, and background are called to military service. The most intriguing and most peculiar recruit he met beside Lenny Kowalski was Wilson Wilder, III.

Wilson the Third, as his mother, father, friends, and relatives called him, was the richest of the rich. He smelled of money, prestige, and social standing. He had never soiled his hands with anything more than a slightly dirty tennis racket or tarnished silver spoon. His father had forced him to join the Army to grow up. After continual run-ins with the law and a string of pregnant socialites, he had pushed family issues to the breaking point.

Nothing mattered in the Army except you were a live body. From KP to digging foxholes, the Army treated Wilson like any other soldier. Because of his father's wealth, Wilson expected special treatment. Wilson Wilder the Second had made millions in the oil business outside Dallas, Texas, and had been recognized as one of the hundred wealthiest people in America. He and his family had butlers, servants, maids, chauffeurs, chefs, and personal attendants while residing in a twenty bedroom mansion on a lavish estate.

To say Wilson had experienced a difficult time adjusting to Army life would be an understatement. He had considered deserting, knowing his father could use his power, money, and political influence to get him off if he went AWOL.

He had decided to try and make it through basic training to get back into his father's good graces and avoid removal from his father's will.

Bravo Company completed a twenty-five-mile hike and returned to the barracks at sunset. They hiked all day, and the soldiers were exhausted. Some of the men stumbled to their bunks and plunged into sleep, not even going for chow.

Smitty and Lenny were lying on their bunks when Lenny's anger started burning. "You know what? I'm so angry I could murder someone." Lenny mumbled and cursed so loud everyone in the barracks could hear.

Smitty moved closer to him and said, "Please calm down. There's not a problem in the world important enough for you to be this upset. Relax and cool it. And by the way, who in the world are you referring to?" asked Smitty. "Can't stand who and can't stand what? You're not making sense."

Lenny replied. "Do you know what Wilson asked me to do after the hike? I swear, he asked me to do his duty."

He became angrier and more agitated by the minute. "He offered me twenty dollars to dig his foxhole tomorrow. He attempted to bribe me for twenty dollars."

Smitty asked, "What did you tell him?"

"No with a capital N! I told him I would not do it for fifty dollars. Then he had the nerve to ask me if I would do it for seventy-five. I told him I would not do it for a thousand dollars. It's not right for the skunk to buy his way out of his duty. Nobody can bribe me, I'm not for sale."

"You won't believe what happened next. Rylee asked what the problem was between us, and I did not tell him anything trying to protect Wilder. Then Wilder tells Rylee, "I offered Lenny money to dig my foxhole, and he declined. Sergeant, would you dig my foxhole if I paid you a hundred bucks?'"

Smitty could not believe Wilson's gall and stupidity and was so stunned he couldn't comprehend what Lenny had said.

He asked, "Did things explode? Did Rylee kill him?" Smitty raised up anxious to hear the rest of the story.

Lenny added, "I thought he had lost his mind or suffered a nervous breakdown. I think he was pushing Rylee to kick him out of the Army. Sergeant Rylee turned every color in the rainbow, ranted, raved, cursed, and swore for twenty minutes. He ordered Wilder from the field to the barracks to await punishment. Wilder will be doing KP, latrine duty, and trash patrol for the rest of basic training and have to come through here again. Rylee is so angry at Wilson I am afraid he might take his anger out on the men in the unit. We're digging foxholes tomorrow and have another hike on Thursday. I'm so mad I could chew nails, and the rest of the unit should be too. Let's shoot Wilder. He's a disgrace to the United States Army."

Smitty felt sorry for Wilder thinking his money could entice people to do anything. Wilder made the mistake of his life attempting to bribe Sergeant Rylee.

"Can you say "stupid"? He asked Lenny as he turned to go to sleep. The other soldiers in our unit will be fighting mad if Rylee takes his anger out on us."

Over the next several days, Wilder looked like death warmed over with Sergeant Rylee determined to whip him out and make him pay dearly for his attempted bribes. For three days, Rylee would find Wilder, hand him a shovel, and order him to dig a four-foot deep foxhole. The area behind the mess tent had several foxholes professionally dug and filled by Wilson Wilder the Third.

Things calmed down after a few days, but Wilson would soon face one of his most stringent tests in basic training when he would match up with Sergeant Rylee on the firing range.

Smitty was ready for arms training and testing but worried how the city dwellers would perform. Many of the recruits had never seen a gun much less fired one. Smitty wondered how they would do firing a rifle for the first time and prayed no one would be wounded or killed.

Smitty thought about The Third. Rylee had given Wilder night guard duty after a full day of KP, knowing he would face one of his most challenging and most essential days in camp without sleep. Trainees had to pass the marksman test to graduate from basic training. Smitty was expecting Sergeant Rylee to make an example of Wilder and embarrass him. He felt the sergeant would humble Wilder to remove his pride and arrogance.

Smitty wondered how much Rylee would chew Wilson's rear and knew it would not be a pretty sight. Wilson had been in Sergeant Rylee's dog house since the first day he rolled into the base in a black limousine, and his personal valet carried four leather designer bags into the barracks.

Wilson did not have a friend in the company, having alienated every man. He was obnoxious, rude, and rubbed people the wrong way. He caused trouble, made people angry, and blamed everything on everyone else. He felt he was never wrong regardless of the situation. And though he had not a single friend, he desperately needed one.

Wilson could not communicate without giving orders and making demands. He had lived his life as a total "me" person and always did what would benefit him. He only knew the rich man's way of doing things and believed money could bring happiness and buy anything.

On the day of small arms testing, reveille blasted right outside Smitty's barracks. Moaning and groaning men were complaining they hadn't had enough rest. The twenty-five-mile hike the day before had taken its toll with everyone's rear ends dragging, except Smitty's.

Smitty leaped from his bed and rushed to the showers to prepare for the firing range as Wilder stumbled in the side door from night duty, hurrying to reach the latrine. Wilder came in cursing and spewing anger. Smitty was concerned with his mental state after listening to his moaning and groaning.

Smitty mumbled, "Has Wilder had a nervous breakdown? Has he gone off the deep end?"

Wilson looked the way Mindy looked at the end of a long, hot day plowing. He did not say anything to anyone, and no one said anything to him. The leave-me-alone-or-else look on his face could not be overlooked. It looked as if Sergeant Rylee might drum Wilson out of the service, with Smitty feeling it could be Wilder's last day in the Army.

The unit fell in and marched to the firing range where they set up field tents. They oiled and inspected their rifles in preparation for the test. If Sergeant Rylee found one speck of dirt or dust on their weapons, it would be woe unto them. They had carried their weapons, and the time had come to fire them.

One by one, the men in the unit approached their firing stations. They were required to shoot from the prone, kneeling, sitting, and standing positions. Sergeant Rylee allowed each man to fire and gave them instructions on what they did right and wrong. After the training, he allowed each man to be tested and gave them their score. He appeared in a good mood, but Smitty knew it would soon be Wilder's turn on the range.

Smitty missed one target, shooting ninety-nine out of a hundred. He had been trained by his friend Johnny, who he considered the best hunter and marksman ever. Sergeant

Rylee smiled and said, "Smitty, you shot a good score. Very few people shoot a hundred. You will rate expert and should win the unit's Marksman Award.

Wilson walked up to the firing range and informed Sergeant Rylee, "I don't need any instructions, I am ready to be tested now."

Wilson became the surprise of the day when he shot a perfect score: one hundred targets with one hundred shots. He placed every bullet dead center of the bullseye. Sergeant Rylee, Smitty, and the men in the unit were blown away by his shooting. Sergeant Rylee never expected Wilder to shoot a hundred percent and had hoped he would be able to hit a few targets.

His performance left Sergeant Rylee speechless. "How in the world can you fire a rifle like that?" Rylee asked Wilder. "Where did you learn to shoot?"

A grin came across Wilder's face. "I've been shooting skeet and targets since I was six and won the Texas State championship nine straight years. I was the National Junior Champion five years in a row. This range is a piece of cake. Can't you give me something a little more difficult?"

Wilder said, "Look at Lenny, he has his rifle too high on his shoulder. He is not going to hit anything. Hamrick has his elbow too far to the side, and Hampton has his head too low. Wilson walked over to Lenny and lowered the gun on his shoulder. Lenny pulled the trigger, and the observer cried, "Bullseye." Lenny grinned from ear to ear and pretended to blow smoke from the barrel of his rifle. The fastest death in the world comes when a soldier can't hit what he is aiming at.

Sergeant Rylee told Wilder, "You've finished your marksman testing, and it would be fine with me if you moved around to give pointers to the non-qualifiers. You know what you're doing when it comes to shooting, and your help would be valuable to the city boys. You are a better marksman than I could have ever imagined. You have to be one of the finest marksmen I have ever tested."

Wilson won the unit's Marksman Award and became the proudest man in the Company. He smiled, laughed, and changed after the day's events. He told Smitty at chow, "I would like to have you and Lenny as friends. I'm sorry for the way I have acted and the things I have done."

Wilson's statements reminded Smitty of what his Sunday school teacher once taught him. Smitty called it the golden rule, "Do unto others as you would have them do unto you."

# *CHAPTER FOURTEEN*

After Smitty hit the halfway point of basic training, he received a four-day pass, Friday morning to midnight Monday. He decided he would travel on the Southern Crescent train to Chattanooga, leaving Columbus Friday morning and arriving in Chattanooga Friday night. He would return to the base by train late Monday night.

Smitty knew he would need a ride from the railroad station to Ringgold. Junior's truck wasn't running and had not moved for a couple of years even though Junior kept saying he would have it repaired. Replacing the blown motor in the old truck would cost more than the thing was worth. They never had enough extra money to pay for the needed repairs, so Junior put the jalopy on blocks after the tires rotted. A tree was growing through the interior.

Smitty realized Roger Brown would be his only option since Roger had agreed to pick him up anytime if he would fill his gas tank. Roger only had to travel seventeen miles each way but would not give him a ride unless he made it worth his effort. Roger would never do anything for anyone without getting something in return. There are givers, and there are takers, with Roger being the most selfish taker he had ever known.

Smitty would have preferred to walk the seventeen miles but knew he would have little time at home if he took that course of action. Few cars traveled from Chattanooga to Ringgold after dark, so hitchhiking was not a consideration. He would need Roger to pick him up regardless of how difficult it was to ask for a ride. He humbled himself and placed a call to Roger.

When Smitty stumbled from the waiting area in the station, Roger was waiting in the parking lot. Smitty's anger blazed when he glanced over Roger's shoulder and caught a glimpse of Janice. Despite his anger, he ran to her, swooped her into his arms, and moved to kiss her. He expected a passionate welcome-home kiss but received a peck on the cheek.

He felt blindsided when Roger got behind the steering wheel, and Janice slid beside him into the front seat. Smitty slouched in the rear seat and questioned Janice's actions and attitude. Janice gave a lame excuse that she would get car-sick riding in the back seat. He could not comprehend Roger and Janice together but realized Janice may have jilted him for the rich kid. It looked as if Roger had taken full advantage of Smitty's time away. He hated Roger Brown and even hated the ground he walked on.

Roger drove through Ringgold and headed for Maple Road. Smitty thought he would visit with Janice, but she never moved from the front seat. She said, "I have a headache, and I'm not feeling well, so Roger will take me home."

As Roger slowed to drop Smitty off, Janice looked at Smitty, "See you later." He discerned Roger had stolen Janice, and he would have to pay. There would be a whipping.

As soon as the car stopped, Smitty realized something had happened at home. All the lights in the house were on, and a black car was parked out front. Smitty recognized the vehicle as the limousine from Jones Brothers funeral home. He saw Junior on the front porch with his head in his hands. Smitty sensed death as he ran from the road to the porch, whispering to himself, "Oh, God, is it Hannah or Maria?"

On the porch, Junior grabbed Smitty and, through bitter

weeping and with a trembling voice, he was able to say, "It's Maria. Maria just died. She had a terrible seizure, rolled onto the floor, and stopped breathing. We tried to save her and keep her from dying, but she died anyway. We did everything we could."

Junior held Smitty in his arms as he sobbed uncontrollably. Smitty had never seen Junior weep with such pain and sorrow, agonizing over Maria's death.

A flood of pain, grief, and sadness slammed Smitty. He pushed open the front door, ran through the living room, and stormed into Maria's room to see Doctor Rogers pull a white sheet over her. She was holding the toy train he had given her.

Hannah kept wailing and crying. "Why, oh God? Why? Why Maria? Why did it have to be Maria? Why not me or Junior? Why, God? Why?"

Hannah ran to Smitty and fell into his arms, sobbing, moaning, and wailing. He joined her with great sobs and a flood of tears. His insides and Hannah's world had been shattered. Grief overcame him. What more could happen, with Mindy dying, Johnny getting murdered, Janice hooking up with Roger, and Maria dying moments before he arrived home? He had returned home for a visit, not to attend a funeral. His homecoming had quickly turned into a dark and sad time.

Smitty tossed and turned most of the night after crawling into bed past two-thirty. The Smith house walls were paper-thin, with his mother's crying and moaning keeping him awake most of the night. He arose at the crack of dawn and stumbled into the living room to think. He was struggling to get a hold on his life, but it kept slipping away as wave after wave of emotions overwhelmed him, pulling him under like a riptide.

He wondered if Janice could help him. He decided to

visit her since he didn't have anyone to share his sorrow and pain. No one was there to give him words of comfort, encourage him, and hold him. He pushed his anger and frustrations aside and decided to seek love and comfort wherever he could find them. In her arms, he might find peace. Tiredness and lack of sleep numbed his feelings as he walked around in a dense fog of sorrow and depression.

After breakfast, he headed for the Millers' house and found Eunice on the front porch arranging flowers.

Smitty walked up and asked, "How are you this morning, Mrs. Miller?"

Mrs. Miller replied, "I'm fine on this beautiful day. Any day is a good day when I'm with my flowers."

He responded, "I'm heartbroken this morning. My sister Maria died last night. She had been sick, but we did not realize how sick she was. She died a few minutes before nine o'clock, minutes before I arrived home from Fort Benning. My family is devastated over her death and will miss her so much. The funeral is scheduled for Sunday afternoon at two o'clock at Shiloh Baptist Church. I hope you and Janice will come."

Eunice looked at him and replied, "Smitty, I'm sorry about Maria. I know how much you loved and cared for her. You and your family will be in our thoughts and prayers. Is there anything I can do?"

He wanted to tell her some of her peach pies would help but kept his mouth shut.

He sat down on the swing and asked, "Where's Janice? I want to tell her about Maria and my Army life. I've missed Janice and everyone in Ringgold. I am lonesome without my friend Johnny and still can't believe he's gone."

Eunice lowered her head without looking Smitty in the eyes as she said, "Janice isn't here. She's gone on a picnic with Roger to the Coosa River. She did not know you were coming today."

Eunice Miller, the queen of gossip, said, "I hate to be the one to tell you the news, but Roger has given Janice an engagement ring, and they're going to be married soon."

His heart shattered like a broken mirror, his thoughts whirled in circles, and he felt lightheaded. He had been blindsided by Mrs. Miller's words and realized he had to face the truth about Janice. He had been such a fool. When he met Janice and Roger in Chattanooga, he did not look at her left hand. He had been so naive. He felt as if he had been gut shot with a double-barrel shotgun at close range. He gasped for breath with pain feeling like he had been stabbed in the back with a butcher knife. He stood up, stunned and speechless, with his world spinning out of control.

After a minute of processing the news, he got up from the swing and stepped off the porch without uttering another word. He was left without a rational thought as he walked away.

# CHAPTER FIFTEEN

Maria's funeral was made horrible by pouring rain, howling winds, booming thunder, and lightning flashing. It was as dark as midnight in the middle of the day with Smitty feeling the darkness was attempting to cover the earth.

A strong tropical depression had slammed Florida and moved up through the center of Georgia battering Ringgold. Smitty didn't know how a hurricane in Florida felt but thought they had to be experiencing one. People had umbrellas, but with the rain blowing sideways, they arrived at the church soaking wet. Due to the inclement weather and so few people knowing Maria, a hand full of people attended the funeral. There were family members, the faithful from the church, eight friends, the pastor, and the musician.

Maria's funeral ranked as one of the saddest days of Smitty's life. He had lost his mule, freedom, best friend, sister, and love of his life in a couple of months. He struggled to hold his hope and purpose for living.

At the visitation Saturday night at the funeral home, Smitty walked to Maria's casket, opened her small hands, and placed a toy train and a used red pencil in them. He had been right when he had felt he would not see Maria alive again. He felt Maria had now touched the hand and the face of God.

He questioned how much pain and sorrow he could experience and felt he was dying from a broken heart. He knew his faith was being tested and wondered if he could pass the test. He had failed so many trials and hated the failures that persisted in his life.

After the funeral, Janice came and gave him an impersonal hug. She hung her head and looked at the floor as she apologized, "I'm sorry about Maria, and I'm sorry mama had to tell you about Roger and me being engaged. We're going to be married as soon as we can get our wedding plans worked out."

Her saddened face brightened as she lifted her left hand. "Look at my diamond ring! Isn't it the most beautiful thing you've ever seen? Roger made a special trip to Atlanta to buy it. I would've told you sooner, but I did not want to hurt you before you left for the war. I could not wait for you and could not have stood it if you got killed. I know you won't be coming back to me. I have strong feelings you'll be killed and never return home. I have to go on with my life, and my life will go on with Roger."

Janice reached and touched his hand, not a touch of love, but friendship. Smitty knew Janice had moved on, fallen for Roger, or his money, power, and social standing. Janice was a conniver and a manipulator like her mother. Smitty knew she was looking out for Janice first.

He decided he would be better off without her, knowing her supposed deep love for him evaporated when Roger entered the scene. She was playing her cards to get everything she wanted. Smitty came to the conclusion Janice only had lust for him and not love. He realized Janice was only in love with Janice. Her empty talk was nothing but lies and exaggerations and left him feeling like a fool.

He grew angry, remembering Janice had attempted to seduce him even after her engagement to Roger. He asked himself, "What kind of a sorry woman would run after a man while being engaged to another? That's it. Janice Miller is history."

He slammed and locked the door to that relationship

and knew it would never open again. Good riddance!

Smitty called Sergeant Rylee and informed him of his sister's death and found Sergeant Rylee had a heart. Rylee spoke with kindness and compassion when he said, "Smitty, I'm sorry. You lost your best friend, and now you've lost your sister. I'm extending your leave until Tuesday, but you have to be back by midnight. Keep your faith, soldier. Things will get better."

Smitty did not care if he ever saw Sergeant Rylee or Fort Benning again and wanted to crawl in a hole and die. He realized he had to face his life issues and overcome them to get set free.

His visit home had been filled with pain, sadness, and grief, with Hannah crying and moaning, and Junior drunk and passed out on the couch. Grief, depression, and sorrow buffeted Hannah as she sat in her grandmother's rocking chair and stared into space. She felt lost without Maria. Hannah had battled depression, and Smitty could see it attempting to pull her back into the pit.

His dreams of a happy homecoming were shattered by tragic events. He realized he had lost most of what he valued, and there was little left for him in Ringgold. He hated the Army but knew he had to return to the only life he now had.

After Smitty re-boarded the Southern Crescent train in Chattanooga, he realized he would be returning to Columbus with his life in shambles. His thoughts and feelings were tormenting him and forcing him to feel like the most miserable person in the world.

He fell asleep on the train and woke up as the train pulled into Brookwood Station in Atlanta. He looked at the Atlanta skyline and realized he was a few blocks from the Martinique Club, where Johnny had lost his life. He wondered if Lila Leigh was still headlining there and if

Gino Marcellie had lived, died, or been confined to a wheelchair? Was he locked up, or had he made bail? Smitty hoped and prayed Gino had not died or been left disabled.

He still thought it would have been better for God to remove Marcellie from the earth than to destroy someone else. The law did not mean anything to evil men like him.

He replayed the Atlanta events in his mind knowing Mindy's death and Johnny's murder had changed the course of his life. He wished he could go back in time and change what had happened.

As the train pulled from the station and headed south, Smitty realized the tremendous loss he had experienced in Atlanta. If he never saw that city again, it would be okay with him. He never wanted to hear the name of Atlanta again.

He signed in at the Fort Benning gate at eleven fifty-five. He fell into his bunk, slept in short naps, and each time he woke up, he cried. By daylight, he could not cry anymore but realized he had to move forward or die.

For the remainder of basic training, Smitty o went through the motions. He experienced sadness and depression to the point he did not care about anyone or anything. His problem was not in his head but in his heart. He wanted to get to the front and fight, not caring if he lived or died.

At the completion of basic training, the Army held an inspection parade before a guest dignitary and inspector. The inspector would be a big-wig from Washington who rode a desk at the Pentagon. The camp commander would present his best show to prove the United States Army produced the best fighting men in the world. The guest inspector congratulated the men and gave them a pep talk before dispatching them. He challenged the men to do their best, do their duty, honor God, and fight for their country.

He focused on freedom, family, and the war ahead. In the end, he called the trainees to be brave soldiers, to never be a coward, and to always fight without quitting or surrendering.

The soldiers dreaded the end of basic training because it hastened the issuance of orders and being shipped out to combat duty. The men knew most of them would be deployed to battle areas for the duration of the war. Some felt they might die on a distant battlefield with Smitty sharing some of those same feelings.

The band played, the soldiers formed parade array, and six thousand trained soldiers marched down the parade field. The latest group of America's finest fighting men moved forward, carrying out their last element of basic training. They were graduating and would be promoted into the Ground Infantry ranks of the United States Army. They were ready, trained to fight, and would give the Japs and Nazis all they could handle. The trainees would remain at Fort Benning until their orders were processed and then be dispatched to their duty stations worldwide.

The graduation ceremonies were impressive. Then Smitty received the shock of his life. Camp Commander, Colonel Oscar Witherspoon, announced, "The winner of the Most Outstanding Soldier at Fort Benning is Private Smitty Smith of Ringgold, Georgia."

Smitty walked to the stage and accepted a beautiful plaque with his name engraved and an elegant symbol of the United States Army. Thousands of soldiers and hundreds of visitors applauded him with a standing ovation. Sergeant Rylee smiled with satisfaction that one of his trainees had won the most prestigious award given at Fort Benning.

Smitty did not know how to feel and could not feel anything. He decided to mail the plaque to Hannah and make her the proudest mother in Ringgold, knowing she would take the award to Shiloh Church and brag on her son.

After the ceremony, Patricia Owens ran to him, hugged him, and gave him a kiss. Her smile and presence brightened his day and added value to his life.

"I am so proud of you. I knew from the moment I met you that you were someone special. Being the finest soldier at Fort Benning is a tremendous honor. I can't wait to tell my dad I am friends with you. You are the best soldier I have ever met."

Smitty had made his preparations for war, knowing he could soon kill or be killed. He thought he might be better off to die.

Sergeant Rylee summoned Smitty into his office and asked, "What's wrong, soldier?"

Smitty replied, "Nothing, Sergeant. There's nothing wrong with me."

Rylee knew he was lying and advised him. "You need to take some time to rest, get out, do something fun, and enjoy life. It's not the end of the world. Things will get better. I promise you things will look different in a few days."

Smitty did not want to hear the sergeant's words, feeling it was his life, and he could live it any way he wanted. He did not need anyone giving him advice or telling him what to do. The terrible thought occurred to him that he was acting like his brother Bobby.

Sergeant Rylee said, "You made me proud, with your selection as the outstanding soldier in this class. Being number one out of six thousand men is quite an honor. You might be the best soldier I've ever trained. I've put you in for a promotion, but it might be after deployment before it comes through. Where would you like to be assigned? I can work your orders and get any duty you want. I want to offer you a position to stay at Benning and serve as my administrative assistant. I guess it's too much to ask, but I wish you would give it consideration."

Smitty realized he could have easy duty the remainder of the war by accepting Sergeant Rylee's offer. He knew if he stayed at the base, he would never see a battlefield. At that moment, Smitty did not want anything safe, with so much anger and aggression in his life.

Before giving the offer any consideration, he stood and said, "I want to go to France and fight the Germans. I can leave today if you can work it out. My time here is finished, and I'm ready to move on. I would appreciate it if you can get me shipped out as soon as possible."

Sergeant Rylee reached into a wire basket on his desk and picked up a brown envelope with the words, "Orders for William Bryan Smith, III."

Sargent Rylee handed Smitty the envelope, knowing he would not have to change Smitty's orders. Smitty felt Sergeant Rylee knew his answer before asking his question.

Smitty scanned his orders. "You are hereby ordered to report by train to Norfolk, Virginia, to the *USS Vermont* bound for Sterling, England. Your final orders are to report for assignment with the United States Ground Forces in France."

Rylee knew he could not persuade Smitty to change his mind. "You have your wish and will be heading to Virginia first thing in the morning. You have your orders, and I will make sure you get shipped out tomorrow. You are the kind of soldier that makes my duties here worthwhile, and I will never forget you. I hope our paths will cross again someday. Drop me a letter if you ever think of me. May God go with you."

# *CHAPTER SIXTEEN*

Smitty arrived at the railroad station ready to board the early morning train and was shocked to find Patricia Owens searching for him. She had come to say goodbye and had brought him a few gifts from the Base Exchange for his departure. As she handed him the bag, she hugged him and kissed him on the cheek.

Tears were flowing from her eyes when she said, "I hate to see you go. My time with you has been a blessing, and I will never forget you. Please write to me, and I will do the same. Let's remain friends and see what life might hold after you return home. My thoughts and prayers are with you on your journey. You will hold a special place in my heart and will always be my friend. Goodbye, Smitty."

Smitty lowered the window and continued waving as the train pulled from the station. He kept shouting, "Goodbye, Patricia. Goodbye, my special friend. I will write soon."

He would miss Patricia, and he was saddened at the possibility of never seeing her again. He had more goodbyes, "Goodbye Fort Benning, goodbye Sergeant Rylee, goodbye basic training. I am shipping out to the war."

The lengthy train excursion from Columbus, Georgia, to Norfolk, Virginia, took all day and part of the night, with stops at every town and station. Smitty leaned back in his seat to sleep, but the noise of the wheels rang in his ears. He found the seats worn with the cushions so flat he could not rest or sleep

Due to his early departure, he had not eaten at the base

and decided to have a lavish meal in the dining car. To his amazement, he glanced about and discovered Lenny Kowolski at the back table. He grabbed Lenny from behind and lifted him from his seat. He and Lenny laughed, joked, and reminisced about their days in basic training.`

They discovered they had been issued identical orders. They had been ordered to Norfolk, then to England, with a final destination in France. Smitty questioned how two close friends could have received identical orders. They would cross the Atlantic on the *USS Vermont* together. He wondered if Sergeant Rylee had anything to do with the arrangement.

He was ecstatic to see Lenny. He could use a friend. His heart ached as he thought about how much Lenny reminded him of Johnny.

He thought to himself, "If only Johnny could be here to share this journey. I don't have Johnny as my best friend any longer, but I do have Lenny, and I believe Lenny is crazier than Johnny ever was."

They arrived in Norfolk and discovered they had been granted a few days liberty before the *Vermont* sailed. On his first day in the city, Smitty decided to kill time walking the harbor and inspecting the ships. He had never seen anything like the ships in Norfolk port, and even though he had seen pictures of ships and boats in books, he was awed at seeing the real thing.

As he walked the harbor, he marveled at the number and size of the ships under construction. Crews worked twenty-four hours a day, seven days a week to complete and launch the enormous ships. To win the war, the United States had to deliver soldiers, supplies, and ammunition to both the European and Pacific fronts. The Germans were sinking cargo ships faster than the United States could build them. With a new design and around the clock assembly, the shipbuilders had constructed some finished vessels in as little as forty-two days. He concluded the men and women in Norfolk were committed to their duties and were doing their part.

Many of the soldiers visiting Norfolk used their free time to drink, gamble, chase women, and sow their wild oats before shipping out. Norfolk was a military town filled with crime, sin, and pleasure-seeking. There were so many bars, joints, and dives around the city, Smitty could not count them. Thousands of sailors and soldiers tried to drown their sorrow or find courage in alcohol.

Smitty avoided a night visit to Norfolk, as he recalled the tragedy at Club Martinique. Visiting night clubs and drinking had no appeal to Smitty. After hours of trying, Lenny broke Smitty's resistance and persuaded him to go out for a night on the town. Smitty was feeling down, without any desire to remain in his barracks and wallow in his sadness and sorrow.

"Okay, Lenny, I'll go to Norfolk, but I want you to know there are places I will go and places I will not go, and you have to give me complete freedom. I once gave in to a friend's insistence; it cost my friend his life, and I never want to experience another tragedy. You can do whatever you want, but I have made my decision and that decision stands."

They rushed to the bus stop and boarded a bus for downtown. Stepping off the bus, Lenny eyed the RevUp Bar and headed for the front door. Smitty walked to the door but could not go in, feeling like an invisible force prevented him from entering.

He called Lenny back and said, "I can't go in there, it brings back too many painful memories of my friend Johnny's death. I promised myself I would never go to a place like that again and would never drink alcohol. I won't go in under any circumstances. You go and do whatever you want. I'm going to walk around town, and I'll meet you here at midnight. Stay out of trouble. I do not want to have to bail you out of jail."

He strolled by bar after bar, joint after joint, dive after dive, with all of them looking and smelling the same. None of the places drew his interest with him feeling if he had seen one, he had seen them all.

Between the Derby Club and a place called LuLu's, he heard the sound of beautiful music. It sounded like "Leaning on the Everlasting Arms," a hymn the choir sang at Shiloh Baptist Church. That was the last thing he expected to hear on the Norfolk strip. He found it difficult to believe he was in the center of drinking, partying, nightlife, and sin, listening to a beautiful hymn.

He looked down the sidewalk and spotted a sign painted on the window of a storefront, "Norfolk Union Mission. Jesus Loves You." He decided to take a closer look at the mission.

Smitty walked to the door and paused to listen. After taking a closer look at the piano player, he realized she wasn't anything like Bessie Truelove, the lifetime pianist at Shiloh Church. Miss Bessie had played the church piano for over sixty years, was over eighty years old, and was as ugly as a pit bulldog. The church kids called her Bulldog Truelove, a strange name since she lived her life single without finding one true love. Smitty concluded there wasn't a man alive who could live with Bessie and felt she might be more challenging to live with than Eunice Miller.

As Smitty walked into the mission, his eyes locked on the beautiful piano player with her jet black hair and smooth skin radiating a warm glow. She was dazzling in a simple white blouse and a black skirt, without any jewelry. His gaze was drawn to the prettiest green eyes he had ever seen. He had to take a deep breath to restore his breathing.

He sat down on the third row. Noticing only nine people were in the mission, he was amazed the young lady played and sang with such talent and passion. She could have sung from the Norfolk phone book and made it a symphony. A young man with a Bible was seated at the front. Smitty concluded they were a husband and wife team. After all, such an attractive woman would have to be married.

Smitty felt peace and just wanted to sit, listen, and gaze at one of the most beautiful women he had ever seen. Her beauty exceeded that of Janice and Lila Leigh. After meeting Lila, he had felt she was the most beautiful woman in the world until he saw the captivating woman before him. She had captured him with her beauty and snared him with her countenance.

The young man at the front stood up to take an offering, and no one moved. Smitty reached into his pocket and removed a five-dollar bill, reminding himself that he still had the five spot in his sock. He felt blessed as he dropped the money into the offering plate. His mama would be pleased that her son gave a generous offering to the mission.

"My name is Smitty Smith, and I'm from Ringgold, Georgia," Smitty told the young minister after the service.

"I'm John Davis," the young man said. "And this is my sister, Gina Davis."

Smitty rejoiced to discover she was his sister and not his wife! He was shocked she wasn't married and verified his belief by checking her ring finger. Confirmed. She was single.

Smitty tried not to focus his attention on Gina when he asked, "Would y'all like to have a cup of coffee? I'm being shipped out to England in a few days and would enjoy some company tonight."

John hesitated and said, "I'm sorry, I can't. I have to go home to my wife and sons."

Gina said, "I would love to have a cup of coffee with you, Mr. Smith. The Mayflower Cafe is a block down the street, and they serve the best coffee in Norfolk."

She turned to her brother, "Would it be alright if I accompanied Mr. Smith for coffee? I haven't been out for a long time, but it is your decision."

John frowned, but after a long pause, he nodded. Smitty thought it must have taken a miracle from God for John Davis to consider him safe enough to allow Gina to spend time with him. He hoped it wasn't because he put five dollars in the offering plate. Gina smiled at Smitty and had an even broader smile as they walked from the mission.

They strolled to the Mayflower Cafe. The restaurant operated between supper and the time drunk servicemen ventured in, heading off their hangovers. There were two people at the counter, so he and Gina took the last booth in a quiet corner. As Gina slid into the booth, Smitty marveled at her beauty. Everything about her made his heart pound, and he chastised himself for thinking how easy it would be to fall in love with her. Love at first sight was not a very real concept to him. But could it be happening despite his belief? He knew that thinking of love with a girl he had just met and would probably never see again was bordering on craziness. It was best to consider this a one-night-and-done evening.

"What's a nice girl like you doing on the strip in Norfolk Union Mission?" Smitty asked.

"Helping people, Gina replied. John and I are continuing the work our grandfather, Carl Davis, started years ago. The Davis family has been serving in the Union Mission for over forty years, ministering to servicemen, ship workers, and migrants just after the turn of the century."

Gina had been truthful about the coffee, but he barely tasted it – he could not take his eyes or mind off Gina.

She looked at Smitty and said, "Tell me about yourself."

Smitty told her about Mindy, Johnny Little's death, Maria, Junior, Hannah, and Lenny Kowalski. He just mentioned Janice Miller when he told her about his life in Ringgold. He could not stop talking, with Gina showing so much interest in him. He found her easy to talk to and loved her smile when she listened.

Smitty lost track of time, and when he glanced at his watch, he was startled to discover it was eleven forty-five. He remembered his arrangement to meet Lenny outside the RevUp Bar at midnight. He took a close look at Gina and saw everything he ever wanted in a woman.

He had prayed most of his life to find a beautiful and special woman like his mama. He saw his mama's beauty and ways in Gina and felt she could be the perfect answer to his prayers.

"Gina, I have to meet my friend Lenny and find a room, so I have to go. I don't want to leave. I've had a wonderful evening, and you have made it one of the best nights of my life. Is there any way I can see you tomorrow? I'll be shipping out soon."

Gina paused and answered, "Maybe."

She scribbled her phone number on a napkin and said, "Call me in the morning, and I'll let you know if we can meet."

Smitty wanted to hail her a cab, but she declined, saying, "My daddy's car is parked across the street. Our home is a few blocks from here."

She was driving a black '40 Ford, a real beauty. Gina slid behind the wheel, shook his hand, and said, "It's been a pleasure to spend the evening with you. By the way, my family doesn't allow me to see servicemen. I'll have to make sure tomorrow will be acceptable, and I will let you know their answer when you call."

Smitty said, "I have always loved history. Do you think we can visit some historic places? I've spent a lot of time reading books, and I know Virginia is loaded with places to see."

Gina smiled when she said, "I'll be waiting for your call, say, around 8:00?" She shook his hand again, gave him a million-dollar smile, shifted the Ford into low gear, and roared off waving goodbye.

Smitty thanked God for his wonderful evening and prayed he would see Gina again.

# CHAPTER SEVENTEEN

Lenny was waiting outside the RevUp Bar, and he wasn't alone. He was hugging two ugly women he had picked up, and he was two sheets in the wind drunk, and talking loud.

With slurred speech, Lenny boasted, "Look what I found. Ain't they beauties? This is Barbara, and this is Delilah. Barbara is for me, and Delilah is for you. Let's find a motel. There's one around the corner called the Paradise Motel, and I know we're going to find paradise at the Paradise."

Barbara was a peroxide blonde with brown roots showing through straw-like hair. She was young but looked old like she had more miles on her than a worn-out sedan. She had a shapely body and the most considerable bosom Smitty had ever seen, even larger than Bertie Seymour's. Smitty laughed when he thought of Johnny Little's mongoose hitting Bertie Seymour in her huge chest.

All that could be said of Barbara was, "She's a woman."

Smitty felt he could not add another quality to her appearance. He surmised Lenny had to be lonely, desperate, or inebriated to classify Barbara and Delilah as beauties. Seeing Lenny drunk brought memories of Junior hitting the bottle.

Delilah was a skinny redhead with hundreds of freckles she attempted to cover with thick makeup. Smitty didn't know her age. However, she looked like a recent high-schooler who had met the wrong crowd in the big city. She had snow-white teeth and a pleasant smile, with her red lipstick making the teeth appear even whiter.

Smitty pulled Lenny aside, "I don't feel right about this. You do what you want, but I am not going to get involved. Lenny, think about the training films at Fort Benning and how the doctors taught us about syphilis, gonorrhea, and how easy it is to get a woman pregnant."

Lenny pleaded, "I promised them a place to stay, and I can't put them on the street. You don't have to do anything but sleep. You or Delilah can sleep on the floor. If something happened to them, I would feel responsible. Come on, Smitty, have a heart."

Lenny sounded and acted like Johnny and badgered Smitty into finding a motel room for them and the girls. Smitty concluded the hustlers had picked Lenny up. He realized Lenny talked all the time but seldom had anything of value to say.

The pink Paradise Motel sign blinked on and off with a small purple neon sign at the bottom flashing VACANCY.

Lenny volunteered, "I'll pay for the room."

When they checked into the office, they were informed servicemen were required to post a twenty-dollar damage deposit. The rooms and furniture had been damaged numerous times by angry and frustrated servicemen.

Lenny reached into his pocket, pulled out a twenty-dollar bill, and said, "I'll pay the room deposit, too. This night is on me, and I want it to be a night to remember."

The night clerk glanced at the soldiers, looked at the girls, sneered and said, "You soldiers had better be careful, or you might get more than you bargained for with those two."

The clerk's warning sounded grave, but Lenny was already nibbling on Barbara's ear and wouldn't be distracted. He was moving as fast as a runaway freight train headed for disaster while ignoring the Danger, Bridge-Out sign. Smitty felt they might be headed for a major train wreck at the Paradise.

Smitty raised his voice as he pleaded, "See there, Lenny, that's what I told you, and he's confirming how I feel. Getting a room for us and a separate room for the girls would be the safest and best thing. This doesn't feel right."

Lenny was rubbing Barbara's neck and back, and Smitty saw his determination to spend the night with the two loose women. He would have taken a bus to the base, but the last bus had left Norfolk at 11:00 PM.

Smitty wanted to kick himself for being manipulated and allowing Lenny to persuade him to do something he knew he shouldn't do. He was aware he would regret his decision and was angry; he had placed himself in another fiasco like Atlanta.

The room at the Paradise smelled of mold, mildew, and years of dirt with the place worse than Smitty had expected. It was a dump. He asked himself, "What was I expecting from a three-dollar a night room sometimes rented by the hour?"

The room was furnished with two beds and a small chest without any chairs or places to sit. The lights of the Paradise Motel sign lit the room with every flash, and Smitty knew he was in for a long night. He had thoughts of fleeing like he had with Janice, but his friendship with Lenny constrained him.

The bathroom would accommodate one person, and Barbara hit it first. Smitty could not wait for the bathroom after three cups of coffee at the Mayflower. He knew it would take a while for Barbara to undress, so he walked outside past the Motel sign and relieved himself in the bushes like he sometimes did on the Smith farm. His thoughts turned to home and left him wishing he could be in Ringgold, at the base, or anywhere besides the Paradise motel.

As Smitty returned to the room, he mumbled, "This isn't right. Don't do it, or you will regret it later. Get your own room now. You're in for a ton of trouble if you don't leave."

He could hear his mama's voice, "Make me proud, son. Remember who you are and where you came from."

He wanted to do the right thing and honor his mama's request. He had always wanted to make his mama proud and was aware Hannah would never approve of Lenny's plans. He decided to confront Lenny and tell him he was going to rent another room.

When he reentered the room, Lenny didn't even notice him. He knew Lenny would never listen, so he decided not to even try.

Smitty became frustrated and agitated but calmed down and decided to make the best of a bad situation. Against his better judgment, he decided to stay to pacify Lenny. To save his money his day with Gina, he decided he would not rent another room. He'd have to make the best of a bad situation.

Smitty undressed, folded his uniform, and placed it on top of the chest. Delilah came from the bathroom with her clothes folded in her arms and laid them on top of Smitty's uniform. As she slid into the bed, Smitty walked over and whispered, "It's not you, it's the principle of the thing. I hope you won't be disappointed, but this isn't what I want, and I'm not going to do it."

Smitty took a pillow and stretched out on the floor between the bed and the wall. He realized a handshake from Gina was better than anything Delilah could give him in a cheap motel room. He thought back to meeting another woman named Lila, who shared blame for his special friend's death.

He kept wishing he had not agreed to stay in the room. His conscience was gnawing at him, and he wanted to run.

He did not have any desire to participate in or condone Lenny's actions. His thoughts accused him, "Smitty, here's another fine mess you've got yourself into. When are you ever going to learn your lesson? Are you insane?"

He planned to wake up early, call Gina, and pray her family would allow them to see each other again. His mind was racing with anticipation and excitement.

Smitty slept restlessly in the cheap, smelly room. His troubling dreams were filled with sounds, whispers, and bumps in the night.

Sunlight was shining through the window when Smitty woke up to go to the bathroom. Coming out of the tiny lavatory, he saw his bed empty and Lenny alone. Drawing a deep breath, he realized his uniform was gone. He ran back into the bathroom, without finding any signs of the girls or his uniform.

Smitty shook Lenny and yelled, "We've been rolled! Barbara and Delilah have stolen our money and our uniforms! Wake up, Lenny! "

Smitty stood in his government-issued boxers while Lenny sat up groggily.

"What?" he muttered, looking around the room. What's going on? Where are the dames?"

"What in the world do you suggest we do, lover boy? They robbed us and fled."

Lenny fumed, cursed, and screamed, "When I find those broads, I will tear them apart limb by limb and kill them with my bare hands. All the money and valuables I have in this world were stashed in my uniform. I had my orders and over two hundred dollars in my wallet. They even stole my grandfather's pocket watch my dad gave me when I left home.

Smitty responded, "They'll stay out of sight until they think we have shipped out and will be back on the streets after more unsuspecting servicemen. There's no need to call the law. By the time they are apprehended, we will be in England or France and unable to return for their arraignment and trial. Without someone to testify, they will be turned loose for lack of prosecution. We don't have any idea how and where to find them."

They knew they would never see Barbara, Delilah, or their money again. Smitty told Lenny, "I can see them having breakfast on the other side of town laughing about rolling two stupid jerks who thought they were real men."

Smitty opened the door to see if there were any signs of the women. To his surprise and amazement, their folded uniforms lay outside the door. He had been spared from seeing Lenny wrapped in a bedsheet attempting to buy new clothes without any money. The two hustlers were smart enough to know stealing Army uniforms would be a felony with a lengthy prison sentence.

Stepping back inside, he tossed Lenny his uniform. "At least, they were decent enough not to leave us naked!" he carped.

Smitty went through the pockets of his uniform without finding anything. Forty dollars and his orders were missing. He breathed a sigh of relief, knowing he had left most of his money in his footlocker at the base and had made a wise decision by sending most of his money home. He hoped Lenny had learned a lesson because his lesson cost a lot more than Smitty's.

Smitty was overjoyed to discover they had not taken his Bible and felt they must have been convicted about stealing it. He could replace the money and his orders, but could never replace the Bible. His shoes were under the bed with his five-dollar bill still in his sock. He knew Delilah could not get past the odor to check his socks and shoes.

"At least I have five dollars," he announced. "That's

better than nothing."

Lenny continued his temper tantrum, spewing anger and screaming threats. He asked, "What do we do now? We've got little money, no friends, and no help."

Smitty remembered checking in, "Thank God for the damage deposit! At least we have twenty dollars for breakfast, lunch, and a bus ride to the base. Get your clothes on. We're going to eat breakfast and decide what to do next."

Smitty rushed to the desk to retrieve the deposit. When he walked into the motel office, the night clerk put his morning newspaper aside and chuckled.

"Hope you guys slept well and didn't get more than you bargained for. Those dames leave a lot of unhappy, angry, and agitated servicemen here."

The clerk inspected the room and handed Smitty a twenty-dollar bill. Lenny hid in the bathroom, not wanting to face the clerk.

"I tried to warn you soldiers, but I could see the big guy had his mind made up. They're professional prostitutes and thieves that never get arrested and jailed because nobody stays around to press charges. My boss won't let me put them out because he does not want to lose their business. They are some of our biggest moneymakers. I hope you boys come and stay at the Paradise next time you're in Norfolk."

Before Smitty left, the clerk added, "Remember, you boys might want to get checked by the doctors when you return to the base."

Breakfast at the Sunrise Diner was much better than Army chow, with Smitty having two eggs over well, bacon, toast, and coffee for fifty cents. Lenny's breakfast cost over two dollars. Lenny had a massive hangover and looked like death warmed over. Smitty could still smell the cheap whiskey he had consumed at the RevUp Bar. Every few minutes, Lenny mumbled more threats against the women.

Lenny felt guilty for causing Smitty so much trouble and had difficulty looking Smitty in the eyes. He wanted to do something to make it up for his deplorable actions.

After breakfast, Lenny went to the bathroom. When he returned, he handed Smitty a ten-dollar bill from the breakfast change and told him, "You go and do what you want. I'm going to find somewhere to sleep off this hangover. My head feels as big as a basketball, and it sounds like someone's beating a bass drum inside. I'll catch the bus later and see you at the base tonight. He hesitated and added, "If I live through the day."

Before Lenny walked away, he lowered his head and said, "I'm sorry about last night. I know I should've listened to you. I made a mistake, and I feel terrible this morning. I can see how sin brings loss and death. I hate the way I feel inside. I know you're sending money home and did not keep much cash for yourself. I promise I'll pay you back and then some."

Lenny walked away, holding his head with one hand and scratching himself with the other.

# *CHAPTER EIGHTEEN*

At 8 o'clock, Smitty strolled to a nearby payphone to call Gina. He was on pins and needles waiting for her answer. Maybe her parents would disapprove of them seeing each other again. He realized he was one of thousands of soldiers passing through Norfolk.

He asked himself, "Why should I be any different from thousands of other servicemen? I know it won't work out, so I wonder if I should even call?"

He picked up the phone and dialed her number anyway, with it taking forever for someone to answer.

"Good Morning," the cheerful voice answered. "This is the Davis residence, Gina speaking."

The sound of her voice made his heart race, and he realized he would have crawled across a thousand miles of broken bottles just to hear her say "good morning" over the telephone.

"Good Morning, this is Smitty Smith. Do you remember me from last night?

"Yes, Smitty," she answered. "How are you?"

"I'm doing okay," he said. "What about today? Can we spend some time together? I'll be happy to come to meet your parents."

A thousand questions rolled through Smitty's mind with his anticipation soaring as he waited for her answer while praying her answer would be yes.

"My brother John called mom and dad last night and told them about you. He let them know he had agreed for us to go the Mayflower for coffee. He liked you and thought it would be fine for us to see each other again. I could not believe my parents agreed. You made a good impression on John, and he's a great judge of character. He felt you were a fine Christian man and a nice well-mannered person. Mom and dad trust John's input, and he is seldom wrong when it comes to people. He is very discerning when it comes to good and evil."

Smitty was filled with happiness and relief when he requested, "I have always wanted to visit historic places. Do you think we can spend the day taking in some history? I've read a lot about Virginia, and I would love to see the sites since I may never have another opportunity. Does that sound like a fun day for you? I don't know how we can go since I do not have transportation. We may have to settle for a day around Norfolk."

Gina answered, "My dad is playing golf with friends, so I'll bring the Ford. We will have to fill it with gas." For a moment, his mind flashed to Roger Brown. She sounded excited about their day when she added, "I'll have to return late this afternoon for my duties at the Mission. Is that acceptable to you?"

"That's more than acceptable," muttered Smitty. He knew it was an answer to prayer. Let's go for it. It's going to be a wonderful day we will remember forever. Spending the day with you will thrill my heart."

"I agree. Let's make plans. We have an entire day to share, and I believe God made this beautiful day for us. Look at that bright sunshine and blue sky. I'll pick you up outside the Sunrise Grill on Bradford Street."

Before hanging up, he added, "I'll be counting the seconds until you arrive."

He could not imagine how much he would enjoy his time with Gina, expecting it to be a red-letter day on his life calendar.

After he hung up the phone, he thought about Lenny,

lying somewhere feeling like he would die. He had probably lost his two-dollar breakfast somewhere. Smitty did not want to think about Lenny's other possible problems. He knew he had paid a high price for a few hours of pleasure and would not know the final cost until he visited the camp doctor.

Smitty folded the five-dollar bill from his sock, added it to the ten Lenny had given him, and searched in vain again for any stray bills the girls might have left in his pockets. He was concerned with having enough money for lunch, drinks, snacks, gassing the Ford, and bus fare back to the base. He decided to make every dollar count without looking cheap.

Regardless of the cost, he was determined to buy Gina some roses to express his feelings and wanted the flowers to show he cared. He would keep his eyes open for a florist on their travels.

He decided to tell Gina about losing his wallet but would not give her the details. He was too embarrassed to tell her about his Paradise motel episode.

Smitty paced Bradford Street, walking corner to corner. His stolen orders were causing him concern. He knew he would have to go to headquarters to have his orders reissued and wondered if he would be in hot water. He would never disclose his orders had been stolen by a couple of prostitutes.

Gina pulled up in the Ford and blew the horn. Smitty slid into the front seat, closed the door, and reached for her hand, wanting to touch her snow-white skin. Her beauty overwhelmed him with her red dress accented with a red and black scarf. The dress made her black hair look blacker, and her green eyes sparkle like emeralds. She was knock out, drop-dead beautiful, and he looked forward to spending the day soaking in her beauty.

He felt at ease with Gina driving since he had never driven an automobile on the Georgia highways. He had never applied for a driver's license since he never had access to a vehicle. He walked wherever he needed to go in Ringgold.

Gina drove them to Williamsburg to explore the city, and Smitty's mind filled with excitement seeing and experiencing Virginia's history. He never expected to be in Virginia, much less in Williamsburg. The old city had fallen into ruins with little to see, but the town came alive in his imagination. He was walking where patriots and heroes had walked in the past.

When he and Gina walked through the battle lines and trenches at Yorktown, he realized he could soon be fighting for his life in similar trenches in France. He pondered what could happen and had a bad feeling about the war.

During the time he spent with Gina, he experienced great joy despite the reality of his impending departure. As the day progressed, Smitty and Gina grew closer in friendship and relationship. While eating a boxed chicken lunch under an oak tree, Smitty held Gina's hand, and it took his breath with its softness. They talked as though they were lifelong friends. He knew he would walk through fire to have her love.

Smitty had never met anyone like Gina. As they walked hand in hand along a river near Jamestown, he could feel love growing in his heart. But he had to face the possibility he would sail to France and never return.

The day passed, and neither of them wanted it to end. Smitty wanted to slow the sun and make time stop. Since he met Gina, he had not thought of his past relationship with Janice. He made a final decision to forget about her since she couldn't compare to Gina's looks and class.

They kept the day simple. Simple things seemed fine to

Gina since she lived without excessive desires or demands for expensive items. Smitty was impressed with her values and graciousness.

As they drove into Norfolk, the sunset painted the sky with radiant reds, oranges, yellows, and golds with the heavens declaring it had been a wonderful day. Smitty made sure they would return in time for Gina to have dinner and reach the mission. Smitty wished he could be with her, but he knew he had to report to the base and replace his orders.

Gina pulled the Ford to the sidewalk on the north side of Bradford Street. To Smitty, the day had seemed like a moment, but also a lifetime. Smitty pulled Gina close and kissed her. She looked into his eyes and declared, "Thanks for a wonderful day. This has been one of the best days of my life, and I'm happy we could share it."

"I have to hurry, or I'll be late for the service. Goodbye, Smitty."

He was filled with emotions as he told her goodbye and watched her drive away. It was one of the most painful goodbyes of his life.

Smitty felt he would not need a bus to return to the base. He was soaring sky-high after kissing one of the most beautiful women in the world.

In his excitement, he had forgotten to ask Gina if he could see her again. He had her phone number and would call her from the base. He wanted them to visit the harbor and stroll around Norfolk.

He experienced a sudden rush of emotions, feeling like he was riding an emotional roller coaster. One moment he felt on top of the world, and the next, he plummeted into the dumps. Sadness came at the thought he might have seen Gina for the last time, and he wanted to cry.

Smitty had filled the Ford's gas tank and saved enough

change for bus fare. He returned to the base with a dollar and three cents in his pocket. He would be challenged to live without funds during the coming month but would do whatever was necessary. Whatever he had spent to be with Gina was worth every penny.

Upon his arrival at the base, he went straight to headquarters to replace his orders. There wasn't a problem since reissued orders were common. He left headquarters, walked to his barracks, and found good news and bad news.

Notice came that the *USS Vermont* had mechanical issues, and her departure had been delayed from five to seven days. The bad news was that his unit would be housed in tents on the base while repairs were made.

To Smitty, it would be like basic training again. He didn't care for the tent stay but celebrated the ship's delay since it meant a chance to see Gina.

The next morning he was deflated to find he had been assigned kitchen patrol and would not be going anywhere. When he called Gina, he learned she would not be home. Mrs. Davis told Smitty, "Gina is babysitting John's children so he and his wife can visit their doctor. They are hoping for another child. We might have another grandchild on the way."

After breakfast, Smitty reported to the mess hall, praying Lenny would be there. KP was easier if Lenny had duty since he kept things moving and worked like two or three men. Lenny wasn't there, but an energetic, egotistical enlistee took it upon himself to hand out assignments.

Smitty sat down in a chair at the back of the mess hall and remained quiet. The bossy soldier assigned duties but failed to issue assignments to him and one other soldier.

After the men reported to their work stations, Smitty strolled outside for some fresh air and to think of Gina. He decided he would find a work station after a break.

Smitty's thoughts moved to Gina, with him feeling he was falling in love. He had thought he was in love with Janice after realizing everything in their relationship had been a product of lust and youthful dreams. His relationship with Gina was a different story that seemed so right, leaving him wondering how his life could change so fast. His growing love for Gina was making Janice seem more like a poor choice for a friend.

Smitty said to himself, "My love for Gina has made Janice a faint memory and an acquaintance. I am over her, and I swear I will never pursue a relationship with her again. It is over, and it is finished!"

He was propped against an outside wall with his eyes closed when a sergeant named Riddle rambled up and snapped, "What's your name, soldier?"

"Smitty. Smitty Smith, Sergeant," he replied in a firm voice as he straightened himself.

"What are you doing outside the kitchen? Have you been assigned KP?"

"Yes, Sergeant."

"Do you think you're too good to work in our kitchen?"

"No, Sergeant," Smitty yelled.

The sergeant chewed him out with words he had never heard before. The sergeant's face was blood red as he shouted at the top of his lungs.

"You're going to learn a lesson, and I'm going to be your teacher. You'll be on Kitchen Patrol until you ship out. I'll teach you to be a slacker. For the next few days, the kitchen will be your home. Is that understood?"

"Yes, sir!"

The discipline crushed Smitty. Choked up and devastated, he realized he might not see Gina before he sailed. He started to appeal, but knowing the nature of hardcore military NCOs, he decided his best course of action was not saying another word. He had learned the best thing to do in life after you mess up is to fess up. He stepped up to take his punishment.

Despite his devastation, he would follow orders to the letter. Smitty walked into the kitchen, picked up a pot brush, and started scrubbing. He had experienced a bad day knowing he had made a big mistake with no possible way to change his bad decision and wrong action. He was overwhelmed with disappointment, regret, and loss.

He spent the day and part of the night carrying out Sergeant Riddle's orders. The last pot was washed and stored at 2000 hours military time. It had been a long day of hard work and what-ifs, with the day feeling like it would never end.

After a long and tedious day, Smitty headed to a payphone when he remembered Gina might be at Norfolk Union Mission. Smitty went ahead and called the Davis residence, and Gina's mother answered. She told Smitty, "Gina is out with a friend."

A hundred questions rushed into his mind, what kind of friend? A girlfriend or boyfriend? A new friend or an old friend? When would she be home? He knew he did not have any right to ask them. Instead, he said, "Please tell Gina I called, and I'll call her tomorrow." He wanted to tell Mrs. Davis he loved her daughter but realized he could not allow such crazy thoughts and actions. After hanging up the phone, he walked to the latrine, took a hot shower, and dropped into his bunk with his thoughts rushing to Gina. He was exhausted and facing another day of KP in less than eight hours. He was beaten down and disappointed with tiredness and fatigue from his KP duty forcing him to turn over and fall asleep.

Morning came earlier than Smitty wanted. He felt

groggy, his head hurt, and he had a terrible case of dishpan hands when one of the cooks woke him at 0415 and ordered him to report to the kitchen. His tail was dragging due to his lack of sleep and hard work.

He found himself hating Sergeant Riddle and wishing he would step in front of a speeding truck or bus.

When Smitty reached the mess hall, he had been assigned to crack eggs for the cooks to scramble. Thousands of eggs! The eggs were disgusting, and he hoped and prayed he would never have to break another one. Some of the eggs were spoiled and left him nauseated with the feeling he could never stomach another egg again.

After breakfast, the base commander, Colonel Rodney Green, entered the vast assembly room and informed the gathered soldiers he had news. "Repairs have been completed, and the *Vermont* will sail at 2100 hours tomorrow for Sterling, England. You men need to gather your gear and set your affairs in order. Those shipping out will be off today to prepare to sail, with the exception of those on KP and motor pool."

Twenty-one-hundred hours tomorrow! Smitty had one last hope of seeing Gina. He spotted Sergeant Riddle after the announcement and approached him.

"May I have a word with you, Sergeant?"

"Talk to me, Private."

"I've spent the last two days on KP, and I've worked my tail off. I want to make an appeal and ask if you'll grant me some grace. Is there any way you could release me from KP tomorrow? Sergeant Riddle, I have this girl named Gina, and tomorrow is my last day to see her before I ship out and may be my last day to ever see her. I'd be forever grateful if you would excuse me from KP."

"All right, soldier," Riddle said, as Smitty's face registered total surprise. "I have watched you carry out your duty, and I think you've learned your lesson. You're excused."

He spent the remainder of the day at his post in the kitchen and worked hard, hoping time would pass quickly. He could not wait to talk with Gina. He would call after kitchen duty, praying she wasn't out with her friend, and still hoping her friend wasn't another man.

At 10 PM, he dialed the Davis home and was surprised that Gina answered. "Hello, this is the Davis residence, Gina speaking."

Her beautiful voice melted his heart, and he could barely speak, "Gina, this is Smitty. How are you tonight?"

Gina said, "I'm fine, Smitty. I decided to stay home so I would not miss your call. Mom is filling in for me at the mission."

Smitty's heart filled with sadness, "I wanted to let you know I'll be shipping out for England tomorrow night." Dead silence on the other end of the phone indicated it was tough news for her. She had thought they would have more time together.

Smitty paused, built his courage, and said, "Gina, I know we've only known each other a few days, but I think I am falling in love with you."

The bomb! He became concerned the bomb inside him would explode. His heart filled with so much joy and happiness he could not contain it.

She paused a long time before responding, so long Smitty expected her to chastise him for his forwardness.

"I... I care for you, too, Smitty."

It seemed to Smitty that fireworks were exploding in his heart, and music was playing inside him.

"You do?"

"I do," Gina answered. "With you leaving tomorrow, we'll have to wait and see what happens when you return from France. If you let me know where you are stationed, I'll write and keep in touch. I promise you, I will."

"Wow! Will I? I'll write to you as soon as I can. Why I'll write to you tonight, but I don't have an address yet."

She paused for what seemed like an eternity. "Smitty," she said. "I think I love you."

Smitty could not believe her words.

Had he heard her correctly? He had trouble believing Gina's response. He was so overwhelmed with her words of love he forgot to ask if he could see her before his ship sailed.

They talked past midnight, and Smitty realized he was in love. He knew this was true love and not lust.

He tossed and turned on his cot as he realized he and Gina could be together after the war.

Most of the soldiers in Bravo Company did not sleep well with the tension in the tents growing, and the soldiers restless and concerned. As the night's darkest hours finally passed, rest came, and the morning light chased away the darkness.

After waking up, Smitty realized his future would have to come as it would, and he would have to have strength, determination, and courage to face what was before him. But now, at least, he had a hope and a future.

# *CHAPTER NINETEEN*

Smitty rejoiced for the opportunity to spend the day with Gina, thanks to Sergeant Riddle. He could not get Gina off his mind or from his heart. It took less than an hour for him to pack and complete preparations for shipping out to have the day free. He went to the payphone and dialed Gina's home.

When Gina answered, Smitty took a deep breath and asked, "Gina, I've been given the day off and wondered if I could see you before I ship out tonight?"

"I'm so sorry, Smitty. I have to drive my parents to Washington today. Dad is seeing a specialist about his heart issues. He has been experiencing an irregular heartbeat and wants to get it checked out at Walter Reed Hospital. We are preparing to leave as we speak. I had hoped to see you, but I don't think it will work today."

Her answer devastated him and left him speechless. He had high hopes of sharing the day with her, but it looked like that wasn't going to happen.

"I understand," he said. "I'll see you when I return."

"I'll look forward to seeing you then, Smitty. I am sorry we did not get to see each other before you deployed."

"I love you, Gina. I love you with all my heart."

Gina responded, "I have thought a lot about it, and I love you, too, Smitty."

His hope and spirit lifted again in his sadness.

"Goodbye, Gina," he said.

"Goodbye, Smitty. God bless. May the Lord be with you and keep you safe. I'll count the days until you return."

Smitty hung up the phone, standing motionless and

dazed. He sat down on the bench next to the phone, not knowing what to do or where to go. He didn't want to go back to his tent and lie there as though nothing of consequence had occurred. He could go to the enlisted men's club, but the choices there were to drink, play checkers, or cards.

No, it was his last day in the U.S.A., and he had to do something. If he couldn't see Gina, at least he could go and walk around her town. He decided to take a bus into Norfolk to kill time and calm his mind.

He boarded the bus for the short ride into Norfolk, and after a bumpy ride, he got off outside the RevUp Bar, where Lenny got him into deep trouble. He refused to go near the Paradise Motel. He took the short walk to the Union Mission, and to his shock and surprise, a black Ford was sitting outside the entrance.

As he walked into the Mission, Gina came flying into his arms. She embraced him, attempting to contain her joy and excitement.

"Oh, Smitty, you came to the Mission. My dad became ill, and we were unable to make the trip to Washington. We had to reschedule his appointment for next week. I did not have your phone number, so I prayed you would come here. And you came! You're an answer to my prayer. I felt so disappointed we were not going to be together, but you're here, and we can share a few hours before you sail."

Smitty held her for a long time and never wanted to let her go.

Gina paused for a moment and suggested, "Let's walk to the harbor and share this beautiful day since it may be our last together for a while."

As he and Gina walked arm in arm toward the docks, Smitty was shocked to come face to face with Barbara and Delilah crossing Bradford Street. The women were hugged up with a couple of sailors heading for the Paradise Motel. Delilah took a quick glance at Smitty and ran for an alley. At the same time, Barbara fled the other way to avoid any contact with Smitty.

Gina asked, "I wonder what that was about?"

Smitty glanced down the street and muttered something under his breath.

Gina asked, "What did you say, Smitty?"

"Oh, nothing. I was thinking about how lucky those sailors were when those women ran away."

"Oh, Smitty. That's not funny. Those women looked like they needed to know the Lord, and so did the sailors."

"You're right. It isn't funny." Smitty's anger rushed in with him wanting to chase them down and deliver them to the police station. He felt it was time for them to pay for their crimes.

Smitty decided if he ever returned to Norfolk, he would have Barbara and Delilah arrested, taken off the streets, and put away from unsuspecting servicemen.

They walked the harbor hand in hand, viewing the ships, and sharing heartfelt conversations. After a while, they grew sad and quiet. Pausing in front of the *USS Vermont*, Smitty realized the vessel was prepared to sail. Gina dabbed her eyes with a handkerchief, and when Smitty saw her crying, tears filled his eyes. The time for parting had come with his heart aching at leaving the one he loved. He had searched all his life to find a woman like Gina and was brokenhearted to leave her behind.

They strolled back into the city and ended up outside Norfolk Union Mission. Smitty thought it ironic they were ending where they had begun. Smitty held Gina and gazed into her eyes. In four simple words, he summed up his feelings, "I love you, Gina."

Gina took his hand and whispered, "I love you, too. I

don't understand how I could feel this way after a few days, but something in my heart and spirit tells me you are the man God has placed in my life. I believe it is the will of God for us to be together forever."

They said their final goodbyes after praying together. Gina prayed for his safety and for the guidance of the Lord. Smitty prayed God would keep Gina safe and bless her in all things.

Smitty questioned, "Who knows when a goodbye could be the last one? This very well could be our last goodbye."

Sad and brokenhearted on the bus ride to the base, Smitty felt he had soared to the top and plummeted to the bottom in a matter of minutes. The time of his departure had arrived, with him wishing not to have to sail away from Norfolk and Gina.

***

At 1800 hours sharp, Smitty's bus departed the base after the men of Bravo Company had consumed their final stateside meal. What a blessing from God that he had been relieved from KP on his last day! He had experienced a wonderful day with Gina, one he would never forget.

After a twenty-minute ride on a rattle trap worn-out bus, the soldiers reached the *Vermont*, as giant cranes were loading the final cargo. Buses and trucks were arriving and departing with thousands of Ground Infantry soldiers gathering on the docks. Most soldiers moved slowly, attempting to prolong their stay on American soil as long as possible with their eyes reflecting their emptiness and sadness. A few of the soldiers were excited, but most were filled with fear and dread as they walked up the gangplank.

When boarding soldiers reached the top of the

gangplank, they shouted, "Request permission to come aboard." The response was "Permission granted."

As Smitty reached the top of the gangplank and stepped onto the ship, his journey into the war became real.

He mumbled to himself, "I am shipping out and heading for the war. I hope and pray I will survive whatever this war may bring. I pray to God that he will allow me to be with Gina and my mama again."

The *USS Vermont* was a large ship built to shuttle cargo and soldiers between the United States and England. She would depart Norfolk with over six thousand soldiers and navy seamen aboard, with Sterling, England, her destination.

The soldiers were herded onto the ship like cattle being driven into a barn. Smitty saw strong men struggle under their duffle bags' weight, with some of the bags weighing over a hundred pounds. The soldiers also carried their bedrolls, rifles, and helmets. They were bearing heavy loads, but the physical loads weren't as heavy as the spiritual and emotional loads as they boarded the ship.

The *Vermont,* under the command of Captain Dick Evans, was an older ship showing her age. The vessel had been pounded together as a troop/cargo ship in the Norfolk Shipyard at the beginning of World War I. It was still giving full service in World War II. She had sailed for over twenty-five years as a Navy workhorse.

Cargo ships were necessary to keep fighting men, supplies, and reinforcements transported to various battlefields worldwide. The *Vermont was* scheduled to be retired after the war, with her final destination being the scrap yard. For the *Vermont,* this sailing to England could be one of the last chapters in her faithful and event-filled history.

The most crucial cargo the ship carried was the finest fighting men in the world. She was transporting American soldiers who were dedicated and determined to protect and defend their country. These brave warriors were fighting to keep their families alive and their country safe and protected. On being sworn into the Army, they took an oath to defend their country and the Constitution of the United States of America.

As Smitty walked down the deck with his duffle bag and gear thrown over his shoulder, he was knocked to the deck by a large soldier.

Lenny Kowalski stood over him grinning, and laughing. How odd, Lenny had knocked him down like Johnny would have done! Smitty asked, "How is Barbara?"

Lenny dropped his duffle bag and gear and put Smitty in a headlock, knocking his hat off, and tussling his hair. Smitty was grinning and laughing when he asked, "Are you still in love with her? Do you miss her? I'm sure she is still the most beautiful dame you ever met."

"Don't ever say that name in my presence." Lenny retorted. "I never want to hear the name Barbara again. I've got a knife in my pocket. I'll cut you." Lenny always put up a tough guy front.

Smitty laughed and said, "You're not going to believe this, but I saw Barbara and Delilah this afternoon in Norfolk, arm in arm with two sailors headed for the Paradise Motel."

"Aw! Who cares? Let's find some somewhere to sleep," Lenny suggested as they headed for the ship's lower decks.

Lenny said, "It'll be difficult finding bunks since most of them were taken by units arriving earlier this afternoon. The men in Bravo Company will be sleeping in hammocks since we were the last company to board."

They followed a long line of men through a maze of

hallways and hatches until they reached an area with available hammocks. The sleeping areas were filled with pipes with the deck looking like a pipe forest, with steel hangers, ropes, and canvas hammocks everywhere. Hundreds of hammocks were strung to large pipes three levels high. The way the sleeping quarters were laid out, each man had to adjust his body in his hammock to have enough clearance to turn over. The sleeping quarters on the *Vermont* were horrible, making it impossible to rest or sleep.

To get the maximum number of troops on the ship, space was minimal, and the aisles between hammocks were narrow and jammed. Walking the narrow corridors was like walking an obstacle course, with men maneuvering through the maze. The decks below the water level had limited ventilation, with the temperatures sometimes soaring over ninety-five degrees.

Problems and issues were compounded by the massive number of men in such confined areas. It was smelly, uncomfortable, and tension-filled with the close quarters creating continual problems and conflicts.

Lenny laughed and said, "Now I know how a sardine feels jammed into a sardine can, and it even smells like an open sardine can down here. Are you sure we haven't lost our way and found the garbage deck? It stinks to highest heaven down here."

Smitty and Lenny searched until they found two hammocks together on the third deck. They were determined to avoid the levels below the waterline. In case of an emergency, they wanted to be able to evacuate.

Smitty and Lenny were aware the ship would be exposed to constant danger from submarines, mines, and torpedo planes. They were relieved to see escort vessels surrounding the vessel and were ready for their voyage to

England.

The captain wanted the men to spend the night with the ship tied to the dock to depart as early as possible and have a full day at sea.

At 0800, the ship's horn sounded, and the men knew the *Vermont* was ready to sail. Smitty and Lenny scurried to the main deck to enjoy the ship's departure from the harbor.

As the tug boats pushed the ship from the dock, Smitty spotted Gina in the crowd waving her arms and screaming, "I love you, Smitty. I love you!"

He waved and shouted, "I love you, Gina. I love you, Gina. I'll be back soon."

Smitty could not believe his eyes when he recognized Barbara and Delilah waving from the last dock. They had come to see the ship depart and make sure their victims were shipping out and no longer a threat.

Smitty looked at Lenny and asked if he'd seen the two women. Lenny nodded his head, too embarrassed to reply.

"Lenny, I know what you can do. Why don't you take those beautiful dames to England with you?"

Lenny grabbed Smitty and pretended to throw him over the side of the ship. Smitty broke into laughter, realizing Lenny was acting like Johnny again.

Gina and the crowd faded to specks barely discernible on the docks. Smitty shuddered when Gina vanished from his sight, though not his heart. He fought back the tears realizing he had left the girl of his dreams behind.

Smitty's heart raced when the ship's engines roared with her course set for England. After the *Vermont* cleared Norfolk Harbor, Smitty took the time to explore the ship. A limited number of life vests were available and were supposed to be worn on deck. Still, few men obeyed the rule, and most considered it useless.

The *Vermont* would sail through the North Atlantic as the centerpiece of a large U.S. convoy. The ship struggled under a heavy load averaging about seven knots an hour, covering about a hundred and fifty miles a day.

Open space on the deck was limited, with crates, vehicles, and containers stacked everywhere. Soldiers and sailors had to search for areas to relax, smoke, and congregate. The men had to settle for any available location to have privacy and quiet time. For some, the shipping crates, boxes, and vehicle hoods served as gambling tables for blackjack, poker, and dice.

After exploring the ship, Smitty felt he was on a floating bomb instead of a troopship. The boat had been overloaded with bombs, small arms ammunition, grenades, explosives, dynamite, and diesel fuel. He realized one match or spark would blow the ship to pieces. The explosives, diesel fuel, and flammable materials were a significant concern.

The *Vermont* cleared the harbor and sailed northward up the eastern seaboard. She would sail north to reach her designated heading and then turn east for England.

The *Vermont* changed course several times daily as evasive maneuvers to avoid being stalked on a fixed heading. The skipper believed these evasive actions would prevent enemy submarines from plotting their future coordinates.

The captain's caution could pay huge dividends in case of an enemy attack and might help thousands to survive.

# CHAPTER TWENTY

Smitty loved his time on deck, observing the massive ocean and stunning blue sky. The first few days of the voyage were sunny and drew him to the main deck for fresh air. The sunshine brought renewal and peace to his spirit as he found time alone.

After a few days, the weather turned horrible as the remains of a Florida hurricane blew into the North Atlantic. The *USS Vermont* plowed through the storm with her goal of safely delivering over six thousand fighting men to England. Smitty hated days when rain and bad weather forced him inside. Bad weather days were long, filled with misery, and were some of the longest days of his life.

Smitty learned the ship's routines and operations, with the continual movement becoming monotonous. Seasickness was rampant, but Smitty endured the rough seas without issues.

Even though they were tedious and bothersome, he and Lenny attended the captain's training classes and evacuation drills, feeling they might help them survive an emergency.

Smitty visited the chow line daily for meals. They were nothing like Hannah Smith, Louise Little, or Eunice Miller served. Smitty missed home cooking. Chow time on the troopship was an unforgettable experience with two meals a day instead of three. Serving so many men in such a short time required waiting in long lines to even enter the dining area. The chow line crew slung the food toward trays as the men jostled along the serving line. Most of the time, more food missed the trays than hit them. The servers called their job "slinging hash." The serving line never stopped moving during meals.

The servers filled the trays on chest-high counters running the length of the ship. The men received their food and ate as they walked, needing to finish their meal before reaching the serving line's end. There wasn't a single table in the dining area. Smitty was amazed at the continual movement of the chow line with several thousand men being fed. He had never seen so many men eat so much food.

At the end of the serving line, the men washed their trays and silverware, then placed them in racks to serve the next group. Some days Smitty and Lenny finished their meal and met on the deck to reminisce about their Army training and KP days. Smitty decided he would avoid kitchen duty on the ship like avoiding a plague.

The food was far from tasty. It was horrible, with many of the men avoiding particular meals, like liver and onions. The meals were cooked by men who were not cooks and served by men who knew little about serving. The troops found all kinds of items in their food, including bugs, hairs, cigarette butts, nose boogers, scabs, paper, and other unidentifiable and unmentionable objects. Liver and onions, beef stew, hash, and canned meats were the main menu items. What was left from one meal was served the next with some dishes warmed up and re-served several times.

Smitty laughed and said, "I now know why they label the food on this ship SOS, same old slop. I fed our hogs better food than this on our farm. We called our hog food slop, and that's what this food is. I would give my monthly army pay to have a couple of fried peach pies."

There were days Smitty could not take the look or the smell of the food and would not go for chow. Lenny never missed a meal and often asked Smitty for his leftovers. He begged others around him for any uneaten food. Lenny had an iron stomach and was ignorant of the taste of home-cooked food. Smitty felt Lenny would kill himself at Hannah Smith's or Eunice Miller's table. He would've thought he had died and gone to heaven and would've eaten a week's groceries at one meal.

The only thing worse than the ship's food was the showers that stayed jammed day and night. Most days, the showers were never turned off. One soldier stepped in when another stepped out. There were no hot water heaters on the ship, with the water freezing cold. The showers *used* saltwater since the vessel could never store enough fresh water. Some days the men showered without soap, and even the available soap was rock hard and wouldn't lather. It was horrible when the salt from the seawater dried on their skin, causing the men to feel dirtier after the shower than before.

The *Vermont* was carrying hundreds of passengers more than it had been rated for, with every square foot overcrowded. The men were in such close contact, the long journey to England put everyone on edge. The number and severity of arguments and fights increased daily with men injured, hospitalized, and some killed from continual altercations. Most men endured the journey with patience, feeling it was a small price to pay for serving their country. Lenny, Smitty, and many others realized they had a duty to perform and would carry it out to the best of their abilities.

Smitty often felt the trip across the Atlantic might be a picnic compared to conditions they could soon face. The men on the ship heard rumors of soldiers on the front lines starving and freezing to death due to the Army's inability to deliver supplies. Smitty thought it would be a shame to starve or freeze to death on a battlefield.

Most nights, the constant humming of the ship's engines caused Smitty to fall asleep. One morning at 0330, he woke up with his hammock swinging wildly and a queasiness in his stomach worsening by the minute. He moved toward the head, but the line outside and the noise inside caused him to sprint for the main deck.

The *Vermont* had sailed into a squall line, with swells topping twelve feet. Smitty opened the exit door, and the wind and rain pounded him. Every bite of supper left his stomach headed for his throat as he plunged through the wind and rain. Before he reached the rail, he vomited onto the deck.

He was bumped by a large man rushing for the railing. Lenny shot by him like a bullet, making strange noises. Poor Lenny threw up into the wind, and all the undigested liver and onions from his supper splattered him from head to toe. Lenny headed for the showers after learning a valuable lesson: never puke into the wind.

Soaking wet, weak, and feeling like he was going to die, Smitty rejoiced he was in the Army and never considered joining the Navy. He would thank God when the night was over, with him feeling like Satan had drug him through hell. He decided he was too sick to die.

Smitty told Lenny, "My mouth tastes and smells like the entire German army marched through it barefooted."

Lenny replied, "My mouth smells and tastes like newspapers from the bottom of a birdcage."

They both laughed at each other's joke, and Smitty grabbed Lenny in a headlock.

The winds and waves lasted three days and three nights. Smitty remembered Jonah's story from his Sunday School days and thought he might have fared better in the belly of a fish than the belly of the *Vermont*. The hell inside the ship was unbelievable and unbearable with the smells, the fights, the cursing, and the seasickness affecting every man.

On the morning of the third day, the problems took a toll on Smitty and Lenny, with both men slumping around in terrible moods. Smitty spent the entire day in his hammock to avoid all humanity. At times, he had to resist taking his feelings out on Lenny and whipping him just for spite. He understood why there had been so many fights and altercations. Smitty told Lenny, "Brave sailors never become heroes by only sailing on calm waters, and this is definitely not calm water."

The ship rocked and rolled in the turbulent waters with the days dark and the nights darker. Each second, each minute, each hour, each day, brought the men closer to their destination. Their journey continued with America and England a lifetime away.

* * *

After midnight the weather turned colder, with the nip of winter in the air. In the early hours of the third watch, the peace and quiet found most of the crew and the majority of the soldiers asleep. All hell broke loose, shattering the stillness of the night. Satan and his hordes of demons had been unleashed from his domain and dispatched toward the cargo ship.

A mighty explosion rocked the ship as though it had struck a North Atlantic iceberg at full speed. At 0235 hours in the control room of the *Vermont,* a cry of panic rang out.

"Torpedo to starboard! Torpedo to starboard! Battle stations! Battle stations! General Quarters! General Quarters!"

Sirens blared the warning. The *Vermont* was under attack from a German submarine.

Alarms continued to wail after the first torpedo

slammed into the hull of the slow-moving ship. A second torpedo found its mark, and a third blasted the heart of the vessel.

The destroyers and mine sweepers escorting the *Vermont* filled the sea with depth charges attempting to execute vengeance on the Nazi submarine firing the torpedoes.

Captain Evans exploded with anger after the destroyers and escort ships assigned to protect the convoy had failed in their duty. He knew someone had been derelict, careless, or asleep on watch. He was livid and perplexed about how the destroyers failed to detect an enemy submarine. They had radar. The sub had slipped into the middle of the convoy and mistaken for a U.S. vessel.

Damaged steel groaned from the belly of the mammoth ship. Smitty could not comprehend the force of the explosions and damages that now staggered the ship.

Smitty had not prayed that day, but prayers broke forth from his mouth and his heart. He prayed, "Yea, though I walk through the valley of the shadow of death, I'll fear no evil, for thou art with me."

His mama had taught him to pray those words in times of trouble.

Smitty glanced toward Lenny's bunk and heard "Hail Marys" and "Our Fathers" shaking his body like the torpedoes had shaken the ship. Smitty could not believe Lenny was praying, knowing it was a matter of life and death for him to pray.

The warning sirens screamed as crew members scrambled to the decks. Hundreds of men were fighting for life vests and rushing the lifeboats. Some of the men remained calm, trying to secure vests and follow evacuation procedures. Most of the men had felt the evacuation drills had been unnecessary and needless, but their value became real. Smitty realized the drills would help save hundreds if not thousands of lives before the night was over.

Smoke drifted through some of the compartments with small explosions rattling the floors and shaking the walls. The torpedoes had struck the ship's right side, forcing the boat to take on water and began listing.

***

The frightening order rang out, "Abandon ship! Abandon ship! Abandon ship!"

Precious minutes passed with thousands of endangered men struggling to escape. The Navy crews continued rushing to emergency stations to distribute life vests and load injured men into inadequate lifeboats.

The men on the ship below deck knew that being trapped in a sinking ship would result in a horrible death. From the time the first torpedo exploded, many men realized they would not survive the attack. It was certain that not every man on the *Vermont* would be saved.

Soldiers scattered in every direction, tripping, staggering, and falling with the throes of the ship. Men were being trampled and killed, while others sustained severe injuries inflicted by panicked men fighting for survival.

Gun crews rushed to the guns but were unable to locate a visible target. They fired anyway, spattering the ocean with lead. One gunner started firing, and the other gunners followed suit, but the submarine had submerged to escape through the center of the convoy.

The Navy brass in Norfolk had made a terrible mistake in limiting the number of lifeboats to make room for additional equipment and supplies. Injured men filled the cramped lifeboats, taking more space than those uninjured.

The lifeboats were filled with hundreds of seriously injured soldiers and sailors. After the last lifeboat was launched, the men started panicking and rushing the rails to abandon the ship.

The Navy's horrible decisions would cost thousands of lives with hundreds of burned and injured men scattered on the decks without lifeboats or means to evacuate. Smitty realized the casualty count would be unbelievable.

After the evacuation order had sounded and with all the lifeboats launched, the Navy crew began forcing men to abandon ship. Mass hysteria hit the main deck, creating a mob scene with men shoving, fighting, and killing to survive.

Without lifeboats, survivors were left to fend for themselves in the cold, dark, death-filled ocean. Some men froze with fear on the main deck and had to be thrown over the rails. Men were wandering in a daze filled with terror and resisting all attempts to remove them from the ship.

The sounds of the ship breaking apart and the groans of buckling steel terrorized the men. The ship was folding like a pocket knife. The creaking and groaning brought a chill colder than the cold water of the North Atlantic. In a panic, men scrambled over the rails as the brine began sloshing over the decks. Desperate men continued clambering from the ship's belly, reaching the upper decks and diving over the rails.

Men in the water were fighting to climb into already filled lifeboats with two desperate soldiers overturning a lifeboat filled with injured men. In an attempt to save their lives, they had taken the lives of others. It was a fight for survival without rules where some men would win, and many would lose. This battle for survival was more dangerous than any conflict in Europe or the Pacific. The men were fighting their final enemy, death.

Frantic efforts continued, but it was inevitable that not every man on the *Vermont* would be saved. Each passing moment affirmed thousands would not be evacuated. The crew worked diligently, but death was widespread, with bodies piling up and sliding to the decks' low sides.

Screams of agony and horror were resonating from every part of the ship. The decks exploded with panicked humanity as the world appeared to be coming to an end. Hundreds of men, trapped in the lower levels, were searching feverishly for any way to escape. Smitty and Lenny were two of those desperate soldiers.

Smitty heard weapons fire as men trapped in the lower took their lives instead of drowning in the ship's depths. They had decided suicide was their only escape from the death they were facing.

In Shiloh Baptist Church, Smitty had often wondered what hell was like. Pastors and evangelists who preached at the church always favored a hellfire and brimstone sermon. Smitty had sometimes questioned the reality of hell, given that God is a loving God whose mercy endures forever and never fails. He always accepted whatever the preachers preached as absolute truth and never questioned anything. In the middle of such horror and death, Smitty had a hundred questions he would like answered.

Smitty believed he had been cast into a place worse than hell and was not prepared for the screams for help, the deaths, or the burning flesh surrounding him. The ship's starboard side was blazing, and life-threatening issues were escalating. Words blasted over the intercom striking fear in him and the men on board.

Captain Dick Evans was weeping when he uttered his final command, "All hands, abandon ship! All hands, abandon ship!"

The destroyers kept lobbing depth charges into the

water with massive explosions around the *Vermont* as she struggled to stay afloat. She was losing her battle as the listing increased with her sinking lower into the water.

As Smitty and Lenny stumbled upward through the second deck, they were overwhelmed by the tragedy and the heartlessness of war. To Smitty, the idea of combat had been exciting, adventurous, and enticing, but in those moments, he found war was hell and without mercy.

When he exited the hatch onto the main deck, he found the situation worse than he feared. Men were screaming and begging for lifeboats that would never come and searching for life vests they would never find. He and Lenny had started from the third deck together but were separated on the second level. He hoped Lenny had not been trampled in the panic with men fighting like wounded and desperate animals in their attempts to escape. He prayed Lenny would survive.

Navy personnel on the deck kept throwing men over the side, screaming, "Get away before the fire hits the diesel tanks and ammunition magazines! You have to abandon ship now!"

It was a tricky jump from the ship's rails to the chilly water, and what appeared to be a leap of death to most of the men was easy for Smitty. He had jumped from the jagged rocks at the Hubbard Rock Quarry into the blue hole many times. It was a much higher leap into the blue hole than off the top deck of the ship. The abandoned rock quarry had filled with water so deep it appeared dark blue in the sunlight. Smitty and Johnny spent many hot summer days swimming, jumping, and diving at the blue hole. You were a sissy and a chicken in Ringgold until you proved your manhood by making the jump.

Smitty rushed and pushed to the edge of the deck, climbed onto the third rail, took a deep breath, and jumped.

Fear flooded him as he plunged under the cold water without being able to see where he was jumping. After what seemed like hours struggling beneath the water, he felt he might not regain the surface. He shot from the water to witness men jumping from the ship landing on others in the water. In some cases, one or both men never resurfaced. Smitty realized the sea never takes any prisoners.

He swam as fast and as far away as he could from the fire, death, and horrors of the burning ship. He pulled away from the crowd toward a dark object looming in the distance. Swimming closer, he saw an entangled mass of wooden crates. After dragging himself onto a large crate, he lay atop it, shivering and praying for the other men. His first action was to thank God he had survived and prayed he would continue surviving his horrible nightmare.

Diesel fuel and oil were flowing from the ship covering the sea. A fire had erupted with the oil and fuel burning like brimstone on the water and making it appear the whole world was on fire. Burning flesh filled the air with a pungent odor causing many of the survivors to vomit.

Smitty would never forget the horrible night with its screams of pain, death, and the smells of burning hair and flesh. He lay on the crate, watching pain and death like a spectator on an athletic contest's sidelines.

Men were jumping from the ship when fire penetrated the ammunition magazines and diesel tanks. The explosions lit the night sky and sent at least a thousand soldiers and sailors to their immediate death.

Fire consumed everything around the ship, as Smitty watched in horror and amazement. He observed the struggles for life as the battle against death was lost by innumerable souls. He gasped and cried out as the *Vermont* took on more water, rolled on her side, and vanished from sight.

It had taken twenty-four minutes from the first torpedo strike until the *Vermont* sank. Smitty grieved that hundreds of men had been trapped in the lower decks without any way of escape. He felt the Vermont's sinking would go down in history as one of the country's worst naval disasters.

Other swimmers reached the crate, and he pulled them to safety. A large soldier floated by fighting to keep his head above water. Smitty took a closer look at the darkened form struggling in the water.

"Lord God Almighty, it's Lenny!"

He pulled Lenny onto the crate and worked to get a response. Lenny was exhausted, almost unconscious, white as a sheet, and in shock. He was breathing deeply and mumbling something Smitty could not understand. Smitty placed his ear near Lenny's mouth to listen. With one deep breath from his abdomen's lower reaches, Lenny blurted, "Sharks, sharks, sharks."

Smitty shook as chills and fear overpowered him. He tucked his arms and legs tighter to his body and rolled into a ball on the crate. Portions of his crate were above water, and Smitty was concerned it might sink. After thinking about Lenny's size and weight, a part of him wished he'd never pulled Lenny from the water. He feared rescuing Lenny could cost him his life, but he kept hoping they would be saved.

Fresh blood in the water drew hundreds of sharks from all around into a feeding frenzy. Smitty was horrified to see men escape a burning, sinking ship only to have their hands, feet, arms, or legs ripped off by sharks. He became nauseated and sick at his stomach from the horror he witnessed. He leaned his head over the side of the crate and lost last night's supper. A large shark burst through the water's surface from the middle of his vomit, attempting to pull him from the crate. The shark grazed his arm as he screamed out in terror.

Even though Lenny was exhausted, he kept helping. He would rest a moment and then struggle to assist in the rescue. Smitty kept encouraging Lenny in his effort to regain his breath, find strength, and press on.

Smitty and Lenny lashed more shipping crates together and pulled more men from the water. As Smitty reached to pull an injured sailor onto the crate, a large shark tried to bite his hand. He experienced his second shark attack within minutes. He was so frightened by the close call with the shark he wet his pants like Birtie Seymour did when Johnny showed her the mongoose.

Lenny fell to the crates, unable to assist, and other men stepped up to take his place. Lenny lay exhausted on the crates moaning and groaning.

Smitty was nearing exhaustion but fought on with his life-saving efforts. He pulled at least twenty more men from the water who could have drowned or been eaten by the swarming sharks. The crates could not hold any additional men. Still, he continued to work tirelessly to save as many lives as possible. He pulled in more containers and strapped them together as he struggled to drag more comrades to safety. With an exhausting and heroic effort, Smitty saved fifty-three desperate men.

Smitty later learned the enemy submarine had been sunk by depth charges from the destroyers. He felt the murderers had received their just rewards and everything they had coming to them. They had reaped what they had sown...death and destruction.

Smitty was sobbing and shaking with terrifying emotions. His feelings were overwhelming him, and he was devastated when he looked over the ragtag entourage on the crates. He thanked God for the men who had survived and prayed they would be rescued.

The desperate men were panicking and screaming, and Smitty sought to calm them. He started singing a song he had learned at church, thinking some of the desperate men might remember it. As he started singing "Amazing Grace," many of the men joined in. As they sang, peace and comfort came in their storm.

The Navy destroyers had initiated their search for survivors, with Smitty and Lenny among the first rescued. They were located after a lookout on the deck of a destroyer heard singing. Their singing drew the rescuers' attention. They rushed to pull the survivors from the crates and deliverer them from the waters of death.

# CHAPTER TWENTY-ONE

After boarding the destroyer and taking a short rest, Smitty and Lenny were enlisted to care for the burned and injured survivors. Volumes of books could never describe the horror and death from the sinking. Smitty was disheartened and disillusioned after thousands of America's finest fighting men died and entered eternity without firing a shot in the war.

All day and into the night, Smitty and Lenny labored caring for the wounded and dying. They were assigned to transport patients, change bandages, and dispatch medical supplies. The injured were dying due to the shortage of doctors, medicine, and precious time. Portions of the destroyers' deck became temporary operating rooms and morgues with the stench of death filling the destroyer and making breathing difficult.

Over twenty-eight hundred soldiers and sailors had died in a matter of minutes, and many others would die in the coming days. Many of the dead men would never be found, with many soldiers ending up in unmarked graves at the ocean's bottom.

The convoy was halfway to England, and a major decision had to be made. Navy officials had to choose whether to sail on to England or return to the United States. The Navy commanders parleyed and decided to dispatch two destroyers to England with able-bodied fighting men. The other two destroyers would return to Norfolk with injured soldiers and Navy personnel.

Smitty felt the wide turn as the destroyer reversed its course and headed west toward Norfolk. Tired and emotionally drained, he sat on the deck, leaned against the ship's railing, and fell into a deep sleep with romantic dreams of Gina. The war in France could wait; he would soon be with the love of his life.

His dream turned into a horrendous nightmare filled with screams, moans, groans, sharks, fire, explosions, and dying men. He awoke to the bone-chilling sounds of dying soldiers shaken with the reality of the dream.

Smitty and Lenny continued serving as temporary medics. When Smitty had a reprieve from the chaotic work giving medical care, he often read from the Bible he kept in his shirt pocket. When he had first retrieved it after his rescue, he had discovered seawater had seeped in and soaked the outer pages, but had not ruined the print. He had placed it in the sun to dry and hoped it would not fall apart.

The absence of morgues on the destroyer required drastic measures in the disposal of dead soldiers. Smitty and Lenny wanted the bodies taken back to Norfolk, but the risk of disease and unbearable living and medical conditions required immediate actions.

There were daily funerals at sea, with a few words from the Captain, a passage from the Bible, and a flag-draped body lowered into the deep. Each day the number of survivors dwindled. Smitty counted the dead for a while but lost count and eventually stopped. Smitty told Lenny, "If we don't reach Norfolk soon, there won't be any survivors to bring home."

It crushed Smitty to see some of the men he trained with at Fort Benning die, and he regretted they never reached the battlefields. One of the critically injured soldiers he first treated kept drawing his attention. The soldier had first and second degree burns over sixty percent of his body with his face burned beyond recognition. Smitty was beside the soldier when he died and removed his dog tags to send to his family. He was shocked and stunned at reading the dog tags. The soldier was Wilson Wilder, III. He was crushed and grieved, realizing the Wilders' power, prestige, and money could not deliver their son from death. Smitty sat down beside Wilder's cot, prayed for him and his family, and sobbed.

He was heartbroken and emotionally exhausted after experiencing another loss in his life. Despite Wilson's shortcomings and obnoxious personality, Smitty cared for him. Wilson had been his friend.

***

In Norfolk, Gina removed the morning paper from the box. Walking up the driveway, she froze in horror at the headline. Fear gripped her, and her heart skipped a beat. She burst into tears, feeling nauseated in the pit of her stomach. Across the Norfolk Times front page was the headline, "*USS Vermont* Sunk by Nazi Submarine. Thousands Dead at Sea."

She settled down on her front steps to read the full story shaking with panic and terror. Fear like she had never experienced slammed into her, with thoughts of Smitty being hurt or killed. She had hundreds of questions. Had Smitty lived or died? Had he been hurt or drowned? Had he been killed or injured in a shark attack?" Her mind raced as she contemplated Smitty's situation.

Wave after wave of fear and panic rose in her, leaving her lightheaded and faint. Tears filled her eyes, blurred her vision, and left her unable to finish reading the newspaper. After regaining her composure, she scanned the rest of the newspaper for any news about Smitty.

Her knees were weak, and her mind racing as more

questions flooded her thoughts. Had he been killed in the sinking ship? Where was he? Would she ever see him again?"

Her thoughts and doubts were running wild. She folded the paper, walked through the front door into the living room, and fell into her mother's and daddy's arms, sobbing.

Her dad asked, "Gina, what's wrong?" She opened the paper and showed him the headlines.

"I know he's not dead. He can't be dead. I know he's alive. I pray he survived the attack. I'm going to the harbor to make sure he's alive. I have to see Smitty again."

Gina continued struggling with the possibility he could've been injured or killed in the Vermont's sinking, but she avoided facing the situation. She was struggling to hold on to her faith that he was alive and would return.

She read in the newspaper that families, friends, and Army and Navy personnel had set a vigil at Norfolk Harbor and would remain there until the *Vermont* survivors returned. She decided to take part in the watch and remain at the harbor to see him return home.

***

A few days later, when the shout, "Land ho!" came from the bridge, Smitty broke down and cried. He decided this was a chapter he wanted to be removed from his life story.

Once the ship docked, medical assistants, nurses, and doctors flooded the destroyer, and Smitty and Lenny were no longer needed. They descended the gangplank with no belongings and little strength as though they were entering another world. As they stepped off the ship, Smitty found Gina waiting for him on the dock.

Lenny lagged behind as Smitty moved to meet her. The tears in her eyes could not deter the beautiful, dancing light they held at seeing him alive. She rushed to him, hugged him, and kissed him again and again. She kissed him with a burning passion and left Smitty thinking she might never release him. She held his hands and said, "I'm so glad you're safe! I'm thankful the good Lord heard and answered our prayers."

Flashbulbs peppered the trio as reporters attempted to capture the sorrow, grief, and fatigue in the service men's faces.

A reporter shoved a microphone in front of Smitty's face and asked, "Are you Smitty Smith? How does it feel to come home a hero?" The reporter pressed on, "It's been reported you saved over fifty soldiers and sailors in the *Vermont* sinking."

"It was the Lord who saved us, sir," Smitty replied.

"Our information indicates you saved those men from drowning or being attacked by sharks. What a brilliant idea to strap crates together for life rafts! America is waiting for the details of your heroic effort."

Smitty shook his head, overcome by the massive death toll; he wanted to get away from anything reminding him of details.

"I did what any soldier or sailor would have done. I did my duty."

The reporter turned to Lenny and tried his questions with the big man, but Lenny waved him away.

Smitty felt a tug on his arm and turned to see a boy about ten, clutching a photo with tears in his eyes.

"Hey soldier, I am looking for my brother Robert. He sailed on the Vermont, and I am trying to find him. He is sixteen and is my only brother. My mama is in shock and sent me to bring him home. Take a look at his school picture. Do you know him, or have you seen him?"

Looking closer at the picture, Smitty was devastated when he recognized the young man as the soldier he had held, prayed with, and released into the ocean after he died. He still had his dog tags in his pocket. Tears filled his eyes and grief-filled his heart.

"You will have to check with the medical staff. They will let you know about your brother."

Smitty did not have the strength to break the news to the lad that his brother had lost his life. He fought to control his emotions and decided he would not allow sadness and sorrow to steal his joy of coming home.

Sergeant Riddle was waiting for them and a few other soldiers at the dock. When Smitty, Gina, and Lenny walked by, he stood at attention and saluted. Smitty and Lenny returned his salute. He said, "Well done, soldiers. You have made America and the Army proud."

Riddle handed them duffle bags with new uniforms, razors, supplies, and toiletries and brown envelopes containing seven-day passes.

Smitty responded, "Thank you, Sergeant Riddle. This means more to me than you can imagine. By the way, Sergeant, this is Gina Davis, the woman I wanted to see when you gave me a reprieve from KP. Isn't she the most beautiful creature you have ever seen?"

Smitty beamed with pride and wanted people to know how blessed he was to have Gina by his side.

Sergeant Riddle answered, "She's as beautiful as any woman I've ever met. Smitty, you're one blessed man, and I can see why you wanted to be excused."

After urging Lenny to find someplace at the base to rest, Smitty walked with Gina to her father's Ford. Gina drove them to the Davis home, an older brick house on an oak-lined street, a picture-perfect street with pruned shrubbery, friendly dogs, and apple pie niceness.

Gina parked the car in the driveway. An older gentleman, who Smitty took to be her father, was raking leaves with Gina's mother taking her husband a cold glass of lemonade. On seeing the car, Mr. Davis laid down his rake, and the couple walked up the driveway.

Gina introduced them: "Smitty, this is my dad, Carl, and my mother, Anna. Mom and Dad, this is Smitty Smith."

Extending his hand to her father, Smitty said, "Nice to meet you." After shaking hands and apologizing for his appearance, he said, "I've looked forward to meeting you. I think a lot of your daughter; she is the nicest and most beautiful woman I've ever met. You sure did an excellent job raising such a wonderful person."

"It's nice to meet you," her father replied. "Gina has told us about you, and we're thankful you lived through such a horrible tragedy. Anna and I are upset at the loss of so many lives."

It had been days, but Smitty felt it had been a lifetime since he sailed from Norfolk. He had tried to forget the events of the sinking and push down his feelings and pain. Any time he heard the name *Vermont* he wanted to cry.

"Yes, sir, I am very thankful I was spared. God surely protected me."

Mrs. Davis said, "I know you're starving, so I'll go and prepare dinner. I have pot roast, vegetables, and fried peach pies for dessert. Would you like a fried pie while they're warm?"

"Fried peach pies! God is so good!"

After stuffing himself at dinner, Smitty sat in the front-porch swing with Gina. He thought how different it was to sit with her instead of Janice. He realizing Gina and Janice were worlds apart in every way.

He slid close to Gina placing his arm around her. Gina snuggled up to Smitty and asked, "Do you want to talk about the *Vermont*? It might help release your hurts and wounds by talking them out. I'm willing to listen."

"I don't want to talk about it, but it might help you know what I lived through. I'm going to do my best to leave a lot of my junk here." Reluctantly, Smitty began his story.

He took in a deep breath, and with strong emotions, dread, and distress, he spoke in a slow and soft voice just above a whisper. "The conditions on the ship were horrible, with too many men in cramped quarters. There were hammocks stacked on top of each other. The food, the showers, and the temperament of angry men were unbearable.

The torpedoes struck the ship in the middle of the night. Gina, it felt like the world had come to an end. The blasts shook the boat, and I knew it would sink."

He paused as he thought about the terrifying explosions that tossed him from his hammock and slammed him to the floor. He had lost consciousness for a moment but fought to get up and get out.

"The decks filled with soldiers struggling to wake up and gain their bearings. Some of the men were knocked out, and others were trying to escape despite injuries. Three torpedoes struck the ship, and each blast brought more destruction. Men were screaming, crying, and calling out to God, their wives, their girlfriends, their mothers, their pastors, or other loved ones.

"It was a living nightmare. I thought I was going to die. Men were trampled to death in the evacuation without an opportunity to escape from the lower decks. I had to climb over dead bodies and injured men to get out.

The ship rolled onto its side and sunk deeper into the water. I called on the name of Jesus, asking Him to save me.

I found some life vests stowed behind two crates and distributed them to the men who had fought their way to the top deck. I gave them all away and could not believe men were fighting and killing each other over safety devices. I wanted other men to survive, so I gave my life vest to an older soldier.

Jumping from the ship was the only option I had to save my life. I had to jump without a life jacket since there weren't enough of them or lifeboats. The water was covered with diesel fuel that had not caught fire. I realized it would be a matter of time before the ship became a hellish inferno consuming everything within its reach. I was terrified it would catch fire and burn me alive.

It was tragic watching men jump from the ship landing on other men with the impact killing one or both. Some men who jumped from the boat never resurfaced." Smitty paused for a moment, then began to sob at the pain of reliving the event.

Gina held him tight, reassuring him she loved him and telling him he would be fine. Smitty took a deep breath, laid his head back on Gina's shoulder, and continued his account.

I swam as fast as I could to move away from the ship so I would not be pulled under when it sank. The ship's engines were idling as it moved away from other survivors and me. By the time the ship sank, it was almost a half-mile away. I cannot tell you the depth of horror and fear I felt when the ship plunged under the water and disappeared.

My eyes burned. I struggled for every breath, as diesel fuel covered every inch of my body, and my eyelids stuck together when I closed them. They would stay shut until I forced them open with my fingers. I swallowed some diesel fuel, became nauseated, and felt I would die. I got so weak I thought death might be my best course of action. I stopped swimming and went under a couple of times before my inner desire to live took over.

The ocean around me was filled with crates, wooden boxes, and debris. The sounds were horrific, with soldiers moaning, crying out, begging for help, and screaming in pain. The salt in the water made my wounds burn and feel like the fires of hell. I am still tormented with the screams and cries of dying men. I can't forget them. And I keep hearing them over and over in the depths of my soul. I can still see the bodies of dead and mutilated soldiers floating in the water around me, and I can't remove them from my mind."

Smitty saw Gina's tears and felt her powerful grip on his hand. He knew if he would take control and ownership of his life issues, they could be solved. He continued his story.

Smitty fixed his gaze on Gina and said, "Your beautiful face and my desire to hold you again were the reasons I didn't give up and let go of the crate. When I realized how much I loved you, I promised myself I would hold you again."

Gina squeezed his hand and touched his face. She held him close and gave him a comforting kiss.

I found refuge on a large wooden crate and felt God had provided me an ark. I don't know how I found it in the darkness, but that wooden box saved my life.

I saw a young man struggling to stay afloat, so I grabbed him and held him. He was a boy about fifteen or sixteen who had lied about his age to join the Army. I'm sure his family needed his Army pay to survive. He had severe injuries and floated by without a life jacket. I pulled him close and struggled to keep his head above water. He moaned, screamed, and died in my arms. I prayed for him, removed his dog tags, and released him into the water. That young soldier was the brother of the young boy we saw at the harbor today. I could not bear to tell him the truth or to see his grief and sorrow.

It was a miracle I found Lenny and pulled him from the water. I then had an idea to strap more crates together to construct a large life raft to rescue other survivors.

We pulled every man we could rescue onto the crates while the waters churned with sharks in a feeding frenzy. The sharks would take an arm here and a leg there. We witnessed men slammed under the water by one shark to be torn to pieces by several others. The water turned red with fresh blood and attracted more sharks from miles away with at least several hundred of them swirling in the water."

"Thank God you saved so many lives," Gina added. "Your life touched and saved so many men who would have died. You should be encouraged that so many men and their families will be blessed by your actions."

Smitty dealt with deep emotions realizing his surviving a sinking ship had changed him forever no matter how he struggled to put his torments in his past.

"We did what we could, but our best efforts could only save a few. We worked with the wounded and buried the dead in watery graves. I pushed dead men toward the sharks so those still alive could escape. I prayed with those who were dying and encouraged those who were hanging on. I had to make decisions about who would live and who would die. I am torn apart by doubts about whether I made the right decisions with men's lives. I feel so guilty. There were so many, I could not save them all. I removed dog tags from dead bodies to send to their families. My spirit and my world were crushed with the magnitude of death and suffering.

After the *Vermont* sank, I started singing 'Amazing

Grace,' and many of the men joined me. We were the first survivors rescued after our singing drew the rescuers to our crates.

When I saw the searchlight, I knew I would be saved and return to you.

My Grandpa Everett always told me, 'Your struggles will make you stronger and the changes in your life will make you wise. Life is a never ending adventure with plenty of trials and struggles along the way.'

I hope he was right."

"Smitty," she said softly, "You were a hero. You will always be my hero. You had a duty to accomplish, no matter the cost. I now realize what it cost, and you made the right choices. Some people have a God- calling on their lives that echoes through the ages. You carried out your calling. Honor and courage are matters of the heart."

"I don't feel like a hero. Sometimes there is only a fine line between being a hero and being a monster. I know any fool can become a hero when it is kill-or-be-killed in a battle. There are only two results, victory or defeat, with nothing in-between."

Smitty and Gina were weeping. As they held each other, Smitty felt peace. He closed his eyes and fell asleep in her arms. He realized he had never been this close to anyone before. It was uncharted territory, and his love for Gina pushed him to the limits to gain and keep her love and affections. Smitty was at a crossroad with his emotions and had a choice: he could move forward or fall back.

# CHAPTER TWENTY-TWO

Time passed quickly for Smitty and Gina as they shared days of laughter and love. Being with Gina and her family felt like home, and Smitty would have been content to stay with the Davises the remainder of his life. He had been blessed beyond measure in his time with them.

On their final day together, Smitty's heart filled with dread, knowing he had to report to the base by 1800 hours.

He said his goodbyes to the Davises, "I'm going to miss you. You've been like my family, and I've grown to love you. You are special people, and I have enjoyed every moment I have spent here. Your love and care have helped me deal with my tragedy and provided healing to my soul.

Mr. Davis shook his hand. "I wish you well, Smitty. May the Lord bless you and keep you every step of your journey. I'll be praying for you while you're away. I pray God will see you through."

Mrs. Davis cried as she hugged him. "Smitty, we've grown to love you, and we know you have been the best thing to ever happen to Gina. We've never seen her so happy. You take care of yourself, and I, too, will be praying for you.

She handed Smitty a brown paper bag and said, "I got up early this morning and made some peach pies for you to take to the base. I know you love them, and I wanted you to have them when you sail. I will think of you every time I make fried pies. Please think of us and pray for us in the coming days."

"A penny for your thoughts," Gina said as they drove toward the base.

Smitty reflected a long time before he replied. "I was thinking I would like to spend the rest of my life with you. I want you to marry me and become Mrs. William Bryan Smith."

"I would be honored to marry you, Mr. Smith," Gina whispered.

Smitty was stunned and asked, "Really, does that mean you'll marry me?"

"Does that mean you're asking?" Gina inquired.

"I'm not asking; I'm begging," Smitty replied. "Marrying you is what I want most in this world."

"Then yes, I will," Gina responded. "A hundred times, yes. A thousand times, yes. A million times, yes. Marrying you would make me the happiest woman alive."

Gina pulled the car onto the shoulder on Norfolk Highway, and they embraced, laughed, kissed, and cried.

Gina said, "Smitty, I'll wait for you, but you have to promise me you'll come home, be my husband, and the love of my life." With teary eyes, she whispered, "No matter what happens, promise me you'll come home."

Smitty raised his right hand, nodded, and said, "I do solemnly swear. You are my world."

Smitty glanced at his watch and saw it was almost 5:45 PM and was concerned they were at least twenty minutes from the base. He told Gina, "I think I am going to be late checking in." Gina drove like a race car driver, pulling into the base at five after six. He was late reporting for duty and was concerned he could be in hot water.

The guard at the gate looked at his papers, saluted, and said, "Welcome home, Smith. We appreciate your heroic actions on the *Vermont*."

Smitty leaned in the driver's side window, gazed into Gina's emerald eyes, and gave her one last kiss he hoped would keep her until he returned. Smitty hated goodbyes, and this was his most difficult and painful separation.

Gina's green dress sparkled in the sunset and created a life moment with him realizing she would never be more beautiful. After one last kiss, he determined he would always remember the gorgeous green dress and the beautiful woman wearing it. This memory would sustain him through the war, giving him the determination to return to make Gina his wife.

He regretted being unable to give her an engagement ring, with little time and money, but he knew he would give her a ring at their wedding. He was overwhelmed at the thought of their marriage.

# *CHAPTER TWENTY-THREE*

Smitty had a sense of *déjà vu* walking up the *USS Iowa* gangplank, a newly christened ship capable of carrying over eight thousand men and a full cargo. The *Iowa* was the largest ship he had viewed in Norfolk harbor and one of the Navy's largest cargo ships. Everyone in Ringgold could fit in one small compartment in the vessel and have room for many more. The *Iowa* had been completed, commissioned, and launched from the Norfolk shipyard for her maiden voyage a few days after Smitty sailed for England.

Smitty remembered how he and Gina had seen the ship being completed when they walked the harbor. The ship did not appear as large at a distance as when he walked her deck.

The ship would sail in a large flotilla of destroyers, troop transports, and submarines. The convoy would also include two cruise ships pressed into duty to transport additional troops. Smitty wished he and Lenny could've experienced the luxury of sailing on a cruise ship with beds and tables in the dining rooms.

Smitty felt confident the ship would be protected by the destroyers and submarines. The mistakes of the *Vermont* sinking should not be repeated, and Smitty prayed he would reach England safely. When the *USS Iowa* sailed for Sterling, England, from Norfolk on a beautiful winter morning, her decks were filled with soldiers. While she carried ammunition, vehicles, and crates of supplies, the cargo was not on the decks. And to Smitty's great relief, the ship carried an abundance of life vests and lifeboats.

The ship was loaded with the safe maximum of men and cargo, and yet it was far from being overloaded. Things were not going well for the American and Allied forces, and the winds of war had to change, with the future of the free world at stake.

As the *Iowa* departed, bands played, people cheered, and thousands waved American flags. Smitty thought of the Fourth of July parades his family attended in Chatsworth. He recalled the music, soldiers marching, food, and children's games. He loved freedom celebrations and parades with soldiers marching in unison. A flood of memories rushed in to remind him his life had seen good times and a loving family, and all had not been tragedy.

The ship's horn blew and startled Smitty. He scanned the dock for one last look at Gina, but could not locate her in the overflowing crowd. She kept shouting to the top of her lungs, "I love you, Smitty, I love you, Smitty, I love you, Smitty."

A voice inside Smitty said, "You've seen Gina for the last time; you will not return. You will never see her again. You're going to be killed on the battlefield in France."

He battled his thoughts but lost. Sadness and loneliness hovered over him, leaving him with a heavy heart and bad feelings about the days looming ahead. He was fighting the good fight of faith, but doubt seemed to be winning the war. He had learned a man cannot have a positive life while living with negative attitudes and fears. Smitty tried to hold a truth his Grandfather had spoken to him, "Worry is a waste of time. It steals your faith and joy, and you should never pay interest on a debt you don't yet owe."

Smitty walked the decks to make sure the *Iowa* had

been equipped with adequate life vests and lifeboats. It had. The Navy brass in Norfolk made sure the ship was prepared for any emergency after the *Vermont* disaster. As the ship cleared the harbor, he broke into a cold sweat with fear and past memories flooding his mind. He was tormented with the screams and cries of dying soldiers and sailors on the *Vermont*. He questioned if the flashbacks would ever stop, feeling the screams might haunt him, battle him, and torment him the remainder of his life.

He went down one flight of steps and turned to escape back to the main deck, but staunched the urge when he realized he had to be brave and strong. He knew he had to overcome past memories and torments to win his battle. Fear was a strong and every present enemy, and he knew that fear never stops death; it stops life. He had been fine when the ship was tied to the pier, but the open water was pressuring him to panic. He knew he had to conquer his fear if he wanted to regain his life.

He wanted to bunk with Lenny but had not been able to locate him in the chaos of the night before when thousands of soldiers rushed for bunks. Smitty walked to the starboard side of the ship and rambled down two levels to the third deck. He heard someone shouting, "Seven, come eleven! Papa needs a new pair of shoes." The voice sounded familiar.

About a dozen soldiers were on the floor, gambling with Lenny kneeling in the middle of the pack shaking the dice in a crap game. He was clinching a wad of money in his left fist as he rolled the dice, and everyone moaned as he rolled another seven and raked in the dough. The soldiers were amazed at Lenny's gambling prowess. Smitty had been dreading the day when he bet everything and got called.

He eyed Smitty and wanted out of the game, Smitty's

appearance giving him the perfect excuse to take his money and run. Lenny said, "This is my buddy, Smitty, and I've got to help him find a hammock near mine. We've bunked together since basic training."

The moaning, groaning, and complaining confirmed he hadn't made any friends. In fact, he had made quite a few enemies among the sore losers who had lost their Army pay before they left sight of land and before the ship sailed from the harbor.

Two large soldiers grabbed Lenny to whip him, and two additional soldiers stood by to assist with the beating. Smitty stepped in and said, "You had better let him go, or I'll knock you into next week. This soldier is my friend, and if you lay a hand on him, you will have to answer to me. He and I can lick all of you, so you had better move on now."

The losers decided it would not be to their advantage to take on two soldiers their size. Though the soldiers griped and complained loudly, they released Lenny and walked away.

Lenny hugged Smitty and placed him in a headlock. He reached into his pocket, pulled out five crisp twenty-dollar bills, and handed them to Smitty.

"I told you I'd pay you back. Remember the Paradise Motel episode? I'm paid in full and never want to hear about it again. That case is closed, and I never want it reopened. Put a lock on it!"

They shoved each other and broke into hysterical laughter. Lenny scratched his crotch, rubbed his head, and pretended to throw up. They laughed until they could not laugh anymore, staggering around like a couple of drunks.

Smitty felt his tension lessen at being with Lenny since Lenny could brighten any day. Lenny had left Norfolk on the train to visit his family in Chicago, so Smitty had not talked to him. Smitty had forgotten to give him Gina's phone number so they meet up again in Norfolk. They had a lot of catching up to do and news to share with so many things happening.

Smitty had spent his time with Gina and her family while Lenny had helped his family remodel their home. Lenny looked exhausted from his travel and hard work.

Smitty decided to send the hundred dollars to his Mama, hoping the money would be used wisely. He was concerned Junior might use it to buy moonshine. A hundred dollars would buy food, clothing, and coal for the winter. Smitty was relieved Hannah would have emergency money.

Smitty and Lenny had difficulty finding a place to bunk together. Lenny paid a soldier five dollars to give Smitty the hammock next to his and helped Smitty transfer his gear to his new area. Lenny knew he would win his five dollars back later in a crap game. Their hammocks were above the engine room but below the water level. Even though they found it almost impossible to talk over the engine noise, they realized they had few choices.

Smitty shouted and asked Lenny, "How does the Navy expect us to sleep in a room filled with hundreds of snoring men, smelly feet, flushing commodes, and engines bumping and roaring? It's going to be a long voyage, but I'm happy we have hammocks together."

When Smitty had opened his duffle bag the night before, he discovered Gina had packed him a letter. He had smelled her perfume and found "SWAK" in large letters on the back of the envelope, reminding him it had been sealed with a kiss. His heart had pounded in anticipation as he had ripped open the envelope.

In the last few hours, he had read her letter at least ten times and paused to reread it.

"My darling Smitty,

"From the night you walked into Norfolk Union Mission, I knew you were the man I wanted to marry. I believe it is meant for us to be together, and I believe it is our divine destiny.

"You've made me happier than I've ever been. I'm going to miss you, but I know you will return safely. I know it. I will count the days until you are in my arms again. I love you and will look forward to spending my life with you.

"You are the joy and love of my life. I look forward to becoming Mrs. William Bryan Smith, and I will wait for your return. I send you my love and prayers.

"Love always, Gina."

Each time he read it, he shouted, "Praise the Lord! Praise the Lord! Praise the Lord!

The men around him would stare at him like he was crazy, but he did not care. He decided he would carry the letter wherever he went and through whatever he encountered. He would keep it near his heart so he could feel Gina's love. He pondered how to keep the letter from being damaged or destroyed and decided to use his metal-clad Bible. He would carry her words in Junior's Bible, the one he would use and return to his mama.

He folded the letter, placed it in the Bible, and pushed it into his shirt pocket over his heart. He wanted her message in a safe place to have it when he returned home.

The *Iowa's* Atlantic crossing was uneventful, and Smitty was overjoyed at the safe passage. They sailed through blue skies and calm waters, but the North Atlantic weather had been chilly. He spent time on deck looking at the ocean as he imagined future times with Gina. The sparkling green water reminded him of Gina's emerald eyes and the beautiful green dress she was wearing the last time he saw her.

He decided he would take Gina to Ringgold to meet

Junior and Hannah and flaunt her beauty. Janice would be out of her mind with jealousy when she met her. He suspected Janice would have a couple of kids, gained fifty pounds, and be like her mother.

Twenty-eight days after leaving Norfolk, "Land Ho!" blasted from the ship's speakers as a tiny dot appeared on the horizon. Smitty got his first sighting of England, and his mind raced with excitement and anticipation. He had never been away from home a single night until he entered the Army. He had read about England, but never dreamed he would travel there.

Smitty said to himself, "I can't believe I'm doing all this foreign travel paid for by Uncle Sam."

He knew from reading The Grit paper that over sixty million people were projected to die from the world being at war and prayed to God he would not be one of them. Nevertheless, he had determined he would fight to the death to defend his country against the Axis of Evil, fight for his family, and fight to protect Gina.

He despised Germany and hated all German soldiers. Germany had become the primary instigator and driving force in the war. Even though Germany was one of the world's most powerful nations, with great wealth, status, and power, they would not be satisfied until they ruled the world.

He hated Adolph Hitler and his coldblooded killers. To him, Adolph Hitler represented Satan in the flesh, a madman without an ounce of love, kindness, compassion, mercy, or grace. The world had become a cup of hatred and evil, with the Third Reich soldiers willingly drinking from that cup.

Smitty knew his hatred for Germany came from Junior and his service in the war. He remembered Junior labeling the Germans as killing machines who often slaughtered innocent civilians in cold blood. He had read about their concentration camps and how Hitler wanted to rid the world of the Jewish race. He had thought he might be one of the soldiers to take revenge for the Germans' atrocious actions.

When he was drafted, he did not have any idea where he would serve, whether in the Pacific theater, to fight the Japanese, or in France, Italy, or North Africa. Smitty was relieved he had not been ordered to fight the Japanese like Larry Garth, and preferred to fight in France instead of jungle warfare. Smitty preferred France because Junior had fought there and had shared his Army life through the years. He realized Junior had a considerable influence on him regarding the Army and this war.

Smitty determined he would not hesitate to kill someone in battle. He understood he would have to shoot his enemy, or his enemy would shoot him and realized he would soon be a warrior in a kill-or-be-killed struggle.

# CHAPTER TWENTY-FOUR

When the soldiers disembarked in Sterling, the gangplanks quickly filled with soldiers and their gear. Leaving the ship, government entry, and processing took hours. The line of waiting soldiers circled the deck five to six times. Every soldier had to be examined, questioned, and verified by English intelligence officers to deter spies, informants, and undercover agents from entering England illegally. The men were angry that England would not accept them with their Army identifications. After all, they were supposed to be allies and friends.

Each soldier was responsible for his Army gear and personal belongings, and every duffle bag was to be inspected. The long inspection lines were causing the men to become restless and ready to move on. Smitty had never heard so much griping and complaining and shuddered to think what Johnny would have spewed out.

After the processing was completed, Smitty and thousands of men were allowed to enter England. Buses transported them to the base at Sterling, where they would be briefed and prepared for duty. As Smitty's bus drove through the gates, he thought the area had been damaged by an earthquake. Most of the buildings and barracks were in ruins.

A pile of broken blocks, bricks, and rubble was all that remained of the administration building. Huge craters were everywhere. Thousands of men were housed in pyramid tents and huts scattered throughout the camp resembling Fort Benning when it was a tent encampment.

The bus driver told the newly arriving soldiers, "When

you hear air raid sirens, run for cover and avoid open areas. We have been experiencing bombing raids most days and many nights. Germany apparently decided to stop the flow of soldiers at the source, and Sterling is that source."

The reality of war dawned on Smitty, and he prayed for his protection and safety from the bombing raids. He had gained a firsthand view and eye-opening picture of the destruction war could bring.

Tension, fear, and danger filled the base as the war came to Britain, centered on London and Sterling. The base at Sterling was a strategic location for the Allies.

After the soldiers settled into their temporary quarters, Smitty and Lenny walked to the nearby town. They found the city a war zone with sandbag barriers stacked at most buildings. Bomb shelters and bunkers had been constructed for people to seek safety from ongoing air raids. Gas masks were stored in the shelters for utilization in possible poison gas attacks.

Every night the people prepared for night bombing raids with sandbags refilled and replaced, debris and destruction removed, and areas cleared. People even conducted funerals and buried the dead after dark. Activities people could not do in daylight had to be done at night.

Most people in the area limited their travels after dark, except for what was required. A few cars and trucks crawled through the streets without headlights. Most of the population stayed inside with blackout curtains over their windows. No outside lights were allowed, and most residents went inside at dusk and came out after sunrise. People entered Sterling in the morning and left before sunset when the town became a ghost town.

After continual air raids, a few shops and small stores were all that remained. The few undamaged structures had little to offer. Many of the pubs and restaurants closed at sundown while a large number had permanent closing signs in their windows. It was nothing like the military town Smitty had sailed from. Sterling had almost been leveled and looked as if someone had attempted to wipe it off the map.

The continual roar of airplane engines seldom left Sterling in peace since most aircraft on sorties departed to France and Germany. The warplanes and bombers took off every few minutes as squadron after squadron risked their lives for freedom.

Smitty often cried, seeing or hearing a damaged or disabled aircraft attempting an emergency landing. He grieved after the explosions when landings fell short, indicating a plane had crashed, and men had died.

Smitty lost count of the air raids as they raged most days and many nights. The soldiers on the base seldom experienced peace and quiet. Even the air-raid sirens blared long after attacks ended. False alarms were frequent, but Smitty and Lenny sought cover at all times.

Squadrons of Allied fighters and bombers flew overhead and, after a while, were seldom noticed. Troop transports loaded and unloaded their cargos of fighting men, some leaving for France and others arriving from the front lines.

Hundreds of buses rolled into the base daily, bringing in replacement troops. Large ships would bring men into England, and smaller ships would transport them out. It was a never-ending process of moving in and out, and for a majority of the soldiers, Sterling would be their last stop on free soil.

The Germans knew closing Sterling would be a significant victory and would damage the replacement-troop pipeline. Without replacement troops, the Allied forces would be destined for defeat.

Smitty and Lenny met soldiers who had fulfilled their duty on the front lines, the stories about life on the front troubling them much. They did not want to hear about the thousands of men being wounded or killed. They had seen death on *the Vermont* but were unaware of front line battle conditions with what they heard serving as a wake-up call.

Bravo Company had been informed Allied forces had taken portions of France. Still, the Germans were organizing a more massive thrust to rid the country of all enemy soldiers. A substantial German assault force was gathering to move through France with everyone concerned England might be invaded.

Smitty had a reoccurring nightmare about his future. He experienced numerous dreams of being shot and lying in knee-deep snow. The dreams were so real he could feel the pain. After waking up from the dreams, he would be sweating as if he had run several miles on a summer day. He was unable to shake what he thought might be a premonition.

Duty assignments were given with Smitty's company assigned supply duty. Smitty was angry and could not believe his orders. He had joined the Army to fight and had been relegated to drive a deuce-and-a-half, a two and one-half ton truck. While these trucks were the Army's workhorses and the best-made pieces of equipment in the war, he was upset and disappointed he could spend his Army career as a truck driver.

He would be devastated if people in Ringgold learned about his truck-driving duties. He would never want Gina to discover he was a truck driver and not a combat soldier. He hated the thought of being another Roger Brown, delivering groceries. He knew Junior would not be pleased with his duty, since he wanted Smitty to follow in his footsteps into combat. He would be disappointed and feel Smitty had let him down.

Adding to Smitty's disappointment, truck drivers were not assigned weapons while driving in England. He was livid at being unarmed and unable to fight. Without a weapon, he did not feel like a soldier but resigned himself to being an unarmed truck driver. He decided he would perform his duties to the best of his ability.

On the first morning of his transport training, Smitty was ordered to drive his truck into a warehouse area and back up to a loading dock. Smitty did it with ease, and Sergeant Robert Kilgore complimented him on his driving. Kilgore was in charge of all transportation units.

"What's your name, soldier?" asked Sargent Kilgore.

"Smith, Sir. Smitty Smith," he answered.

"Where did you learn to drive a truck?" The sergeant inquired.

"My Uncle Alvin drove over-the-road trucks and would let me drive them around our farm when he visited. I spent hours driving over our open land, and I always loved backing into tight places."

Sergeant Kilgore hailed from Gainesville, Georgia, and was familiar with the people and the area around Smitty's hometown after visiting Ringgold numerous times. Mr. Robert Hamilton, an attorney in Ringgold, was Sergeant Kilgore's uncle. Kilgore knew the Browns, the Hamiltons, and other prominent families there." I don't care for the Browns or their son Roger. He is a spoiled brat," Kilgore confided. "They are rich, but they don't have to act like God made them rule the world. That family is way too uppity for me."

From that moment, Smitty liked Sergeant Kilgore, and Kilgore decided to look out for Smitty, with him becoming one of Kilgore's favorites.

Day after day, Smitty and the other drivers carried out their duties. Smitty lost count of the days and functioned like a zombie driving the truck over repetitive routes. He lived in a rut and determined his rut was like a grave with both ends dug out. He longed for a change and hoped he would not die of boredom.

# *CHAPTER TWENTY-FIVE*

One morning after breakfast, Sergeant Kilgore announced, "Listen up! There will be an assembly at 0800 this morning in Hangar 9, and all drivers must assemble. Colonel Shepherd will be briefing us on the progress of the war and our involvement. You need to start preparing to be shipped to the front. It's your time and your day to fight for freedom. This is your hour, and I challenge you to seize the day."

Sargent Kilgore called the assembly to attention as Colonel Thomas, "T-Bird" Shepherd, the highest-ranking American officer at Sterling, walked to the front of the hangar. The men snapped to attention and saluted their ranking officer with the Colonel returning their salute. He was from Dallas, Texas, and a cowboy in civilian life. His family owned and operated a cattle ranch outside Austin, Texas, called the Triple T. He was a tall, well built, stone-faced professional soldier. He was a highly decorated leader who had earned his rank in battle. Not only did he know he was tough, but everyone around him knew it. He had power, knew it, and used it. He was life-and-death serious about his duty and was a soldier's soldier.

"At ease!" Colonel Shepherd said. "Be seated."

Not a single soldier moved as he stood and surveyed his audience.

"Men, things aren't going well for us in France, and we are having a difficult time holding our positions. The Nazis have turned back our assaults and brought in tanks and troops to push our men from France back to Spain and England. The Germans will soon launch a major offensive to defeat all Allied forces, and the next few weeks will be critical to our success or lead to our defeat.

Our fighting men on the front lines are running low on food, supplies, ammunition, and replacements. We must deliver these things to enable them to continue fighting. You men have been assigned the task of delivering what our troops desperately need. Your efforts will involve going to the front of the battles and driving into heavily fortified enemy-held territory.

You may think your task is minimal, but you men are one of the keys to whether we hold or lose France. He paused for a moment to allow his statements to sink in.

I'm asking you to do whatever necessary and make needed sacrifices to keep our soldiers in the field. You and your trucks will be targeted by enemy planes, tanks, and infantry patrols. They know if they can stop our supply trucks, they can and will retake France. If they retake France, England and the United States could be next.

I want you to know the cost of your orders. Some of you could die or be wounded in the next few days and weeks, but we must succeed at all costs. No price is too great. Right now, I'm asking you to be brave and courageous. This is the time for you to come forth as freedom fighters. In light of upcoming events, I want us to pray.

Colonel Shepherd's words had been startling and sobering, but when he offered to pray, Smitty and most of the soldiers felt encouraged.

"Our Father Who Art in Heaven," Colonel Shepherd began praying the Lord's Prayer. Most of the men joined in while some stood quietly.

After Colonel Shepherd and the men finished the prayer with a loud "Amen!" the Colonel asked, "Any questions?"

No questions were raised, so he continued.

"Bravo Company will sail for France at 0900. I pray God will watch over you and help you through this mission. God speed! May God bless you, our soldiers in the field, and bless the United States of America."

The room grew quiet without any movement for what seemed like an eternity. As the Colonel exited the hangar, Smitty realized how foolish he had been looking at his assignment as a third rate truck driving job. He no longer felt like a grocery delivery boy.

He was elated to be transitioning from truck driver to combat soldier. Smitty had kept a quote from General Omar Bradley in his helmet and would read it when he witnessed replacement soldiers leaving Sterling. He would think of it when he saw wounded and battle-worn soldiers returning from the front. He read it in preparation for his journey to France.

"The rifleman fights without promise of either reward or relief. Behind every river, there's another hill and behind that hill, another river. After weeks or months in the line, only a wound can offer him the comfort of safety, shelter, and a bed.

Those who are left to fight, fight on, evading death, but knowing that with each day of evasion, they have exhausted one more chance for survival. Sooner or later, unless victory comes, this chase must end on the medical litter or in the grave."

Smitty didn't know why this always touched his heart when he read it and often prayed he would not end up "on a medical litter or in a grave." He was fighting a dark spirit and struggling to keep a positive attitude. His inner conflicts were raging more than the battles he could be facing.

The squad leader in charge of the post office came to the

center of the hangar and shouted, "Mail call."

He delivered mail to the soldiers in Smitty's squad. The soldier called Smitty's name and handed him two letters, one from Gina and another from his mama. He read the letter from Gina, reread it, and savored every detail, seeking to know everything about her.

He ripped open his mama's letter and started reading.

> Dear Smitty,
>
> I'm sorry to inform you your daddy died last night in his sleep. He bought a fifth of liquor from the Kendall boys, got drunk, and went to bed. He has been hitting the bottle a lot since you left. Doctor Rogers felt it was a heart attack, a stroke, or whiskey poisoning. I feel like his body wore out. By the time you receive this letter we will have conducted your Daddy's funeral at Shiloh Baptist Church and buried him in the church cemetery. I do not know what I am going to do now that I'm alone. I have peace that you will make it through and return. I need you to come home since I don't know how long I can live like this.
>
> By the way, Roger and Janice Brown had twin girls last week. She was three months pregnant when they married, gained forty pounds, and looks and acts like her mother. She stopped by to visit and check on you. She told me, "Smitty is still my favorite man and the love of my life. I wish I had married him instead of Roger. He will always hold a special place in my heart.
>
> We got the news Larry Garth had been killed by machine-gun fire when his unit stormed the beach on some island. The report said he was in the first wave of men to attack the Japanese bunkers. His

> death made me even more concerned about your safety. Please stay safe.
>
> I'm doing all right, but the house is so empty, I stay lonely, and life is hard. Pray for me and write soon. I'm praying for you. Remember you can make it through.
>
> Love forever,
> Mama

Smitty shed a few tears over Junior's death, but his heart broke for his mama's sorrow and grief. Despite Junior's faults, Hannah loved him. She never liked being alone, and Smitty wondered how she would handle her loneliness and the farm's responsibilities. He hoped she would not experience another nervous breakdown and end up in a mental hospital like she did after Maria's birth. She fought hard while suffering through that most difficult and darkest time of her life.

After Smitty returned to his quarters, he did what his mama asked him to do. As he opened his mouth to pray, he began to cry, feeling the hurt, pain, and loss his mama felt. Smitty thought she had shed enough tears, sorrow, and loss in a few months to last a lifetime. He choked out a short prayer, and his thoughts returned to Gina, knowing that, other than Gina, he loved his mama more than anyone in the world.

***

"All right, let's move out," shouted Sergeant Kilgore. "Get up and get going!"

The moment had arrived for Smitty to ship out, and he approached the sailing with mixed emotions. He was challenged to go into battle with a war raging within him.

Sergeant Kilgore delivered the news Smitty he had been promoted to Corporal. He was honored by the promotion and elated with the pay increase providing additional money to send home. He was satisfied with Hannah's provision after his pay increase.

Smitty had been disappointed his promotion has been delayed after Sergeant Rylee had requested it after basic training. He realized with all the issues facing the Army, his advancement was not very important compared to winning the war. Victory was far more critical than any promotion.

His promotion to squad leader assigned him a group of nine drivers with Lenny assigned to his unit. At first, Lenny did not like taking orders from Smitty and felt he should be in charge. He later accepted Smitty's promotion and told him, "Smitty, you're my squad leader, and I'm honored to serve under you. You're my horse, and I'm going to ride with you, even if you never win another horse race." Lenny tussled Smitty's hair to show he had signed on.

The next morning the men were bused to Liverpool, a port on the English Channel, where they drove loaded trucks up steep ramps and arranged them on the ship. The men stayed below deck protected from the howling winds, the bitter cold, and blowing snow. It was a dark, frigid, and dreary day leaving most of the soldiers feeling hopeless and depressed.

Snowflakes fell like tears, from so much pain, sorrow, and death on the earth. Smitty's heart was burdened as his thoughts skipped from Norfolk with Gina, to Ringgold with his mama, to France with the men who would soon welcome them and the needed supplies.

The Germans had initiated an all-out attempt to annihilate every ship leaving England. They were employing submarines, destroyers, fighters, and every weapon in their possession to stop, delay, or destroy any vessel bound for France.

Smitty knew the ship could encounter minefields and U-boats before reaching their destination. Germany had dispatched vessels from their powerful fleet to intercept and destroy all Allied vessels. The Americans and the British were no match for the German's killer task force with Germany utilizing some of the most powerful ships in the world. Smitty prayed they would not encounter any attacks on the crossing, believing he could never survive another sinking ship.

German aerial patrols and spotter planes searched the Channel daily for ships. Simultaneously, the mighty German Luftwaffe dispatched fighter planes to destroy anything in the shipping lanes. Some of the Allied ships sailed at night without a single light burning.

The Germans had prioritized the destruction of eastbound ships loaded with men, supplies, and weapons, but still gave limited attention to ships departing France. Most returning vessels were empty, with some carrying small numbers of wounded, worn-out, and exhausted troops. The enemy's goal was to destroy everything sailing into and out of England.

Smitty and the members of Bravo Company would sail on the *RMS Winston.* The *Winston* had been assigned to ferry men and equipment across the channel, as it was one of England's most dependable vessels.

As the *Winston* prepared to depart, Smitty strolled to the main deck for a breath of fresh air and solitude to deal with his emotions and feelings. His thoughts drifted to Gina, to home, and the people he had lost from his life.

He stood by the railings for a few minutes staring into the dark gray water with his thoughts centering on what would lie ahead. He was carrying a heavy burden feeling his death was near. The stiff winds and the white caps breaking across the channel left him feeling sad and lonely.

Breaking the silence and stillness, two German planes had been spotted in a steep dive toward the ship.

"Enemy aircraft at eleven o'clock! We are under attack! Battle stations!"

The ship's deck guns fired anti-aircraft bursts at the incoming planes. Two Hurricanes escorting the convoy were on their tails, and four British Spitfires were closing. One of the German planes bearing down on the ship was blasted and spiraled into the ocean.

Panic exploded as the ship's spotter screamed, "Hit the deck! Hit the deck! Hit the deck!"

The remaining German plane was streaking toward the ship with a golden opportunity to damage or sink the *Winston*. Anti-aircraft guns were booming with round after round directed at the airplane, yet the German pilot held his course. He had emptied his machine guns on the gun batteries and had flown through the heavy anti-aircraft fire to drop his bombs. With death bearing down on him, Smitty fell to the deck praying.

The first bomb missed the ship and burst in the water with the explosion rocking the boat and soaking Smitty. A second bomb screamed toward the ship and slammed into the deck about forty feet from Smitty. It struck the ship with a huge thud and failed to explode. It slid under the trucks, bounced to the end of the deck, and slid harmlessly into the water without exploding.

Smitty jumped up, shouting, "It's a dud! It's a dud! Thank you, Jesus!"

Smitty could not believe the bomb had not exploded and blown him off the face of the earth. His life and the lives of countless soldiers and sailors had been spared. Smitty rejoiced. He had prayed for safety before his journey began and was thankful his prayers had been answered, and his life saved.

Seconds later, American and British planes blasted the attacking enemy plane from the sky.

Sailors ran to inspect for damage with a Navy captain, the first officer to arrive. Glancing at Smitty, he muttered, "You're one lucky son of a gun; that bomb should have blown you to smithereens. You must have a good luck charm around your neck or a rabbit's foot in your pocket. It must not have been your time to die."

"It wasn't luck. It was prayer," Smitty said. "God was with me."

Smitty looked up, smiled, and thanked God for delivering him from certain death. He reached up and touched the Bible in his shirt pocket, feeling that Hannah, Gina, the Davis family, or someone had been praying for his safety.

After the attack, it was smooth sailing across the English Channel to their landing at Le Havre, France. They had taken a longer southern route attempting to avoid any attack.

They sailed up the coast of Spain and southern France to reach their destination. It worked as they arrived safely and without danger.

As they landed, those on the docks cheered, screamed, and celebrated, welcoming the Americans like conquering heroes returning from an extraordinary victory. It was heart-warming to feel their welcome and appreciation while delivering the critical supplies they had been desperately needing. Smitty and his men drove the trucks from the ship, covered them with camouflage nets, and waited for orders.

The landing area was filled with thousands of soldiers, most assigned to the front lines as replacements. Some men were waiting to return to England after completing their tours of duty. Those returning from the front appeared weary and exhausted, and Smitty could see in their eyes how the war had taken its toll. He had tremendous respect for foot soldiers and realized a battle is won or lost by the infantry's fighting.

Smitty knew these soldiers on the dock were regular people. The soldiers were someone's family member, someone's friend, or someone's next-door neighbor. Some of the soldiers had been farmers, salesmen, pastors, factory workers, doctors, lawyers, shop keepers, mechanics, welders, or school teachers. They were average men called to be above average soldiers. The soldiers' most important goals were to survive the war, fulfill their duty, and return home to their families, jobs, and former lives.

Smitty was honored to be counted among the strongest and best fighting men in the world. He was a soldier in the United States Army.

# CHAPTER TWENTY-SIX

Upon his arrival in France, Smitty was assigned to a forward base camp called Camp Lucky Strike, one of several camps named for American cigarette brands. These cigarette names created confusion when the enemy intercepted radio messages with German intelligence personnel confused about why Americans talked about cigarettes on their radios.

The camp got its name when an advanced patrol stopped at that location. The Sergeant told his men, "This is a good place to rest, so let's stop here and have a Lucky Strike."

From then on, the location was named Camp Lucky Strike. And subsequently, the camp had served as one of the most strategic Allied positions in France, with the camp functioning as a supply depot receiving and delivering needed men and supplies. It was a center of life, with men and supplies continually moving to and from the front lines.

The worst thing about deliveries from the battlefronts was the vast number of dead and wounded. After months of intense fighting and essential battles, hundreds of casualties returned daily. Camp Lucky Strike served as a focal point for men withdrawing from the front for needed rest and relaxation, known as R&R.

At times, entire squads were shipped from the fronts to allow men to rest in safety with the camp serving them in numerous ways. The men in the camp worked extended hours to replace losses in combat and resupply thousands of soldiers.

When Smitty first arrived at the camp, he was amazed at its size and activity. The base was many times larger than Ringgold, with its buildings, barracks, and tents. It appeared to be larger than Chattanooga, with thousands of men and women living and working there.

There were different types of support units in the camp functioning like a well-oiled machine. As part of the transportation unit, Smitty was committed to being the best driver he could be.

When Smitty and the men first reached the camp, their tents had been erected, a new mess tent had been constructed, and all needed elements were waiting. Their trucks had been packed with thousands of items for delivery, with everything from toilet paper to hand grenades. Tons of needed supplies would be distributed from the camp.

The camp had thousands of six-man pyramid tents with dirt floors. After each rain, the dirt floors would become mud holes making life miserable for the soldiers. Smitty, Lenny, and four other soldiers were assigned to tent L13. Smitty did not like the number 13 but did not have any say in the matter. There was canvas as far as the eye could see.

The constant roar of airplane engines was as nerve-racking as it had been at Sterling, with American and British planes providing a "safety net" to protect the camp's critical mission.

Smitty grew to hate the camp, with its clouds of death, pain, and loss that hovered over it like a thick fog. The men coming from the front lines were exhausted, mentally spent, and depressed, while those leaving for the front were filled with fear, dread, and apprehension. Feelings were heightened by the presence of so many dead and wounded soldiers.

Smitty had another reason for hating Camp Lucky

Strike. The mess tents at the camp were massive, where hundreds of cooks and servers prepared and served thousands of men and women. When he wasn't driving, he was assigned to KP. Even though he wanted to stay busy to keep his mind off the war, he had no desire to be on regular KP duty. He solved part of his problem by requesting assignment to the motor pool servicing and repairing equipment. Smitty was an outstanding and skilled worker who stayed in high demand. Working kept his mind off fighting and dying since the most protracted days in a soldier's life were days he had nothing to do but think about the war.

His assignments transporting men, equipment, and supplies to other camps were tiresome but somewhat dangerous. Smitty volunteered to drive to the front lines, where the soldiers were desperate for supplies. Driving a truck seemed easy and insignificant, but it was hazardous duty. At times, drivers had been dispatched and never returned. Smitty had lost two drivers from his squad.

It was not unusual for the drivers to have small arms fire hit the sides of the trucks. On one occasion, Smitty was delivering a load of ammunition when his convoy came under attack. His front windshield was shattered after a bullet slammed through the cab of his truck. He didn't receive any cuts or wounds and was amazed the round missed the ammunition cases in the back. He could have been blown to kingdom come. He experienced several close calls carrying out his duties.

He had been attacked with small arms fire several times but had never experienced an aerial attack or an assault by tanks. He was thankful, too, at not having driven through land mines. Smitty had observed trucks blasted into oblivion after striking a mine. One of the greatest dangers to the drivers was mines buried on secondary roads. The drivers were without any protection against mines since the army could not sweep every road. He always drove the lead truck and was exposed to the most danger. He felt God would keep him safe and help him to overcome the fear of danger and death.

Smitty's truck often stayed on the road twenty-four hours at a time, and some days, he would get in a truck as another driver was getting out. At times the truck engines ran continuously and were never turned off. Smitty was serving as part of the third wave of the Army. First came the scout patrols to explore the area. Next came the infantrymen, to secure the area, and then the supply trucks delivered soldiers and supplies to hold the site. Without supplies, it would be impossible for fighting men to stay in the field. At times, a combat unit suffered without food, water, supplies, and ammunition until a driver could deliver them.

The drivers also served as messengers carrying dispatches and orders from camp to camp. The drivers joked about being a modern-day Pony Express without horses, and with the threat being Germans instead of Comanches. Smitty kept feeling the truck drivers at Camp Lucky Strike would soon be moving deeper into combat areas. He realized they would be in the fight of their lives when they were assigned double duty as combat soldiers.

The war continued to heat up near Lucky Strike, with the Germans dug in, fortified, and holding ground until they could move forward. Their ground offensive was ready to be launched to unleash thousands of well-trained troops gathered from all over Europe.

# CHAPTER TWENTY-SEVEN

Lenny Kowalski was a professional gambler who grew up in Chicago's Polish neighborhoods, where gambling was a way of life. Lenny had perfected his gambling skills, was lucky at dice and won most of the time. Smitty had never seen Lenny lose. He was so skilled and lucky, most losers accused him of cheating. Smitty had observed him gambling and knew Lenny wasn't a cheater. He had witnessed Lenny win extra food, cigarettes, watches, jewelry, and large sums of money. He would have losers polish his boots, wash his uniforms, and take his assignments. This was quite a change from his anger over the foxhole episode with Wilson Wilder in basic training.

Most soldiers in the camp liked Lenny, but a few didn't. His gambling created enemies who accused Lenny of conning them out of their money and valuables using loaded dice. They were stupid to keep playing with Lenny but kept gambling, attempting to win their money and valuables back.

Late one night, Smitty and a soldier named Mark Ross were walking through the camp and heard a scuffle at the rear of the mess tent. They first thought a German infiltrator had penetrated the compound and was being apprehended. They rushed toward the commotion and found an angry mob of soldiers cursing and beating another soldier. The victim was on the ground motionless, as numerous men kicked and stomped him. Smitty and Ross moved closer to see what was happening.

The soldier on the ground was rolled up in a crumpled ball, moaning and groaning in pain. He had his arms over his head, attempting to avoid injury, but blood gushed from his head and face. Smitty became angry and horrified after he recognized the soldier on the ground was Lenny.

Smitty and Ross pushed closer, tossing angry soldiers aside and forcing their way into the fight. One soldier attempted to strike Smitty, but Mark decked him with a right cross that knocked him out. The rest of the mob decided they had exacted their revenge and backed away cursing.

Just as Smitty reached Lenny, four MPs rushed in and took control. Smitty, Ross, and an unconscious Lenny remained in the center of a group of onlookers running to observe what was happening.

Two of the MPs took statements from bystanders and witnesses. Medics arrived and rushed Lenny to the base hospital, where numerous stitches were required in half a dozen locations. The doctors taped his broken nose without any attempt to straighten it. Lenny already resembled a street thug, and his damaged nose added to his prize-fighter image and reputation. He looked even more like a fighter who had fought too many rounds.

After Lenny was carted off, two of the MPs remained. "You guys saved his life. He could have been killed with that mob out for blood."

Lenny received treatment, and the doctors admitted him to the medical center for observation should he have a concussion. He was required to stay overnight in case he experienced a brain bleed.

After his medical treatment, Lenny returned to his tent the next day, looking like a defeated boxer. He had a death-warmed-over look but had not suffered any permanent damage. Smitty laughed and said, "If there was any permanent damage, how could anyone tell?"

The beating caused something miraculous to happen in Lenny's head. His personality and outlook changed. He was no longer an obnoxious loudmouth filled with bragging, insults, and foul language. He ceased his rudeness, bad manners, and sarcastic remarks. The changes left Smitty believing the blows had knocked some sense in and some stupidity out.

He had told Lenny, "You need to learn from other's mistakes. You will never live long enough to make all the mistakes yourself. You are as hard-headed as my brother Bobby."

Lenny thanked Smitty and Ross for rescuing him and often said, "These are friends who saved my life and fought to deliver me from my enemies. I owe them my life, and they will always be my friends and brothers."

One of the greatest blessings in Smitty's life occurred the next day. Lenny called him aside and said, "I could have been beaten to death last night. At one point, I could feel my life flowing out of my body. I saw a bright light and heard someone calling my name. I felt surrounded by peace. Smitty, I believed it was Jesus, and I answered Him. I determined right then I wanted to be saved and baptized. I am the first Christian in my family, and I hope the rest of my family will be saved someday. I have been listening to you and Ross read your Bibles. I don't know how to do it, but I want to be saved and go to Heaven."

Smitty broke down and cried like a baby as he prayed with Lenny. He could not believe he wanted to be saved and baptized. He had witnessed a major miracle knowing if God could save Lenny, he could save anyone.

Lenny told Smitty and Ross, "I want to be baptized right now. I don't want to wait, so let's go see the chaplain and let him handle it."

The chaplain could not believe Lenny had come to him wanting to be baptized. Chaplain Henson looked at Smitty and asked him to do the baptizing. Smitty was beyond happy to handle it. Even though the baptismal water was freezing, Lenny was baptized in the name of the Father, the Son, and Holy Ghost. It was for real.

Lenny was transferred to another unit to avoid further trouble. However, Smitty still saw him when he and Mark ate breakfast with him or visited after supper.

The three made plans for after the war, agreeing they would never forget each other, that they would stay in touch and remain friends. They discussed forming a trucking operation to run from Atlanta (Smitty) to Chicago (Lenny) to New York (Ross) if they could beat the odds and survive the war.

Mark Ross was a committed and dedicated soldier and the most likable person Smitty had ever encountered. Smitty met him by accident at the latrine when they physically ran into each other while walking intersecting boards placed across a mud hole. Coming from different directions with their eyes focused downward, they collided where the boards joined and fell headfirst into knee-deep mud.

Instead of being angry, they pretended to wrestle and fight. A crowd gathered, and soon other GIs were rolling in the mud laughing and screaming. Somehow, being covered with mud from head to toe caused the heaviness and weight of war to dissipate in their laughter and horsing around. Smitty and Ross crawled from the mud and embraced one another, with many others continuing to wrestle, play, and laugh.

After Ross and Smitty showered, they visited the mess tent for breakfast. Smitty learned Ross was a hardcore, big city New Yorker, Yankee accent and all. Even though

Smitty was a dyed in the wool Southern farm boy with the heaviest southern drawl a person could have, the two became friends. Except for Lenny, Ross became Smitty's closest and dearest friend with Smitty loving Lenny and Ross like he had loved his friend Johnny.

***

Ross had fought in several battles with his units outnumbered and surrounded by German soldiers. He had fought bravely, surviving every battle. He was captured behind enemy lines with five other soldiers, marched halfway through France, and taken across the border into Germany as a prisoner of war. The Germans forced him in a hellhole POW camp, incarcerating him in far less than humane conditions. Even so, he escaped through a horrific blizzard on a stolen motorcycle. He was a brave and courageous soldier who had fought in intense, confusing, and chaotic combat and always stood strong.

Mark shared his life, heart, and battle experiences with Smitty, relating how he hated every moment he had endured with the Germans. The horrors of the camp were unbelievable, with prison life unbearable. The lice, rotting food, dysentery, malnutrition, starvation, cold, filth, and stench broke the soldiers' spirits and wills to live. Many of the prisoners ended up taking their lives to escape the torture and abuse.

The prisoners were forced to work from sunup to sundown seven days a week performing various duties. Some days they worked on mechanical things and repaired equipment while, on other days, they would cut and split firewood. They had spent days doing laundry, cooking, cleaning latrines, digging graves, and whatever the German soldiers demanded. They had loaded and unloaded trucks and trains in the snow and brutal cold without coats, gloves, and even boots.

The prisoners were taken to a train and forced to unload bodies for two days without gloves or protection. The bodies were rotting and beyond any human resemblance. Mark cried over every child and baby he removed from the railroad cars. They were forced to stack the bodies in piles for the Germans to burn to stay warm in the cold. Ross and his fellow soldiers found out the dead were Jewish victims of Hitler's hatred and goal to kill every Jew in Europe.

Smitty told Mark, "I'm amazed at the story of your capture and daring escape. I admire your bravery, determination, and heroism, and I hope and pray I can be as brave as you were. You are a hero."

Mark and Smitty shared hours encouraging each other as they talked about their past, future, families, homes, and dreams. Mark had a beautiful wife named Julie and six-year-old twins, Robby and Michael. Mark always carried a picture of his family in his shirt pocket and showed it to everyone. His wife and children were his life, and anyone who knew him knew his deep love for his family. Whenever he shared his treasured picture, tears would flow from his eyes. He longed to hold his wife and hug his boys again and was counting the few days remaining until his tour of duty would end.

Mark and Smitty became inseparable friends, eating meals together, sharing Bible studies, and praying. When you saw Mark, you saw Smitty and vice versa. They stayed together until Mark received orders to the front. He and about a hundred other soldiers were given special duty. It was his final assignment before shipping home. His tour of duty would end in a few days, and he would be discharged.

Smitty wanted to face battle the way Mark did, with

courage and bravery, even at the cost of his life. He knew he could soon be tested.

After Mark shipped out, Smitty fought loneliness with his days long and his nights longer. As a result of his loneliness, he decided he would hold off making friends, feeling the pain of loss and separation too difficult to bear.

A few days after Mark left the camp, Smitty was summoned to Chaplain Henson's tent. He prepared himself because the chaplain usually delivered bad news. He dreaded every step to the chapel, holding his breath as he went.

His mind raced with questions. "Could it be Gina, his mama, or Lenny? Is it Mark or someone in my family or Gina's family?"

His runaway fear of bad news could not be halted, and with a lump in his throat and taking shallow breathes, he pulled back the tent flap and walked into the chapel.

Chaplain Henson embraced him and spoke softly, "Smitty, I know you've been through a lot, and I have heard stories of your bravery. It breaks my heart to tell you Mark Ross has been killed. He was one of the bravest soldiers I've ever known. He sacrificed his life for his men last night. When he shipped out Monday, he had been ordered to one of the most dangerous locations on the front lines. He was on duty at La Caroche Bridge, his unit ordered to hold the bridge at all costs.

A German infiltrator wearing an Army uniform slipped by the guards and tossed a grenade into the middle of Mark's unit. He was the closest soldier to the grenade, and, without hesitation, he dove on top of the grenade to save his men.

I know you hate to hear this, but I thought it would be better coming from me than through camp scuttlebutt. I know you and Mark were close friends, and you loved him like a brother. Another reason I called you is Mark left something for you."

The chaplain handed him several letters. With tears in his eyes, Chaplain Henson said, I was close to Mark. He was the first soldier I prayed with when I came here. I considered him one of my spiritual sons.

Mark left the letters and these instructions and told me to give you these if he did not return. He said the instructions would let you know what to do."

As Smitty took the letters and turned to leave, Chaplain Henson added, "Ross's orders to return home came into Headquarters late in the afternoon on the day he was killed. If only his orders had come sooner."

Chaplain Henson could not finish the sentence. He composed himself for a moment before speaking again. "God bless you, Smitty, and may God keep you safe in the coming days. Don't give up. It may be tough, but God is going to be with you every step of the way. You will make it through."

Smitty realized Chaplain Henson had spoken the exact words his mama had spoken to him the day he left for the Army. He confirmed what his mama had said to him, and the chaplain's words gave him some comfort and peace.

Smitty returned to his tent, hurting and feeling numb inside. His heart was breaking with him feeling it might tumble from his chest and shatter. He was filled with sorrow and grief over Mark's death and kept telling himself the news had to be a mistake. He shook himself as if he was trying to wake up from a bad dream.

Smitty cried, realizing Julie Ross would never hold Mark in her arms again, and his boys would grow up without knowing their father. He found a quiet place, sat down, and opened his letter.

Dear Smitty,

Thanks for being my friend and brother. I've enjoyed sharing our journey. You helped make this war bearable, and I've seen in you some of the finest qualities a man can possess. You're the type of man I pray my sons grow to be. Your friendship made a tremendous difference in my life. As you read this, I'm now at the front of this war. I feel I won't make it through. I've had several dreams with a massive explosion happening before I wake up. I feel like I am nearing the end of my journey, but I don't fear death because God's perfect love casts out my fear.

If anything happens to me (and it has, if the chaplain has given you these letters), I ask you to mail my wife, Julie, her two letters and send the other to my sons. I pray you might consider visiting my sons someday to tell them about my love for them and my life as a soldier. I would appreciate it if you would pray for them.

I hope you will post a letter to my family someday telling them how much I loved and valued them. I would like for you to say to them I did my best to return home and fought as hard as I could to survive this war.

This is the end of our friendship on Earth, but I know we'll meet again in a better place. I'm not looking at my death in terms of an ending, but a beautiful new beginning. To be absent from the body is to be present with the Lord.

Keep your faith, stay strong, keep believing, and keep reading from that small Bible we studied. It contains the keys to life.

I pray the Lord will watch over you, keep you safe, and deliver you through this terrible war. I am asking

God to be with you even if you walk through the valley of the shadow of death, as I have, that you will fear no evil, for He will be with you. I know beyond a shadow of a doubt you will survive. It may get tough, but you will make it through.

We are blood brothers through the blood of Jesus Christ. I'll love you forever as my friend and my brother,

Mark Ross

Smitty folded the letter and placed it in his shirt pocket with his Bible. He would post the letters to Julie and the boys in a few days. He walked to his tent and reached for the red pencil Maria had given him but teared up, remembering he had given it back to her at her funeral.

He found another pencil and sat down to write the letter with a broken heart. Through flowing tears, he began, "Dear Julie."

***

News of Mark's tragic death plunged Smitty into despair and depression and brought sad memories of other losses and deaths. A cloudy, dark spirit came over Smitty, leaving him feeling he and many other soldiers from Camp Lucky Strike would soon die.

Smitty's nightly dreams were filled with blood, death, and horror. Each day, he slid deeper into a hole he could not escape from. He had fallen into a deep ravine filled with hopelessness and depression, feeling there was no way out. He realized the strongest prison in the world is a closed heart. Smitty thought he had suffered enough losses to last a lifetime, but another tragic death soon occurred.

Leroy Huckabee was from Greenville, Alabama, and a

driver in Smitty's squad. He had been one of Smitty's bunkmates when the two had sailed on the *Iowa*. His nickname was "Huck," but Smitty called him "Bama" because he talked so much about the Crimson Tide football team. He had grown up a farm boy and pure Alabama redneck. Smitty shared with him about God and taught him from Junior's Bible. They shared their faith and prayed for each other. After losing Mark, Bama had filled part of the void in Smitty's life.

One morning while Smitty was inspecting his truck, a massive explosion rocked the camp. Smitty learned that after breakfast, Bama went for a cigarette break. He stepped into a storage building, and his cigarette ignited an open barrel of gasoline. The explosion scattered Bama and the building across a large portion of the camp.

Smitty cried for days after he rushed to the scene to find Bama killed in the explosion. He boxed up Bama's belongings and penned a letter to his folks. He wasn't able to send Bama's dog tags home; they were never found. Bama was a good, hard-working country farm boy like Smitty and Johnny Little, and his death added to Smitty's sorrow and depression.

Smitty asked himself, "Who will die next? Would it be Lenny? Another member of my squad? Could it be me?"

He felt he could not survive another death of someone he loved - first Ross and then Bama. It seemed as if everything and everyone he valued in his life would be taken from him.

# CHAPTER TWENTY-EIGHT

Days seemed to last forever as the drivers carried out daily orders. The men rose at 0430 and were on the road before 0600, often returning to camp after 2100 hours. They were on the road seven days a week with driving a truck becoming more difficult than Smitty had imagined.

The roads were a continual problem, with mud up to the fenders of his deuce-and-a-half with trucks having to stay in six-wheel drive. The weather left many roads impassable, with the drivers having to push the trucks to solid ground when the convoys bogged down. Most of the time, the trucks could not travel more than five to ten miles an hour. Smitty felt if he never drove another truck on another muddy road, he would be happy. He had driven enough muddy roads to last a lifetime.

Day after day, Smitty labored behind the wheel of his truck. He thought he might be going crazy when he could not remember his location or where he had driven. He operated like a robot doing what his job required. Each night, Smitty went to sleep, thankful he was another day closer to returning to Gina's arms and seeing his mama.

His life brightened when Lenny transferred back to Bravo Company. He needed a friend. Lenny took Bama's bunk next to him, and Smitty was elated to be sharing the journey with Lenny again.

One cold, dreary Monday morning, the men did not receive daily orders when they arrived at the shipping depot. The men of Bravo Company had been ordered to assemble outside the headquarters tent. The enormous tent was filled with maps, graphs, and charts. Smitty had observed the officers studying the maps and knew something huge was coming down.

Colonel Bob Franklin was a West Point honor graduate and the commander of Camp Lucky Strike. He walked to the front and called the men to order. He emptied the tobacco from his pipe and addressed the soldiers.

"Men, I have news. Many of you have wanted to get to the front, and you will have your opportunity. You have been ordered to transport relief forces and supplies to combat areas east of Paris, the hottest combat zone. You'll rest today and leave at first light in the morning. This will be your most dangerous mission to date and could be your most hazardous war mission. You have done a great job, and today I'm asking you to go the extra mile or maybe two.

You might want to set your affairs in order and write home. Captain Wagner will be in charge of this mission. I wish you safety and success in your duty. Good day, men."

The men spent the day contemplating the seriousness of their orders. Aware of the risk to their lives, most soldiers were silent, their tents funeral-home quiet. Some of the soldiers were filled with anxiety, wondering about the mission, and questioning if they would survive. Smitty was one of those soldiers.

The night seemed as if it would last forever with Smitty experiencing his reoccurring nightmare. He saw swarms of German soldiers storming over snow-covered hills. No matter how many he wounded or killed, they kept advancing. No matter how hard he fought, the enemy soldiers over-running his position, he could not stop them. When an enemy soldier pulled the trigger to take his life, he was roused and awakened by a soldier next to him.

"Man, you've been having a nightmare. You've shouted, screamed, and woke everybody in the tent. It's 0230, and we have to be up in two hours. If you can't sleep without nightmares, stay awake for the rest of the night."

Smitty tried to go back to sleep, but his dream troubled him. He felt it was a warning he would soon die at the hand of a German soldier.

The trucks rolled at first light, with their destination about a hundred fifty miles from the camp. They would travel through areas under Allied control. Some sections were no-man's land, where armies were battling for control.

The drivers had been ordered to keep their weapons ready and be prepared to use them after being assigned double duty as combat soldiers. Smitty felt like a soldier with his M-1 by his side.

The convoy roared through Loren with the road sign for Benet pointing straight ahead. Captain Wagner was at the head of the convoy and gave the command to proceed full speed forward. The captain failed to verify the direction and was unaware the road to Benet turned right. Without anyone's knowledge, an infiltrator had reversed the road signs. The convoy was no longer heading for its ordered destination but rolling toward the German's largest troop concentration in Europe.

The convoy passed burned-out railroad tracks, blown up bridges, and even dead horses, sheep, and cattle. They passed destroyed vineyards and fields of burned wheat and grain left in ashes. Smitty was awed and saddened by the deserted towns and villages leveled to the ground, shuddering at how many innocent people had lost their lives without any involvement in the war.

They roared across an expansive bridge with Smitty questioning how the bridge was standing. He estimated at least a hundred armed American troops were dug in to protect and defend the bridge. Smitty wondered if this could be the bridge where Mark Ross was killed. He choked up at the thought. Smitty started weeping when he read the sign on the bridge, La Caroche. He would have given anything to see Ross alive on the bridge. His tears helped release some of the feelings and sadness that had been pressing him.

He thought the bridge might cause trouble for the convoy if it was overrun before they returned. Without the bridge, they would be cut-off from Camp Lucky Strike, so Smitty prayed, asking God for the bridge to remain under Allied control.

The convoy made swift progress without any German opposition, giving Smitty the feeling something was wrong. He had a premonition they could be heading into a trap. As the convoy proceeded toward what they thought was their ordered destination, they came under fire.

Long-range cannon fire erupted over the convoy. When the captain radioed headquarters for support, the cannon fire ceased. American batteries had been firing at their own convoy! Friendly fire could have destroyed them before they reached their destination. On learning an unscheduled American convoy was passing through their target area, headquarters failed to realize the mistake and order them to reverse their route. Their failure was the second critical error in this fiasco.

The journey became even more frustrating when they encountered a washed-out road. The drivers spent over three hours making the road passable. Filling the area with dirt using picks and shovels took a long time and a lot of hard work.

After another fifty miles, Lieutenant Lewis Watson asked Captain Wagner about the route, expressing concerns about the direction of travel. He said, "I do not think we're traveling the right way."

Wagner was a prideful man, a hardheaded know-it-all who would never admit he was wrong. He exploded, shouting strong curse words and threats at Watson.

"Who do you think you are, questioning my orders and my authority? I'm in complete charge of this mission, and I resent you thinking I don't know what I'm doing. May I remind you, you are to follow my orders and never question any order I issue. Don't you ever challenge my authority again. I know where we are and where we're heading. I am insulted and offended at your actions, and we will discuss them when we return to camp." Captain Wagner was always right, even when he was wrong.

After the strong words, the captain waved his hand forward for the convoy to move ahead for what he thought was Benet. They traveled faster and farther behind enemy lines without the captain realizing they were traveling in the wrong direction. Snow began to fall with flakes as large as half dollars, and the quietness and stillness left Smitty apprehensive and concerned.

Smitty continued feeling something was wrong, with many of his drivers thinking the convoy should have reached its destination. They had not seen a single directional sign, but the captain still felt he did not need any signs. He felt the map was inaccurate, or they had been detoured. The convoy continued driving in the wrong direction toward a massive enemy stronghold.

Smitty was concerned they had not seen any GIs in hours and had not seen a single human being. They moved deeper into enemy territory, with danger increasing by the minute. As darkness began to fall, the captain's error became apparent, and he called the squad leaders together.

"We should have reached our destination by now. I've made a mistake, and it seems we have been traveling in the wrong direction. I do not know where we are or the distance to our destination, but we'll have to backtrack at first light. Let's get things battered down for the night and get some sleep. We do not need to tell the men since it might make them anxious and keep them from sleeping. Let's find a safe place to stay the night."

The snow fell from the darkening gray skies as thick as Smitty had ever seen it fall, covering the trucks in minutes, so thick the drivers could not see the road or ditches. Huge flakes covered the landscape, creating additional hazards and dangers for the convoy.

The captain ordered the men to bed down in a pass between two hills, the logic being the hills might prevent them from being spotted by the Germans. The lieutenant did not like being hemmed in between two high places, but could not express his opinion to his superior. He always wanted to fight from high ground. Captain Wagner repeatedly said, "I know what I'm doing. We need to be hidden from the enemy." Wagner was compounding his directional mistake.

Around 2400 hours, a shot rang out, then another, and another. A sentry shouted, "It's the Germans. We're under attack." German machine guns barked, with small-arms fire screaming from the convoy. Those sleeping in and under the trucks awoke quickly as if responding to a fire alarm. They answered the enemy fire with round after round from their carbines. Cries and screams from wounded and dying men on both sides rose above the gunfire. The Germans fired flares to light the night sky, exposing the trucks like midday.

Smitty realized the German soldiers were the finest in the world. They were armed with the best weapons, had been given the best training, and were the most experienced and battle-tested soldiers anywhere. Death was the only language the Germans understood, and to them, there was no law but the law of the strongest.

It looked like he and his fellow soldiers were left with little chance of survival in a battle for their lives in the freezing cold. He was sweating profusely with his heart racing faster than a thoroughbred running the Kentucky Derby. He felt like he was in the middle of a hangman's noose, waiting for the inevitable. He did not have much time to be afraid; he was too busy finding targets. He quickly learned that men will fight and kill to save their lives and remain free. There is nothing wrong or prohibited in a battle; everyone fights for their survival without holding anything back. Bravery, honor, and courage are heart matters and always show what a man is made of.

Smitty no longer worried about his actions in combat. He realized it was kill or be killed, and he had no desire to die. It was his time to kill, and he stepped up. He knew an ax never mourns a tree it fells.

The Germans attacked in waves, charging from all sides. Out-manned, out-numbered, and out-gunned, the American soldiers' only hope was to hold out until morning and pray reinforcements would come.

The battle raged without any signs of the Germans withdrawing. They seemed reluctant to use grenades, mortars, or bazookas, which could quickly destroy the trucks. Smitty figured they must need the supplies in their trucks, therefore using only small arms fire. The last thing he wanted in life was to end up in an unmarked grave from a huge blast.

The Germans held the advantage of position and apparently planned to fight with small arms until the Americans were killed or surrendered. The American soldiers were face to face with the most experienced and most honored enemy soldiers in Europe.

Smitty thought to himself, "We have two chances for survival, slim, and none. We are in the fight for our lives, with the odds stacked against us. We will be fortunate if we can even hold out a few hours more. My mama told me I would make it through, and I hope she was right."

The convoy was surrounded, and its men pinned down by constant enemy fire. Men kept falling around Smitty, some killed instantly, and some with serious wounds that would prove fatal. Smitty, Lenny, and other drivers had pulled their trucks between rocks to provide some safety. Trucks caught in the open without cover were being blasted. By the law of war and the odds against them, the men of Bravo Company would die before dawn.

Snipers were picking off soldiers when a stray tracer bullet hit the fuel tank in the last truck. The explosion shook the entire convoy. Fourteen men died in the blast, burned beyond recognition. The battle raged, as hell continued to be unleashed, with Smitty feeling he was being swept away on a tidal wave of heroes' blood.

Smitty's heart plunged when he realized the convoy's medics and all their medical supplies had been destroyed in the explosion. Men kept screaming and crying out for medics who would never come. The medics who died were some of the most important soldiers in the convoy.

Smitty realized the battle was a flashback of his dream from the night before. He said to himself, "I'm going to die on this battlefield. This is not a dream or a nightmare. I'm going to die tonight." It appeared Smitty had dug his grave before he even died.

# CHAPTER TWENTY-NINE

Captain Wagner took a shot to the head just after Lieutenant Watson was blasted in the heart. Sergeant Christopher Morgan was shot between the eyes by a bullet that blew his head open. Sergeant William Norton had been blown apart in the truck explosion. With their deaths, Smitty became the ranking officer in charge of what was left of Bravo Company.

The Germans overwhelmingly outnumbered the Americans and continued attacking with small arms fire from machine guns and rifles. They continued attacking from all directions but concentrated on the exposed rear trucks. The Germans were taking heavy casualties with their soldiers exposed in the open without cover.

The GIs hoped there might be Allied troops in forward positions near them that would come to their aid or contact headquarters for assistance. Smitty kept praying the Germans would continue withholding their most potent weapons, remain cautious, and keep firing above and below the diesel tanks.

Another tremendous explosion rocked a truck behind him, leaving him horrified. He lost his hearing for a moment, thinking they had been shelled by a Panzer 4 infantry support tank. He shuddered when he realized a stray bullet had hit the ammunition truck and blown it into oblivion. He was thankful it had been separated from the remainder of the trucks, and the men had been moved as far away as possible. So much for the needed ammunition at the front! He knew it was a costly loss that would result in the loss of many lives.

A few of the killed and wounded had been shot upon crawling from under the trucks to find better cover. The number of dead and wounded on both sides mounted. Smitty was concerned with so many of his men drowning in the waters of death.

A young soldier in front of Smitty took a shot to his stomach and cried out in anguish. Smitty knew he would not survive with a bullet in his gut. His blood spilled like an overturned glass of red wine as the snow under him changed from white to blood red.

A soldier next to him caught a bullet in the groin, and his manhood disappeared. Jimmy Ramsey, one of Smitty's bunkmates, took a shot in his stomach and screamed for a medic. Two men covered him in snow, hoping the cold would slow his hemorrhaging. Smitty knew Ramsey did not have long to live, so he crawled to him, held him, and prayed. He removed his dog tags after he exhaled his final breath.

Lenny told Smitty, "I don't think we stand a snowball's chance in hell. We have killed at least five hundred Nazis, and they keep coming. How many Germans do you think are out there? There must be thousands, and they all want us in their sights."

Lenny placed him in a headlock and whispered, "You've been the best friend I've ever had. A man is blessed to have a friend like you. I want you to know I love you."

As Lenny hugged him, he felt Lenny's tears on his face. Lenny's tears broke his heart, and he began to cry. They held each other for a moment without speaking a word. Smitty hoped the last face he would see before he died would be his friend.

"Looks like we've got the Germans right where we want them," Lenny joked as he popped a fresh clip into his carbine.

They raised their weapons and fired at five German soldiers rushing forward. The charge ceased after three of the soldiers went down, and two retreated. Smitty wished there were more than eight cartridges in his clip.

Smitty stopped firing and looked at Lenny, "No matter what happens, we have experienced friendship and love few people find in their life journeys. Let's take every German we can to the grave with us."

The radio operator kept sending SOS messages for troop support and immediate air cover. The unit was under fire, in desperate need, and facing huge problems. No one in the convoy or anyone at headquarters knew their exact location.

Smitty remembered Captain Wagner had carried a map in his field jacket. He secured the blood-soaked map from the captain's pocket and slid under a tarp with a flashlight to search for their location. He located a waterfall they had passed, and an abandoned monastery confirmed the convoy's approximate location. When he found the two hills where they were pinned down, he calculated the map coordinates and handed them to the radio operator. The operator transmitted the information to headquarters, and Smitty felt help would soon be dispatched to their location. He prayed to God that Command would send immediate assistance and not wait until morning. Sunrise would be too late.

The Germans fired another flare, lighting the night sky, as hundreds of screaming Nazis charged down the hill, shouting at the top of their lungs. Smitty shot one after another, no longer wondering if he could take someone's life in battle. His gun barrel was glowing red when the Germans abandoned the charge, leaving hundreds of German soldiers scattered in the snow.

He saw figures moving bodies around, not dragging the

wounded back, but stacking bodies into a wall. Smitty knew they were desperate for supplies to sacrifice so many lives and take such desperate measures. They were paying an exorbitant price for supplies when they could've destroyed the convoy and killed every American soldier if that had been their goal.

After the first, second, and third onslaughts, many Germans pulled back from the shallow wall of corpses to reorganize and plan their next move. They had underestimated the determination and courage of the truck drivers and supply troops. With their overwhelming numbers, they felt the Americans would surrender after their first attack. They had sent three waves of attacking soldiers, and the GIs were standing strong without any signs of retreat or surrender.

Smitty organized his remaining troops and pulled wounded soldiers to the center of the convoy. The men stacked corpses for protection from snipers and random enemy fire. The wounded's moans and groans brought images of ghouls and evil spirits roaming the road, with the men feeling they were in a horror movie. Many of the men still alive were riding on a tidal wave of hero's blood.

The temperature had plunged and was chasing zero degrees. The Germans withdrew to tents, cozy fires, and hot coffee. Smitty realized the Germans were waiting for the soldiers to freeze to death and had decided to use the freezing temperature to finish them off without firing another shot.

Smitty grew concerned when he could not feel his right foot or lower leg. He had ignored his condition and looked to his men's needs, showing greater concern for his soldiers than for himself. He determined he would walk through the fire for the sake of love. His love for Gina and his mama burned within his heart and kept him fighting for his very life.

He asked Lenny, "How are you making it? This makes me wish I had been sent to a warm, beautiful, and sun-filled island in the Pacific. We should've gone to a tropical beach with Larry Garth."

Smitty felt guilty about his Larry Garth comment, knowing he was wrong to disrespect a brave soldier killed in battle.

Lenny said, "I'm all right for the moment, but I have been hit. I'm losing blood and growing weaker. This could be the end for me, and I want you to know it will be my highest honor to die with you. We have put up a gallant fight without surrender, but I am not sure I can fight anymore."

Smitty was stunned and shaken when he saw Lenny's blood dripping on the snow. The sight left Smitty speechless with memories of losing Johnny filling his mind. He determined he was not going to lose Lenny.

He held Lenny and said, "Fight on; you are not a quitter. You will survive this battle; we will make it through, and we will live a long and happy life. Keep fighting, and you will make it through. He grabbed Lenny's outstretched hand and said, "If you are inclined to pray, now would be a good time. Looks like prayer is the only way to get out of our last stand. Just one of us is allowed to get frightened at a time, and right now, it's my time."

He stopped and heard Lenny praying, asking God to save him, Smitty, and the other soldiers. He told Smitty, "I have prayed and made my peace with God, and I will see you up there soon. Mark Ross, Bama, Wilder, and I will be waiting for you."

Smitty stopped and prayed God would spare Lenny's life. He was a valued treasure, one he wanted to keep. His eyes brimmed with tears at the thought of Lenny's death, knowing he had to face the reality that both he and Lenny could soon die. He felt the big cat would not move until the little mice had been annihilated. The Germans were playing a game of cat and mouse, and they were the big cat. It was yet to be determined who would win the cat and mouse game.

Smitty was whispering his prayers to God when he began to feel the prayers of others. Smitty felt his mama was lifting up his name in prayer from the Smith farm or Shiloh Church. He felt his worry and hopelessness lessen as warmth flowed inside his chest.

With his foot numb and frostbite creeping in, he kept moving to stay warm, crawling from truck to truck on his stomach, encouraging the wounded and counting the dead. He searched for someone with rank to take command, but his heart sank when, nearing the last truck, he realized he was the commanding officer. The last thing in the world he wanted was to be in charge and have responsibility for hundreds of men's lives.

Unaware of any actions he could pursue to save his life and his men's lives, he kept searching for a way to save the wounded and dying soldiers. He positioned the soldiers without wounds on the perimeter of the middle ten trucks. He stacked bodies to construct a barricade like in the old west when they used flour barrels, crates, and anything they could find to fill holes around a wagon train.

After placing the wounded men in safety, he removed coats and clothing from the dead to protect the wounded from the cold. He kept encouraging them, "If you can take it, you can make it. You will make it through. We will choose death before dishonor."

The men needed heat, and Smitty was determined to find a way to fill the need. They needed a heat source, but he knew light or burning flames would enable embedded snipers to sight the men. He could start the trucks, but the carbon monoxide would asphyxiate the soldiers underneath the vehicles. Running the trucks was not a viable option leaving the remaining soldiers to die from the freezing cold.

Smitty kept praying and asking God to allow them to see the first light of a new day when the temperature would warm with the rising sun. Smitty kept feeling God had sent him to this battlefield to find the meaning of life and understand the value and price of freedom. He felt God saying, "If you want to survive this night on this battlefield, you will have to go to your knees."

Smitty realized his fiercest and most formidable battle was not with the Germans but against mighty enemies battling his soul. He had to defeat and destroy them to set himself free.

The darkest and longest part of the night had passed, and many of his men remained alive. He felt they could survive if help arrived.

He kept shouting encouragement to his men. "We have made it another hour, and we are closer to the dawn. We have reached headquarters on our radio and relayed our position. I know help is on the way, and we will be rescued soon. You have to be brave, courageous, and stand against our enemies. Keep telling yourself you will make it through."

Many of the wounded soldiers grew tired of moaning and screaming for help. Some of them yielded in their struggles and pain and surrendered to death. Some closed their eyes, went to sleep, and drifted away. A few soldiers were praying and calling for their wives, children, mothers, friends, or pastors. Some were calling on God to save them or take them as they uttered their final prayers. Smitty could hear the continual screams for medics that would never respond.

Smitty knew his men could not survive the bitter cold, so he prayed again. He remembered a verse from his Bible that said, "If any man doesn't have wisdom, let him ask God for some." He was counting on the God of light to work in the darkness, the God of light to appear in the darkness.

Smitty prayed and sought wisdom. He asked God, "What can I do to save my life and my men's lives?"

They needed heaters to keep warm and avoid freezing. He remembered the trucks had diesel heaters in their fuel tanks. The heaters were designed to keep diesel fuel warm for the trucks to start in freezing weather. The heaters operated on truck batteries to heat the engines and facilitate cranking. Smitty crawled into his truck, careful to avoid exposure to snipers. He turned on the diesel fuel heater and waited for what seemed like hours before feeling the heat. It was not as warm as a regular heater, but it might sustain them. To a freezing soldier, even a little warmth could mean life. He moved from truck to truck, turning on the heaters and moving the injured and wounded men directly under the fuel tanks.

He was aware that gathering the men under the tanks involved risk. One tracer round could bring instant death, but with no more certainty than freezing to death in the bitter cold.

He kept moving and checking his men. He removed a shirt from a frozen body and wrapped it around a hat's head. He removed socks from dead soldiers for the men to use as gloves to warm their hands and protect them from frostbite. He found a parka under a truck's seat and used it to cover a shivering young soldier with a leg wound – no older than sixteen or seventeen. Smitty stopped for a moment and thought back ten years before when youth still burned in his eyes and heart. He had always considered himself invincible and expected to live forever. Those were unrealistic dreams and expectations. With him now facing a harsh reality, his life could soon be over.

Smitty instituted every action he could to stay alive and help others survive. He continued crawling from one end of the convoy to the other, continually in motion, keeping life-giving blood flowing through his veins. The diesel heaters were working; his men began responding to the added warmth. Some soldiers risked a sniper bullet drawing up on their knees to get closer to the warmers.

Smitty was brokenhearted, knowing the cost of the frigid cold would be high. With some, the price would be paid later in amputated fingers, arms, legs, and toes. Some soldiers had already paid the full price immediately with their deaths. Whatever a man will kill for, he is also willing to die for. Men must have the ability to know what is worth giving their lives for and what is not. To the soldiers in this battle, freedom was worth giving their lives.

Each minute of survival came at the expense of another life. Some of the wounded soldiers ceased their moanings and cries for help, the gurgling sounds of death breaking the night's eerie silence. The warriors fought to keep their courage as soldier after soldier took his final breath. Death filled the battlefield, and Smitty knew, after witnessing the deaths of his men, he, too, could soon be facing his death. How fine the line was between coward and hero! Without weakness and fear, there could be no bravery. He knew he had to be right at the right time and for the right reason if he would survive."

In the darkness of night on a snow-covered battlefield in France, Smitty looked at his life. He felt he was living his final hours and, if he had to die, he wanted to die in peace. The temperature was hovering near zero degrees. With death surrounding him, he closed his eyes. In the winter night's stillness, with his thoughts rushing through thousands of days and nights, he spent his final moments reliving his simple, blessed life.

Facing death was enabling and empowering him to live. He looked up and said, "God, I am placing my life in your hands, and I trust your will to be done." He felt a warmth inside, as the presence and peace of God poured upon him. He believed he was being strengthened and saved by prayers of faith. He knew a praying warrior was a mighty warrior. He was a prayer and a gallant soldier. Prayer gave him strength and courage as he fought the giants in life and his enemy on the battlefield.

He remembered how the Greeks stood steadfast in war and were some of the world's bravest soldiers. After their battles, they returned home with their shields or on them. He held his conviction and belief that he would return home with his shield in his hand.

The dawn's first glimmer of light broke through, revealing the extent of death and destruction. Many of his soldiers were experiencing their first day in eternity, and he questioned how many of the men had prepared for this day. He cried over the sacrificial death of courageous soldiers. Still, He knew the worst causalities from a battle are not always those who are killed, but those who would survive the hell. He realized his time in the Army had fed the wolf inside him.

Smitty was still wrestling with fear and distress, knowing he was prepared to die, but wanting to live. He believed honor and courage were matters of the heart and soul. There are only the defeated and the victorious and nothing in between. He wanted to win the battle.

The temperature began to rise, bolstering his hope after they had survived the night. He continued reassuring his men they would make it through.

A few of the men confronted Smitty about surrendering. He was not a quitter and would never consider withdrawing from the battle. Knowing the Germans executed many of their prisoners, he knew he needed to stir the soldiers' fighting spirit and determination. He started screaming, "We have survived the night, and we can hold on until our deliverance comes. I believe help is on the way! It could arrive anytime! We have to fight on, and surrender is not an option. We will win this battle, and we will win the war. We will fight for good, for honor, for freedom, and for America.

It's time to rise up and seize the day, time for victory and not defeat, and time for men to stand up and be real men. Listen up, it's not the size of the dog in this fight; it's the size of the fight in this dog. We are going to fight like mad dogs, and we're going to tear our enemies to shreds or die trying."

He pressed on. "This is our time to decide to live and not die. We will not surrender, and we refuse to die. Fight on. Fight on, men. Help is on its way. We will make it through."

He realized some people were given an ancient calling that echoes through the ages. He felt his calling might require him to sacrifice his life for his men and his country. He had read in his Bible that "many are called, but few are chosen. He thought, "God has called me here for such a time as this."

He was well aware Satan was using the German army to manipulate, intimidate, and discourage the soldiers. The devil wanted to control, create fear, and horror, and dominate. Smitty drew a line and decided he would resist with everything within him. He bound Satan in the name of Jesus. He knew he was a weak person with a very strong and powerful God.

He detected activity on the hills that suggested the Germans were preparing for an imminent attack, but they continued waiting for Mother Nature to finish the battle. The enemy delayed their attack and kept holding back. It was if the hand of God was holding them back and postponing their onslaught.

Smitty stretched out in the snow under his truck and covered himself with a tarp. As he removed the Bible from his shirt pocket to read, the letter from Gina fell out. Switching his flashlight on, he read it for the hundredth time. He cried as he folded the letter and placed it back in his Bible after reading some verses about Heaven he had underlined. He prepared himself to face death with his final thoughts of God and Gina. He was struggling to hold on to his dreams, but remembered what he had once heard, "Whether it's big dreams or little dreams, some dreams end up getting shattered."

# *CHAPTER THIRTY*

Lenny was clinging to life but growing weaker from blood loss. His bleeding had slowed, but his complexion was as white as snow. Smitty loved Lenny like a brother and could not face his death. After discovering a couple of blankets stuffed behind a truck seat, he wrapped Lenny from head to toes. Smitty was shivering but would not take one of the blankets. He wanted the warmth but remembered a truth from his Bible. "No greater love has any man than to lay down his life for his friend." Lenny was his friend, and he was willing to lay down his life and his blanket for him.

Every few minutes, Smitty would rub Lenny's arms, legs, and hands to keep his circulation flowing. Lenny was semi-conscious but unable to talk. They lay near each other in silence for added warmth without either of them speaking. Smitty could see Lenny's love and appreciation in his tear-filled eyes. He knew if help did not arrive soon, they would all die. Every last soldier in Bravo Company would give their lives for their country, paying the ultimate price for freedom. He knew he was frail, but his God was powerful.

Sunrise broke over the mountains and streaked the newly fallen snow with golden rays and gray shadows. In the morning light, the snow glistened and sparkled like glimmering diamonds. The sunrise was so beautiful and peaceful Smitty felt he could have been anywhere in the world besides the middle of a battlefield.

Smitty had pondered a run for safety, knowing the trucks' fuel was warm and ready. The trucks would crank and move out, but he realized snow packed in the draw could cause issues. He scrapped the idea after realizing a well-placed mortar shell fired into the lead truck would render the escape attempt foolish and suicidal. He knew he could never abandon his men, so he decided: life or death, he was staying to the end. The end was drawing near. The only help they could hope for would have to come from God and headquarters.

Suddenly, the Germans shattered the peace, screaming orders with movement in their camp escalating. No doubt, they believed the cold had finished its work as they prepared for an all-out attack to crush the convoy.

Smitty had conducted a hurried body count in the early morning light. Of the six hundred men who started the mission, only one hundred ninety-one men could fire a weapon. Many men had died. Others were too wounded to fight or were in the throes of dying from the killing cold.

Smitty snapped a fresh clip into his carbine and waited. He decided he would spend his final moments destroying the trucks to prevent the Germans from plundering the supplies and ammunition. He thought about his sworn duties to his country. "Duty first, duty last, duty till I die." Death before dishonor was his motto. Like Mark Ross, he would fight to the end without surrender. He was not without fear but determined he would not allow his fear to diminish or defeat him. He resolved he would fight until he breathed his final breath, realizing his most potent weapon was the determination in his spirit.

He whispered, "This is it. It's death time. Goodbye, Gina. Goodbye, Mama. Hello, God."

He felt his next few minutes would be his last on Earth and could hear his mama's words. "It's going to get tough, but you can make it through. I'm praying for you. You will make it through."

Her words kept running through his thoughts, "You will make it through."

He determined the way he could make it through might just be through to Heaven. He had learned to never question God's actions or timing. He felt God and satan were fighting on the battlefield for the hearts and lives of the warring soldiers.

The first shots from the German attack came as the sun rose above the eastern hills. Simultaneously, two dozen fighter planes roared over the trees, dropping bombs, and plowing up the snow-covered ground with machine guns blazing.

A dozen British Spitfires followed, unleashing death, fury, and judgment on the Germans. An additional twelve American P-38s were delivering hell and destruction to the enemy soldiers surrounding the convoy. Smitty's men heard the roar of deliverance, with bombs and bullets sounding like beautiful music and deliverance songs. Smitty felt ground reinforcements could arrive at any moment.

The planes crisscrossed the hills, death riding on their wings, cutting the Germans down like a combine in ripened grain. They had surprised the Germans in the open, without cover or protection. The planes ripped them to shreds, killing hundreds with bombs and bullets. Deliverance had arrived from headquarters and from God.

From the other side of the plateau came the roar of trucks and tanks, growing louder by the second, bringing critical reinforcements and medical assistance. Their radio message had been received, and help had been dispatched when their location had been determined. Smitty thanked God that headquarters had not waited until dawn to send needed reinforcements. The convoy's men and urgently needed supplies were important enough for the Army brass to act immediately. Orders had been issued for all available planes, tanks, trucks, and reinforcements to be dispatched to save the convoy.

The planes flew dangerously close to the trucks as hundreds of German soldiers were obliterated. The Heaven-sent planes buzzed directly over the soldiers' heads as bomb after bomb found its intended target. The bombing attacks and aerial strikes continued for what seemed like an eternity. The soldiers could feel the bombs' blasts, the force of the explosions, causing them to cover their heads. Smitty felt the explosions could cause some of the soldiers' eardrums to burst, destroying their hearing, but knew it was better to lose hearing than life.

The Germans retreated in force, running for their lives. Smitty could hear bombs exploding and machine guns firing in the distance when the retreating Germans ran into a trap set by American and British ground forces. The Allied soldiers had dug in overnight, waiting for the enemy to retreat. The last thing the Germans was an ambush.

The German forces found themselves between a hammer and an anvil. Planes reaped destruction near the convoy, and ground forces were pulverizing the Germans in their retreat.

This battle would result in a massive defeat for the German army and weaken their offensive to retake France. Smitty's convoy had been the impetus for the German military to overplay its hand. The attack on the convoy produced a significant victory for the Americans and a tremendous defeat for the German forces.

Smitty became so elated when the planes roared in that he crawled from under his truck to scream and cheer. The moment he left his cover, a wounded German soldier lying in the snow lifted his infield rifle and shot Smitty in the chest.

The impact of the bullet slammed him against his truck. He struggled to stay upright with a death grip on the truck mirror before tumbling into the blood-stained snow. He raised his hand to his chest, touched the wetness, and held it up to see blood dripping from his fingers. The sky spun as Smitty lost consciousness realizing the difference between life and death was a single breath.

# *CHAPTER THIRTY-ONE*

"Here's another one alive," the medic shouted as he stood over Smitty. He's shot in the lung, but his heart is beating. The cold temperature has slowed his bleeding, or he would be dead by now. Let's see if we can get him stabilized."

Another voice screamed out, "Blankets! Bring blankets and morphine! Stat! Plasma! We need more plasma!"

Another medic shouted, "You won't believe this. Come and see what happened to this soldier. Take a look at a miracle."

The medic shook his head as he lifted the small Bible a bullet had ripped from Smitty's shirt pocket.

"The bullet struck the metal cover on this Bible and careened into his lung, barely missing his heart. That bullet missed his heart by half an inch, the medic said, lifting two fingers to indicate how close the bullet came to blasting open Smitty's heart. "This Bible saved his life."

***

The last thing Smitty remembered was the boom of a rifle, burning pain, and the ripping open of his chest. He remembered the sounds of planes, tanks, and reinforcements. His remembrances were like experiencing a slow-motion dream, living out a nightmare.

In his final moments, Smitty had a vision of someone holding a colossal hourglass in their hand. With only a few grains of sand waiting to fall, he was aware his time was running out. He saw a passageway with light streaming from a distant door. He knew he was being given a choice to go on or come back. He chose to return with his love for Gina and his mama, the only things that brought him back and made him want to live.

Closing his eyes, his thoughts went back in time. He traveled to Ringgold, riding in a new buggy and playing hide and seek with his brothers and sisters. He returned to the Smith farm and visited Hannah, Junior, Maria, Johnny, Mindy, and Janice.

He could smell fried chicken and hot fried peach pies on Hannah Smith's table. He saw Maria with the toy train and sat on the front porch swing with his mama on a hot summer night. He returned to the chilly days of fall, the snowy days of winter, and little flowers growing in the springtime.

A sudden bump returned him to reality, with soldiers shouting and screaming. He fought to raise up, but the medics stopped him and said, "Lie still. You've been wounded. You're going to make it, soldier, so stay calm and do everything we tell you. We are transporting you to a field hospital for surgery. You've lost a lot of blood, but you will survive. Don't die on us!"

The medics packed Smitty's gaping wound with gauze and wrapped a tight bandage around his chest, applying pressure to the injury. They worked furiously, even though they felt Smitty would die. The medics knew the odds of his surviving were not in his favor, with his survival being 50/50 or less.

Smitty lost consciousness again, with his mind exploding with horror and death. He saw his first dog die in his arms and Johnny Little's dog, Worthless, being shot by Old Man Beasley. Johnny was in his arms on the floor of the Martinique Club. He returned to Maria's funeral, with the wind and rain on a stormy Sunday afternoon, and stood before Junior lying in a casket in his overalls. He witnessed Mark Ross being blown apart by a grenade. He felt the explosion that caused Bama's horrible death, and he held Wilson Wilder as he died on the destroyer. He relived the horror of thousands of men dying in the Vermont's sinking and hundreds of soldiers being slaughtered in the convoy, dying horrible deaths.

He traveled to Shiloh Baptist Church and looked up from a casket with a military flag draped over it. His mama, his brothers and sisters, and some uniformed officers were gathered around the coffin. The Davises were there, as were his friends and neighbors. Janice and Roger Brown were there with their children. Gina was leaning over the casket, telling Smitty how much she loved him and how she would miss him. He was trying to crawl out of the casket when he was blinded by a bright light.

***

For a moment, Smitty thought he was standing before God in Heaven. The light was so bright it hurt his eyes, he turned his face from it, screamed, and everything went black. Numbness had crept into his fingers and toes, and he panicked at not feeling his leg or foot. He woke up with his right foot and leg submerged in warm water and a bright light warming his body. The medics had cut Smitty's boots loose and discovered his foot was frozen and swollen twice it's normal size. Smitty had been trained to never remove his boots in combat because it would be difficult to get them back on. Smitty's feet and legs were in terrible condition.

The doctors struggled to keep him from losing an arm, a leg, a toe, or even a finger to frostbite. They had completed the surgery on his chest wound, patched his lung, and kept him alive, despite his tremendous hemorrhaging.

Doctor Oliver Holmes was one of the field surgeons who operated on Smitty in the MASH unit. While visiting with a group of doctors in the mess tent at breakfast, he held up a small Bible and shook his head.

"The good Lord wanted to keep this soldier alive," said Holmes. "Take a look at his Bible and how the bullet struck the center and careened downward. Had it not been for this Bible in his uniform pocket, the bullet would have hit the lower chamber of his heart and killed him instantly. He shook his head solemnly at the other surgeons.

"I'm going to put this aside and see he gets it when he's on his feet again. I mean, if he gets back on his feet. I'm worried about him keeping his right leg. His right leg and foot are in terrible condition from extensive frostbite, and time will tell if he ends up with one leg or two."

***

When Smitty opened his eyes, he thought he was seeing an angel.

"Hello, soldier," the beautiful, golden-haired nurse said. "Welcome to the land of the living. No, you're not dead, and you're not dreaming. You are alive after surviving a major chest wound, but you are doing fine."

Smitty caught himself staring into the most beautiful, sky blue eyes he had ever seen and was lost in them. The nurse's blue eyes were as beautiful as Gina's green eyes and Janice's pale blue eyes. The bright lights made her blonde hair shine like twenty-four-karat gold, and Smitty found her beautiful beyond imagination.

He attempted to rise and asked, "What's your name?"

"Mary Lou Brown," she answered. "Of the Georgetown, South Carolina, Browns. I'm your nurse."

Her gleaming white teeth and beautiful red lips made Smitty want to reach out and hold her with her like a magnet pulling him to her. He felt crazy and thought he was dreaming with feelings he had died and gone to Heaven. His thoughts rushed to Gina, and he ceased his wayward thoughts about the nurse. He was in love with Gina and wanted her to be the only love in his life.

Smitty wished Mary Lou's name wasn't Brown. He still hated Roger Brown for stealing Janice but often thought Roger had done him a huge favor removing Janice from his life.

"I'm glad you're alive this morning. We kept thinking you would hemorrhage and bleed to death during the night. No matter what happened, you would not stop breathing. It was as if someone or something kept preventing you from dying during surgery. Your heart stopped a couple of times but started back on its own. Do you remember getting shot?"

Smitty nodded. He remembered the pain, the flashing of his life before him, and the burning in his chest. "How long has it been? Where am I? What are my condition and chances of surviving? Will I live, or are you just keeping me comfortable until I die?" He had a thousand questions.

Mary Lou took his hand. "You have to rest. You'll need all your strength to get back on your feet."

Smitty drifted off to sleep, savoring her perfume's sweet smell and the touch of her hand gently stroking his face. He felt if he had never met Gina, it would be easy to fall in love with Mary Lou. She was as beautiful as Gina, with the same gentle and loving spirit.

Later in the day, his surgeon stood beside his bed and told him, "If you had not been healthy and robust, you would have died in transport. The cold temperature slowed the bleeding and helped keep you alive. It is a miracle you lived to reach the operating room. Some of your surgeons and nurses from last night have come by to see if you survived. None of them thought you would pull through. We seldom see a fighter like you. I've never seen such determination for someone to stay alive.

Smitty realized it was his love for Gina that had brought him back with him wanting to hold her in his arms again.

Doctor Oliver Holmes moved to the corner of Smitty's bunk. He stood silent for a long time before he spoke." I'm afraid I have some bad news. We've done all we can, but you're going to lose your right leg. The frostbite was extensive; gangrene has reached your ankle and is heading for your knee. We have to move quickly. We will amputate your leg below the knee, but if we don't operate within four to six hours, you will die tomorrow. It's your choice of losing your leg or losing your life. I'm sorry to be the bearer of such devastating news."

The room started spinning as Smitty lost his breath and tried to deal with the knot in his stomach. He lost his breath again, struggling even harder to breathe. Doctor Holmes said, "I'll be back in an hour for your decision."

When Smitty looked up, Mary Lou was standing beside his hospital bed with tears in her eyes as she reached for his hand. "It's not the end of the world even though it looks that way. Everything will turn out alright. Wait and see. I'll be with you, take care of you, and walk with you every step of your journey." Mary Lou had said she would walk with him, but what if he never took another step? He could not believe he would soon be a one-legged man, without hope or a future.

Doctor Holmes returned well before the promised hour. He reached into his pocket, pulled out Junior's Bible, and handed it to Smitty. "You might find help in here," he said.

This Bible saved your life and kept you from being killed. If you had not had this Bible in your uniform pocket, you would be dead." He turned and walked from the room, questioning why so many good soldiers had to pay such high prices to serve their country and fight a war.

Smitty remembered his mother's words the day she gave him the Bible: "It's going to be tough, but God is going to help you. You can make it." The Bible had saved his life, and Smitty knew he would need its strength to help him through his time of testing, trials, and struggles. He prayed God's Word would heal his heart and strengthen his spirit. Smitty opened the book, turned to the Twenty Third Psalm, and read it aloud. He had read this psalm almost every morning when he was growing up.

"The Lord is my Shepherd; I shall not want. He makes me to lie down in green pastures. He restores my soul. He prepares a table before me in the presence of my enemies. He anoints my head with oil. My cup runs over. Surely goodness and mercy shall follow me all the days of my life, and I will dwell in the house of the Lord forever."

Some of the words were missing due to the bullet hole, but Smitty had memorized the psalm. He was in his valley of the shadow of death and facing a life-changing decision. He had to make a choice of losing his leg or his life. He could not envision Gina with half a man, a cripple with one leg, nor could he believe she could marry a man who could not provide for her. He loved Gina, but could not face her disappointment when he would be carried off a ship with one leg. How could she ever love a handicapped veteran?

Smitty made the life-changing decision that he would never see Gina again. Conflicted, he knew he should shake himself, open his eyes, and come to his senses. Still, his pride would not allow him to consider any other course of action.

Doctor Holmes opened the door and inquired, "It's time for your answer. What have you decided?"

Though flowing tears, Smitty made the most difficult decision of his life. "I want to live, so go ahead with the amputation." It had taken all the courage and strength he could muster to respond. Even if Gina did not want him, he would go home and care for his mama.

Mary Lou wheeled him into the operating room when Doctor Holmes pulled up his mask and nodded. She leaned over the gurney and kissed him. "Everything will work out, you wait and see. Time and God will do a lot of healing."

# CHAPTER THIRTY-TWO

"Smitty." Mary Lou whispered, placing a cold cloth on his forehead. "You're going to be fine. The operation is over, and everything went well. You need to rest and take it easy. You will be up and around in no time."

Smitty shook his head to clear his mind, but the room was swirling. The ether used to put him to sleep left him nauseated and semi-conscious. He struggled to remember where he was and what had happened, but he was confused and disoriented.

Mary Lou gave Smitty a kiss on his cheek. He thought he was dreaming, but the pain in his chest and right leg slammed him back to reality. All Smitty had ever desired and searched for in his life was for someone to love and cherish him. He questioned if he would lose the love of his life and never find true love again.

He remembered the frostbitten leg, Doctor Holmes' bad news, and Mary Lou wheeling him into surgery. The reality of the operation hit him. He thought he could move his leg and toes, but his body told him otherwise. He raised his head, glanced down, and screamed at the realization his leg was missing below his knee.

Mary Lou held Smitty until he dropped off to sleep. She would not leave his side. She had promised to be with him, and she was determined to keep her promise. Smitty tossed and turned with his nightmares stalking him and was terrified, fighting his fear. He babbled about Maria, Johnny, Junior, Hannah, Janice, and Gina. Mary Lou sat and listened as Smitty traveled to places and times far away. As he drifted in and out of sleep, Mary Lou touched his face and thought she might be falling for Smitty. Time would tell. She cared for him and was determined to walk with him through this terrible turn of events.

Doctor Holmes aroused Smitty as he made his early rounds. He changed Smitty's bandages and made sure the sutured arteries were holding. If anything happened, Smitty would bleed to death. His chest wound was still critical, but he was alive, and the bleeding had stopped. Doctor Holmes knew the healing inside would be more complicated than the improvement of his leg and lung. The battles with his thoughts and imaginations would be more painful than dealing with his physical issues. He knew Smitty could become an emotional cripple rather than a physical cripple if he chose not to fight.

He told Smitty, "Most of the survivors from the convoy are doing well. One hundred-and-fifty-three men survived the horrible ordeal, and they owe you their lives. It is a shame that only a fourth of the men made it out alive. It's difficult to comprehend that almost 450 men lost their lives in the battle. We are thankful to God you made it through."

America desperately needed a hero with a name like Smitty Smith. At the time, Smitty felt like anything but a hero. He felt like a coward who couldn't even defeat his discouragement and fear. Smitty had to deal with his feelings. He would have been better off to have died on the battlefield with his men, and right now, he wanted to be alone to deal with the painful issues in his life.

***

Smitty's emotional swings sent him falling like a late winter avalanche after a major blizzard and then soaring like a high flying kite on a gusty March afternoon. One day, he would spew anger, hatred, bitterness, and violence, and the next day he would become meek, mild, and peaceful. Anger and resentment alternated with peace and calm. Some days he cried like a baby, and other days his raw emotions and anger spilled over on everyone. He found it difficult to control his thoughts and feelings. He was trying to fight his way through an emotional storm.

All the pain, denials, and "what ifs" kept pressuring him to consider suicide. He thought about ripping his bedsheet, throwing it over a metal pipe in the bathroom ceiling, then placing the sheet around his neck and leaping from the commode. His life would be over, and his mountain of pain and sorrow would be gone. He felt through his death, he could find peace but realized committing suicide was impossible since he could not climb anything.

Suicide continued to occupy his thoughts, with him feeling that by ending his life, he would not have to survive as half a man. His life would be over. At times, he wanted to live and return home to the red clay of Northwest Georgia, see his mama, hunt in the woods, and fish the rivers and streams. He knew he would never do those things with one leg and wept, knowing he might never fish the Coosa River again. That life had ended, and he closed the chapter.

His fighting on the battlefield had ended with the victory, but his most difficult struggles loomed ahead when he would have to fight and battle to regain his life.

His heart ached as he found it difficult to tolerate the emotional pain inside him, ripping him apart. Intense pain in his body and emotional struggles in his spirit were shattering him. In his quiet, dimly lit hospital room, he often cried himself to sleep. He was depressed, not wanting to live another day, and wishing he had never been drafted and sent to the war.

On one of Mary Lou's visits, Smitty noticed a small

bottle in her uniform pocket. He saw her dispensing pain pills from the bottle to a wounded soldier. As she leaned forward to kiss him, Smitty slipped his hand into her pocket and lifted the bottle like a professional pickpocket. After she left, he hid the bottle under his mattress. Mary Lou returned desperately searching for the lost pills, but Smitty kept his eyes closed, pretending to be asleep.

She mumbled to herself, "I am in so much hot water. How could I have ever lost those pills? I will be relieved of duty if I don't find them soon. How could I have been so careless? I guess this is the end of my nursing career and my days here."

She realized how much trouble she would be in if she did not find them. She needed to locate the pills. Her carelessness could mean being removed from her position and could enable a depressed soldier to take his life.

Just after midnight, Smitty awoke from another horrifying nightmare. In his dream, he was lying in a casket, and he saw all his deceased friends and loved ones. His nightmares were like Mark's dreams of his death. He believed he was being warned of his coming death with his fear growing stronger after every dream.

He removed the bottle of pain pill from under his mattress. "I can swallow a handful of these, go to sleep, and never wake again. Death will end my pain, suffering, losses, heartbreaks, and tears in a matter of minutes. I am ready to take my life and end this ongoing nightmare. It's time for me to die."

Smitty opened the bottle and counted twenty-one pills into his hand. As he reached for a glass of water, he was face to face with Chaplain Henson standing at the end of his bed. The chaplain had been summoned to pray with a dying soldier and decided to check on Smitty. Smitty thought he was dreaming until the chaplain spoke. "Son, what you are about to do isn't the answer to the problems and issues in your life. You have lived this long and survived a lot of things. If God didn't have a plan for your life, you would be dead, and by all accounts, you should be. God wants your life instead of you taking it this way. Why don't you surrender to Him and allow Him to live through you? "

The chaplain's words hit home and stunned Smitty out of his self-pity as he fell back on his pillow and sobbed. Chaplain Henson held Smitty in his arms the way Smitty had always wanted Junior to hold him.

The Chaplain whispered, "You're the kind of son any man in this world would be proud to have. You're a son any father could hold up to others and say, 'This is my son, in whom I am well pleased. I have the best son in the world. Of all the sons God could've given me, I'm glad he gave me you.' I wish you were my son, and I would be honored to be your father."

Smitty felt something snap inside as he received the chaplain's loving affirmation, acceptance, and approval. He had never had anyone speak words like that into his life. He had received love and approval from the chaplain and his Heavenly Father.

Smitty knew the chaplain had spoken words from God. How could he have known what Smitty needed to hear? Even Smitty did not know. Smitty felt his personal worth soar after the chaplain prayed for him and encouraged him. He was uplifted as renewed strength and new life flooded him. He gained a renewed will to live and questioned how he could have thought suicide was the way out?

Before the chaplain left, Smitty asked a favor. "Chaplain Henson, will you return these pills to Nurse Brown? I would appreciate it if you would not disclose where they came from. I would not want her to have problems or get in trouble." Smitty slept soundly and woke up the next morning with a new outlook, new feelings, and new life in his spirit.

The two medics that treated him on the battlefield transported a new patient into Smitty's unit and stopped by to encourage Smitty in his recovery. One of the medics shook his hand and said, "Well, look who's here and still in the land of the living! I can't believe you are still alive. Your wound was so severe, and you lost so much blood we never dreamed you would make it through. You are a fighter. Seeing you alive makes our job worthwhile. With a wound like yours, most soldiers would have never left the battlefield. You have a second chance in life, and I hope you use it wisely."

The medic's words forced Smitty to realize he did have a purpose in life. He was alive for a reason, but he did not know what his destiny would hold. He thanked God for the medics who saved him, kept him alive, and rushed him to the MASH unit. He was thankful for Doctor Holmes and his wise decisions and surgical skills. He continued to wish Doctor Holmes could have saved his leg.

Every day he prayed and blessed those who cared for him and thanked God for them. He determined after his release from the hospital, he would find everyone who treated him and express his gratitude and appreciation for saving his life. He felt he should bless those who had blessed him and find some way to repay them.

He was still experiencing times of sadness and discouragement and had to fight negative thoughts about his future. He wanted to live with suicide no longer an option.

He would fall into a deep depression whenever he struggled with his future with Gina. "He could not face Gina as a one-legged, wheelchair-bound invalid and knew he had to end their relationship. He knew he would not live a normal life and felt she deserved a real man. He searched for a way to end their relationship without destroying her. He decided to write and tell her he had fallen in love with a beautiful nurse named Mary Lou Brown. He would express his sorrow their relationship had to end and tell her someone had come into his life, made him happy, and he had decided to marry her. He was going to tell Gina she would have to let him die in her heart. He felt if they married, Gina would be miserable and would divorce him and vanish from his life."

When Gina received his letter, she would probably be devastated but felt she was strong enough to survive. It broke his heart to hurt and disappoint her, but a single hurt was better than a lifetime of pain and sacrifice. He would end the Gina chapter in his life and questioned if he would ever find true love again after losing the girl of his dreams.

He knew it was always best to try to stay on your friends' good side and especially the one you love, but Smitty could not do it. He kept feeling he had lost everyone and everything he ever loved, including Gina.

# *CHAPTER THIRTY-THREE*

"Mail Call!" The tall, slender nurse in a stiff, white starched uniform sang out as she walked into Smitty's hospital room. "You have mail, Corporal Smith!" she announced as she threw the letters on his bed. Smitty picked up the envelopes and inspected them. One was from the President, the second one was from Gina - Smitty sniffed her perfume - and the final letter was from his Aunt Nettie Ann, his mama's sister. He questioned why his aunt would be writing? He paused, preparing for more bad news. His heart raced with fearful thoughts of his mama as he threw the other letters aside and ripped open Nettie Ann's.

> Dear Smitty,
>
> I hate to be the bearer of bad news, but your mama has had a stroke, and we're not expecting her to live. She's in Memorial Hospital in Chattanooga, and the doctors don't give her much of a chance to survive. If you can get yourself home, you might see your mama one last time before she dies. We're praying for you and asking God to keep you safe and send you home soon.
>
> Aunt Nettie Ann.

He understood why he had not received any mail from his mother since the Army notified her of his injuries. His mind filled with urgent questions with him not knowing if she was alive or dead, in a coma, or buried in her church cemetery. He cried out with sorrow, sobbing so loud, three nurses burst into his room. The head nurse calmed him and gave him a shot to help him rest. Smitty went to sleep, wondering how much pain and loss a person could endure. He panicked at the possibility of losing the last precious and most valuable person in his life. He feared his mama might die before he returned home.

He did not sleep well and dreamed he was attending another funeral at Shiloh Church. It was rainy and windy; lightning flashed, and thunder rolled. He walked through the rain to the cemetery, where the undertaker had placed a wooden casket under the funeral tent. He walked over, opened the pine box, and looked squarely into his mama's face.

Panic hit him as he struggled to awaken from the vision. Anger flew through him, and he exploded with rage. He threw everything off his bedside table, scattering bottles, a bedpan, and several small trays across the room. He was upset and ready to take action. He decided he would dress and head home. He would see his mama if she were alive and visit her grave if she wasn't. He slid out of bed, pulled himself up by the bed rail, fell, hitting his head against the bed's corner, and collapsed onto the floor. The fall split his head open, and blood spurted from a deep gash.

Mary Lou rushed into his room, ran to Smitty, and lifted his head. She placed a towel over the cut and held him close. Between his moans, he heard her whisper, "I'm here with you. Everything is going to be all right." The room started spinning as Smitty lost consciousness and blacked out.

The doctors sewed up his wound in a few minutes, and he woke up with a pounding headache making him hurt all over. He struggled to focus his eyes and his thoughts. After clearing his mind, he put the pieces of the puzzle in place and remembered mail call, opening the letter from Aunt Nettie Ann, and attempting to get out of bed. Watching beautiful multi-colored stars exploding was the last thing he recalled. Reality rushed in when he remembered trying to return home to see his mama.

He was aware going home would be impossible until his condition improved, and arrangements could be finalized. He would have to undergo physical therapy to regain his strength before traveling. He knew the treatment would take time. He asked Mary Lou to request the major come by and discuss his returning home. He glanced at the two unopened letters on the night table, picked up the President's letter, and read it.

"Corporal William Bryan Smith, III,

"I want to thank you for your service to our country. In the Vermont's tragic sinking, you fought bravely to save fifty-three men who would have drowned or been eaten by sharks. Due to your heroic efforts in France, one-hundred and fifty-three soldiers were saved from certain death. Crucial ammunition and supplies were withheld from our enemies. You risked your life while receiving a life-threatening wound and the loss of your leg in service to our country.

"I am requesting that you return to Washington for a hero's welcome and full military honors before the United States Congress. At that time, you will be presented two United States Medals of Honor, The French Legion of Valor Medal, a Purple Heart, and the United States Army Medal of Valor.

We will make all the arrangements when you return. I look forward to seeing you in Washington. Please advise me of any family members and guests you wish to attend the ceremonies at the Capitol.

"Sincerely
"Franklin Delano Roosevelt
"President of the United States"

Smitty did not want honors or medals and did not have any desire to be a one-legged national hero. However, he decided if being a hero would get him home, he would take any ride he could get.

He opened the envelope from Gina, drawing in the scent of her perfume again. The wonderful fragrance transported him back to happier, love-filled days in Norfolk, days when he had dreams and plans. The fragrance took him to an emotional place and caused his heart to ache. He removed her letter and starting reading.

Dear Smitty,

I hope this letter finds you well. I think of you always and pray for you every day. I want you to know I miss you and hope we can remain friends. I wish you and Mary Lou the most profound love and blessing-filled marriage this life can offer.

The news of your bravery has been in the Norfolk paper. The whole nation has heard of your heroic actions in France. I was sad to find out you were wounded and about the loss of your leg. I know it must be difficult, but God will see you through.

Whether we are apart or together, I want you to know I still love you. If you change your mind about our relationship, I would still like for us to be married. I promised I would wait for you to return home, and I will keep my promise. My thoughts and prayers are with you. I love you!

Gina

He held the letter to his chest and wept. He loved Gina,

but could not believe she could love him in his handicapped condition. He felt she would pity him and feel compassion for him, but would never love him. He had all the misery he could handle with his emotional plate so full it could not hold anymore. He knew he would never be strong enough to face Gina. He turned over in his bed, covered his head, and cried.

***

When Gina received the "Dear John" letter, she was blindsided and heartbroken. She could not believe Smitty's words and reread the letter with her world crashing in a matter of seconds.

His rejection was the last thing she expected. The news Smitty loved Mary Lou Brown devastated her and filled her with sadness and grief. She loved him more than anyone or anything. She questioned his actions and motives, asking herself, "Why did he ask me to marry him if he would fall for the first pretty face he met? Why did he reject me, hurt me, and wound me? I will love him no matter what he says or does. My love for him is unconditional, and I will not be affected by his actions. Nothing he can do will make me love him any more, and nothing he can do will make me love him any less. I love him!"

Oddly enough, the day Gina received Smitty's letter, someone from her past resurfaced. Immediately after she finished reading Smitty's letter, a former boyfriend phoned. When she attended the University of Virginia for a year, she had a relationship with a young man named Pierpont R. Ransom, Junior. He was a member of one of Richmond's oldest and wealthiest families and the only child of Pierpont R. Ransom, Senior. He had joined Richmond's leading law firm for a successful law and investment career.

People in Richmond believed he would run for President. As the richest and most eligible bachelor in Virginia, he had his sights set on Gina becoming Mrs. Pierpont R. Ransom, Jr. He was good looking, rich, intelligent, filled with personality, and possessed excessive political influence and power. He was tall with coal-black hair and gray eyes and was the most handsome man Gina ever met. He was the total package. There wasn't another man in Ronald Ransom's class. Gina considered Smitty to be attractive but in a different way. If Gina was searching for a strikingly handsome, rich husband with a ticket to success, he filled the bill, but she wanted more than good looks, riches, and success. She wanted someone to love and cherish her like Smitty.

At Ronald's insistence, Gina accepted his invitation for a date. He picked her up in a limousine and escorted her to the Norfolk Country Club for dinner and dancing. Gina enjoyed the evening, but at the end of the night, she realized Ronald wasn't Smitty. She had never known anyone like Smitty and was madly in love with him.

As he walked Gina to her front door, he whispered, "I love you, Gina, and I want you to be my wife. Will you marry me?" He moved to hold her and kiss her, but she withdrew.

"I need to tell you something important. I am in a relationship with a soldier serving in France, and I promised to wait for him. I love him dearly, and I'm hoping and praying he returns for us to be married. I love him like I've never loved anyone."

Ronald had difficulty receiving the news, and Gina was not convinced he would give up. She would honor her commitment to Smitty and hoped he would change his mind about Mary Lou Brown. She would wait until he returned home or until she felt God was releasing her to end the relationship.

Ronald walked away disappointed but with tremendous respect for Gina and would be there if she changed her mind.

# CHAPTER THIRTY-FOUR

Smitty was transferred from the medical unit in France to a large Army hospital in London, with his hero status allowing Mary Lou to travel with him. He wanted to see London, but his only views were from an ambulance and a hospital window.

He liked the hospital staff and loved the rehabilitation team providing physical therapy. The staff treated him with respect and admiration after learning of his heroic exploits in the Vermont's sinking and on the battlefield in France.

Major Phillip Dawson had been assigned to supervise Smitty's care and make sure he received everything he needed. Major Dawson was a former lumberjack from Seattle, Washington. He was a huge man whose hands were so large he could palm a basketball in one hand. He towered over Smitty by at least six inches. He was a tough soldier and leader with a big heart and love for the soldiers under his command. He visited Smitty daily to monitor his progress and make sure he received proper medical care. President Roosevelt had ordered the Army to honor Smitty and treat him like a hero.

Major Dawson entered Smitty's room and inquired with a wide grin, "How are you doing, hero? How are they treating you in this crazy place? Are you ready to blow the joint?"

"I'm doing much better, thank you, major," Smitty replied. "I'm receiving the best care in the world. I did not think I'd make it for a while, but now I'm sure I'm going to survive. Things are looking up."

The major glanced at Smitty's lone leg and said, "I know

you've had a rough time, but I believe things are turning around. Mary Lou told me about your mother, and I sent a message to the hospital in Tennessee. Your mother is holding her own. She's had three strokes, and her second was serious, leaving her paralyzed.

"We're going to send you to Ringgold - VIP treatment - as soon as you are well enough to travel across the pond. The doc says it will be at least another week before you can make the trip. The home folks are clamoring to see you back in America."

The major stepped closer, holding up a magazine. "Look at this cover of LIFE. Smitty took the magazine and examined the cover. He was stunned to see his picture in uniform with the headline, "Smitty Smith, A True American Hero."

He tossed the magazine on the bedside table. He said, "Major Dawson, I don't want honors, medals, ceremonies, or magazine covers. I want to go home, see my mama, and leave this war. I know I'm going to need additional medical care and emotional support, so I want to request that nurse Brown travel with me."

The major winked, "I'll talk with Colonel Shepherd and Mary Lou and see what can be worked out." Things were turning around for Smitty. He and his mama were both alive, America wanted their hero, and Mary Lou might be traveling with him.

Each day, his leg, his chest, and his feelings improved. He moved around the hospital on crutches and realized hundreds of soldiers were fighting for their lives in critical condition. His outlook changed as time passed. His leg was amputated below his knee so that with a prosthesis, he could walk better than without a knee. Things were improving as his faith and hope returned.

***

The day came for Smitty to leave England, and he would depart from Sterling, the same location where he first arrived. The base looked the same as the day he was bussed in and still looked like a hell hole in some God-forsaken foreign land.

At times Smitty considered what things would have been like if Johnny had traveled with him to the front lines. He wondered if he would have survived or been killed. He rejoiced Johnny did not have to experience the hell of war and felt he was spared horrible times and terrible pain by his early death. That feeling was the only good thing he could hold on to after Johnny's murder.

It was a beautiful day, with brilliant sunshine and clear blue skies when the medics carried Smitty up the steps into the plane. The band played as Colonel Thomas Shepherd saluted him and wished him Godspeed. Officers and enlisted men crowded the tarmac to see an American hero returning home. The crowd cheered as the plane taxied down the runway and took off for America.

As the plane lifted off, Smitty looked across the English Channel toward France and prayed he would never visit France again. He wondered how many soldiers had seen France once but never lived to see it again. He rejoiced he would arrive in the United States in a few hours with his heart longing for home.

He was aware the airplane had been built for cargo and not for passengers, so his flight across the Atlantic was uncomfortable with him thinking it might never end. The roar of the engines burned into his ears and mind, with the seat feeling like a wooden stadium bleacher without a cushion. No matter how much redesigning and renovating had been done, it was still a cargo plane.

Smitty's endurance had almost reached its limit when the pilot announced, "Prepare for landing in about forty minutes." They were landing in New York City on a stop-over to Washington, D.C. The plane would be refueled, inspected, and dispatched to Washington in less than thirty minutes.

"Welcome to the USA," co-pilot Lieutenant Jason Rollings said as he paused in the aisle next to Mary Lou. Smitty noticed Jason could not keep his eyes off Mary Lou, and she could not stop eyeing him. He stared at Mary Lou as if he was undressing her with his mind.

"We'll be on the ground before you know it. We have been blessed with a powerful tailwind, and we will arrive before our scheduled landing time."

Mary Lou turned to Smitty, "Welcome home, hero."

Jason Rollings asked Mary Lou, "Would you like to visit the cockpit and see how we fly this crate?" Mary Lou batted her eyelashes and said, "Of course I would. Will you show me the way?" They walked to the cockpit, where they stood in the aisle and talked. Smitty kept watching them and did not like what he was feeling.

The pilot came over the intercom and said, "We have an update on our landing. The airport in New York City has been closed with ground fog and poor visibility. We have fuel to continue to Washington and will be landing there earlier than expected." Smitty settled back, gritted his teeth, knowing he would have to endure the extra flight time without complaining. Mary Lou returned, took his hand, and kissed him. Her kiss made him feel better and helped calm his anxiety. He would be met at the Washington Airport by the President and a host of Washington dignitaries, Army brass, and reporters. He was nervous and not looking forward to the celebration.

***

Smitty did not know what to expect but never imagined over fifty thousand people would assemble to welcome him home. Bands played, and flags waved as Washington's highest brass and most influential people were awaiting his arrival. They came to see a war hero step back onto American soil. As he exited the plane, shouts, applause, and cheers drowned out the plane's idling engines.

A nearby soldier draped an American flag around Smitty's shoulders and allowed him to carry the red, white, and blue with his head held high. The Army band played the Army march as time stood still for Smitty. The welcome was like a dream with him soaking in every second of his special moment.

When the band played "Hail to the Chief," Smitty realized the President had arrived. Flashbulbs flashed, as reporters from as far away as California pushed and shoved to get a photo of Smitty. He was crying like a baby with tears of joy. He believed he had shed too many tears of sorrow and longed for happier days. He still did not feel like a hero. He had not destroyed any tanks, captured any generals, or stormed any machine-gun bunkers, but he was still honored.

Mary Lou had not been away from his side since the day in the MASH unit when she had committed to staying with him. She had become the rock he leaned on for strength and support and had more than fulfilled her promise.

Pictures and stories of the welcome would be on front pages across the country, including the Norfolk Times and Norfolk Free Press. He knew Gina would see him and Mary Lou. It hurt him to know his actions would close the Gina chapter forever and would be the dynamite that would blow their relationship apart.

A soldier pushed Smitty's wheelchair up the ramp onto the flag-draped platform. As he approached the President, Smitty slid himself to the edge of his wheelchair, lifted his hand, and saluted his Commander in Chief. The President returned the salute with tears in eyes after seeing a hero in a wheelchair. The salute had touched his heart.

President Roosevelt reached for Smitty's hand and shook it, pulling Smitty forward and embracing him like a father would his long lost son. When he pulled Smitty close, he whispered, "Thank you, and God bless you. This is a great day for you and an even greater day for America. America desperately needs a hero."

Smitty had difficulty believing a small-town farm boy was meeting the President, and having so many people welcome him home. In his wildest dreams, he could not have imagined what he was experiencing.

The President approached the bank of microphones with the huge audience screaming and cheering. "Smitty, Smitty, Smitty."

"Ladies and Gentlemen," he began, "we are gathered here today in our nation's capital to welcome Corporal Smitty Smith home to the United States of America."

The crowd shouted and cheered, awaiting Smitty's remarks.

"We are honored to have a true battlefield hero with us," Roosevelt continued, "a brave and gallant soldier who risked his life in the service of his country in time of war. In the *USS Vermont's tragic sinking,* this brave soldier saved fifty-three servicemen from the burning, shark-infested waters of the North Atlantic. His bravery in the face of danger will be recorded in the history of our nation.

Months later, Corporal Smith's actions saved one hundred fifty-three men who would have died on a freezing winter night on a French battlefield. He has not only been a hero once but twice. Over two hundred American soldiers and sailors owe their lives to Corporal Smith. We owe even more to this heroic soldier.

History has recorded the mighty deeds and heroic actions of many men and women in our great and mighty nation. It will now record those of Corporal William Bryan Smith. We see before us today a man who risked everything to save others, without regard for his own life.

I'm pleased to announce that the United States Congress has unanimously approved the awarding of two Congressional Medals of Honor to Corporal Smith. I want to be perfectly clear about these honors. In 1918, Congress enacted a law forbidding awarding multiple medals of honor to the same serviceman. I recommended, and Congress voted to make an exception in this case. A soldier seldom has an opportunity to be a hero. Corporal Smith had two opportunities and exhibited courage and valor far beyond what could be expected from any soldier. I feel Smitty Smith is one of the most deserving medal winners in our country's history.

Please welcome home the first soldier in recent history to receive two Medals of Honor!"

A roar like a hundred freight trains rose from the crowd. "Ladies and Gentlemen," the President continued, "would you welcome home Corporal 'Smitty' Smith, an American hero?"

The crowd erupted with applause, cheers, whistles, and shouts. The band blasted the Army march, and the crowd roared with appreciation. "We love you, Smitty," yelled one small boy in the front row of spectators.

The welcome raged like a waterfall. The applause went on and on, with Smitty wanting it never to end. For the first time since he was wounded, he was glad he did not die in the North Atlantic waters or on the battlefield in France. He wished his mama or someone he loved could have shared his special moment. Amid thousands of people, he felt alone.

President Roosevelt lifted his hand, quieted the crowd, and said, "And now a few words from one of the bravest men I have ever met." The President pulled him to the dozens of microphones placed on the podium. Smitty reached for his nearby crutches and stood up. The crowd roared when he saluted them and stood for a moment, honoring them.

His emotions flooded him as he fought back the tears and struggled to find the right words. With a lump in his throat and his mind racing, he paused again, looked across the crowd, and turned to the President. "Thank you, Mr. President, for the honor of being with you and the great people of this nation. You are the reason we fight, and I am honored to stand before you. I am honored to be an American and proud to be a United States soldier."

His voice quivered, and his hands shook as he struggled for his words. Sweat trickled down his forehead, and his palms were wet. He would have preferred facing an enemy assault rifle or firing squad rather than what had been requested of him. He knew he wasn't a public speaker and never would be. He had come to share his heart. Smitty took another deep breath and began.

"When I was drafted out of the hills of Georgia, I dreamed about the war and how it would be to serve my country. As a kid, I believed war was a game and failed to recognize battle involves bullets and death on a real and final battlefield. I've heard people say war is hell. And it is, but it's not nearly the hell our lives would be if we lost our freedom to Hitler, Mussolini, or Hirohito. The crowd roared as flags waved above their heads.

I fought with some of the most courageous men this world has ever known. I was honored to be a member of Bravo Company, the bravest group of soldiers fighting in this war.

I have returned home, but I left a part of me in France. Thousands of American soldiers will never return. Every soldier on those battlefields paid some, but some paid all. Many brave soldiers purchased our liberty and freedom at the cost of their lives. We in America have been free, we are free, and I pray to God we will always be free. All I can say today is thank God we are free!

The Bravo company soldiers fought for good, for honor, for freedom, and keeping America safe. Their bravery, even at the cost of their lives, won a significant victory in the war. With only one in four surviving that snowy night, so many soldiers fought to the death. Some will be remembered, most will not. Every one of those six hundred soldiers should be standing here today. I am honored to be here for them. They were all heroes.

As we stand here today, the war is raging, with our freedom still in doubt. Victory has not yet been won, and our enemies have not been defeated. Every citizen in this great land needs to sacrifice and contribute what they can to the war effort. American soldiers are fighting on battlefields worldwide, and today I'm asking you to be civilian soldiers to carry out our battle on the home front. Whatever it takes, we must all step forward to do our part. America desperately needs you today! At all costs, we will win this war! We will be victorious, the Axis of evil will fall, we will defeat our enemies, and we will stay free. Thank God, America will win, and America will remain free!

Smitty collected his thoughts as he struggled for his words. I would give anything if my mama could be here today. I always wanted her to be proud of me. My mama is in a hospital in Tennessee, fighting for her life. She recently had a stroke that left her paralyzed. I do not know her condition, but if it's all right with you, Mr. President, I want to go home and see my mama.

Thank you, Mr. President, and thank you, servicemen, and servicewomen all around the world. Thank you, people of America, for coming. May God bless you and may God bless America."

Smitty fell into his wheelchair, turned it around, and rolled from the platform. The roar of the crowd grew louder and could be heard a half a mile from the airport. The air was energized with hope, as a spirit of victory and celebration swept through the crowd like a mighty wave. The atmosphere was electric, with thousands encouraged and feeling triumph was at hand.

# *CHAPTER THIRTY-FIVE*

After the ceremony, Mary Lou pushed him to the Presidential limousine and helped him inside. He was physically exhausted from the flight and emotionally exhausted from his speech. People pressed near, reaching to shake his hand. Despite the adoration of the crowd and being with the President and Mary Lou, Smitty felt alone. None of his loved ones had come to share his honors. Gina's absence was his greatest disappointment, and he was crushed that she was not there to share one of his most important life events.

"Great job, Smitty," the President said as he was lifted into his limousine. "You gave a wonderful speech. I want to send you across our country to visit the American people on a whistle-stop tour to speak for our soldiers. What do you say? Can I count on you?"

"Mr. President, right now, I'm exhausted and don't know if I can do what you ask. Would you allow me to go home to rest and see my mama, and I'll let you know when I'm ready? I'm honored you would ask me to represent you and our country. I will honor your request when I am able."

***

If Smitty had looked to his right from the podium, beyond the second section of people pressed against the stage, he would have seen Gina, wearing the same beautiful green dress she wore the day he left for France. She had driven from Norfolk to Washington after hearing Smitty was coming home. She wanted to greet him and fulfill her promise. She had waited for him and wanted to be in Washington when he returned but was lost in the massive crowd.

Gina had noticed the young woman holding Smitty's hand and saw her at his side. She had seen her kiss and embrace him and watched them leave together. Gina came to see Smitty but got an eyeful of Mary Lou Brown. She would have to agree with Smitty; Mary Lou Brown was a beautiful woman.

As she turned from the crowd, tears dripped onto the front of her dress. Seeing Smitty had touched her heart, but her tears were tears of sorrow and loss. She was experiencing the pain and sadness of unreturned love. Smitty's letter and his actions with Mary Lou lessened her hope he would change his mind and suggested she had lost Smitty forever. Seeing them together shattered her dreams.

***

The limousine driver delivered the President to the White House and took Smitty and Mary Lou to the historic Willard Hotel. The Willard was located one block from the White House, and every U.S. president since 1853 had stayed there. Smitty was scheduled to fly to Chattanooga the next morning in the President's private plane, and by noon he would see his mama.

As he and Mary Lou feasted on a gourmet dinner, he was sad with little to say. He had reservations about returning home and realized it was going to be difficult. There wasn't anything left for him in Ringgold except a paralyzed mother and an ex-girlfriend who had left him for someone else.

The next morning, he woke up early, anticipating his flight on the President's plane. He gazed from his hotel window and was unable to see anything through the dense fog. It was like the fog that had prevented their landing in New York City. He could not see across the street and knew he would not be flying out of Washington.

He picked up the phone and called the number the President had given him. A desk sergeant answered and confirmed all flights out of Washington had been grounded. They discussed alternative ways for Smitty to travel to Chattanooga since he did not want to wait for the fog to clear. He feared it could linger two or three days or longer, and he wanted to see his mama without any delays.

He decided to return home on the train. Since the only train to Chattanooga was leaving in an hour, he decided to write Mary Lou a note telling her he wanted to go home alone. He would contact her in a few days and make arrangements for her to join him in Ringgold. He would gather his things and slip Mary Lou a note under her door and not disturb her.

Smitty dressed and packed his duffle bag. As he picked up the bag, his mind returned to the pillowcase sack he carried when he went for his physical in Atlanta. He looked back at some chapters in his life he would like to close. He confirmed his seat on the train with the sergeant requesting the station master hold the train as long as possible. His plans were complete, and he was more than ready to travel home.

The phone rang, and the desk clerk informed him, "Mr. Smith, your car is here to take you to the railroad station. Your bill has been taken care of by the White House." Smitty thanked him and picked up his duffle bag. He took one last look around, sealed Mary Lou's note, and rolled down the hall. The door to her room was ajar, so he decided to drop the message inside.

Easing the door open, he was shocked at the sight of

Mary Lou naked in bed with Jason Rollings. They were sleeping and had been so distracted with their lust, they had failed to close the door. He was shattered as he dropped the note on the floor, pulled the door closed, and whispered, "Goodbye, Mary Lou." He felt nauseated as he wheeled to the elevator, knowing he had seen the last of her.

Smitty questioned what he had done wrong in his life to experience so much pain, grief, and hurt. He had tried to be a good person and live a good life. He realized his mama was very wise when she once told him, "When things go wrong in life, don't ask what you've done wrong, but what you've done right." If that were true, he concluded, he must have done a lot of things right.

He had feelings for Mary Lou and had felt he might be in love with her. He realized he had responded to her care, her kindness, and compassion. He would have fallen for anyone who cared for him and filled the voids in his life. He did not feel broken-hearted like he did with Gina but felt numb.

His feelings for Mary Lou were never the feelings of love he held for Gina. Mary Lou was a beautiful woman. He needed her care and compassion, as well as the encouragement and acceptance she freely gave. He might have married her because she seemed to care for him. If he had believed Gina could love him in his condition, he would never have been interested in Mary Lou. Like Janice, Mary Lou became a thing of the past. In his sadness over Mary Lou's shady character, he wished he could return to Gina. If he could have anyone in his life, it would be Gina, but he knew that was never going to happen.

Mary Lou's betrayal became even worse when he realized he did not have anyone in his life and was alone.

***

"Clickity-clack," the train sang, as it rolled southward toward Chattanooga. Smitty traveled all day and into the night to reach his destination.

He had lunch in the dining car and devoured southern fried chicken, mashed potatoes, green beans, and freshly baked biscuits like Hannah made. He talked with the waiter, and the waiter discovered he was Smitty Smith. The Southern Railroad Supervisor on board came to Smitty, shook his hand, and declared, "We are honored to have you travel with us. Thank you for your war effort. Lunch and supper are on the house. Eat what you want, courtesy of Southern Railroad. What would you like for dessert?"

Smitty responded, "I would love to have a fried pie, peach if possible." In minutes, the aroma of fresh fried peach pies filled the dining car with the cooks frying the pies for Smitty. Some things in life never changed, like the taste of warm peach pies.

When Smitty tasted the desert, his thoughts returned to his mama's pies, cooked on their wood stove using peaches dried in the summer sun on window screens. He thought of the ones Eunice Miller cooked and Mrs. Davis' fried pies he and Gina shared before he shipped out.

He loved Gina more than ever and could not get her out of his mind. He cared for her and pulled her letter from his Bible. He studied the bullet hole through her signature and parts of the letter. As he read it, he yearned for her, with the pain in his heart causing him to tear up. Those memories had taken place a lifetime ago in another life.

Lord, how he missed Gina! He still felt he could never be her husband, lover, provider, and man in her life. Though he loved her, he would have to forget her. In his mind, their relationship would never work. He cared too much for her to ask her to live her life with a one-legged handicapped husband. He hated the thoughts of her taking constant care of him and being unable to carry his load in their marriage.

His anxiety and fears increased as the train neared Chattanooga. Smitty had drifted in and out of sleep, his watch moving so slowly, it appeared time had stopped. He had not made arrangements for anyone to meet him at the train station, so he took a cab to the hospital. He wasn't sure if he would find his mama dead or alive.

"Chattanooga. Chattanooga, Tennessee," the porter sang out as the train slowed. A kind man pushed Smitty's wheelchair to him and lifted him into it. The ticket agent and a large station employee helped Smitty off the train. They almost dropped him and his wheelchair when they slipped on the steps.

Smitty declared, "There should be a better way for handicapped people to have access to trains. Some kind of ramp is needed to allow people like me to board and exit trains safely. I've learned this world isn't made for handicapped people, and I will do something about that someday. It isn't right for people like me to have to endure these barriers."

He paused beside the train, feeling he had arrived home. The air smelled like home, the sky looked like home, and people did not have an accent. He had returned home with peace flowing into his life.

He took a taxi from the railroad station to Memorial Hospital. When the cab stopped, Smitty felt an even more profound sense of relief. The driver retrieved Smitty's wheelchair from the trunk, assisted him with it, and left him on the curb in front of the hospital.

He became frustrated when he could not open the hospital's front door and had to wait about fifteen minutes for someone to open the door for him. As hard as he tried, he could not open the door. "This world makes everything difficult for wheelchair people," he muttered. "Someday, I will do something to make life easier for those struggling in such an uncaring world."

Smitty wheeled into the lobby and rolled to the information desk. He asked the receptionist, "Hannah Smith's room number, please?" The lady behind the desk searched for Hannah's name and was unable to locate her information. She looked at him and said, "Sir, we don't have a Hannah Smith here." Smitty was speechless, and his first thought was his mama had died.

"Sir, did you hear me? We do not have a Hannah Smith here."

"Can you check your records and see what happened to her?"

The receptionist said, "Yes, but this might take some time, so please take a seat."

Smitty laughed and said, "Ma'am, I'm already seated!"

The hospital worker laughed and smiled.

After a few minutes, she returned from the records room and said, "Hannah Smith was discharged and returned home to Ringgold last week. Are you her son, the hero everybody's talking about? I'm sorry, we did everything we could."

What did she mean by, "We did everything we could"? What was her situation? How bad was his mama? Was she dead or alive? How would he deal with seeing his mama as a paralyzed invalid? He wanted to see her, hold her, and tell her he loved her. Everything would be fine as long as she was alive.

# CHAPTER THIRTY-SIX

Smitty faced a problem traveling to Ringgold since taxis stopped running at eight PM. He realized he did not have many choices and decided he only had one option. He would buy Roger Brown a tank of gas if he would come to Chattanooga and take him home. He went to a payphone in the waiting area and had the operator connect him with Brown's Grocery.

"Jot 'Em Down," Roger answered, indicating he was ready to take the next grocery order. This is Roger Brown. May I help you?"

Roger had taken over the store as the new owner and operator of Ringgold's leading business. Roger's father had died of a heart attack and left his money and the store to Roger, who was now the sole owner. Smitty wondered why he was working late and thought he might be avoiding going home to Janice. Smitty often wondered how much Janice would look and act like her mother.

"Roger, this is Smitty Smith. I'm in Chattanooga, and I need a ride to Ringgold. Is there any way you can help me? I'll fill your tank with gas if you'll pick me up. I don't have anyone to call, and I am desperate to get home and see my mama."

Roger replied, "I'd like to help, but I'm busy taking tomorrow's orders, and I can't leave the store."

Smitty's heart sank when he realized he might have to hitch a ride. He said to himself, "Nobody will want to stop and pick up a one-legged hitchhiker in a wheelchair."

Then Roger said, "I could send Janice, but she will have to bring the babies. Would you like for her to pick you up?

Where are you?" Smitty wasn't pleased with the idea but needed to get home, and he did not have any other choice.

"I'm in front of Memorial Hospital, he said. I'll be in a wheelchair."

Roger said, "Fine, and don't forget to fill the gas tank. I only use premium in our new car." Roger had not changed and was as greedy and money-hungry as ever.

***

Janice wheeled the Plymouth into the Memorial Hospital entrance, and two hospital workers lifted Smitty into the front seat.

As soon as they pulled out of the lot, Janice started talking. Smitty was amazed at how much she talked, how much she resembled her mother and how much weight she had gained. He questioned how he could have ever been in love with her. He thought she must have eaten everything in Brown's Grocery. She was huge, but it did not matter because Smitty no longer cared for her. He could sense she had everything she wanted, except love.

Janice turned the interior light on, and Smitty gazed at the two babies in the back seat. The girls looked like Janice with blond hair and beautiful skin. They had little resemblance to Roger, and Smitty thought their mouths and noses looked like Larry Garth. It might have been a coincidence, but Larry Garth had a twin brother and a set of twin sisters. The girls were asleep, and Smitty hoped they would stay that way since he was too tired to deal with screaming children.

Janice talked a mile a minute. She bragged about their new car, new home, new furniture, new twin babies, new dog, and new cat. She bragged about their new store and the money they were making. Everything was new. She had all new things, but Smitty could sense her unhappiness and empty life. Her words were shallow, and her smiles, forced.

She said, "I hardly see Roger anymore. He works all the time and never has time for me." She winked when she said it.

About halfway home, she pulled the car onto an unlit side road. Smitty reacted with shock and outrage when she took his hand and pulled it toward the front of her dress. She asked, "Do you want to finish what we started the day you left for the war?"

Smitty jerked his hand away, pushed her back, and said sternly, "Janice, don't you ever do that again. You're a married woman, and you have babies in the back seat."

He realized he had made a terrible mistake asking Janice to pick him up.

Janice exploded and started screaming and swearing, "If you want to act that way, I'll put your rear out on the side of the road and make you roll all the way to Ringgold."

Her shrieking woke the babies, and they started crying. The screaming set Smitty's nerves on edge.

If Roger ever found out what his wife had attempted, he would leave her. As far as Smitty was concerned, he would be happy if he never saw Janice again.

He did not say another word until they turned onto Nashville Street.

Ringgold had not changed. They rode by Jerry's Sinclair Station, and Janice pulled in for the attendant to top the car off with premium gasoline. Leaving the station, they passed the Ringgold Bank, the old movie theater that closed when Mr. Thompson died, Ringgold School, and Brown's Grocery. Smitty noticed the new storefront and the new sign. It was now Roger Brown's Grocery, and Roger had plastered his name everywhere.

Smitty could see Roger on the phone taking orders.

Janice blew the horn and waved, in case Roger was looking. Smitty wanted to stop and tell Roger what his wife had attempted but decided to leave well enough alone. Junior had taught him to let sleeping dogs lie, and this sleeping dog had awakened him to Janice's true nature and character.

Smitty remembered what Larry Garth said about Janice on the bus trip to Atlanta. He had been unwilling to accept anything Larry said. He should have known it was true when Larry Garth said, "She has a purple birthmark below her naval and one on the top of her right breast." He had played the fool. How could Larry have known about the birthmarks unless he had seen her naked? He had confirmed Janice was a slut and a hussy.

They drove through Ringgold and turned down Shiloh Church road. His heart was pounding in his chest as they neared the Smith farm. They turned onto Maple Road, and Smitty felt he was home. In some ways, he felt as if he'd never left, and in other ways, he thought he had been gone a lifetime. The lights were on in the Smith house, and an old pickup truck was sitting beside the farmhouse, informing Smitty that Uncle Jack and Aunt Nettie Ann were there.

Jack's old Dodge truck was still running even though it had been given up for dead hundreds of times. It was originally black, but with all its rust, it now appeared to be red. It was a miracle the truck was still running with Smitty feeling it had to be Aunt Nettie Ann's prayers and faith that kept it going when it should have been in a salvage yard years ago.

Uncle Jack came to the porch to see who had driven up, and when he saw Smitty, he shouted, "Lordy, Lordy, Smitty has done come home from the war!"

He turned and called through the screen door, "Smitty's come home! Looking back to the car, he called, Welcome home, Smitty."

Uncle Jack was almost ninety but still danced a jig making his way to the car.

Uncle Jack pulled the wheelchair from the trunk and held it steady while Janice assisted Smitty. When Smitty momentarily lost his balance, he grabbed for Janice's arm, missed, and grabbed her breast. He turned bright red with embarrassment as he fell into his chair and sat up straight. Janice had a wide grin on her face, with Smitty fearing she might think he was trying to make amends for his earlier actions. He didn't utter a word.

Janice and Jack had difficulty rolling Smitty's wheelchair across the yard. They made it to the front steps, where they encountered another problem. They could not lift him and his wheelchair up six steps to roll him across the front porch. Smitty knew it would be impossible for him to crawl up the steps.

Smitty remembered Junior had stored some long boards in the barn, so he sent Jack to retrieve a couple. Jack brought two wide boards and laid them up the steps. With great difficulty, Uncle Jack and Janice pushed the wheelchair up the boards and across the porch. They were laboring for breath after the task was over.

Once Smitty got over the threshold, he proclaimed, "Home at last, home at last! Thank the good Lord, I'm home at last! Thank you, Jesus! I have made it home alive."

Aunt Nettie Ann was sitting in his mama's rocking chair, knitting. Smitty could not see his mama.

Aunt Nettie Ann jumped up laughing, crying, and shouting, "Smitty's home! Welcome home, Smitty!"

She grabbed him around the neck and would not let go. Her headlock reminded him of how Johnny used to grab him.

"We are overjoyed you have made it home and

survived the war. Your mama is holding on and would not die before seeing you. She's been waiting for you to return."

Smitty rolled to her bedroom with tears streaming from his eyes. He wheeled past Nettie Ann, Jack, and Janice as he rushed through the doorway.

He wasn't emotionally prepared to find Hannah in a fetal position without any movement. Smitty's heart broke, seeing her so frail and tiny. The light from the single bulb gave an eerie feeling and cast shadows around the room with Smitty feeling gloom, doom, and death.

He rolled to her bed, took her hand, and whispered, "Mama, Mama, it's Smitty. I've come home. I have kept my promise. Wake up, Mama! Wake up!"

Hannah lay motionless without any emotions or signs of life. Smitty did not want to face the fact his mama was paralyzed. He gripped her hand and attempted to wake her again. He thought he saw her eyes open and her mouth move, but realized he was mistaken when she did not respond. He was brokenhearted to find her immobilized and unable to move or speak.

Nettie Ann tiptoed to the bedside. "She can't answer or respond, and she has been this way since her second stroke. She almost died a couple of weeks ago, and the doctors gave her up for dead. We've done everything we could."

Even though she was totally paralyzed, Smitty was upset his mama had been sent home to die. He hated finding her this way and determined he would love and care for her as long as she lived. He had seen her alive, and that was better than finding her dead and buried.

When Smitty came from his mama's room, he thanked Janice for picking him up. He was trying to get past his anger and disappointment. He would forgive her but knew he would never be alone with her again. He was so relieved to find his mama alive that little else mattered. His prayers for his mama had been answered, and he would continue to pray until she recovered.

He thanked Jack and Aunt Nettie Ann for caring for Hannah and encouraged them to return home. He wanted time alone with his mama. They were ready to go home and sleep in their own bed. They had spent several weeks away from home taking care of Hannah, and Smitty was grateful for the love and care.

After they left, he wheeled into his mother's room and talked to her as if she was normal. He told her he loved her, missed her, and how happy he was to be home. He told her about the war, losing his leg, and the actions that had gained him medals and national recognition.

He talked about Junior, Maria, and the rest of the Smith family and reminisced about Johnny and their crazy times. He told her about meeting the love of his life in Norfolk and how he had lost her.

When the sun came up, he was asleep in his wheelchair beside his mama's bed. Even though he doubted Hannah had understood, he had talked to her most of the night. He wasn't sure if she could comprehend anything.

In the bright sunlight of a fresh, new day, things looked different. In the morning light, Hannah looked peaceful, and her countenance had brightened. Smitty felt she knew her son had returned home.

She had lost weight, was thin, and frail, but still looked like Hannah. Smitty wanted her to regain her life and mobility. He felt Hannah had been the best mother in the world, and it was time for him to be her best son. If he never did anything else in his life, he would love and care for his mama.

# *CHAPTER THIRTY-SEVEN*

Early the next morning, Uncle Jack's old Dodge pickup sputtered into the yard. Even though Jack had to roll it downhill to get it started, it ran well. It had not cranked with its starter in years. He was close with his money and preferred putting up with the problem rather than spend money on truck repairs.

Nettie Ann scurried through the front door and placed Smitty's breakfast on the kitchen table. He didn't know how she had kept it hot, but the plate was steaming with grits, country ham, homemade biscuits, and strawberry jelly. It had been a long time since he had eaten country cooking. His last home-cooked meal was with Gina at the Davises' house in Norfolk.

He devoured the food like he was starving, or as Junior would say, like a pig at the hog trough fighting for its share. He ate until he could not consume another bite.

After he finished the country cooking, he knew he was home. He told Nettie, "I believe I will eat Hannah Smith's cooking again."

After eight o'clock, friends and neighbors started arriving, bringing food and warm fellowship to the Smith house to welcome Smitty home and visit a hero.

The pastor of Shiloh Baptist Church visited and shared, "Hannah prayed for you every day. On Sundays and Wednesday nights, she always requested prayer."

She would ask the congregation, "Can we pray for my son, Smitty? I know he's going through some rough times."

The pastor added, "A few Sunday mornings before she had her first stroke, she begged the church to pray for you. She was weeping and moaning when she told the congregation she felt your survival depended on our prayers.

"She told us, 'I believe my son is walking through the valley of the shadow of death at this moment. Can everyone please get on their knees and pray? I believe it is a matter of life and death, so let's pray he will live.' We prayed many times for you and the men in service. Hannah would never let us forget you needed prayer."

After the friends left, Smitty and his family talked until after midnight, remembering past days on the Smith farm. During the evening, at the top of every hour, Smitty would slip away to check on Hannah.

The next morning, after the family members left, Jack and Nettie Ann came to Smitty, "We need to stay home and take care of our place. We did not mind helping, but we've stayed a long time. Y'all need some time together."

Smitty was concerned about how he could care for himself and his paralyzed mother but knew he could not continue to impose on his aunt and uncle. They had gone far beyond what anyone could have expected.

He decided to take a portion of his Army pay and employ someone to cook, keep house, and care for him and Hannah. He wrote an advertisement for a live-in caregiver and had a neighbor deliver it to the Ringgold Tribune.

The ad ran four days without a single response. Aunt Nettie came by, cooked, bathed his mama, and cleaned the house. Smitty knew her age was taking its toll. She was nearing ninety, and hard work was difficult. Her giving heart had driven her to make sure Hannah and Smitty were cared for, no matter the cost.

Smitty was surprised when Miss Bessie Truelove drove

up to inquire about the job. Smitty had known Miss Bessie all his life. She had been his Sunday school teacher when he was a child and had played the church piano for many years. She stayed single because she could never find anyone who could put up with her. She talked more than anyone Smitty had ever known except Eunice Miller. With all her talking, she never had anything positive to say. Smitty did not want to hire her, but went ahead and told her about the job, the pay, and the work required.

She said, "I'll take the job. I can start Friday, so let me know what time you want me here. I'll work days, but you'll have to handle nights."

Smitty quickly replied, "Let me get back to you. I need a full-time, live-in person."

Before she reached the door, Smitty had decided he would not spend his days listening to Bessie Truelove. Smitty knew there had to be someone better than Bessie and decided to wait for the right person.

The next afternoon he was napping on the front porch in the slow part of the day when things grew quiet and still on the farm. He thought he was dreaming when he heard a soft, gentle voice. He tried to wake up, but his eyelids were too heavy to open.

He heard the voice again.

"Hello, Hello," came from the bottom of the steps.

Smitty stirred from his sleep, attempting to focus on his visitor. He saw the outline of a small person he did not recognize standing halfway up the steps.

"My name is Elaine Taylor. I've come to inquire about the job. Is it still available?"

While Smitty was trying to recall who she might be, she spoke again. "My family and I are new in these parts, and I've been looking for a job since we moved here. Can I talk to you about the ad?"

Elaine Taylor was a common-looking young lady, neither pretty nor ugly. She had sandy hair and an abundance of freckles, and her green eyes were like cat eyes, very intense and piercing. She appeared to be sixteen or seventeen, but her physical proportions made her appear older. Smitty noticed she was small-built with an hour-glass figure. She was neatly dressed and seemed to have a pleasant disposition.

"Is the job still open?" she asked again. "I'm interested in the job in the paper - the job for a housekeeper, cook, and caregiver."

Smitty gathered himself and said, "Yes, the job is still open. Come sit down, and we will discuss it."

Smitty proceeded to tell her about the job and wheeled inside to show her the kitchen and his mama. Without comment, she straightened Hannah's bed and wiped her face with a damp cloth from the basin beside her bed. She talked to Hannah as she pushed back her hair.

"My, you're a beautiful woman," Elaine said. "You have the prettiest eyes I've ever seen. I bet you broke a lot of hearts when you were younger."

Smitty made an immediate decision. Elaine Taylor had the job. She had been kind and gentle to him and Hannah. Smitty was worried there could be a major problem. Elaine was near his age - unlike Miss Bessie - and he wondered what people would think of a single, young female moving in with a young man and his bed-ridden mother. He needed help and decided he would deal with that issue later.

"Have you cooked before?"

"I've cooked for my family, and I helped cook in a restaurant in Raleigh. What do you like to eat?"

As he told her the things they ate, she moved into the kitchen, washed the dishes, opened the cupboard, and selected canned green beans, corn, and tomatoes. "I'll make some vegetable soup and cornbread."

Smitty knew he had found the right person when she pulled out dried peaches, placed them in water, and soaked them for peach pies.

She said the key words, "Fried peach pies are my favorite dessert."

"You're hired," said Smitty. "When can you start?"

He watched her glide around the kitchen and said to himself, "Elaine Taylor, you're the person we need."

He was so impressed with her readiness to work that he decided to pay her a dollar a week more. She was worth a hundred dollars more than Bessie Truelove. He knew Elaine would work out fine and was the person he had been praying for.

Smitty said, "Go and get your things. I want you to start immediately."

She jumped up and down with joy to secure a job helping people. She needed the money, and Smitty felt the job would help her have a better life.

After cooking and cleaning, she walked home for her things and was bringing them in when Miss Bessie came to see if Smitty had made up his mind about hiring her. Miss Bessie sat in her car and watched Smitty hold the door while Elaine moved in.

Within an hour, most of Ringgold knew a young woman had moved in with Smitty and Hannah. The tongues did not stop wagging for two or three days. Miss Bessie told everyone in town, including the pastor and members of Shiloh Baptist Church, about sin in the Smith house.

Smitty did not know about the tongue-wagging and rumors until Aunt Nettie Ann and Uncle Jack stopped to check on them.

Aunt Nettie Ann asked, "Do you know what people say about you and that new girl in town? They ain't painting no pretty pictures. They say y'all are sinning right in the house where Hannah is laying an invalid."

Smitty did not care what people were saying. He was doing what was best for him and his mama. If people wanted to talk, let them talk. Nothing was going on, and nothing would go on. He loved his mama too much to disappoint her with inappropriate actions.

***

One of Smitty's most difficult tasks was taking a bath. He had trouble getting in and out of the bathtub Junior installed when he sold some acreage. Unlike other nearby farmhouses, the Smith home had a bathtub, a sink, an inside commode, and running water.

He had fallen several times and decided it was too dangerous for him to get in and out of the tub with one leg. He had been limited to sponge baths in his wheelchair. He hated bath time and delayed bathing as long as possible, but after a week, he asked Elaine for assistance.

He wrapped a towel tight around his waist and tugged at it to make sure it wouldn't come loose. He glanced from Elaine to the tub and back. "Well, here goes."

Smitty turned red with embarrassment, and even his ears were blood red. Elaine noticed his embarrassment and laughed.

"Mister Smitty," she said, "I have four brothers, and there's nothing to be embarrassed about. I look at you like my brother, and I never want to cause you problems."

Her words rang shallow. One night, Smitty was having trouble sleeping and rolled to the kitchen for a drink of water. It took time for him to get to the kitchen and back.

When he returned to his bed, he was shocked to feel the bed move when Elaine lay down beside him.

When he could speak, he demanded, "Get yourself out of this bed right now! Pack your clothes, because you're leaving. First thing in the morning, I want you out of here!"

She left the bed crying and never spoke a word.

He couldn't sleep the rest of the night with his conscience bothering him with how he had reacted. He felt she would slip out, move away, or harm herself. Smitty did not know how to handle the problem but knew she had to go. He tried to account for her youth and immaturity. He would know what to do after he saw her actions and attitudes. He didn't fall asleep until after five o'clock thinking and praying about Elaine Taylor's actions.

He awoke to the sounds of dishes clanking in the kitchen and realized Elaine had stayed and had not slipped out in the middle of the night. He dressed and wheeled out to find her putting breakfast on the table. She had her head down, and her eyes were red.

She rushed to Smitty's wheelchair, fell on her knees, and begged, "Please forgive me. I made a terrible mistake. I love it here, and I care about you and your mama."

She shared a story that touched Smitty's heart and helped him make the right decision.

She related when she turned ten, her Daddy made her come to his bed every night. After her Daddy died, her brothers took turns, making her do the same thing. It was the only life she had ever known. Somehow, she thought her actions were an acceptable way to express her appreciation and give her value.

She said, "I'll pack my bags and leave, but I love the job, and I want to stay. I don't want to go home and have to deal with my brothers. I would be grateful if you would give me another chance, and I promise you, before God, nothing like this will happen again."

Smitty was touched by her story and felt sorry for her. He realized his problems were not as serious as some problems and issues people with two legs had to deal with. He felt people with broken hearts and wounded spirits had more deep-seated issues than he had and felt the more significant pain in life wasn't physical, but emotional and spiritual.

Smitty responded with grace and kindness.

"I'm not going to fire you, but here's what I want you to do. I want you to pack your bags and leave immediately."

Elaine began to cry as she turned toward Maria's old bedroom, where she had been sleeping. She decided she would gather her things and leave. Her head was down in shame, and her heart was breaking. She had made another bad mistake and the wrong decision. She felt she always ruined everything good in her life and set herself up for failure and rejection.

"Hold on, now, Elaine," Smitty said. "I'm not firing you. I will find you a place to live, and I'm going to pay for it. I want you to go to Uncle Jack's and Aunt Nettie Ann's house and stay for a couple of days. Their farm is within walking distance, and they may even have a room to rent. You can keep your job, but we have to work together, and things have to be done the right way."

She wiped her eyes and looked up, "Thank you, and thank God for hearing and answering my prayers."

***

Days passed with Smitty fighting loneliness and emptiness and needing a friend. His thoughts returned to Patricia Owens and the days they spent together at Fort Benning. They had corresponded off and on through his deployment and had kept the friendship alive.

He thought about traveling to Columbus to visit her. He had enjoyed having a friend without issues, problems, and complications. He had not written her during his medical treatment. He had written her when he returned home, and it was a long time before she responded.

Patricia informed him, "My father has been reassigned to Schofield Barracks in Honolulu, Hawaii. My family and I have relocated here, and I love it. It is like paradise. I feel we will be stationed here for the remainder of the war. I have enrolled in college and studying to become a teacher. I think I have found my forever home."

He would always value her caring, friendship, and how she helped him through a dark and challenging time. He realized romance and love did not have to be involved in every relationship and friendship with someone like Patricia would always be valuable in his life.

# *CHAPTER THIRTY-EIGHT*

Dear Mr. President,

I am sorry it has taken so long for me to get my personal affairs in order. My mama is about the same, and I have found someone to care for her. If you still want me to build support for our troops and the war, I'll be happy to do it. Please let me know your plans, and I will be ready to return to Washington after you finalize the arrangements. Thank you for helping me during my trouble-filled days.

I look forward to our visit.

Sincerely,

Smitty Smith

Smitty sent the letter, and President Roosevelt responded.

A week later, there was a knock at Smitty's door. He rolled to the front door and found two soldiers standing with hats in hands. They introduced themselves. One of the soldiers said, "The President sent us to develop an itinerary for you to come to Washington and begin a whistle-stop tour."

The three of them sat at the kitchen table, and the captain said, "We're here to help you any way we can, Corporal Smith. The President is looking forward to your visit to Washington. We will be assigned to you for your travels."

They did not look like Mary Lou, but he appreciated

any assistance he could get and was happy he would not have to struggle with his wheelchair. The soldier gave Smitty possible dates for the medal ceremony and a list of dates and places he would visit on tour. Smitty found it hard to comprehend he would be traveling from Washington to California, east to Miami, and then end up in New York City, making stops in other cities along the way.

He was ready for a lifestyle change since his life in Ringgold wasn't the same as before he left home. Except for his mama, he did not have anything left in Ringgold.

He would start making preparations as soon as possible and verify Elaine would continue caring for his mama. He was sky-high about his new adventure since life on the farm had become boring. Once he had seen the world, his small Georgia town felt dead even for a disabled man.

"The President sends his regards and this notification."

One of the soldiers handed him an envelope with a promotion letter inside. Smitty's heart beat faster as he read his news.

"Congratulations, Sergeant Smith."

Even though he only had one leg, he was still in the Army, on the payroll, and able to serve his country. He had not wanted a medical discharge. He was still an active-duty soldier and was willing to help his country fight on the home front.

The Captain gave him more good news.

"Your first stop will be Fort McPherson in Atlanta, where the Army doctors have developed a new artificial leg made for soldiers wounded in combat. You will be one of the first soldiers to receive the new leg. The doctors say it's the next best thing to having your leg re-attached. This is going to be one of the greatest blessings you'll ever receive, and the new leg should allow you to do whatever you want."

***

Smitty's mind filled with memories, and his heart overflowed with emotions on his bus ride to Fort McPherson. The Army wanted to send a car or plane, but Smitty wanted to take the bus to relive his first trip to Atlanta. His mind raced as he thought back on the events of his past.

He could hear Johnny's voice and smell Lila Leigh's perfume. He sat in the back of the bus and talked to the black passengers like he and Johnny did on their first trip to Atlanta and marveled at how things had changed.

His bus pulled into the Atlanta bus station, and he saw the same green buses transporting new draftees to Fort McPherson. He had been assigned a new Army sedan with a uniformed driver. The driver helped him into the car and placed his wheelchair in the trunk. As Smitty pulled into Fort Mac, he hoped his wheelchair days would soon be over.

Smitty was driven to the medical building and checked in. He went through a battery of tests the next morning with the doctors informing him he was in perfect health, except for missing a leg.

Doctor Robert DeVay entered his room, clutching a measuring tape and clipboard. He measured Smitty's leg, height, foot size, the flap of his missing leg, and everything he could measure. Each time the doctor measured parts of Smitty's body, he muttered, "Hum." Smitty got tired of hearing, "Hum, hum, hum."

The doctor scratched his head, turned for the door, and said, "I'll see you in a few days with your new leg. Make yourself at home at Fort Mac. Take a couple of days off, and

I'll see you day after tomorrow."

Smitty wanted to leave the hospital for a few hours, so he requested a driver to tour the base. The base appeared the same as when he left except for new draftees. Passing by his original barracks, he asked to get out. As he entered the barracks, he came face to face with Sergeant Rylee. When Rylee saw him, he came to full attention and saluted. Smitty returned the salute. Big grins crossed their faces as they hugged like two bears.

Sergeant Rylee had been transferred from Fort Benning to Fort MacPherson after Fort Mac had been designated as an induction center and basic training facility.

"How are you doing, hero?" Sergeant Rylee asked. "I see those stripes on your sleeves. Congratulations."

Rylee nodded to where his gaze went. "How's the leg? I heard the Germans tried to shoot you in the heart, but could not find it."

They laughed and embraced again.

Sergeant Rylee asked, "How about dinner tonight? You have any plans? We can go into Atlanta if you are up to it."

"I'd love to go, but only if we don't visit any nightclubs, joints, dives, or hole-in-the-wall places. I've had enough trouble in Atlanta to last a lifetime."

"Let's shoot for 1800. Can we take your car and driver?"

"I think we can swing it," said Smitty.

"You lucky dog! You're receiving the VIP treatment. You could ride with me, but we'd have to take the bus, and I don't think either of us would be up for that."

"1800, then?"

"Yep. I'll meet you here, hero."

The old friends shared good food and heart-to-heart talk, looking back and looking forward. Rylee asked, "Will you speak to our recruits next weekend if you're here? I would love for you to encourage them and share what they will face in the war."

"I'm not a speaker, Smitty said, but I will share my story."

***

Doctor DeVay pushed the door open and said, "You know they shoot horses with leg problems, don't you? Maybe we should shoot you and get it over with."

"No, that won't work," quipped Smitty. "The Germans have already tried to shoot me."

"You are one tough soldier to survive what you've experienced," DeVay responded.

He padded Smitty's flap, slid on the artificial leg, and strapped it securely. He pulled Smitty from his chair onto his artificial leg. Smitty lost his balance and fell into Dr. DeVay's arms. They both tumbled to the floor, and after a good laugh, Dr. DeVay picked Smitty up.

He handed Smitty a set of crutches. Smitty placed them under his arms and wobbled unsteadily across the floor, moving the artificial leg with difficulty; it had been months since he used his knee. The knee was stiff, weak, and hurt like the devil with the new leg's weight and pressure. He thought his flap had healed, but it hurt as much as when his leg was removed. He was having second thoughts about the artificial leg.

Doctor DeVay removed the prosthesis, measured, hummed, and measured some more. After he examined the device, he concluded, "This is good! This is excellent! It's a perfect fit! Sometimes I surprise myself with my work. This is the best prosthesis I've ever done."

He patted Smitty on the back.

"It's time for you to walk and walk and then walk some more. When you get through walking, walk again. You'll feel like you've walked a thousand miles before this is over. It will be a blessing, and you will walk alone again. You will soon throw the wheelchair and crutches aside and walk without any aid. The more you walk, the more stable you will become."

Smitty followed Doctor DeVay's orders. Clumsily at first and then better, he walked with his crutches and bars. With each step, his confidence increased, and his spirit lifted. After lunch the next day, he experienced pain and burning in his flap. He couldn't walk and fell into his wheelchair.

After a short rest, Doctor DeVay unstrapped the artificial leg and removed it. Smitty's flap was irritated, swollen, and throbbing. DeVay said, "We will give it some extra padding and treat it. Welcome to the world of artificial limbs."

He explained to Smitty, "You'll have to toughen your flap to handle the new leg. It will take time, and there will be pain, but you will whip it like you've whipped everything else in your life."

DeVay rubbed salve on the flap and told the orderly to soak his leg in Epsom salts when Smitty could endure it. The Epsom salts water hurt worse than any torture Smitty could imagine. The burning of the salts on his flap was more than he could take and left Smitty feeling it was more painful than anything the Germans could inflict in a POW camp.

The next day and the following days, Smitty walked as long and as far as he could. He felt he would walk a thousand miles, and despite the pain, he worked to build up calluses on his flap. He looked forward to the weekend and a needed reprieve from his torture.

Smitty had been so busy, he had forgotten his commitment to Sergeant Rylee. He always sweated and worried whenever he was asked to speak. He thought he would be talking to a small group of Rylee's men, but on Sunday morning, he discovered he would be addressing the entire camp. The crowd's size put dread in Smitty, but the men on the base were anxious to hear an American hero.

On Sunday afternoon, Smitty and Sergeant Rylee traveled to the parade grounds. The celebration began with patriotic music and barked-out commands, as graduating recruits paraded in front of the Army brass. Fort McPherson had been recognized for producing quality soldiers like Smitty.

Thousands of recruits came to rest in the middle of the parade ground. All eyes turned to the reviewing stand where General Hershel Goodwell opened the ceremony. The program included prayer, a welcome, and the playing of the National Anthem. The thousands of gathered people stood and recited the Pledge of Allegiance to the American flag.

General Goodwell walked to the microphone, challenged the men to be brave, and moved to introduce Smitty. He told his men, "We are honored here today to hear from a brave and heroic soldier who survived the *USS Vermont's sinking*, saving fifty-three men. Later, on a battlefield in France, his bravery saved one hundred fifty-three servicemen. Over two hundred soldiers and sailors owe their lives to the heroic actions of this one soldier.

"We are privileged to have him with us today. Ladies and gentlemen, I am honored to present to you Sergeant William 'Smitty' Smith."

The General shook Smitty's hand and embraced him for a moment. Smitty moved toward the podium. As Smitty walked forward on his crutches and artificial leg, the crowd erupted. Shouts, whistles, drums, and applause echoed off buildings surrounding the parade ground. Smitty's heart beat in his throat as he stood with tears flooding his eyes while experiencing one of the most memorable moments of his life.

He took a moment to gaze into the faces on the parade ground, and the assembled men stared back in silence. A gentle breeze lifted the American flags and made the men feel honored they were soldiers. It was so quiet you could have heard a single whisper.

"My name is Smitty Smith. I am honored to be here today, and I am proud to be an American soldier. Not long ago, I was a farm boy in this beautiful state. I was inducted into the Army at this very place. When I received my draft letter from Uncle Sam, I was excited about the prospect of being a GI. My thoughts about the war were unrealistic. No one would get shot or hurt in my war, no one would lose his life, and nothing would be destroyed. I saw war through the eyes of an innocent kid. I should have known the horrors of war would go far beyond anything I could have imagined.

Many of you stand here today with similar thoughts and ideals. During my days in battle, I learned some important and valuable lessons, and I would like to share some of those lessons with you.

Live each day as if it were your last. It well could be. Love those who love you and don't miss a precious moment with them. Love your wives, hug your children, kiss your mothers, and spend time with friends. You will be leaving them soon, so don't miss a moment."

Smitty took a deep breath and stumbled over his words as he thought about kissing Gina. His heart filled with sadness, realizing he would never see her again. He paused another few seconds with the realization he would never share another moment with Johnny Little. His mind flew to other losses, but he sucked in a deep breath and went on.

In this conflict, you'll have other soldiers around you on the battlefields to share your life struggles, so don't be afraid to love those men around you as much as you love your family. You will develop into a band of brothers, struggling to keep each other alive and keep America free. You need to watch each other's backs and carry one another when necessary. Cherish the moments and make memories that last forever.

You need to remember everything you have been taught here, because your life may depend on it. I had a tough-as-nails Sergeant named Rylee during..."

The good-hearted groans did not surprise him. He grinned at the men, gave Sergeant Rylee a quick smile, took a deep breath, and continued.

"As I was saying, I had a tough-as-nails Sergeant named Rylee during basic training. I often thought he was a jerk. I didn't like him being so strict and uncaring. I felt he was unfair and sadistic the way he treated his men. To be honest, at times, I hated his guts and wished he would be run over by a truck. I'm sure none of you have felt that way."

Again, the groans and laughter arose.

"I now know he treated me that way out of love and wanted me to live through the hells of war. When my life was on the line, the things he drilled into me saved my life. You've been trained to be a soldier in a world at war, and now you must face whatever the war may bring. You have the highest honor and most excellent title in the world. You are a GI, an American soldier.

"You won't be able to live until you're willing to die. The more you try to save your life, the more you'll lose it. There are things in life bigger and more important than you. The value of freedom, liberty, and democracy can't be measured and are beyond cost. You must be willing to lose your life if that is the cost of freedom.

"Some people call me a hero. I do not feel like one. I'm a soldier who willingly gave his life for what he believed in. I fought for my life, fought for my country, and refused to allow anyone to take my life from me. I offered it willingly for my family, my men, and my country.

"The soldiers in Bravo Company sacrificed their today's for your tomorrows, and they did it willingly and courageously. You must know what is worth the fight and what is not. Our freedom is definitely worth it.

Deep in my soul and spirit, I wanted to live more than I wanted to die. Freedom and liberty are gained at a high price, and now you have been asked to step up. On the battlefields, when one soldier falls, the officers call, 'Next man up.' After today, you will be the next man up."

Some of the soldiers on the field and on the platform teared up. Smitty's sincerity and powerful words released deep emotions. Even Sergeant Rylee had watery eyes, thinking of what these recruits might suffer and how many would die. His heart was breaking with sending young soldiers to their deaths on the battlefields of the world. Rylee loved his soldiers and had always cared for Smitty.

Decide why you fight. If you fight for yourself, your gain, your career, your honor, your promotion, your anything, you will lose. This war is bigger than you. This war is about our freedom, our families, our country, and our future. The most precious things in this world are purchased at the cost of men's lives. At this moment, in places around the world, men and women are paying that price. They're picking up your tab today, and in a few weeks, you will be asked to pay the tab for the soldiers who will follow you.

"During the few moments I've been speaking, hundreds of soldiers worldwide have sacrificed their lives to pay for our freedom. Hundreds have died in these few moments. Our freedom and liberty must be worth your life.

"Nothing great is achieved without suffering and sacrifice. The future of America and the free world has now been placed in your hands, rests on your shoulders, and is your responsibility. You are counting on America, and America is counting on you. We must not lose this war. How you fight this war will determine if we remain free or fall victim to the soldiers and leaders of the Axis of Evil fighting to rule the world.

"A part of me remains on the battlefield in France. I left part of my body there, but my heart never left America. I left home with two legs and came back with one. I left America a kid and came back a man. I left America as a recruit and came back a soldier. I left America free and I have returned to America free."

Smitty breathed deeply and choked out his final words. He took a deep breath with tears streaming down his cheeks, and with a broken, crackling voice said, "I share with you the final words my mama said when I left for the war.

"She said, 'Smitty, it may get tough, and it may look hopeless over there, and you may not think you'll make it, but people are praying for you, and you will make it through.'

"It is my prayer that in your darkest hour and greatest danger, you will remember these words: You will make it through. I pray you make it through. You will make it through and you will return to America free. You will be free.

"Thank you. May God go with you, and may you go with God. God bless you, and God bless the United States of America."

Smitty hobbled back to his seat on his crutches and sat

down. Seconds of silence ticked by, then the parade grounds erupted like an explosion with cheers, shouts, and applause.

Smitty received a standing ovation that seemed to last forever. He lowered his head and thought back to the words he shared. He prayed for the men as he looked over them, hoping his words would make a difference.

A roar of determination filled the parade grounds and spread across the base. Smitty had passed the torch of freedom to the next group of freedom fighters.

He left the parade grounds, realizing he had walked a long and challenging road with a lifetime of trials still looming ahead of him.

# CHAPTER THIRTY-NINE

On Monday, Doctor DeVay increased Smitty's physical therapy. The doctor said, "Today, you are going to walk without crutches."

Smitty said, "In your dreams, Doctor DeVay."

Smitty could not stand on his own, much less walk. Doctor DeVay placed him between two parallel bars and told him to walk back and forth without crutches. Before Smitty began, the physician had an orderly remove one of the bars. He walked with one bar until lunch.

Smitty walked with gritted teeth and sweat and prayed he would have the determination not to quit.

Doctor DeVay reentered the therapy room after lunch, eating an apple, and said, "Are you ready for a huge test? It's time to take away the other bar."

He placed a large orderly on each side of Smitty and ordered him, "Walk!"

When Smitty leaned to one side, an orderly would catch him and push him back. When he went the other way, the other orderly would do the same. Smitty walked the rest of the day with the orderlies' support.

When the day ended, he fell exhausted on his bunk without removing his uniform and slept the night without turning over. When he got up the next morning, he felt like he had been on a fifty-mile hike in full gear.

Doctor DeVay came in early, examined Smitty's artificial leg, and said, "Today is W day."

"What is W day?" Smitty asked.

"W day is Walk day. Today you will walk on your own without assistance or aid. Today you will throw your crutches aside and walk."

Doctor DeVay helped Smitty put the artificial leg on his stub, pulled him from his wheelchair, and commanded him, "Walk, Smitty! Walk!"

To Smitty's utter amazement, he walked unassisted.

When he reached the other side of the room, he screamed, prayed, and cried. With a little more confidence, he might have jumped.

He was walking on his own like he had two good legs. He was elated.

He screamed, "I can walk again! I can walk!"

He shouted, cried, and hugged Doctor DeVay, the orderlies, and every soldier in the rehabilitation room. He prayed, thanking God for his miracle.

He walked around the room, out of the room, down the hall, and back. He could not walk enough. He walked and kept walking. The more he walked, the more he grinned and laughed. His grin grew broader, and his laughter grew louder.

Doctor DeVay hugged Smitty and said, "One more day, and we'll send you home to become an expert on your own. You won't need us or this place anymore. You now have two legs, and you're a complete man. Congratulations, Smitty."

***

Smitty took his time as he rambled from Uncle Jack's truck. Jack had picked him up at the Sinclair bus stop and brought him home. Smitty had decided he would never call Roger or Janice again. He had learned his lesson. If a dog bites you once, shame on the dog. If a dog bites you twice, shame on you. He never wanted to be bitten by Janice again.

Smitty took his time as he walked to the steps. He grabbed the handrail and swung his real leg up on the first step. Elaine Taylor was standing on the porch and started clapping, jumping, and cheering. Tears flowed from her eyes as she screamed, "Look at you, Smitty Smith, walking in here like the king of the world."

Smitty not only could walk, but he could also climb steps.

Elaine saw Smitty's wide grin and said, "Come see your mama."

He walked across the living room floor and found his mama in her rocking chair. He screamed and hobbled to take her in his arms.

"Mama, oh Mama!" was all he could say.

He could walk, and his mama was awake. Life could not get any better.

Smitty was speechless when his mama stretched out her hand and reached for him. He waited for her to speak, but realized she was unable to talk. Even though her right side wasn't moving, her improvement shocked him.

Hannah squeezed his hand, and the left side of her face lifted in a smile. Smitty wanted to fall to his knees and weep. When the initial shock passed, he started talking to his mama.

"Look, I can walk. I am safe at home, and we are going to spend our lives together."

He showed her he could walk and told her the things she missed while in her coma.

Hannah could not talk, so Smitty made signals for her to communicate. She moved one finger for yes and two fingers for no. Her mind was sharp, but she could not speak. Her actions were slow and deliberate, so he had to be patient with her.

The remainder of the day and into the night, Smitty sat

beside his mama's bed talking. He remembered his words to the soldiers at Fort MacPherson, "Live each day as if it were your last. It well could be. Love those who love you and don't miss a moment with those you love."

These were precious moments for Smitty and Hannah.

After they shared a delicious supper Elaine had prepared. Smitty reached into his shirt pocket and withdrew the Bible his mother had given him. He removed Gina's folded letter. Smitty pressed the Bible into his mama's good hand and said, "I'm keeping my promise. I made it home, and I am returning this to you. This Bible saved my life and kept my soul. Without this, I would have died on the battlefield.

"Many times, it was life or death, but I made it through. With your prayers and the Lord's help, I made it through."

Hannah clutched the Bible and wept as tears flowed down her face. She could not speak, but she did not need to say a word; her joy spoke for her. Smitty had challenged the soldiers to kiss their mothers, so Smitty kissed Hannah on the cheek like he had a lifetime ago. A beautiful smile spread across her face as she rejoiced at her son returning home. Her son was alive.

* * *

The day came for the presentation of the Medals of Honor, with Smitty flying to Washington the day before the ceremony aboard the president's plane. He stayed at the Willard and chose not to revisit past events there.

William Bryan "Smitty" Smith, III, stood in the well of the House of Representatives before the president and members of Congress. It was a banner day for the display of courage, bravery, patriotism, and support for the war. He stood alone without anyone to share his special moment. Hannah was the only person left in his life, and she was too weak to travel. He felt it was a shame to have such a timeless moment without anyone to share it.

President Roosevelt called the ceremony to order. The vice president, the House speaker, and the Joint Chiefs of Staff were in attendance. The members of Congress were waiting with anticipation for the ceremony. England had a representative of the royal family and leaders from Parliament. The assistant prime minister came and read a letter from Winston Churchill. Charles De Gaulle had dispatched his top assistant to represent him and to present the French Legion of Valor medal. Many other leaders from all over the world attended the presentation.

The vice president gave a short welcome and introduced the dignitaries. The Senate chaplain prayed, asking God's blessings on the ceremony. The Army Band played the Star Spangled Banner. Everyone placed their hands over their hearts and recited the Pledge of Allegiance.

The president spoke of this great day in America's history. He paused before proceeding.

The side doors of the chamber burst open, and a mass of people rushed in. At the front of the group was Hannah Smith in a wheelchair pushed by Elaine Taylor. Tommy and Ella Smith from Calhoun walked in behind Hannah. Evelyn and TJ. McCord came in from who knows where. They were now Betty and Tim McEver in their new life. Smitty hoped Beatrice Whelchel wasn't anywhere near.

Smitty lost his breath when his brother Bobby walked in, dressed in a suit and tie. Smitty could not believe Bobby was there. He could not comprehend Bobby had been located and felt finding him was a miracle.

Aunt Nettie Ann and Uncle Jack came next. They had flown to the ceremony in the president's private plane with Hannah and other family members. Smitty was glad Uncle Jack had not attempted to drive his pickup to Washington.

His pickup truck would have had a difficult time traveling seventeen miles to get out of Georgia.

Louise Little marched in, taking Johnny's place. Her eyes filled with tears. Smitty wished Johnny could have attended and shared his day. When he saw Louise, he started weeping as his love for Johnny spilled from his heart. He still missed Johnny.

When Hannah rolled to Smitty, she held out her right hand, smiled, and said, "I love you, Smitty. I am so proud of you."

Smitty broke into more profuse tears and sobs, unable to stand the shock. He put his hands to his eyes and wept. His family gathered around him, hugged him, and patted him on the back. They were all crying, and most people in the chamber could not hold back tears. Deep sobs from the president gave evidence of how he had been touched.

The chamber was quiet when the rear doors of the chamber swung open. Lenny Kowalski, Sergeant Rylee, and Sergeant Riddle marched in. Julie Ross was behind them with two handsome boys, Robby and Michael. Mary Lou Brown Rollins walked in with her pilot husband, Jason. Wilson Wilder's parents were there, and Bama's dad had come. Bama's mom died a few weeks after receiving the tragic news of her son's death.

Doctor Holmes had flown in from France, and Doctor DeVay had arrived by train from Atlanta. He was still humming.

The two medics who saved Smitty's life on the battlefield had been located and entered in full dress uniform. They were wearing their Red Cross armbands like they were when they treated him. Smitty would have his opportunity to thank them and bless them for helping to save his life.

Army Chaplain Henson came in his clergy robe to pray

for Smitty.

The president and the Army had done an excellent job of locating and arranging for the special people in Smitty's life to be present for the ceremony. Smitty was blessed to have family, friends, and loved ones to share his special day. He had expected to be alone for the presentation.

He was relieved Roger and Janice had not come. He knew Roger was too tight to miss a day's work, and Janice would not want to face him. Someone had told him she was pregnant again.

Just when Smitty did not think he could take anymore, more was to come. The chamber's rear door banged open again, and in walked Gina Davis, wearing the beautiful green dress she was wearing the last time Smitty saw her. It was the same dress she wore the day she promised to wait for him.

Carl and Anna Davis walked with Gina, and John and Carol Davis entered with their three children. Gina ran to the stage, wrapped her arms around Smitty, and gave him a long passionate kiss. She whispered, "I still love you, Smitty Smith."

He held her close and whispered, "I am sorry for what I put you through. I tried to do what I thought was best for you. Will you please forgive me? I know I hurt and wounded you. I will make it up to you even if it takes the rest of our lives."

Smitty held her close and through tears of joy, said, "I love you more than anyone or anything in the world. Will you still marry me?"

Gina responded, "Yes, yes, a million times, yes! I desperately want to marry you."

The ceremony was called back to order. Chaplain Henson prayed over Smitty and Gina and asked God to bless them beyond measure and give them their hearts' desires.

The president spoke of bravery, courage, and sacrifice. He saluted Smitty as his Commander and Chief, and Smitty stood at attention and returned his salute. The president told the crowd, "Smitty is what every young boy hopes to be like when he grows up. He is a tremendous example to the youth in our nation."

The French Ambassador presented the French Legion of Valor medal. President Roosevelt then presented Smitty with a purple heart, two bronze stars, the Army Medal of Valor, and two United States Medals of Honor. Like his grandfather before him, Smitty had become a national hero. He had often said people always recognize those who are brave but never recognize cowards.

After the speeches ended and the medals were presented, an American hero was presented to the nation and the world. Most of the world would never know the full story of Bryan "Smitty" Smith, III. It had been a long journey from the red clay fields of Ringgold, Georgia, to the nation's capital. What a journey it had been! Smitty knew and believed the best part of his life was just beginning.

After the ceremony, the sun was setting over the capitol building, and the air was crisp and cool. Goodbyes and farewells were over, with family members and friends returning home.

Smitty and Gina walked down the steps of the United States Capitol. As the sun's last rays faded, a beautiful woman named Gina Davis and the handsome, heroic love of her life, Smitty Smith, walked away. After a few steps, they stopped and shared a passionate kiss.

They gazed into each other's eyes and said together, "I love you. I always have, and I always will."

***

Smitty Smith became the most decorated and honored soldier in World War Two. His pictures were placed on recruiting posters throughout the United States, and the War Bond Commission printed his image on everything they could print. His story and face were shown for months in newsreels and in theaters throughout America. His face became the face of the American soldier and the face of the country's war effort. He became famous overnight. The people of the United States loved him, embraced him, and accepted him as their hero.

The principal accomplishments in Smitty's life could not be counted. One of Smitty's most outstanding contributions was to help lead, guide, and direct handicap legislation in the United States. He was an untiring advocate for disabled veterans and people with special needs.

For many years afterward, he worked tirelessly to see the disabled gain full access to public areas. His voice became the loudest voice of all as millions were blessed through the fulfillment of promises he made to himself at a train station and outside the Chattanooga hospital doors.

Smitty Smith died mid-summer of 2011 on a hot July day on the Smith farm. He died in the bottoms, near a giant oak tree where the springs flowed freely. It was the exact spot where the Smiths' trusty mule, Old Mindy, died the day Smitty was drafted into the Army on his nineteenth birthday.

Smitty had spent the morning with his loved ones as they gathered to celebrate his eighty-fifth birthday. Gina Smith was by his side, as well as his four sons and two daughters. Two of Smitty's sons had followed their father into the United States Army and were recognized as outstanding soldiers and military leaders. His two beautiful daughters loved him and had made his birthday a memorable day.

His twenty grandchildren and four great-grandchildren ran and played around the beautiful farmhouse Smitty and Gina had built to replace the old Smith home.

Sitting on the porch was Smitty's newest great-grandson, William Bryan "Smitty" Smith, the VI who would live to carry on the Smith tradition. Greatness had already been written into his life and destiny.

The children had brought back memories of the beautiful times the Smith children ran and played in the yard. Smitty's family had gathered in the knowledge Smitty's life was ending. He had fought a fierce and courageous battle with cancer for five years and knew it was time to surrender. He had lived his life in fullness and felt a new chapter would soon be written.

Smitty had encountered forever friends, strippers, mobsters, preachers, soldiers, and thousands of others he impacted and who had impacted his life. From the richest of the rich to the poorest of the poor, every person who crossed Smitty Smith's path was dramatically affected by a simple farm boy whose early life was spent within twenty miles of his home. His life was a life well-lived.

That morning in bed, Gina held Smitty as tightly as she could, knowing things were not good, with him fighting to stay alive. They shared a special life moment. She turned and held him in her arms as she whispered, "You will always be my hero. I have always loved you, and I always will."

Smitty kissed her as he had thousands of times and whispered back, "You are the love of my life. You have been the most wonderful gift God could give me. I have always loved you, and I always will."

He struggled as he traveled down the worn path to the

Smith's bottoms. Smitty fell to the ground that hot July afternoon. As he did, he saw Hannah and Junior, Maria, Johnny, Janice, Ross, Bama, Wilder, Lenny, and others who had blessed his life. He even saw Old Mindy standing under the oak tree, drinking from the cool spring. He fell to the ground on the pile of stones marking the grave where Old Mindy had died and was buried sixty-six years before.

As he took his last breath, he looked up to Heaven and said to God, "I love you, Father. I always have, and I always will."

Time has now recorded the life and the death of William Bryan "Smitty" Smith, III - A True American Hero.

END

# *ABOUT THE AUTHOR*

Jimmy Hope is a committed Christian, a lover of history, and a devoted family man. He has been married to his wife, Judy, for over fifty-five years. He has worked as a city planner, parks and recreation director, minister, and missionary. A graduate of the University of Georgia, he also has a DTh degree from International Seminary. Jimmy is an avid fisherman, a Georgia Bulldog fan, MG lover and a sharer of the Gospel of Jesus Christ.

Connect with the author at elcid7@charter.net.

Made in USA - Kendallville, IN
1208173_9781642043013
12.08.2020 0830